DAN

SUGRALINOV

HERO

*May every new day
in your life
become a Level Up day!*

Dan Sugralinov

LEVEL UP + 2

MAGIC DOME BOOKS

ALL BOOKS BY DAN SUGRALINOV:

Level Up LitRPG Series:
Re-Start
Hero
The Final Trial
The Knockout (with Max Lagno)
The Knockout: Update (with Max Lagno)

Disgardium LitRPG series:
Class-A Threat
Apostle of the Sleeping Gods
The Destroying Plague

World 99 LitRPG Series:
Blood of Fate

TABLE OF CONTENTS:

PROLOGUE

What a horrible dream! Ones and zeros everywhere... and I thought I saw a two...

Futurama

"OKAY, I'LL PUT IT IN A DIFFERENT WAY. HOW DID YOU kill them?"

"There was this little boy... he suffocated. It just happened! Then there was a girl... she just died too... bled to death..."

The sound of a gunshot almost deafens me. A bullet to the shoulder throws the corrupt government official onto his back. My ears are ringing. I can barely hear Vicky cuss under her breath as she flings the gun aside,

"Bastard, bastard, bastard! How I hate them!"

"Holy crap, Vick, what have you just done!"

Gleb Grechkin, a prominent figure in the Town Hall's Cultural Department, is squirming on the floor, apparently not in a hurry to croak. His wound isn't life-threatening and his Vitality is still in the green as a Bleed debuff ticks away, stripping the pedophile of his Health.

"He's a scumbag, don't you understand? He doesn't deserve to live!"

"Uuugh," he groans, "You're gonna pay for that! I'm gonna wipe you out... Ooooh..."

"Enough! Wake up!" I shake Vicky by the shoulders, trying to bring her back to her senses. "Let's go!"

"Where do you want us to go? We need to finish him off first!"

I'm a bit worried about her attitude but I can see the Fury and Righteous Anger buffs hovering in the tag above her head. I grab her by the hand and drag her toward the door. I also pick up the gun, just to be on the safe side.

I open the trunk of Grechkin's SUV and look for a hose and an empty can. While Vicky inspects the other cars, I syphon off the gas.

"Here, I've found another one," Vicky hands me an empty can.

It takes us some time to fill both. Then I take them and go back into Grechkin's house.

Grechkin's cowering behind the couch. A bloody trail lies in his wake. As I enter, he shudders and starts muttering.

I cuss as I remember something. I reach into my pocket for the handkerchief I'd taken from the corrupt Colonel "Dimedrol"[1], Grechkin's best friend. I pour some vodka over it and wipe the gun clean. Vicky leaves to do the same with the fingerprints in Wheezie and Zak's car: the two junkies who, on Dimedrol's orders, have kidnapped me and Vicky in a dark alley, stuffed us in the trunk and brought us here.

"What are you doing?" Grechkin asks clearly, enunciating every word. "I can't feel my legs. What's wrong with me?"

I peer at the profile of this ignoble non-entity which has already been sentenced to death by the mysterious interface in my head:

Social status level: -1

This has resulted in a dramatic drop in all of his characteristics. His debuffs aren't exactly energy-promoting, either: his Metabolism is deep in the red, his Mobility virtually non-existent. Once he'd confessed to all his crimes, the game system declassified him, changing his social status to negative and issuing me a system quest to eliminate the pedophile.

Which is exactly what I'm going to do now.

I can hear someone moaning nearby but it's not Grechkin. Wheezie raises his bloodied head, his foot twitching. He's still alive but I don't feel like killing him yet. He can stay alive... for the time being.

---

[1] Dimedrol: a sedating antihistamine drug popular with Russian criminals

I glance at the clock hanging above the door. It's well past three in the morning. Trying to stay away from the burning fireplace, I pour the gas over the bodies, the furniture and the pool table, then use the second can to douse the verandah, the hall and the wooden staircase leading to the second floor. The remainder I use to make a hot trail to the house.

I return to the lounge holding the gun in the handkerchief and laid it into Zak's hands.

"Please don't leave me..." Grechkin pleads. "A million dollars... in cash... please..."

I leave the empty cans in the house. Snatching a lighter from the couch's armrest, I survey the scene of our nightmare.

Then I walk outside. Vicky stands next to me and lays her head on my shoulder.

Even if hell doesn't exist, we're going to make a personal one for him: here on planet Earth, in this particular local segment of our Galaxy.

Let it all burn to hell!

Out of the corner of my eye, I glimpse a silhouette appear from around the corner.

The last thing I hear are the claps of several gunshots. As I pass out, Vicky's scream echoes through my mind.

Chapter One

RESTART

Warning! Forceful activation of the Time Cheat Heroic ability following the user's death!
Creating a database backup...
Deleting the logs...
Clearing the user's operating memory...
Reboot in 3... 2... 1...

Augmented Reality! Platform Home Edition

I COULD STILL SEE THE SMOKY CRIMSON FLAMES imprinted on my retinas; I could smell the steely odor of blood and hear someone shrieking; I could taste the gas and the damp loose earth in my mouth when I woke up.

"Phil! I'm home!" Vicky's cheerful voice rang in the hallway, awakening me from my nightmare.

She walked into the bedroom, leaned over me and kissed me.

"Vicky... sweetie..." I rubbed my eyes and stretched, feeling all my bones ache. Then I couldn't help it any longer: I scooped her up and pulled her toward me.

Laughing, she fell into my embrace. Still holding her, I rolled onto her, supporting myself on my elbows.

"You didn't expect me, did you?" Vicky gave me a brazen smile. "I thought you were enjoying your freedom! Maybe not with the girls but you could have gone out with your friends for the weekend!"

"No, I didn't expect you. And no, I wasn't going to enjoy my freedom. You know very well I don't do weekends. I went for a jog in the morning, did some market research trying to work out a few things, then I had my boxing practice and pumped some weights. By the evening, I was so tired I zonked out reading some Adizes. His books are so beneficial they put me to sleep."

She shut me up with a kiss and reached under my T-shirt.

"Why did you-" I began, meaning to ask her why she'd come back from her parents so early — she was supposed to spend all weekend there — but the blood drained from my brain. For the next quarter of an hour, I had no desire to ask her anything.

When we finally lay there quietly, I tried to pull together the tatters of my dream but could only remember a few images. The woods, a cellar, rain, some bad people and my utter helplessness.

I remembered my unasked question. "So what made you come back earlier than planned?"

"You know... we were sitting there at the table having dinner and talking; my parents, my brother and my daughter..." she fell silent, reminiscing. "And all of a sudden I felt I had to go and see you. I felt as if I was losing you. At first I wanted to just give you a call, but then Dad decided to go on an overnight fishing trip and Mum had her own things to do. So I gave Xena a kiss and jumped into the car. I was in such a hurry to get back home before nightfall I very nearly had an accident. I skidded into the opposite lane just when a white Land Cruiser sped right past me..." she droned as if it didn't happen to her. "Then I walked in, heard you wheezing in your sleep and felt a whole lot better straight away!"

Impressed by her story, I pulled her toward me. That was my Empathy at work: I could physically sense the potential loss and something truly terrible that could have happened to us but luckily didn't.

For a while, we lay in silence. Then Vicky lifted her head from my chest and sprang back to her feet. I got up too and followed her into the bathroom, unable to take my eyes off her well-rounded backside.

"How about we have dinner?" she asked as we took a shower together. "Mom sent us over a whole heap of pies."

"Are they deep fried?"

"No, she sent them raw!" she lashed out at me with her sponge. "Some are egg and onion, some are cabbage and the others are potato!"

"I only asked!" I said, ducking out of the way. "Give her my thanks! Okay, okay, I give up!"

Her reaction was pretty understandable: she was sick and tired of my lecturing her about healthy eating. What did you expect me to do if every time I took a bite of French fries, the system showered me with warnings and debuffs? If you listened to the interface, everything fried increased the risk of cancer and raised your cholesterol levels. It would have been okay but every time I saw my Health drop even one-thousandth of a percent, it eroded every pleasure I had in eating.

While Vicky was getting dressed, I managed to slice some fresh veg for our dinner. That was the only way I could neutralize the effects of fat food, courtesy of the system.

"Listen, Phil," Vicky came back into the kitchen. "My Mom has been pestering me about you. I'd have loved to tell her something but what can I say? I can't keep explaining to them that you're such a nice, reliable, intelligent guy, then drop the bombshell that you're unemployed. Should we go and see them together next week, maybe? It's about time I introduce you to them..."

My parents had indeed liked her. When we'd arrived at their place together a couple of weeks ago, they'd been lost for words because they'd expected me alone. But as soon as the effect had worn off, Mom began squawking,

"Don't just stand there on the doorstep, son! Come in and introduce us!"

"I'd like you to meet Vicky," I said. "We're seeing

each other. We met at work. Vicky, these are-"

"I'm Kira, this wanker's sister," my sister gave Vicky a hug. "Come in, don't stand on ceremony! Make yourself at home!"

It had gone well. But now I was a bit worried how the meeting with her parents would go.

As I pondered over this, Vicky switched over to another sore subject, "Listen, so what's on your agenda? Have you made up your mind? You sure you don't want to try White Hill, Ltd? I know their HR manager. They're major distributors in their field but their sales reps don't last long so they're constantly short of staff. How about you give them a try? Even an average rep earns a decent living there and you're one helluva salesman. I could talk to them..."

"Please sweetie, don't start. I know you're used to only relying on yourself, so allow me to do the same. I've got a business idea and I'm sure it's gonna work. But I still need a little bit of time to prepare everything and start everything properly. I'm not just doing all this market research for nothing..."

"But you never even talk about it! Why can't you tell me? Could it be that you don't even have an idea? Or are you not only trying to fool me but also yourself?"

"Yes, I do have an idea-" I began.

A telephone call interrupted me.

"Wait a sec, I'll get it," I said.

I looked at the phone screen. Well, well, well. Look who's calling! Alik, as large as life! I hadn't seen nor heard from him for quite a while, almost since I gave him my old apartment.

With an understanding nod, Vicky got up and started doing the washing up. I walked out onto the balcony so that the noise of the running water didn't drown my voice out. "Hi there."

"Good evening, Mr. Panfilov!"

"Evening, Romuald! Why are you so official?" I asked, slightly baffled by his formal manner. It had never happened to him before.

"There's something I need to ask you, Mr. Panfilov," he drawled glibly. "What's with our business? When is the launch?"

I realized he was half-canned. "I can't talk to you right now. We're gonna start any week now. I'll give you a call."

I could hear a woman's laughter in the background and his own voice whispering, "We'll start any week now! You're gonna be my secretary!"

Then he switched back to me. "Mr. Panfilov? Well, just make sure it's all sorted! Because if you don't-"

"Right," I said. "I've no idea who you're with or where but I suggest you split and call me back later. Over."

I hung up. I really didn't like the almost condescending tone of his voice. I stayed on the balcony waiting for him to call back.

"Everything all right?" Vicky's voice came from the kitchen. "Who was it?"

"It's okay. I won't be long."

I waited a couple of minutes until finally the screen lit up again, showing Alik's toothy grin: it was the picture of him I'd taken for his phone book profile.

"Phil, I'm alone now, just like you asked," Alik said in his normal voice. "What's up?"

"You'd better tell me who you're out boozing with. What did you want from me?"

"Eh, sorry if I upset you. Today's a day off so I've had a few drinks with the guys from work and I'm just sitting here socializing. There is this girl, Irina... I think I like her," Alik paused, reluctant to go on.

"And?"

"Well, I told her I was going to quit and start my own business. Like, I was your partner. So she started nagging that she wanted to be in it too. And I-"

"I see. I'd like to ask you about something. Before you promise anything, please run everything past me first. Otherwise nothing will pan out. Agreed?"

"Word up. Sorry, Phil. You shouldn't think I'm crocked. I've only had a few beers. I'm gonna get Irina now and we'll go to my place."

"Where do you live?"

"I've rented a place next to work. It's really run down but at least it's cheap, five grand[2] all in. Listen... so do you want me to quit? And the guys as well?"

"Which guys?"

"My guys, the lads who very nearly beat the crap out of you, remember? Tarzan and the other two? I got them working with me. And if we do have to quit, we've still got a month's work in front of us."

'Okay, just let them work for the time being

[2] $75 a month which is extremely cheap even by Russian standards

seeing as you've got them already. But I might need your help very soon so you can quit from this Monday onwards. It'll take us about a month to get the show on the road."

"Yes, boss! Sorry for having troubled you. Don't hold it against me!" he hung up.

By my calculations, three weeks should have been enough to finalize everything we still had to do to launch our little enterprise. I'd had a lot of ideas but they all summed up to a few things: to bring my physical stats above average, level up Insight and wait for Optimization. Once that done, I could concentrate on my business.

I planned to start with just one thing: opening a recruitment agency. One activity was much easier to promote than several. Also, I'd already had a few successful referrals like Alik and Fatso. And once our agency had made a name for itself, we could start broadening out the range of our services.

There were two more factors at play there. Firstly, I still didn't know what kinds of perks I could receive at the next level of Insight. You never know, I might be able to see hidden treasures by looking at maps, or even new plutonium deposits. And secondly, processing a large flow of job seekers would allow me to hand-pick the best people for my own company.

I went back to Vicky. She'd already poured out the tea and was sitting at the kitchen table hugging her legs, glued to her telephone. On seeing me, she looked up quizzically.

"That was Alik," I answered her silent question.

"He asked me the same thing as you: when we're gonna start the business."

"Alik? Who's that?"

I realized they hadn't met. They'd never had the occasion.

"Just a friend," I said, unwilling to go into details. "He's gonna help me with the business."

She didn't seem too convinced but she didn't show it. All I could see in my interface was her slightly deflated mood and her prickled interest.

"You're gonna meet him as soon as I get the chance. And as far this business is concerned..." I chuckled. "This isn't just an idea. I know exactly how to launch and develop it. All I'm asking you for is a little bit of patience. You won't be disappointed, I promise."

"Phil, I'm only worried about you, don't you understand? I just can't work out what's going on in your head. I'm afraid you're thinking about going back to your old lifestyle..." she lowered her gaze.

"Look me in the eye, sweetie," I pressed my hand to my heart. "I swear on everything that's holy that I haven't even thought of anything of the kind! I'm following a plan, and this plan is going to bring success to our family!"

There was a spark of surprise in her eyes. A smile lit up her face. "Are we a family, really?"

"Yes, we are. And next weekend we're gonna see your parents just as you suggested."

"In that case..." she said slyly as if she was up to something.

She suddenly dropped her head, letting her hair

fall over her face, then stood up, holding her outstretched arms in front of her, doing an impersonation of that girl from *The Ring* movie. "You'd better watch out! The ancient evil has awoken in me! It wants you!"

* * *

EVEN IF MY RELATIONSHIP WAS GOING WELL, my leveling up strategy wasn't. All I'd achieved in two weeks was a level 13 in social status, +1 to both Strength and Agility and +2 to Stamina. Just as I'd planned, I'd invested the three system characteristic points into Perception (+2) and Intellect (+1).

Even if I'd become any smarter, I hadn't noticed it. But my heightened Perception had immediately made my world a lot brighter. I now had 20/20 vision, my hearing was excellent and so was my palate. I was even capable of telling the difference between various types of tea and coffee which I'd never noticed before. Just think that I used to equally enjoy that instant powdered crap and proper freshly-ground coffee!

As for my eyesight, the only thing I'd been able to see in the night sky without glasses was the North Star. And now... now I derived a particular pleasure from studying the heavens. How fragile planet Earth was and just how insignificant was humanity! You never know, maybe it was true about all those senior races visiting us from thousands of light years away and the mysterious Vaalphors who looked suspiciously like horror-movie demons.

I hadn't yet touched the system skill points I'd received for leveling up so now I had a total of five. It wouldn't have been wise to invest them now because the initial skill levels normally don't take much time to achieve. Which was why I was waiting for the Learning Skills optimization period to expire so that I could invest all the available system points into it. If I'd calculated everything correctly, touch wood, then I might be able to learn new skills and level up my existing ones at a truly cosmic speed, almost like in WoW. I only had ten days left to wait.

Philip "Phil" Panfilov
Age: 32
Current status: unemployed
Social status level: 13
Class: Book Reader. Level: 8
Divorced
Children: none

Main Characteristics:
Strength: 9
Agility: 7
Intellect: 20
Stamina: 9
Perception: 11
Charisma: 14
Luck: 10

At 8 pt., my Reading skill had already overtaken Empathy. These days, I wasn't perusing sales manuals anymore. I chose the books relevant to my skills as I'd already found out, through trial and error, that knowing the theory of a given skill — be it boxing or vending — considerably increased its leveling rate. I hadn't yet attacked Martha Stewart's cooking books but I fully intended to, because a high level of Cooking just might allow me to prepare buff-rich food.

Heh! Wouldn't it be cool to eat a hearty bowlful of borsch[3] knowing that it gives you +2 to Strength and 30% to Satisfaction for three hours!

These days, I was cooking much more often compared to the time I'd lived with Yanna, which had allowed me to make another level in Cooking.

Now, whenever Vicky was at work I concentrated on XP grinding. We'd get out of bed together and have breakfast sharing our plans for the day or discussing a movie or a series we'd watched the night before. Then she'd leave for work and I would head off to a dilapidated school stadium nearby, its soccer pitch with lopsided netless goal mouths overgrown with yellowed weeds.

Grass peeked out of the holes in the rubberized running track which I used to circle every day, trying to improve my distance. With every training session and every fraction of the skill gained, my running felt increasingly easier.

One fine morning I'd discovered that I was already on my fifth mile and I wasn't even out of breath. Nothing was hurting. If someone called me on my

---

[3] Borsch: Russian beetroot soup

phone, I'd be able to speak to them normally without them even noticing I was running. I'd raised Running three more points and made level 5.

Once I'd realized that it took me very little time to restore — thanks to the booster — I started going to the gym every day. Ditto for my boxing sessions. Even though my Strength wasn't growing as fast as in the beginning, I still had less than 20% left to the average 10 pt. which was about a week's training.

I'd also received a new skill: Athletics. It came without a description so I'd had to ask Martha about it. Apparently, unlike in Morrowind where Athletics only conditioned a character for running and swimming, my game system used it as the ability to compete. In other words, having this skill activated meant that the system now considered you a proper athlete (albeit an amateur) and not a wimp.

Admittedly, I was starting to feel like an athlete. My six-pack might still be concealed under a layer of fat but there wasn't much of that fat left, either. When I'd put my old glasses on just to check if my increase in Perception had indeed improved my eyesight, they refused to stay put. In actual fact, my goofy mug had thinned out so much that it now fit in the proverbial mug shot. If Kira were to be believed, I'd "shed a few years". The only thing which still reminded me of my past was my admittedly shrunken belly which, although it had stopped pouring over my belt, was still visible unless pulled in.

Last time I'd seen Alik was when he'd moved out of my old apartment. That day, I'd gone there early to make sure everything was hunky dory. He hadn't let me down. The place looked fine; he'd even managed to do some repairs. The only thing my former landlady found to complain about were the claw marks in the couch left by Boris the she-cat. We came to a reasonable agreement about this, considering the couch's ancient history.

The same day, I'd come across Fatso in the yard. He'd changed an awful lot. Maybe not on the outside but his Vitality had considerably grown and his Mood figures were high. The stable job seemed to have instilled a bit of discipline in him. It had also calmed his wife down, disabling her built-in Scold mode. Altogether, it had improved his Satisfaction, pacifying the formerly unemployed juicehead and considerably improving his Health.

Last week I'd received an invitation for a birthday party from Cyril Cyrilenko, my ex-coworker from Ultrapak. I'd wanted to invite Vicky along but she'd refused saying she wouldn't feel comfortable after what had happened with Marina and Dennis. So in the end I went there alone.

Cyril had chosen a modest but cozy venue with attentive waiters, cold beer, good food and upbeat live music. There were about ten of us, all his friends and colleagues. I didn't know some of them so I sat at a table between Greg and Marina. Their trial period had nearly come to an end but neither of them seemed to be too worried about it. Seeing as Dennis had been fired for sexually harassing Marina, and as I had also left the company, Pavel was likely to keep both trainees

— especially as their sales results had been excellent. Greg was one of those people who could sell sand to Arabs while Marina was enthusiastically working her way through the client list I'd compiled for her, working on the "not a day without a sale" basis.

After Greg had made up with his pregnant wife Alina, his paternal instinct seemed to have kicked in. Having sat with us for a couple of hours, he apologized to Cyril and went home. As for Marina, she'd brought a date along, some postgraduate or other.

I was truly happy I'd been able to help my friends and change the course of their lives in some way. Who knows? Maybe this small readjustment would change their lives dramatically for the better. Or was it already doing so?

By the way, the system had classified my attendance as a socially meaningful action and rewarded it with some XP points. Apparently, the ability to always stand by your friends in good times as well as bad was considered a virtue.

I hadn't heard from Yanna even though my Mom had called her mother for some unknown reason and asked how she was doing. That's my Mom for you: she's constantly worrying about everyone. As far as I understood, their conversation had been curt and brief, ending with Mrs. Orlova's demand to "leave her family alone".

Mom had accepted this with comprehension. I'd only found this out by pure chance from Dad when the two of us went to our summer cottage one weekend to help build the bathhouse[4]. I'd used the occasion to weed the vegetable garden, bringing my Agriculture skill to level 2. I'd also used the hand pump to water the whole garden. No amount of time in the gym can compare to hand-watering a garden. My muscles were still indignant of the fact, remembering all the effort.

One morning on my way back home from my run I'd met Mr. Panikoff, the dear old-age pensioner. I tensed up: by then, the whole dark incident involving Valiadis and Khphor had already begun to fade from my memory. Deep inside I'd been expecting something like this to happen. Still, my worst expectations hadn't come true. All that had happened was he'd issued me another quest. Apparently, his children had given him a tablet with his favorite sports newspaper app already installed — but it stopped working whenever his Wi-Fi was out of range. As soon as I walked the old gentleman back to our building's door and within range of his Wi-Fi, the app started up and the quest was closed, rewarding me with 5 more Reputation points and a negligible amount of XP.

I'd bought myself a mid-range laptop, perfect for writing and doing online search. It was lightweight with a wide screen and a long-life battery. I'd developed the habit of taking it with me in my sports bag so that I could pop into a café on my way back from a gym

---

[4] A steambath house is a Russian version of a sauna heated with a wood burner, common in the Russian countryside. It is a small one-story log hut usually located some distance from the main house, normally at the back of the garden, preferably close to a source of water such as a river or a stream.

practice and do a bit of writing. This had become my favorite time of the day. I was yet to tackle novel-length manuscripts but at least my vignettes and short stories had found their reader, harvesting likes and comments. That in itself was motivation enough, not to mention the fact that they improved my ranking on that particular writers' portal.

I'd gone as far as to write the story of Alik and Fatso whom I'd rolled into one character. It had become a one-day wonder, hitting the portal's "most read" list. The readers demanded a sequel which I didn't have because the story's prototypes were too busy working and basically leading an uneventful life. If it went on like this, I might write a sci-fi story in which the MC would receive the same kind of interface as I now had.

Like about some puny guy who was too scared to fight. Why not? It might be interesting.

In any case, my Writing and MS Word skills kept leveling at a rate of knots. That showed both in their numerical values and in the way I felt. Words came easier; my fingers flitted over the keyboard and ideas seemed to come out of nowhere so that I'd even had to start a special file in my smartphone to jot them down.

The change in my lifestyle had also indirectly affected my other skills: Self-Discipline (+2), Self-Control (+1), Perseverance (+2) and Long-Term Planning (+1). Indeed, these days I found it easier to follow my own plans, nipping all attempts at procrastination and cowardly moments of "I don't feel like it" in the bud.

The major part of XP I now had I'd amassed by

leveling up skills and characteristics — but some of it I'd also received for completing the tasks I'd set for myself. Any athletics-related goals counted (like an effort to run a hundred meters more than the day before), as well as helping my family with their everyday tasks. For instance, helping my Dad at their summer cottage that day had resulted in me receiving a hefty 500 pt.

What upset me a little was that I still couldn't level up Insight. I'd already got into the habit of IDying everything in sight. It had become as involuntary and automatic as turning round in the street to double-check a pretty woman's posterior. Still, it didn't seem enough.

The skill seemed to have frozen at about 40% halfway between levels 2 and 3. All the hundreds of object identifications I performed every day garnered me a fraction of a percent.

Ditto for using the interface map. Whenever I asked Martha about it, her response was like a Catch-22 situation: my level of Insight wasn't enough to receive the answer to the question of how to level up Insight.

I had this idea that its leveling rate could increase whenever I used the interface for the benefit of society. Alternatively, the skill's level cap could be tied to the current social status level — but I had no means of checking out these two theories yet.

But the biggest improvement, apart from Running, had proven to be my Boxing skill (+3) which had brought the total up to level 4.

Main Skills and Abilities:

Learning Skills: 3 (a primary skill currently undergoing Optimization: +4)
Reading: 8
MS Word: 7)
Empathy: 7
PC skills: 7
Vending: 6
Communication Skills: 6
Creative Writing: 6
Russian language skills: 6
Running: 5
Intuition: 5
Cooking: 5
Online search: 5
MS Excel: 5
Boxing: 4
Perseverance: 4
Decision Making: 4
Hand-to-Hand combat: 4
Self-Discipline: 4
Self-Control: 4
Seduction: 4
English Language skills: 3
Long-Term Planning: 3
Speed Typing: 3
Manners: 3
Driving: 2
Pushbike riding: 2
Leadership: 2

Marketing: 2
Map reading: 2
Public Speaking: 2
Fishing: 2
Agriculture: 2
Power of Persuasion: 2

...

Athletics: 1

...

Playing World of Warcraft: 8 (a secondary skill currently undergoing Optimization: −8)

System Skills:
Insight: 2
Optimization: 1
Heroism: 1

System skill points available: 5

But as for the money, I was slowly but surely running out. After I'd paid the rent on the new flat and bought the laptop, I had to shell out a lot for my individual boxing lessons — and I also took Vicky out from time to time.

I had put a certain amount away for a rainy day but I loathed to dip into it, determined to level up financial discipline. Spending is easy; saving and making the money grow is much harder.

* * *

THE TWO GRAND I HAD TO PAY MY COACH FOR EVERY boxing session was quickly depleting my budget. If I wanted to continue training with what little money I still had left, I had to join the group. It would certainly be wise and much cheaper.

So once the next session was over, I stopped him. "Mr. Matov, I need a quick word with you."

"What is it?" he glanced at his watch, apparently in a hurry. "Go on then but make it quick."

"Do you remember when I first came you refused to let me join the group? Do you think I'm good enough now? Am I ready?"

He frowned. "When you're ready I'll let you know. In my personal opinion, you're still a while behind the other guys. You'll be holding them back. You've made some progress, I agree. You're night and day compared to what you used to be. But they're young guys who've been training since early childhood and you're still a wimp. Every boxer that's worth his salt will punch your lights out."

"Yeah but-"

"Are you serious? Listen, I have an important tournament coming up and I won't have the time to mollycoddle you in the group. It's one thing when you pay for your own training and quite another when you start impinging on the time of the really promising guys who work hard to prepare for the competition. It's absolutely out of the question. Carry on for another six months and then we'll see."

"But I don't have money for another six months, Sir! I could pay you for another couple of sessions and after that, I'll either have to quit or look for another gym."

"Does that mean you're stopping with the one-on-one training?"

"I'm afraid so. Two more sessions is all I can manage. But I don't want to give up boxing."

"Now listen. I have to run. There're people waiting for me. I have two groups: one trains Mondays, Wednesdays and Fridays, the other Tuesdays, Thursdays and Saturdays. Both start at 7 p.m. Come and we'll see. If you can't keep up, I'll kick you out, as simple as that. You sign up and pay at the reception. That's it, I need to rush. See ya!"

He left, leaving me to decide how to fit it into my schedule. I wanted to keep the weekend evenings free, just in case I wanted to take Vicky out. So it looked like it would have to be Mondays, Wednesdays and Fridays.

Consumed by these thoughts, I headed to the locker room when some jerk barged past me, knocking my shoulder.

"Is the corridor not big enough?" he asked, swinging round. "I could cut you down to size a little bit, if you want."

I decided not to make a big thing of it. "Sorry. I was miles away."

"Yuri!" another guy called him from the boxing hall. "We're all waiting for you! Get your ass in gear!"

"Coming!" Yuri shouted, then turned back to me. "Listen, are you the guy who trains with Matov?"

"Yes, and what of it?"

"Aha, I see now! You're the daddy's boy who takes private lessons every day. Fancy sparring with me?"

"No, thanks."

"As you wish. See you around... wuss," laughing, he disappeared into the hall.

Yeah right! I don't think so! He had Boxing all leveled up. Compared to his 7 pt., my four were a joke.

I looked at the calendar on my smartphone. Without it, I wouldn't be able to stick to a strict schedule. I wouldn't even know which day of the week it was. Aha! Today was Wednesday which meant this had been the group which I wanted to join. No, I didn't fancy training with such a bunch of uncourteous and unfriendly individuals.

Having thus come to a decision, I headed for the reception and laid the magnetic locker bracelet on the desk.

A petite blonde called Katia scooped up the bracelet and gave me my card. "Are you all done, Phil?" she flashed me a pearly smile. "How did it go?"

"Everything went fine, thanks. Listen Katia, I'm stopping one-on-one training with Matov and transferring to his group. Can you sign me up for Tuesdays, Thursdays and Saturdays?"

"Just a minute. When are you starting?"

"Next week. I'm leaving town for the weekend. I'll finish up the one-on-ones for this week if it's possible."

"Of course," she replied, tapping something into the computer. "Now: evening boxing sessions starting

Tuesday at 7 p.m. Don't be late, otherwise Matov might not let you in."

"I know," I smiled, remembering his proverbial *'one minute late and it's finished!'*

"Are you gonna pay straight away? It's four thousand a month."

"I'm afraid I don't have it on me. I'll pay just before the session."

"Very well. See you, then!"

BACK HOME, I WAS GREETED BY BORIS THE SHE-CAT WHO complained bitterly, peppering her diatribe with a feline equivalent of f-words. I'd been out the whole day and she'd missed me. Having said that, she was probably just hungry.

"Can I at least change into something dry?" I begged. "I'm soaked through!"

Still, she wouldn't leave me alone, rubbing against my legs.

My conversations with Boris — and with Richie the pooch before that — probably didn't fit the pattern of a completely sane person. But I couldn't help it. I understand that it's probably naïve and stupid to see a human being in every man and animal. But that was just me.

I opened the kitchen cupboard. The shelf where I kept cat food was empty. I'd forgotten to buy it again. I had this urge to get dressed and rush out to the shop but hesitated. I really didn't want to get wet again.

"Go and drink some milk," I remonstrated with the cat.

Contrary to stereotypes, Boris wasn't fond of milk. No idea why but she'd always preferred industrial cat food to milk and even meat. Could they be indeed lacing it with something? Nevertheless, her hunger was so strong she attacked her milk with gusto.

Still, unwilling to upset her, I called Vicky.

"Hi," she replied. "I'm coming over to see you soon."

"Great, I'll be waiting. Can you go past the shop for me?"

"Easy. What do you need?"

"Just some coffee and a bag of cat food. Could you bring that?"

"Not a problem. Kisses! See you soon!"

I turned on the TV for some ambience, peeled off my soaked clothes and threw them in the washer when I overheard an anxious voice off-screen,

"An all-points alert has been put out for Joseph Kogan, a six-year-old boy last seen in the local mall... dressed in... please contact the search and rescue team..."

That was the mall where I did my shopping! I hurried into the room to catch the precious snippets of identification data: the boy's picture, date of birth... description and height. Now I had enough KIDD points.

I opened the map. He was alive. He was out of town though, somewhere in the north east.

I zoomed in to the max on the house. It didn't look like a posh villa. I surveyed the outhouses and the

---

fenced-off yard. A white SUV was parked by the house. I didn't observe any movement; the boy's marker was quivering on the map indicating that the object was moving around slowly inside.

I reached onto the bookshelf and pulled out a fat encyclopedia, reaching for a sturdy well-used Nokia stashed behind it. I'd bought several such antiques in a seedy phone repair shop by an underground crossing specifically for occasions like this.

I got dressed, slid the phone, the charger and a SIM card into my pocket and went outside, calling Uber on the way.

So as not to get wet, I waited for the cab in the doorway. After about five minutes, a battered old Lada pulled up. The driver's rating was very low and I saw why the moment we'd pulled away. He started grumbling, complaining about everything.

"Jesus Christ, I've just washed the car and now it's bucketing down! It'll take me ages to clean all those muddy footprints!"

I gave a sympathetic chuckle which he must have taken as me being contrary.

"Something you don't like?" he snapped. "I'm in my own car! I can do what the hell I want! Where to?"

"I gave my destination when I booked you," I said, slightly annoyed. I was trying to word a search query and he was distracting me.

"Is it so hard to give me an answer?"

"Absolutely not. Vernadsky St. 306."

"Which Vernadsky is it?" he decided to show off. "The geoscientist?"

"Dunno. Maybe."

"That's young people for you these days! Nobody knows the history of their own country! When I was young..."

My phone vibrated in my pocket. It was Vicky.

"Where've you got to?" she laughed. "Did you go out yourself to get cat food? Was Boris too impatient for her dinner?"

"I'm going to go and look at an office," I adlibbed. "It's a good offer, I don't want to lose it."

"No way! You don't mean it! How cool is that? Okay, I'll wait for you. You tell me about it later. I'll cook something for dinner. Love you."

"Likewise," I took the telephone from my ear.

"He's gonna look at an office!" the driver muttered under his breath. "Everyone's a businessman these days. All those iPhones, offices, businesses... Everywhere you turn, it's nothing but commerce!"

I tried to distance myself from his grumbling. I'd already come far enough to do what I'd intended to do when I'd left the house and ventured back into the rain.

I inserted the battery into the phone and waited for it to boot up. Then I typed a text message,

You can find the missing boy Joseph Kogan at a house located on the north east highway 20 miles from town. The exact coordinates are...

I sent the message to the two numbers I had for the search and rescue team, pulled the SIM card out, broke it, removed the battery, opened the window a

---

crack and flung everything out by the roadside.

"Are you hot?" the driver asked, casting an unhappy glance at the window.

"Me? Yes, it's a bit stuffy in here. Could you take me somewhere else instead? I've changed my mind. I won't be going to Vernadsky St."

Having lied to Vicky, now I had to lay the groundwork for my fib. I opened the map and searched for all business centers with rentable premises. I then narrowed my search to the offers of less then 500 square feet, security and cleaning staff included, in the immediate vicinity of my house with a rentable value between...

I found a suitable offer six blocks away from my place. I Googled it, then dialed the number given on the site but nobody picked up.

Never mind. Even if there was no one in administration at this late hour, at least I could go and see for myself. That way I'd have something to tell Vicky.

That's it, then. Let's go there!

The driver kept grumbling. I looked up.

"Hello!" he demanded. "Where to now?"

"Chekhov St. 72, please."

The moment I leaned back in the seat and tried to relax, my phone rang again.

The number didn't show. For a while, I just stared at the screen wondering if I should answer it. It wasn't as if I was afraid of phone calls from strangers but I was a bit reluctant to talk to the likes of Police Investigator Igorevsky just now.

Finally, I decided that the uncertainly was worse than taking the call from a potential police officer.

The driver, too, was getting annoyed. "Are you gonna pick it up or what?"

I did.

"Hello," a strange male voice said. "You've just phoned our number."

"That's right. Is this Chekhov business center?"

"Yes, go on, I'm listening," the voice urged, impatient. "What was it you wanted?"

"I called you about office rental. Could I come now and take a look?"

"What exactly do you have in mind?" he asked, all businesslike. "What surface area?"

"Something around five hundred feet."

"We do have something to offer you. But I'm leaving in half an hour, do you think you can make it?"

"I'll be there in ten minutes."

"Good. I'll meet you at the entrance."

Even though he'd never introduced himself, he was apparently happy to land a potential customer. I too felt slightly elated. The initial reason for my phoning — my desire to justify my sudden disappearance from home — had already taken a back seat. I was curious to see the office where I might possibly start my first real business. What if I actually liked it?

We finally arrived at the center. The driver pulled up by the curb without continuing to the parking lot.

"Have a nice day," I sincerely wished him. He

could use some positivity.

Not bothering to reply, he pulled away sharply as soon as I closed the door.

I took a good look around. The parking lot was almost empty if you didn't count two rather shabby cars parked in the slots for the company administration.

The four-story Soviet-era administrative building was rather squat and unpresentable. A massive staircase faced with crumbling tiles led to the front doors. Two flowerbeds lined the entrance; a long-unkempt hedge grew along the fence. A cumbersome concrete awning overhung the façade, sporting an unassuming sign of vinyl letters, Chekhov Business Center.

I climbed the stairs and leaned my weight against the heavy wooden door.

I was greeted by a typical office smell. The hall still preserved the aura of a Soviet-style government building, complete with the local version of Maxwell's demon: an old lady doorkeeper sitting at a flimsy desk with an ancient rotary-dial telephone. Her kind usually decided who deserved the right to be let in. Although apparently dosing off, she was nevertheless vigilant, my arrival provoking a knee-jerk reaction in her.

"Where do you think you're going?" she asked cantankerously the moment I'd crossed some invisible threshold.

"Good evening! Sorry I don't know your name," my Empathy prompted the right approach: as long as I showed respect to her age, everything would be fine.

"I'm Auntie Ira."

"Excuse me, Auntie Ira, I'm here about renting some space. When I called, they told me to come here for a viewing."

"Who told you that? You know what time it is? There's nobody here now!"

"Some guy but I don't know his name."

"Come tomorrow," she announced, then mumbled under her breath, "I should have locked the doors, lazy cow..."

While she was still grumbling, complaining about all sorts of folk who kept "coming and going at every ungodly hour", I dialed the number again. Before it even started ringing, the old lady waved her hands and exclaimed,

"Mr. Gorelik! You still here?"

"I am," a man mumbled, walking down the stairs in the company of a woman. "Do me a favor, Auntie Ira, and try to at least pretend you're not asleep."

"God forbid!" the old lady exclaimed with another wave of her hands.

The man left his companion and headed over to me with a spring in his step. "Was it you who called me about the space?"

"That's right. I just spoke to you not long ago. My name's Phil."

"I'm Stephan Gorelik. I'm the manager here."

His female companion — an ample peroxide blonde with hair permed into tight curls — walked over to us. "Are we finished, Steve? I need to be off. My husband keeps calling."

"Yes, thank you very much, Mrs. Frolova," the man said with a faint smile. "I really appreciate your help with the paperwork."

"You're very welcome," she replied with a blush, then left.

While Gorelik watched her leave, I quickly studied his profile.

Stephan Gorelik.
Age: 46
Current status: manager
Social status level: 6
Class: angler. Level: 5
Married
Wife: Maria Gorelik
Children: Vasily, son. Age: 25
Criminal record: yes
Reputation: Indifference 0/30
Interest: 58%
Fear: 14%
Mood: 49%

The fact that his interest in me was pretty high was quite clear. When you have available premises that don't pay for themselves, every new tenant is a feather in the manager's cap. His rather average Mood could be explained by the long working day and possibly a missed lunch break. But fear? What could he be afraid of? Could it be just a light anxiety brought about by his adultery? Possible.

Not wanting to increase his anxiety by focusing

on his unzipped fly, I elected not to say anything.

"Come and have a look," he called me.

As we climbed the stairs, he asked, "What kind of company have you got?"

"A recruitment agency."

"How many staff?" he asked, wheezing.

"At the moment, just myself," I replied, then added, seeing the surprise in his face. "We haven't started yet."

We went up to the third floor. My eye fell on the ubiquitous fire hazard regulations on the wall next to a fire extinguisher. An endless corridor stretched out on both sides of us.

"To the right," Gorelik wheezed.

He stopped by a metal door painted a cheerful light blue which admittedly didn't look very serious.

"This one was previously occupied by some MLM guys," he explained. "They sold makeup, perfume, that sort of thing. Things went well for them so they moved to the center."

He sorted through a bunch of keys, found the right one, unlocked the door and gestured me inside, "Come in, please."

As I stepped in, a faint wave of excitement swept over me. Behind my back, the manager flipped the light switch, flooding the room with a cold fluorescent light.

"It's just been recarpeted," he said. "The blinds are new. They even left a couple of desks and chairs behind as part of their rent. If you need the landline, you'll have to have it reconnected."

"And the Internet?"

"They'll do it at the same time as they connect the landline. We have a permanent contract with the providers so they'll get it all done within twenty-four hours. In total, it's under five hundred square feet which will cost you forty-six rubles[5] a square foot," he produced his phone and made some quick calculations. "In total it's twenty-three grand a month[6]. If you pay for an extended period, I can give you a discount."

"What kind of period? And what kind of discount?"

"If you pay upfront for the first quarter, we could make it twenty grand a month."

"I'll have to think about it."

"Think but not too long. A lot of people come and ask us about available premises and this office is the best we have. Would you like to look at something else? Something cheaper, maybe?"

I took another wander around the room to check out all the little things that might need fixing or redecorating. The walls were a bit shabby in places, one of the plinths had come away from the wall; there was also an oily patch on the floor and a window catch that didn't work.

"A thorough cleaning will cost you a couple grand," the manager said. "And you can count the same for a paint job."

"Thanks," I said sincerely. Considering my lifestyle over the last years, I was a total noob in

---

[5] About $0.70 per square foot
[6] About $350 a month

everything concerning cleaning, painting and decorating. If I made up my mind, I'd have to have a chat with Alik. He might know someone who could use a little job like this.

"Do you want to look at anything else?" the manager said impatiently. "I really need to go."

"Yes, why not? Just to compare."

Ten minutes later, we went back downstairs. Their other offers hadn't impressed me at all. In fact, they shocked me. One of the rooms hadn't been redecorated since Soviet times. Its parquet floor had sunk, its walls painted a ghastly dark blue to shoulder height, its window frames loose and crumbling. Another room was too big and a third one too small, resembling a broom closet. Having viewed this last one, I decided to do a bit of haggling for the first one.

"So," I summed up, "is this all you have?"

"Not really. We have another room on this floor and four more on the fourth floor."

"Could I venture a guess that they're even worse than the ones we've already seen? This place is really in a state."

"Well, you know, the owner won't lay out anything for decoration," he complained. "He says, let the tenants do it themselves. And you know what tenants are like these days... they can barely scrape together enough money to pay the rent and even then they're late."

"So seeing as you have so many unrented premises which bring nothing in, maybe you could bring the price down a tad for the first one? You know which one I mean, don't you?"

"How am I supposed to charge less? It's at rock bottom now! Twenty grand for a great office! All inclusive: the electricity, the heating, the cleaning and even security."

I laughed. "Security? You mean that old lady by the front door?"

He gave me a bitter grin. "It's up to you. I don't have anything else to offer you."

"I'd say, thirty rubles per square foot is all it's worth. So taking into account the relatively recent decoration, the cleaning and security in the form of an ancient old lady, I suggest fifteen grand a month."

"What do you mean, fifteen?" he seethed with indignation. "A great office like this with cleaning and security can't cost less that nineteen grand a month! And that paid quarterly!"

In the end, we agreed on seventeen and a half. Gorelik gave me a week "to think it over", promising to hold it for me for a symbolic advance.

In fact, I'd already made up my mind. The only thing I still had to "think over" was how to come up with $750 for the first three months.

My initial plan hadn't counted on paying the advance; furthermore, I'd naively expected to talk him into being able to pay at the end of the month, hoping to find a few clients and make a bit of money. But the more I looked into the finer details of my idea, the more I realized I'd be lucky if I broke even straight off, with or without the advantage of the interface.

Which was the reason why I kept delaying the

launch, telling myself I had to level up a bit more.

The system registered the new task as a matter of course:

Find the rent money, sign the rental agreement and pay the Chekhov Business Center for the first three month. Deadline: July 1.

I paid Gorelik the two-thousand advance which went straight into his pocket, considerably improving his Mood.

Once back downstairs, I noted his cell number and bade my goodbye to him. As I headed for the door, I heard him giving the security babushka a good dressing-down for having let in a certain Veronica who apparently was a persistent non-payer.

"But that wasn't me!" the old lady replied indignantly. "That was during old Tamara's shift!"

As I rode home, I remembered the missing boy and checked the map. He was on his way back to town in an ambulance. Excellent. I just hoped he'd be all right.

Still, I kept getting this nagging feeling that all was not well with the boy.

Chapter Two

Meeting the Parents

*The man who is fortunate in his
choice of son-in-law gains a son;
the man unfortunate in his choice
loses his daughter also.*

Democritus

HAVING ARRIVED AT VICKY'S HOME TOWN, WE TOOK A
walk in the courtyard where she'd spent her childhood.
Everything about it was depressing; even my old yard
complete with Yagoza and his alcoholic buddies looked
brighter and more lively in comparison with the junk-
filled yard of this old house.

Even trees didn't grow here. A discarded plastic
bag rustled in a sickly-looking bush, caught on one of
the branches.

The entire town in general with its population of
less than twenty thousand exuded an aura of

42

depression. During the couple of hours that we'd spent driving there, Vicky told me that young people used every opportunity to leave the place the moment they'd finished school. They settled in big cities and moved their parents over which was why with every passing year the town's original population shrank, replaced by newcomers from the ex-Soviet Asian republics.

Nobody came out to greet us. As we climbed to the fifth floor of the dilapidated prefab remnant from Kruschev's times, the more disheartened Vicky grew. I could see that her relationship with her parents wasn't the warmest. Still, they doted on Xena, their granddaughter, which remained the only link between the parents and their daughter.

Vicky's mood proved to be contagious as I started worrying about our meeting's outcome. I could already list all the reasons why they wouldn't like me. I had neither a job nor a place of my own, I didn't have a car, and on top of it all, I was divorced. The list could go on — but still I decided to carry on to the end and do everything correctly like a good mensch.

The moment we'd stepped in, it became painfully obvious that nobody here was happy to see me. Everything pointed to the fact: the brusqueness of her parents, the grim "Hi" mumbled by her brother Victor, not to mention my interface Reputation reading: *Dislike.*

As Vicky was talking to her daughter and her parents in the kitchen, I was sent "to wait" in her brother's room. Victor hospitably hid behind his computer, engrossed in Counter Strike. Over the next hour, we only exchanged a couple of meaningless phrases. Then they called us.

We all sat around a cramped table and waited for Aunt Toma to serve up the *pelmeni*[7].

"So you're not working, are you?" Uncle Alexey asked grimly, stabbing a *pelmen* with his fork.

"Dad, didn't I tell you just now that Phil is starting his own business?" Vicky piped up.

"And you should hush up when men are talking!" Aunt Toma chastized her daughter.

"I suggest you take Xena and go out for a walk," Uncle Alexey suggested. "We'll carry on without you."

Vicky and I had spent some time discussing how I should address them before we finally settled on Uncle Alexey and Aunt Toma. I didn't want to address them formally but was reluctant to call them Mom and Dad which was admittedly a bit too early. Like this it was nice and neutral.

Without saying a word, Vicky rose from the table and went to get Xena dressed. Her daughter seemed to be the only one who'd received me well. We'd immediately found common language, discussing her favorite cartoons while I was introduced to everybody else and found my bearings in this new situation.

But as for her parents and her younger brother, things hadn't gone as smoothly. Vicky's dad was a working-class man who'd spent all his life busting his

---

[7] Pelmeni: Russian meat dumplings, a popular and much loved dish. Can be bought readymade in supermarkets but every Russian cook worth his or her salt have their own family recipe.

hump for a construction company. For him, stability and reliability were the cornerstone virtues. Her mother worked for the same company as a bookkeeper and completely shared her husband's views. Up until now, they'd never stopped blaming Vicky for the breakup of her first unsuccessful marriage when she'd got hitched practically with the first guy who'd asked her. In their opinion, she'd made a completely irrational and improper choice. They even derived a particular gleeful pleasure from her current status as a divorcee and single mother, as in, "We told you so!"

"Eat!" Uncle Alexey commanded. "These are real pelmenis, Toma's spent all morning making them. We made the stuffing last night, so you can't get any fresher than that. Come on, pour some sour cream over them! That's real stuff, not like that crap they sell in town. Eat!"

"I am eating, thank you. And very nice they are, too!"

"Help yourself! So what about your job?" he got back to his original question. "From what Vicky told us, you didn't even last a month at her company."

"And why did you split up with your ex?" Aunt Toma inquired, placing more salads and starters on the table.

I switched my attention to her, then looked back at him, wondering whose question to answer first. The father decided it for me,

"Give it a break, Toma! Go sit down and stop fussing about!"

She perched herself on a chair. Both of them

looked at me, awaiting an answer.

"At the moment, I don't work. I quit Vicky's company because I decided to open my own business. They asked me to stay but for me, it was now or never. That's why I left. I'm going into..." I paused to fill my mouth with pelmenis, realizing that Vicky's father probably wouldn't appreciate my recruitment agency idea.

"What are you going into?"

"Just some business."

"Monkey business," young Victor snickered as he stuffed his face with food. He seemed to be the only one who felt comfortable in this oppressive atmosphere.

Vicky's father gave him a sonorous slap on the back of the head. "Shut up and listen when your elders are talking!"

Victor lowered his face over his plate. His ears went red. His Mood had plummeted as his father had humiliated him in front of a stranger.

"So what kind of business is it?"

"In the service sector," I replied vaguely.

"What's that, peanut salesman?" Uncle Alexey insisted. "Or someone who wipes other people's asses for them?"

"It's more like a supply and demand sort of thing."

He chuckled away his discontent as he waded through his pelmenis. My Reputation with him had dropped to the lowest possible Dislike reading. One more faux pas on my part could result in unbridled

Animosity.

I had my work cut out for me, I could feel it. Boring me with his glare, the fifty-year-old Uncle Alexey frowned his ample eyebrows. He looked impressive. Now I understood where Vicky had got her shapely body. He was a huge man almost seven foot tall with arms used to hard physical labor. My potential father-in-law sat straight as a ramrod, towering over us at this small kitchen table like a mythical giant. The fork in his calloused bear paw looked like a child's toy. It took all of my self-restraint not to lower my eyes first.

'Very well," he summed up. "You've made everything very clear. Meaning, nothing is clear. I'm not sure you know yourself what you want. You're just leading Vicky up the garden path."

"You really shouldn't talk like that, Uncle Alexey," I said. "I have everything sorted. We'll never go without. I just don't like talking about things that aren't even done yet. Once I do it, I'll tell you everything. But now it's pretty pointless."

He chuckled. "Yeah right, pull the other one, it's got bells on. Okay, let's leave it like that. And what kind of person are you? Tell us a bit about yourself. What's your trade? Who are your parents? Vicky said, you used to be married."

"I was. I met my first wife online. She was still at college."

Victor pricked up his ears, apparently interested. Aunt Toma craned her neck so as not to miss one word. Then she jumped up and exclaimed,

"Wait a sec, Phil! Let me pour the tea first and

then you'll tell us!"

She was a fragile petite woman two years her husband's junior who was visibly afraid of him — but still had boundless respect for him, obeying his every word as if it was set in stone. Being a mother, it didn't stop her interfering in our conversation.

As she was fussing with the kettle and the teapot, scalding the tea leaves with boiling water and slicing the cream cake we'd brought along, I'd finished my plate and thanked her. Indeed, her pelmenis were exceptional. And the whole time I sensed the appraising stares of my potential father-in-law.

Which was why I couldn't read the quest message that had suddenly appeared in my view without my face making funny grimaces. I was forced to minimize the window and leave it until a more appropriate time.

"Dad, are we going to watch the soccer? It's Croatia versus Argentina!" Victor asked, then switched his gaze to me. "Are you watching the World Cup?"

"Oh yes. That would be great."

He smiled and gave me a satisfied nod.

Your Reputation with Victor Koval has improved!
Current Reputation: Indifference 5/30

"You can talk about soccer later," Uncle Alexey said. "Come on, mother, sit down. Carry on telling us about yourself, Phil."

"My parents are quite ordinary," I said. "My dad is a fireman and my mom's a school teacher."

Your Reputation with Mr. Alexey Koval has improved!
Current Reputation: Dislike 20/30

Your Reputation with Mrs. Tamara "Toma" Koval has improved!
Current Reputation: Dislike 5/30

I fought the temptation to look at the system messages flickering in my view because I'd have hated them to have thought that I was shifty-eyed. In any case, my parents' professions apparently seemed to have passed the litmus test so I had to continue in the same vein trying not to tell any lies.

"What does she teach?" Victor asked.

"Russian language and literature. They're both retired now."

"So they're retirees, then," Uncle Alexey came to some conclusions only apparent to himself.

"And what kind of pensions do they hand out these days!" Aunt Toma exclaimed. "They're a joke! Do you help them out?"

"I try to, as much as I can," I replied, remembering my gardening stint at their summer cottage. I wasn't exactly lying but I felt some pangs of conscience because she did mean financial help. "I also have an elder sister, Kira, who works at the bank."

"Is she married?" Aunt Toma interrupted me. "You sister, I mean?"

"She's divorced. She's raising a son who's slightly younger than Xena," I replied willingly, trying to satisfy her curiosity.

Still, I didn't like the straightforwardness of her questions. I felt I was being interviewed for the position of son-in-law.

"Come on, keep going," Uncle Alexey said. "You're not a spring chicken anymore. What have you done in your life?"

"Take our Vicky, for instance," Aunt Toma began. "Who would have thought that she would have made a career in the city. Now she's a *deputee* director at a factory!" she said proudly.

"Deputy director?" I repeated mechanically.

"Of course!" She gave me a look of disbelief at my apparent naïveté. "You must know, seeing as you two worked together, no?"

"Just give him a chance to tell us about himself!" Vicky's father snapped.

"I won't say a word more," she made a mouth-zipping gesture.

All this time, Victor had been busy stuffing himself with the cake. Seeing as nobody had been watching it, he'd already demolished a third of it. He could certainly work his jaws! But as for Vicky working as a "deputy director", I might have to have a word with her in order not to burst their bubble.

Her parents were sitting expectantly, waiting for me to reply. I plucked up my courage and began,

"I finished college where I studied economics. It's true that since my internship, I've never worked in this profession. So for the last ten years, I basically just went with the flow. You know what they say about turds never sinking?"

I caught the faint glimpse of a smile on the man's lips. Apparently, he appreciated a little self-deprecation.

My next words I chose just as carefully as if I were negotiating a mine field. "So basically, I was in sales for some time."

Uncle Alexey pulled a sour face. "What do you mean, as in shop assistant?"

"Not exactly. I didn't have to stand behind a counter. I moved around a lot offering various goods and services."

He squinted sardonically at me. "Goods *or* services?"

"Depending who I worked for, Uncle Alexey. Do you qualify satellite dishes as goods? And advertising them in a paper — is it a service? I wasn't particularly successful though which was why I moved on to writing."

"And what is it that you wrote?" Vicky's mother asked in surprise.

I could understand her. It's not every day you get to entertain a real author in your kitchen. "I didn't mean it like that, Aunt Toma. I wrote articles for various websites and businesses..."

Seeing as they'd stopped interrupting me, I finished up in one breath in all sincerity, albeit omitting my gaming past. "I didn't earn much doing that, either. That's exactly why my first wife Yanna left me. She put up with it for four years, waiting for me to either make it or get my act together. But it just so happened that I finally got my act together only after I'd lost her. I still remember that day last May. It felt like I'd been hit by a ton of bricks. I walked out onto the balcony and took stock of my life asking myself what I'd done with it. The answer was, I'd done nothing! I turned thirty-two last winter and what did I have to show for it? I didn't have a job or a place of my own, I didn't even have children. And now I'd lost my wife as well! You can't imagine how I felt. I was gutted."

Resting her cheek in her cupped hand, Aunt Toma listened to me open-mouthed, enthralled by my story as she mechanically continued to stir the long-dissolved sugar in her cup. Uncle Alexey silently gnashed his teeth. Even Victor froze with a piece of cake in his mouth.

Come on, Charisma, give it your all! Communication Skills, get on with it! Empathy, do your job!

"I was so gutted that it felt as if a switch had been flipped on in my head. I started running in the mornings, I found a job straight away, I signed up for a gym and started boxing and pumping iron. Workwise, things went just fine. Vicky can tell you. I was a successful salesman. Our boss paid me large bonuses and wanted me to stay — but by then, I'd already decided I was done working for a boss," I used this last cliché to make sure the phrase was imprinted in their brains. "I already found an office the other day. I'll be launching in two or three weeks, depending on how fast I can register the company. So basically, I just got my act together.."

The deadly silence was broken by the sound of Aunt Toma's teaspoon falling to the floor. As I awaited their response or at least any coherent reaction to my story, I picked up my mug and took a sip of strongly brewed tea to wet my whistle. I could hear the front door open.

Vicky's voice rang out in the hallway,

"We're back! Have you finished interrogating Phily?"

"*Phily!*" Victor rolled his eyes and dissolved into broken-voiced teenage laughter.

'Gran, I'm thirsty!" Xena announced, appearing in the kitchen.

Aunt Toma jumped up to pour her some water. Victor rose from the table too. "Thanks, Mom. It was great. Dad, can I go and play now?"

"Sit yourself down!" Vicky's father barked. "We're not finished yet! Victoria, come back here. This concerns you too."

As Xena was drinking her water, Victor surrendered his place to his sister. She sat down looking at our faces, very concerned.

"Now," Uncle Alexey summed it all up. "Victoria, I've listened to your fancy man and had a think. He sings a nice song, very pleasant to listen too, only I have no faith in him at all. You're a grown woman now, you've been married before so it's up to you how you want to live your life. All I want to say, don't expect us to give you our blessing for a match with this loafer!"

"We won't! Don't even ask!" Aunt Toma enthusiastically nodded her agreement. "We don't believe him and you shouldn't, either!"

"You keep your mouth shut, Tamara! No one wants to know your opinion!" Vicky's father slammed his fist down on the table and pronounced his verdict in a voice ringing with indignation. "A fucking *salesman*! He calls himself a businessman! At his age, your mother and I already had a small place of our own! We had a car and a summer cottage! You wanted for nothing and Victor was already on the way. And all this we did ourselves, your mother and I! Our whole lives we've been working hard without ever complaining! And what is this guy? He's piss poor! He's trying to get out of the crap he got himself into through his own laziness by sponging off you! I bet it was you who found him that job in the first place! And then your bosses must have realized what a big mouth he was and kicked him out by the scruff of his neck! And you believe all his bullshit? Or are you covering up for him on purpose? You should think with your head and not with your pussy! That's exactly what he's counting on! He wants to make you fall for him and marry him All he needs is a free ride and someone to warm his bed in place of his ex-wife! He just saw you were pretty, had a good job and a place of your own so he decided to turn on the charm, nothing more! He won't be coming here anymore!"

He uttered the last words slowly and calmly which added an additional gravity to his words. You could tell he wasn't speaking lightly. This was a man who'd thought everything through in his own way and made his final decision.

Your Reputation with Mr. Alexey Koval has decreased!
Current Reputation: Animosity 10/30

You've been dealt critical damage: verbal injury
-50% to Spirit
-50% to Confidence

"Uncle Alexey," I closed the devastating messages and made one last attempt at righting the unrightable.

He shook his head, unwilling to listen. "I've said everything," he said softly. "Get out of my house."

I rose slowly, still in disbelief this was actually happening, then very nearly collapsed on the floor. I was feverish and nauseous, almost fainting. My vision blurred; I wanted to rub the strange haze from my eyes.

I closed the Reputation message with Vicky's mother without even reading it. She would agree with everything he said or did, anyway.

Supporting me by the elbow, Vicky sat straight as a rod and said in a level, mechanical voice staring fixedly in front of herself,

"Phil, wait. Xena, get your stuff together. We're going home."

"What's that now?" her mother protested. "The child has no business living under the same roof as a strange man! That's a scandal!"

"Mom!" Vicky exclaimed, a tear rolling down her cheek.

"I've been your mom for thirty years now! I'm not

giving you Xena! Once you've split up with him, you can have her! The school is on vacation, anyway, she has no business being in town! At least here the food's decent and the air's better!"

"Mom, please don't cry," Xena tried to console her.

Vicky gave her a peck on the cheek and eased herself away. Kicking the chair away, she rose and dragged me to the door.

"Vick, wait," I tried to stop her.

She snatched her hand away. "I'll be waiting for you in the car."

With those words, she left.

Me, I couldn't do the same without giving some answer to her father's slanderous assumptions. I knew very well that my every word could be conceived as a feeble attempt to redeem myself but I wanted to pour some oil over troubled waters, unwilling to burn any bridges.

"There is some truth in what you've just said," I told him. "I'm not going to justify my behavior. I can't prove anything to you now, anyway. The time will come when you realize you were wrong. Thank you very much for your hospitality. Aunt Toma, your pelmenis are out of this world. I've never eaten anything like them."

No one replied. Vicky's mother had demonstratively turned her back on me, rattling the plates as she cleared away the table. My once-potential father in law was rolling a cigarette, ignoring me entirely.

"All right. All the best, then."

Staggering (what was it with me?), I headed for the hallway and began putting my shoes on. Victor was the only one of them who came out to see me off.

"What a shame you're gonna miss the soccer," he whispered. "It's starting in an hour and you'll be on the road for at least two or three hours."

"I might make it for the second half. See you, Victor. Nice to have met you. Don't play too much Counter Strike. Stay in touch with the real world."

He grinned and shook my proffered hand.

I softly closed the door behind me and left their hospitable abode. Stumbling, I managed to negotiate two flights of stairs before my legs gave way under me and I slid down the wall to the floor. I felt weak and lethargic. Could this be the consequence of him having critted me?

I reopened the closed messages and carefully read through them.

Aha. It had nothing to do with the crit. While we'd been busy eating pelmenis, I'd received a system quest. It was the first time I'd ever come across such an ad hoc system ability to generate quests. And to top it all, the quest description seemed to run forever.

System quest alert!
Family Bonds I
This is the first part of the quest chain concerning the Koval family.
You need to win their trust and approval, bringing your Reputation with each family member to not less

than Amicality.
Current Reputation:
With Victoria's father Mr. Alexey Koval: Animosity 25/30
With Victoria's mother Mrs. Tamara "Toma" Koval: Animosity 10/30
With Victoria's brother Victor: Animosity 10/30
With Victoria's daughter Xenia: Indifference 0/30

Rewards:
XP: 2,000 pt.
Reputation with Victoria Koval: 30 pt.
Current Reputation:
Psychological Reputation: Amicality 25/30
Emotional Reputation: Love 1/1

Penalties:
Reputation with Victoria Koval: 20 pt.
Current Reputation:
Psychological Reputation: Amicality 25/30
Emotional Reputation: Love 1/1
XP: 2,000 pt.

Warning! A decrease in your Reputation with any one family member to Animosity or lower will result in your failing the quest!

The quest message showed my old Reputation numbers with them. I had a funny feeling I knew what the next messages would be about. Nevertheless, I read them too.

System quest alert: Family Bonds I. Quest failed!

Your Reputation with Victoria Koval has decreased!
Current psychological Reputation: Amicality 5/30
Current emotional Reputation: Love 1/1

XP lost: 2,000 pt.
Current level: 13. XP points gained: 8700/14000

Ouch. That was tough. So that's how the system "rewarded" a user for failing quests and the loss of XP? By making them feel sick? Oh well. This was the proverbial carrot and stick, I suppose. I've already consumed quite a few carrots and I'd finally got a taste of the stick.

Frankly, I didn't wish to repeat the experience. What I felt could be best described as an extreme case of alcohol poisoning coupled with a fever and high blood pressure. Was the system indeed capable of controlling my body's biochemistry? Was it possible for it to synthesize some nasty substance and inject it into my blood stream? Some kind of toxin, maybe?

What I also found strange was the division of Reputation into psychological and emotional. With Yanna, it hadn't been like that. Nor with Kira or my parents, come to think of it. Their readings were simple: *Love 1/1*, period. What was this now, some new approach offered by Insight? But it hadn't reached level 3 yet. Or was the system capable of self-learning so it could now tell the finer aspects of human relationships?

I might have to ask Martha about it. At the moment, it was all academic.

I clambered back to my feet and staggered down the stairs, holding tightly onto the banister so as not to fall flat again. I still felt awful but the system didn't seem to think so. It rewarded me with the same debuff I'd received when I'd just started tackling the interface.

> *Apathy*
> *Duration: 18 hours*
> *You're emotionally drained. Your central nervous system needs some rest. We recommend that you get some quality sleep, a balanced diet and some exercise.*
> *Warning! The state of Apathy can easily escalate to Depression!*
> *-5% to Satisfaction every 6 hrs.*
> *-1% to Vitality every 5 hrs.*
> *-6% to Vigor every 6 hrs.*
> *-2% to Metabolism every 6 hrs.*
> *-5% to Confidence every 6 hrs.*
> *-2% to Willpower every 6 hrs.*

I clenched my teeth and, mustering the last of my strength and willpower, stumbled out of the front door toward the car.

Everything was fine. Everything would turn out well. Come to think of it, what had happened just now? Just a misunderstanding, that's all. I would go home now, open my business, employ Alik and start working.

Clients would come and with them money would start coming too. We'd make a name for ourselves. And then Vicky and I would come back here. I might ask my own parents and also Kira to come with us to lend it more weight. The main thing now was, I had to get my act together and make sure I didn't lose what was left of Vicky's Amicality.

Strange. Whenever had I lost her Respect? I met so many people these days I made a habit of closing Reputation messages without even reading them. One day I was absent-mindedly crossing the street and I was absolutely flooded with Animosity messages from all the drivers. More than likely, that was how I must have overlooked the message informing me of Vicky's drop of Reputation.

By now, I was shivering and shaking all over. I staggered over to the car, grabbed the passenger side door handle and yanked on it several times before I realized that the door was locked and there was nobody in the car.

Where was Vicky, dammit?

Then I heard someone scream.

Chapter Three

I'M FREE!

You couldn't wipe it out, no matter how hard you tried:
Freedom is just something I carry inside.

Sergei Shnurov. Freedom

I LOOKED AROUND, TRYING TO LOCATE VICKY, BUT I couldn't see her. Some children were playing in a sandpit; a young mother on a bench was looking anxiously right and left. She must have heard her scream too.

Suddenly I felt a whole lot better. My fever, weakness and nausea were gone. Apparently, the penalty for the failed quest had just expired.

The pain from the stick was much worse than the pleasure derived from the carrot. It was out of all proportion, really: they only rewarded you with a couple of seconds of pleasure for reaching a new level while this agony had lasted for a good five minutes.

The scream definitely seemed to have come from the row of doors at the far end of the apartment block. I took another look around and ran over to them.

I had to go almost to the end of the building when I noticed a group of people by one of the many front doors. Only then did I take the situation in and breathed a sigh of relief.

Vicky was standing there surrounded by women, chatting to them cheerfully. No, she only appeared to be cheerful because her Mood was still not too hot after the visit to her parents.

"Vicky?" I asked.

"There he is!" she said to the women and only then turned to me. "You okay?"

"I'm fine," I nodded, looking at her friends.

I'd overestimated their age at first glance. Now I could see they were the same age as Vicky but slightly worse for wear. Two of them — Irina and Olga — resembled little sheep with their hair permed short in an old-fashioned way. Their clothes, too, befitted women in their forties or older. The third one — Natalia — was probably considered a raving beauty by local standards: she was wearing an acid pink track suit, her long raven-black hair pulled back in a ponytail. She had Botoxed lips, thickly painted eyebrows and the waxen complexion of an Instagram doll.

All three sported high Interest in my respect, Natalia's being the highest at over 60%. I had to play it cool with them considering Vicky's jealous streak.

"Okay girls, we've gotta go," she said to her friends. "I'll see you around!"

"Wait a sec, Vic! Aren't you going to introduce us to your fiancé?" Natalia pouted her lips. "Please!"

"She's right, Vic," Olga nodded. "Introduce us."

Vicky nodded her permission.

"My name's Philip," I began. "And you must be Vicky's friends, of course."

"I'm Natasha," the dark-haired girl said languidly.

"Olga... Irina..." the two little sheep echoed.

"Was it my imagination or was one of you screaming just now?" I asked. "Because it was really loud. That's why I came running. I thought someone was hurting Vicky."

"As if!" Natasha chuckled. "She could see most people off if she wanted to. She knows how to defend herself! It was actually me you heard screaming. Or not even screaming, I was just happy for her. You've just proposed to her, haven't you?" she said with a wink.

"Yes, he has," Vicky replied for me. "So have you all introduced yourselves now? We need to go."

"Where are you rushing off to? Just because you've had an argument with your parents? We thought you were coming for the whole weekend," Natasha butted in. "Let's go to my place. I live alone.

There's nobody there to pester you. We can sit down for a chat and a drink and get to know each other a bit better. I have some martini left, how about that?"

I didn't need my Intuition to tell me it wasn't such a healthy idea. I already knew — from my experience with Vicky among other things — that this elevated Interest from the opposite sex toward a complete stranger was bad news. And seeing as this girl was apparently either Vicky's best friend or sworn enemy, I had to tread very carefully.

Still, I felt a degree of guilt toward Vicky about our failed meeting with her parents. So I left it up to her. If she wanted us to go, fine; if not, we could just go home.

In any case, I'd already decided to spend all weekend with her. As it was, I'd been busy every waking moment pushing myself to the limit, afraid of missing a single second without having leveled up, so by now I felt completely depleted. A change of scenery would do me a world of good.

Then I noticed some shopping bags loaded with groceries on a nearby bench.

"Are those yours?" I asked Olga. "Would you like me to take them up to your apartment for you?"

She appeared scared. "Oh no, it's all right. I can manage."

"Her husband is really jealous," Irina explained. "He'll punch your lights out first and ask questions afterward."

"Vick, that's one knight in shining armor you have!" Natasha commented on my attempt at chivalry. "Can I borrow him? Joke."

"Yeah right! Dream on!" Vicky quipped, ignoring the fact that it had been meant as a joke. Her voice rang with the unfamiliar tough notes of a street urchin. "Thanks for the invitation though. We have to be going."

"Look who's talking!" Natasha stood with her hands on her hips, speaking louder with every word. "We're a big city lady now, aren't we? Nose in the air, and not just your nose? Too squeamish to visit your childhood friend? She's got a posh job in a big company, a car and a place of her own! And now she's getting married to a big businessman! What did you do to deserve that? You couldn't study at school to save your life! Where's the justice here? Some people have it all!"

"Zip it," Olga said quietly. "Don't start."

"Natasha, please don't," Irina concurred.

"I don't mind!" Vicky joined in. "Let her speak! It's perfectly clear what she's implying. But who's she to judge?"

She turned to me and handed me the car keys. "Go down and wait in the car!"

The attention of all the girls turned to me.

So that's how it was, then. Quite an eye-opener.

Once back in the company of her old street friends, our cute girl next door had reverted to the role of an alpha bitch in our nascent family.

Without saying a word, I took the keys from her. "Nice having met you, girls," I smiled and nodded. "See you around."

"Likewise," Natasha replied for everyone. "Bye, Phil!"

As I walked back to the car, I wondered if I'd jumped the gun with my proposal. As she had just shown, I didn't really know the real Vicky at all. Could it be that I'd trusted the system's Reputation reading too much? *Love 1/1*, yeah right. But what was love, anyway, but a biochemical process in the body? A psychological attachment, maybe? In any case, a romantic infatuation wasn't exactly love.

My father had always tried to impress upon me the importance of looking before you leap. And once you'd made up your mind, you just had to go for it. With my impulsive tendencies, explosive character and inability to think ahead, I was his exact opposite. He would have spent another couple of years checking all available scenarios; and once he'd decided on a potential mate, he'd spend another two or three years checking out whether she was right for him. According to my parents, they'd been friends for already three years before they finally started dating. The dating stage lasted another year until finally my Dad had proposed to her.

Well, I was nothing like my father in this respect. Until today, nothing in Vicky had made me feel uncomfortable. She'd appeared to be a good and faithful friend, a trustworthy ally, a consummate lover and an excellent housekeeper. Also, she'd promised me to be a good wife.

All of this was indeed true — and until now, it still outweighed the vague yet undefined feeling that something wasn't quite right in our relationship.

I sat in the car and turned on the radio. Without really listening to the DJ's happy chattering, I tried to work out what had just happened at her parents'.

Had all this taken place a couple of months ago when I still hadn't had this weird game interface in my head, I would have acted differently. I would have exaggerated my achievements, unhesitant to sugarcoat my questionable accomplishments in order to endear myself to her parents, and would have undoubtedly stooped to blatantly lying to them if the situation had required it.

In those days, I used to do a lot of things differently. After that first night we'd spent together, I probably wouldn't have invited her to the movies at all.

Now that I had this crazy software in my head, I seemed to be doing things that I'd always wanted to do but never had.

Being honest, correct and sympathetic is only easy in our dreams. That's how we like to view ourselves and that's exactly how we try to justify some of our more than questionable actions. We tell lies in order "not to rock the boat"; we half-heartedly apologize as we unflinchingly deny help not only to strangers but also to the people that we hold dear. Gradually, the borders of the lie we live in begin to expand as we become brazen with impunity — or just fear to face the truth. We live with spouses we don't love, we go to a job that we hate, we flatter our idiot boss; and then we even have the temerity to "love" ourselves the way we are.

But the main object of our lie is inevitably ourselves. We lie to ourselves in little and large ways. We promise ourselves to do tomorrow what we didn't feel like doing today. We assure ourselves we'll start a new life but we never do. We quit smoking, then start up again. We stop drinking, then reach for a new bottle because there's always an occasion. We decide to start working out and read useful books — but instead, we glue ourselves to the couch leafing through cheap novels, the names of their heroes easily forgotten and replaced by those from yet another fantasy world. We decide to briefly check our social media feed, then spend hours scrolling through it in anticipation of those tiny micro doses of happiness hormones, a.k.a. new likes and comments.

This is our right, isn't it? We all study and work hard; some of us have a house to keep. We do get tired. We need some rest, after all. Everybody does it. Come to think of it, we're doing fine, aren't we?

But still, this hamster wheel conceals an oppressive feeling of self-deceit. We admit it during our rare moments of lucidity when we make new to-do lists, read motivational articles, count calories, pack our gym bag, upload a Top 100 list of the best

---

books of all time fully intending to read them all; we quit smoking, find a new job and start taking new courses and seminars. Then we report it all on social media, replacing the beautiful expectation of a new successful life with more microscopic injections of happiness derived from the more likes we receive for our post about us starting a new life.

I of all people knew the ugly truth about all these great unfulfilled plans and new starry-eyed beginnings which are doomed to fail.

I'd needed an appraisal from an impartial piece of alien software in order to see myself for what I truly was, not the imaginary Phil I'd believed myself to be. As they said in the movie, "You have been weighed, you have been measured, and you have absolutely been found wanting."

Which meant that today's bout of idiotic honesty with Vicky's parents was rooted in my recent interface experience. Who knows? Had I read the system quest message straight away, I might indeed have reverted to being devious and telling lies to them. At least I wouldn't have opened up so much in front of strangers. But now the cat was out of the bag.

The strangest thing was, I knew perfectly well I wouldn't have lied to them. Sooner or later, the truth would out anyway, and I didn't want to start a family with lies, half-truths and exaggerations. Honesty was indeed the best policy, even with oneself.

When I'd heard Natasha scream, my first

thought was that it could be some incredible new development courtesy of the program. I'd thought I'd recognized Vicky's voice, imagining her to have been attacked by some hooligans and hoping to use my newly-acquired fighting skills to defend her. Her father would see it and change his opinion of me; he'd shake my hand, invite me back into the house and we'd sit and watch the soccer game all together.

I smiled at my own naïveté and my belief in fairy stories.

The yard appeared deserted. Friday night was here but the sun was still high in the sky. Tonight was the longest day of the year. At least it definitely felt that way to me. The groundhog days I'd been living just lately — jogging, training, reading, leveling up, a quick dinner and a bit of downtime with Vicky, then it was back to bed — went so quickly I didn't even see the passing of them. It seemed that I'd get out of bed, and then it was time to go back to sleep again.

But today felt long, stretching like treacle and seemingly having no end.

I glanced at my watch. I'd been waiting already for half an hour. I got out of the car, locked it and decided to go see Vicky and find out if everything was all right.

Halfway there, I saw her coming toward me. Her head hung low. She walked quickly, stooping. I could see she was in a bad mood.

"Vick? Are you okay?"

She looked up at me and nodded, then turned

toward the car. I followed her in silence.

As we drove back, she didn't say a word. To all my questions and attempts to strike up a conversation she replied with a curt "yes" or "no". I wanted to leave her alone but decided to give it one last try.

"Listen," I said, "what's all this about you being a deputy director at some factory? Did your dad mean Ultrapak?"

"Why do you ask? Have you got a problem with that?"

"It's just that all his accusations were based on this little untruth, that's all."

"Were they really? And I thought that he was talking about you being a useless unemployed loser. I don't think it had anything to do with my job."

It hurt to hear this from somebody you loved. Still, I suppressed the bout of anger. All she'd done was say it loud and clear, whatever I might have thought about it.

"I just asked," I said. "Do you really think I'm a loser?"

"I don't think anything! Just leave me alone!" she tugged on the steering wheel to overtake a car. I said nothing until she'd finished the maneuver.

She tensed up, white-knuckling the wheel. I could sense her unwillingness to talk. I could see in her profile that she was afraid. Her Fear was at 14%: not much but still. Was it the fear of an inexperienced driver on the road? Or was it the fear of our potential confrontation?

"Okay, let's not talk about me," I tried again. "Why are your parents so sure-"

"Shut up. Please. The more you speak, the worse you make it."

"Vicky, if we can't clear the air in moments like these, how can we live together?"

"What do you want to hear?" she asked listlessly, leaning back in her seat.

I remembered what her father had said about her having made a career. She'd bought a car and an apartment. I also thought about Natalia's accusations.

Then I remembered what Vicky had told me about herself: *"It's been three years I've been working for Ultrapak,"* she'd said. *"I started as office manager. Than they transferred me to HR."*

No matter how hard I tried to dismiss it, something just didn't sum up. How can an office manager buy an apartment in just three years? Seeing as her father had made a point of telling me that she'd done it all on her own. Especially because before that, she could barely make ends meet.

"Are you telling lies to your parents because of the apartment?" I asked, putting all of my suspicions into one sentence.

"I didn't lie to them," she replied. "For them, an HR manager is a big shot because she decides whom to hire."

"An HR manager? Your father told me you were a deputy director."

"So what if I did tell them that?" she snapped,

furious. "What's that got to do with you? Does it hurt anyone? And they feel great that their daughter has made it! All my childhood they were pushing me around. All my younger years they were shitty with me. And now they're proud of me. Is that enough for you? That's nobody's business! Least of all yours!"

Your Reputation with Victoria Koval has decreased!
Current psychological Reputation: Indifference 25/30
Current emotional Reputation: Love 1/1:

How was it possible? How could a person be indifferent to someone she loved? What kind of love was that?

For the first time I doubted the adequacy of the program's rating system. What could a heartless artificial intellect possibly know about the explosive cocktail of human feelings if it had to rely on the data downloaded from the universal infospace? What kind of oversimplification was that? Or could it just be that my Insight skill wasn't yet up to scratch?

I left her alone, not having enough courage to ask her about the source of her managerial income which was apparently enough to buy her an apartment. An oppressive silence hung in the car. I finally fell asleep to the rustling of the tires on the tarmac.

I was shaken awake. "Get out. We've arrived."

I climbed out of the car and stopped, waiting for her to follow me. Instead, Vicky rolled down the window. "I'm going to my place," she snapped, then sharply pulled away, leaving me in the yard.

I stood there a long time, not having the power to decide whether I could take such behavior. What was I supposed to do now? Should I try to make up with her straight away? Or should I give her some space?

My heart was heavy. I felt like shit.

The program was going crazy, creating and deleting new tasks:

Make up with Vicky
Get Vicky back
Go to Vicky's
Speak to Vicky
Sort it out with Vicky
Split up with Vicky

In the end, all the tasks mentioning her name disappeared, leaving only the one about me raising the money for the office rent.

I got home and cooked myself a simple dinner, all the while thinking I'd jumped the gun after all. I'd had my fill of emotions and relationships for this particular stage of my life. Regardless of whether Vicky and I made up or split up, my efforts in this respect would take way too much time and energy. Her style of bringing me close, then pushing me away was pure manipulation. And it wasn't going to work with me anymore.

For the second time this month — the first being her ungrounded bout of jealousy over Marina — I decided to take a break and see how things panned out. She could always come back to me if she wanted to. And if she didn't, her priorities would be clear.

The program disrupted my train of thought, rewarding me with 2000 XP for a socially meaningful action. What could that be for? I scrolled through crime reports. As I methodically looked through the local news on our city portal, I stumbled across a message reporting the finding of the six-year-old Joseph Kogan. The identity of his abductor hadn't been disclosed "in the interests of the investigation".

Still, something in it had awoken a vague memory of my earlier nightmare about the pedophile official.

I spent the whole night writing up the concept of my agency.

I envisioned vending as our main source of income at the initial stage. Yes, exactly the same as I'd formerly done at Ultrapak. I might not have my own warehouses or logistics but I did possess what was valued the most in this world: information. By varying search filters, I could work out who needed something and what kind of price they were prepared to pay for it; I could also see who had this particular thing up for sale.

This was basic commerce, the kind that Vicky's father had described as a "peanut salesman". It also included broker's services, matching large suppliers up with equally large buyers.

The social purpose of my business was going to remain the same: a recruitment agency. Although I wasn't going to make millions doing it, it could kill three birds with one stone: it would provide me with some initial income and allow me to accrue some XP, but most importantly, I — or my agency, rather — would make a name and a reputation from it.

And after that, we could start tackling bigger business, like the recruitment of top management for leading brands. The most valuable resource of any company is its workforce.

What was it Comrade Stalin (may he rot in hell) once said? "Workforce is key" — in my case, this couldn't have been truer.

And once I had a name, money would follow. Then I might start thinking about opening a sports department.

But I could only do that if I could somehow extend my license for the program. I could start talent scouting in soccer, ice hockey, tennis, boxing and other sports. I could also work with socially vulnerable kids from disadvantaged or single-parent families and orphanages. I could match them with understanding coaches or sports schools which would be beneficial to them.

And this approach could work in other areas, too! How many talented artists, writers, singers, dancers or actors were wallowing in obscurity? Very few could make it big.

And then there were medical diagnostics, missing persons' search, bounty hunting, the tracing of dangerous criminals, a detective agency... Lots of things to do — but I couldn't possibly pull them all off alone.

And what if I could use the initial agency only as a starting point? That way I could accumulate some funds and gather a team of the best minds in the most promising scientific fields. And then...

I stopped myself from daydreaming. No good trying to plan too far ahead. Still, I made a mental list of things worth looking into: augmented reality, the Universal Infospace, biotechnologies, blockchain technologies, wetware... I could create an international company, choose a few of the most promising fields, then find some good investors (which was piece of cake with my interface).

All the prospects took my breath away.

All I needed was time. The countdown till the end of my license was ticking.

Dammit! What had I wasted all this precious time on? On building, then successfully ruining my relationship with Vicky? Or on running around like a headless chicken selling packaging materials to all and sundry? On boxing? Or spending hours jogging around the stadium like a donkey on a millstone? Or on leveling up Cooking and Agriculture?

The realization of my own stupidity was sobering.

In three days' time, Optimization would have

run its course which would bring my Learning Skills level to 7. I had 5 available skill points I'd saved during the last five level ups and I fully intended to invest them into Learning Skills too. That would bring it to level 12, giving me +450% to skill development rate. Add to this the 50% bonus to the development of primary skills and that would bring it to five hundred. If we multiplied it by the stat booster's effects which tripled your XP gained from skill use, that would give us 1500%. That meant that I'd be able to develop any skill fifteen times faster than an ordinary person.

I might try to choose some totally undeveloped skill like soccer, shooting or a foreign language and level it up for a couple of days just to see how fast it would go. And if it worked...

My lips stretched into a smile at the thought. This might end up being the craziest leveling stretch both in my gaming experience as well as in real life.

And I still had the activation of Heroic skills to look forward to.

On top of all that, I was waiting for more new offerings from the system like a kid on Christmas Eve. What else would I learn about the Universal Infospace once I'd reached the next level of Insight?

The mere thought of all those goodies, so dear to the heart of any gamer, calmed and reassured me in anticipation of the new day — and possibly, also a new life — without Vicky.

I relegated the memory of my failed visit to her parents to the trash can of my memory, complete with her father's illogical and unfair attacks as well as the strange behavior of Vicky herself.

Regardless of how much I loved her.

Chapter Four

THE RIGHT THINGS AREN'T ALWAYS THE BEST

Making a decision was only the beginning of things.

Paulo Coelho. The Alchemist

THE NEXT DAY, I AWOKE AT 10 A.M. RECENTLY, I'D ONLY needed six hours of sleep even though at the time of my gaming raids nine hours hadn't been enough. In those days, I'd had no incentive to get out of bed. On the contrary: once I'd awoken and had breakfast with Yanna, I would go back to bed and lose myself in colorful, perfectly logical dreams. Back then, I would have never said no to a few extra hours of sleep.

But not now. Whether it was due to my working out, my steady schedule or my improved recovery rate courtesy of the booster — but all in all, these days I jumped to my feet the moment I awoke. Which gave me an additional three hours to my daytime, allowing me to accomplish so much more. And today, I'd only slept a little more than four hours.

The moment I was awake, I impulsively took out my phone and checked the message notifications to see if there was anything from Vicky.

There wasn't. That was a relief. My phone screen was pristine these days, free from all the icons as I'd removed all the games and deleted all the social media apps. They might be convenient information-wise but on the other hand, this convenience provoked a Pavlov's dog reaction, constantly prompting you to check out this and that. It might sound funny but I used to reach for my phone even during sex just to see who'd written what.

I spent the first hour of each day doing mundane chores — not the kind that we are conditioned to consider monotonous and boring but something totally different. To me, it was a sequence of habitual actions necessary to steer my day to its maximum productivity.

Put the kettle on, feed the cat, brush my teeth, splash some water on my face, have a shave, take a shower, do five minutes of exercise, collect and take out the garbage, sort my washed clothes and put them away, pack my gym bag — all this took me just over half an hour.

After that, I'd make a light breakfast. By then, I'd finally start getting hungry as normally I had no appetite after I'd just got up. I'd top up my fuel tank with proteins, fats and carbs, eating unhurriedly without pausing to look at the newsfeeds in my phone.

Later, I'd drink my first and only mug of coffee for the day — large with just one sugar, both for the taste and to give my brain a glucose boost — while making a mental list of all the important things to do today as well as those that could wait till tomorrow.

So these were my plans for the weekend:

I set aside two hours a day for Stamina, Strength and Agility training, plus another hour to get to the gym, get changed and come back again. My one-on-one boxing sessions with Matov had finished and the group training wouldn't start until Tuesday. That meant six hours of physical training this Saturday and Sunday.

I also had to go to our summer cottage to check up on my parents. And if Kira managed to do the same, I would see her there too. That was a minimum of five hours but if they needed some help, I might spend the whole day there. Leveling up was all well and good, but my parents were quite old now and I had no idea how much longer they might last. My every visit strengthened their bond with this world, giving them a charge of positive emotions and consequently, a reason to live.

I scheduled my trip for tomorrow. Today I had too many other things to do.

On top of everything else, I had to work out a few potential Insight development scenarios. It had been quite a while since I'd last received quests from strangers. It might be worth my while taking a walk around town looking to see if I could find anybody sporting the exclamation mark of a quest giver hovering above their head.

I scheduled this task for tomorrow as well.

Also, the office rent couldn't wait any longer. I absolutely needed a place where I could start to receive my unemployed clients — because I viewed the unemployed as my main target market, and we had officially over a hundred thousand of them in our city alone. Naturally, some of them still worked somewhere undeclared, receiving under-the-counter payments but some of them were bound to be truly without work. Especially because those who already had work were unlikely to give my new unknown agency a try. People like them aren't normally in a hurry; they upload their CVs to employment sites and wait for the best offer.

The program duly classified this task as a priority, shoving my visit to my parents into second place.

I had a week until the rent payment deadline. All kinds of ways of earning a quick buck passed through my head. Playing online poker seemed like a relatively easy way to do so but my heart wasn't in it. The very idea of making money through gambling met with some sort of inner resentment and rejection, even though the possibility of using poker to check my post-Optimization leveling rates seemed more than attractive.

I could try and raise some money through bounty hunting. According to the official website of the Ministry of Internal Affairs of the Russian Federation, they promised a million rubles[8] for each criminal

---

[8] About $15,000

caught. Still, I had no idea how I was going to explain my knowledge of their whereabouts, especially if they were located in different parts of the country.

I set this idea aside as a last resort. What a shame I couldn't assist justice without having all these reservations. Why couldn't I just email them the coordinates of all these wanted crooks from my computer? Was it because every such letter would provoke an investigation, triggering an unhealthy interest in me? As in, who was I? Where did I get my information from? What connection did I have with the criminal?

So generally, I did want to help them — but I wanted to do it so as not to attract the attention of all the intelligence services.

Having said that... wait a sec!

We lived in a globalized world, didn't we? Why was I focused on our country alone?

Gripped by excitement, I brought my laptop to the kitchen.

Within a minute, I'd found the Rewards for Justice site. This was a program created by the US Department of State in order to fight international terrorism.

One of the site pages read,

You may submit information anonymously. The personal information requested is not required, although it will help us to contact you in the event that there are any questions.

All information you provide will be kept strictly

confidential.

You may be eligible for a reward. In addition, you and your family may be eligible for relocation if necessary.

I tried to listen to the voice of my intuition but it didn't seem to protest. Just to be on the safe side, I Googled some information about the program. Apparently, it had already helped to arrest a number of terrorists and a reward had already been paid out to those who'd tipped them off. I read a few discussions which confirmed a few cases when the reward had been paid out within a few weeks.

Oh well. It might be worth a try.

The list of the most dangerous terrorists was split into regions. I checked them one by one, initiating my own search every time. Not all of them could be located due to a lack of information.

The first one was a Jabar Aziz Haqqani, 52 years old, a terrorist with Yemeni roots who'd lived a long time in the States. I had all the information about him. He'd sponsored various terrorist organizations in the US, including Al-Qaeda. He was involved in the explosions in NYC and Chicago with over a hundred dead.

The reward for the information about his current whereabouts was five million dollars. And judging by some other sums mentioned on the site, it wasn't the limit. The information about Abu Bakr al-Baghdadi, one of the ISIL leaders, had been valued at twenty-five million!

When I'd Googled Haqqani's name, one of the first listings was the link to his profile on the FBI site. There, I had more than enough KIDD points. Ditto for Wikipedia. The date and place of birth, photographs taken at different times in his life, his height, weight and family information...

I committed it all to memory.

A new marker lit up on my internal map, showing a small Saudi town Al Kharkhir almost on the Yemeni border. Haqqani was in a large house in the north of the town, not far from the power station. I jotted down his coordinates, returned to his profile on the Rewards For Justice site and pressed the *Submit a Tip* button.

I entered the house address and the coordinates into the form. After some deliberation, I also entered my name, email address and phone number. I made a mental note about leveling up some English in case they called me. Having said that, an organization like this was bound to have Russian-speaking staff.

I was fed up with having to lie and hide all the time. Hundreds and thousands of psychics — authentic as well as charlatans — worked quite happily and advertised their extrasensory abilities, real as well as invented ones.

Having made up my mind, I pressed *Send* with a light heart. After a moment's hesitation, the browser offered the following text:

Thank you for the tip. If you've left your details on the site, we might contact you again for any additional information.

If your tip results in the criminal's arrest and court judgment, you might be eligible for a monetary reward. In applicable cases, you and your family could be subject to relocation.

All the submitted information will be treated in strict confidence.

I finally breathed out. That's it, Phil. Now you should be prepared for anything.

Still, something was nagging at me. It wasn't even the fact of me disclosing my identity but rather something I hadn't done yet. I couldn't quite place it, so I went back to my plan.

Having sent them the data worth 5 million bucks, I then spent quite a bit of time trying to come up with a way of quickly raising 50,000 rubles for the rent, discarding different ideas one after the other.

For instance, debt collecting agencies offered hefty rewards to those who gave up the whereabouts of certain debtors. Like a Vakha Salamgadjiev who'd siphoned off about two million dollars from the bank accounts of some private company. Anyone who could report his whereabouts was promised 10% of all the assets he'd stolen.

It didn't take me long to locate Vakha in Chechnya — or the Chechen Republic of Ichkeria, as it was called these days.

I was about to send them the data when my intuition screamed a desperate warning, alerting me to some sort of mortal danger and completely discouraging me from pursuing this route.

Without having decided anything, I dashed off to the school stadium for a run. Dashed being the operative word. I'd seen enough overweight guys who'd taken the elevator to the gym on the second floor just to walk unhurriedly on the treadmill. Hats off to them, of course, for trying to conserve energy before their training but this wasn't my case. I invested every effort into my continuously progressing Stamina.

The midday sun was blazing so hard in the faded sky that I could feel my exposed skin burning. My breathing, light and level at first, soon dried out my throat, becoming wheezy and laborious. The old rubberized coating of the running track flashed underfoot; its every dent and crack were like old friends to me.

My Stamina training didn't go easy. No matter how many long miles I'd run in my life, every new one would still be a challenge despite having stronger legs, a second wind, and the constant injection of endorphins into my bloodstream.

As you run, you don't have any deep thoughts, only instincts: to drink, to breathe, to jump over an obstacle. Still, my mind kept working on autopilot, processing its tasks. Snippets of ideas coursed through my head, all of them centered around either some sort of gambling or missing persons' search.

Finally I stumbled across the seed of something more practical and dependable. I remembered how I'd earned my first money after Yanna had left, offering copywriting services via some freelance portal. Last night, Vicky had left me too — so was it worth trying again, maybe?

Although this route didn't promise much money, it was also risk free. Especially if you took payment upfront.

I couldn't quite finish these thoughts because my heart was too busy pumping hundreds of gallons of seething blood as I ran. My body had no intention of wasting precious energy on whatever mental considerations I was busy with, investing every bit of it into my survival.

Ten interminably long miles of running and a gallon of water later, I finally got the precious new Stamina level I'd been after.

Task status: Running Practice
Task completed!
XP received: 300pt.
+5% to Satisfaction
Current level: 13. XP points gained: 8730/14000

Your Stamina has improved!
+1 to Stamina
Current Stamina: 10
You've received 1000 pt. XP for successfully leveling up a main characteristic!
Current level: 13. XP points gained: 9730/14000.

Congratulations! You've unblocked one of the requirements for the Stealth and Vanish heroic ability: Stamina (level 10+)

Having finished my training, I went to do some shopping.

The guard by the door stepped in my way — or rather, tried to but was too late, so he just shouted threateningly at my back, "Sir! Excuse me, sir! I'm talking to you!"

I kept walking as if I hadn't understood he was addressing me but I had a funny feeling he wasn't going to let it drop.

"Hey, mister! You!"

I stopped and turned round with a long-suffering expression on my face. "Are you talking to me?"

"Yes, you!" he nodded vigorously as he came closer. "You can't come here dressed like that!"

"Like what?"

"Eh..." he paused, trying to remember the word. "Unhygienic!"

Okay, what did we have here? *Name: Alexander. Age: 23. Social status level: 3. Intellect: 5.* The picture was pretty clear.

I pretended I was reading his name tag pinned to his T-shirt. "Listen, Alex, bro, I'm parched. We had a bit of a shindig with the guys last night. I won't be long, all I need is some water and grub. Your till's working, I take it?"

His narrow forehead furrowed. He'd already grasped my situation which was way too common. Also, the unwritten street code demanded he did me a favor. On the other hand, he could get what-for from his superiors.

Furthermore, this was the legendary big man syndrome in action: he was drunk on his power which allowed him to either stop me or wave me through.

"Alex, please, be a mensch!"

"Okay. Just make it quick."

I smiled, nodding. "I'll be back in a flash! Thanks!"

Congratulations! You've received a new skill level!

Skill name: Communication Skills
Current level: 7
XP received: 500

I'd chosen how to address him instinctively — and it had worked. Had I started to read him my rights, demanding to see the manager or look at their dress code rules for customers — that might have worked too but it might have taken infinitely more time.

I did some shopping and carried it all home, throwing the bag over my shoulder. As I walked, I entertained myself by opening my interface map and adjusting its transparency so that I could view it out of the corner of my eye, then spinning the globe in search of any old friends, mentally zooming in on cities from Antananarivo to Zurich.

Once back home, I took a quick shower to wash away the sweat, then cooked lunch as I drew the office layout on a sheet of paper. My visual memory worked fine, allowing me to plot out the position of the furniture and working places.

I spent some time pondering whether we would need a receptionist who'd answer the telephone and greet visitors, but decided against it for the time being. Once we had a steady flow of customers, we might have enough money to expand. In the meantime, there was only me and Alik for whom I still had to find something to do.

I estimated a rough budget. Fifty grand for the rent and another thirty for some decent furniture which I was planning to buy second hand. We needed some desks, chairs and a couch for any visitors. I already had a laptop but we might have to splurge on a printer to print out our contracts with clients. We also had to have the Internet and a landline installed and buy the phone itself, which also was going to cost money.

And finally, the most important thing was to advertise our services. Opening an office wasn't enough; we had to attract a clientele which would actually come.

And how exactly were they supposed to come if they didn't even know we existed? In an ideal world, we'd need a signboard and a couple of sidewalk signs which we could place on both sides of the street.

The cheapest but arguably the most cheerful way of making ourselves known was by plastering the whole city with posters announcing "100% Employment Guarantee". Yes, we'd have to compete with the numerous MLM and pyramid schemes but that would give me hope for some popularity through the grapevine. Everyone who'd found employment through us would surely tell others about us.

In total, I reckoned it was about a hundred thousand[9]. Some I could invest by depleting my bank account and the rest I'd have to find.

I remembered my long-neglected freelance portal account and decided to check it out.

I had several unread messages from potential clients. Judging by the dates, the orders were long gone but still I sent each of them a quick message, apologizing for the belated reply.

The home page of the site advertised a large competition project, offering 50,000 rubles to anyone who could write up a book-size biography of some local public figure for his anniversary.

The rules were simple: contestants had to write the first chapter based on the materials provided, after which the person's children would choose who to make the contract with.

The minimum word count of the finished biography had to be 35 thousand words. That was about half the size of an ordinary book. If I only did that, I could finish it within a couple of weeks.

And — they promised a 50% advance!

That could actually work. If they did hire me, I could always top it up by emptying my bank account and pay the rent to the business center manager which was the most urgent matter. The rest could wait.

Once I'd made that decision, the program duly recorded a new task:

---

[9] About $1500

Write the first chapter of the biography of Mr. Vladimir Koutzel and enter it into the competition.

I downloaded the archive with all the materials and opened it, leafing through scan after scan of yellowed childhood and teenage photos, newspaper cuttings and articles as well as testimonials by his friends, family and fellow workers.

I spent about an hour reading through them, soaking up the information and trying to put myself in his shoes. Then I picked up my gym bag and headed for the fitness center.

I worked through my weightlifting schedule mechanically, thinking about what should go into the first chapter. Where should I start? Should I begin by telling the mundane story of him starting school? Or by describing his parents meeting at a metal working plant where both had worked at the time? Or should I really list all of his titles and achievements, then flash back to his childhood?

Task status: Weightlifting Practice
Task completed!
XP received: 30pt.
+5% to Satisfaction
Current level: 13. XP points gained: 9760/14000.

Deep in thought, I finished training and headed for the locker room packed with strangers. I brushed against someone's gym bag on the bench. It dropped to the floor.

"I'm sorry," I picked up the bag and set it back on the bench.

"Whoa, dumbass! Are you completely blind?" the bag's owner — a squat stocky Dagestani refused to accept my apology.

"Cool it, Mohammed," a small sinewy guy next to him said.

"What's that to you?" another Dagestani guy butted in. His name was Zaurbek, according to his name tag. "Do you know him or something?"

"You should watch what you're saying, Kostya," Mohammed added threateningly through clenched teeth.

My interface identified the two Dagestanis as the Kichiev brothers. At 24, Mohammed was the elder of the two, Zaurbek a year his junior. Both were boxers, as was the guy who'd just taken my side. His name was Konstantin "Kostya" Bekhterev, 21 years old.

Having received no answer from him, Mohammed returned his attention to me, towering over me and staring me out.

I rose, locking my eyes with his. "I already said I was sorry."

"So what?" he said challengingly.

"That's all."

"What's all?"

"Right, Kichiev, give it a break," the coach commanded, entering the locker room. "Phil, meet your group. You're starting Tuesday, aren't you? Boys, this is Phil. He'll be joining you."

"Who, him?' Zaurbek couldn't conceal his

surprise. "He's too old!"

"Are you serious, coach?" Mohammed asked.

Matov shrugged. "Let him try. I already told him he won't make it. There you see," he turned to me, "even the boys are doubtful."

"I can do it," I answered, even though by then I wasn't really too sure. The guys' Boxing skills were at level 6 and 7, all of them. With my meager 4 points I might find it heavy going.

'It's up to you," Matov summed up, then gave a sharp hand clap. "Right! Focus! What are you waiting for? Get training! Bekhterev, why are you hanging around?"

In a few seconds, I found myself alone in the room. Finally I could strip off to take a shower for the third time today.

Languishing under the jets of hot water lashing my back and shoulders, I checked my Strength. I'd almost managed to bring it to 10 during this last session. I only had a couple percent left which meant I might be able to make a new level today.

I gulped down a large serving of a carb and protein shake in the gym bar which must have had the desired effect.

Back home, as I was sitting by my laptop, laboring over the biography of Mr. Koutzel, our distinguished local luminary, I finally received the system message:

Your Strength has improved!
+1 to Strength

Current Strength: 10

You've received 1000 pt. XP for successfully leveling up a main characteristic!

Current level: 13. XP points gained: 10760/14000.

Congratulations! You've unblocked one of the requirements for the Stealth and Vanish heroic ability: Strength (level 10+)

Still, the long-awaited improvement to my Strength didn't make me happy. Something wasn't quite right. Words didn't flow. I still couldn't quite place the premonition that had kept following me ever since I'd pressed *Send* on the Khaqqani message. Something elusive which had something to do with missing people.

Trying to put my finger on it, I opened Google search and entered the keywords "search", "rescue" and "missing person". Immediately I came across a public group on VK[10] which belonged to some rescue team in Izhevsk[11]. They were looking for a missing old lady suffering from amnesia. She was so old she might have seen Comrade Stalin in his diapers but still they were actively involved in her search. Dozens of volunteers continued to comb the local woods 24/7 under the pouring rain but by now, nobody believed anymore in a positive outcome. Considering the search

---

[10] VK — VKontakte ("In Touch"), a popular Russian social media site similar to Facebook

[11] Izhevsk: A provincial Russian city used here as an example of a far-off backwater

had been on for three days already, she could have frozen to death because the summer was quite chilly over there this year.

I had plenty of data — which allowed me to locate the granny almost straight away twenty miles to the north of the search area. Even though I didn't see her behind the trees, she was alive judging by the fact that the marker was moving.

I created a fake account via TOR and sent her coordinates to the group's admins, then used one of the cell phones I'd bought in the underground crossing to dial the search team's leader's number.

"Yes?" a voice snapped.

"I want you to write down the coordinates of the missing old lady."

"One moment. Go on, then."

"Latitude: five, seven, dot, zero, one, four, six, nine. Longitude: five, two, dot, nine, two, six, one, eight. The old lady's still alive but won't be for much longer."

"Accepted. What's the source of your information?"

"I'm Phil Panfilov. I can't explain it to you. You wouldn't believe me, anyway."

"Who are you, a psychic? It doesn't matter, anyway. Thanks."

I could hear him barking orders even before he'd hung up.

A wave of relief flooded over me. That's what had been bugging me!

When I'd decided to help foreign secret services,

I hadn't done so anonymously. I hadn't used any anonymizers and all that proxy shit, I'd just entered my personal information into the form. My name, my email address and even my phone number. And was I too much of a coward to do the same to help my fellow countrymen?

Enough lurking in the shadows. There were people to be saved who would otherwise die if I kept my head down. They were still someone's family.

So what if I made myself known? Catch me if you can!

I closed the Word document with the first page of the biography of Mr. Koutzel, that yet-unsung functionary hero, and started leafing through the many social-media groups and sites of rescue teams all over the country.

The city of Minsk: *Angel Search and Rescue*
The Don area: *The Night Watch Rescue Group*
The city of Tver: *The Owl Volunteer Rescue Team*
The cities of Novosibirsk... Voronezh... Tambov... Kazan.... Vladivostok... Orenburg... Dnepropetrovsk... Almaty... the list went on and on.

A missing child. A missing man... Missing people...

I'd find them all. I would help them all.

CHAPTER FIVE

ME, ME AGAIN AND
MARTHA

*People are always asking me if know
Tyler Durden.*

Fight Club

THOSE WERE THE MOST DIFFICULT HOURS OF MY LIFE,
steeped in other people's pain, desperation, exhaustion
and disbelief.

I'd finished my search well after midnight when
my Spirit was finally completely depleted. I'd located
over forty missing people, seventeen of whom were
already dead, then passed on the coordinates of all the
others. Some of the postings had long since expired
and judging by the lack of any messages reporting
either their successful completion or the abandonment
of the search, there was no point in persevering. But

still, I'd looked into those cases too — and even found quite a few... most of whom were already dead.

Apart from impassively showing me the missing people's markers on the map, the program hadn't shown any other signs of life. I'd received no rewards or quest completion messages, neither anything informing me of having performed "a socially meaningful action".

I'd made and returned dozens of phone calls to anonymous search coordinators and rescue group volunteers whose voices betrayed the exasperation and disbelief of people who'd seen everything in this world. Then I went to bed completely drained and slightly uneasy about the potential repercussions of what I'd just done.

Still, I fell asleep almost instantly — most likely, because of last night's lack of sleep, but especially due to my Spirit being at zero. The only thing I'd thought of doing was switching off my potentially dangerous clandestine telephone.

I had another illogical dream full of strange details but couldn't remember any of it when I'd finally awoke, desperately trying to nail down the elusive images, one of them a girl whose face I couldn't recognize.

When I woke up, I didn't check either the computer or the clandestine phone, too wary of having to bog myself down in more endless dialogues and uncomfortable questions.

Instead, I phoned Kira right after breakfast, just to feel I wasn't alone.

"Hi there," she replied. "How are you? How's Vicky?"

I was so happy to hear her warm voice. "Hi. Vicky... she's okay, I suppose. We've had an argument."

"What's all that about? You had it so good, you two."

"I'll tell you when I see you. How are *you*? How's Cyril?"

"Fine, thanks. Just business as usual. We went to the movies yesterday and you know what he told me?"

As she kept on about how they'd spent their weekend, I listened to the smooth flow of her voice, plucking up some spirit — which, by the way, had completely restored in the course of the night.

"Listen, Kira," I finally said, "How about we go see the old folks?"

"Eh... let's have a think," Kira paused. "Okay, but let's make it closer to lunchtime. I've got a whole heap of things to do at home. I have washing and ironing to do, then I have to clean the house... Will lunchtime do? I'll come and pick you up."

"Great. I'll see you then."

That was it. I'd done everything I'd planned for this morning. Now I could go for a run but I was curious about how the search was going. Had they already found anyone?

I gave the clandestine phone a long look, took a deep breath and switched it on.

The few minutes after its activation seemed to last forever, then I was inundated by text messages.

The majority of them were about missing calls but some were from rescue workers. Apparently, not being able to call me, they'd texted me instead.

We found the girls exactly where you said they'd be! Thanks!

The missing woman was located at the coordinates provided by you. Thank you for your cooperation!

We couldn't get hold of you. We're very happy to tell you that the boy was found near the place that you'd indicated. He's in a bad way but he's gonna make it.

Unfortunately, we only received your message today. We haven't located the missing person at the coordinates you provided but we've been searching through the surrounding area. Do you have any updates for us?

Good morning,
We've just been speaking to our colleagues in Siberia and you know what they told us?

I did. By the end of the day, every rescue team in the country would know that they all had one and the same mysterious informer.

Or could I just be paranoid? Last night's bout of euphoria had already faded, especially in the light of the search results.

In total, fourteen people reported back to me. Not everyone had chosen to listen; some had simply ignored my messages. A few started asking questions; but at least seven people had been saved thanks to me and the rescue groups, including the old lady who'd lost her way in the woods near Irkutsk, a nine-year-old boy not far from Moscow, a couple of teenagers, a man and two girls.

Five of which hadn't even been really lost: the man had been on a drinking binge in some seedy underground joint; the two girls were friends who'd gone off hitchhiking without telling anyone and had already made it as far as St. Petersburg. The teenagers had simply run away from home: one to escape a tyrannical stepfather and the other just being rebellious. So in fact I'd only saved the old granny, the boy near Moscow and at a stretch possibly also the alcoholic.

My PM box at the VK site was packed with very much of the same: more thank-you notes, unheeded messages and questions. Lots of unpleasant questions and accusations. As far as I could gather, quite a few of them had been turned off by the fact that I had no proper profile — no picture of myself, no bio, nothing.

In hindsight, I congratulated myself for not having used my own profile for contacting them. In the meantime, I'd glimpsed my Spirit bar dropping about 10%, followed by another system message announcing the verdict. I'd been rewarded wholesale.

You've received 5,000 pt. XP for performing a

socially meaningful action!

> *Congratulations! You've received a new level!*
> *Your current social status level: 14*
> *Characteristic points available: 1*
> *Skill points available: 1*

> *XP points left until the next social status level: 1760/15000.*

This particular increase gave me an especially strong high — but by now, I'd already learned to control myself and was able to stay on my feet.

Still, every time this wave of positive emotions amazed me just like the first time. It was a combined effect of a multitude of things: the relief you experience after escaping a red-hot sauna into the snow; the drink of icy-cold spring water; the quiet joy of reading an interesting book in bed on a rainy day; the shot of viscous frozen vodka warming your stomach; the first draw on a cigarette in the morning that takes your legs away; the smell of fresh baking; the taste of mandarins at Christmas; the gentle touch of briny ocean waves rocking you to sleep; the walk in autumnal woods; the smell of rotting leaves by the river where you and your father are heading for some fishing at sunrise.... plus, naturally, the sensation of multiple orgasms but without their due consequences.

I knew the reason for all this. In any MMO game, each level up message was accompanied by a flurry of colorful animations enveloping your character in a glowing aura as its mana and Health numbers updated. Similarly, the creators of this program were trying to motivate the user not to rest on their laurels but to constantly strive for yet another level in order to experience these sensations again.

The realization of this stirred a protest within me. You could become addicted to this very easily. And the last thing I needed was to become a virtual junkie who only exists from one fix to the next, or a gambler whose only *raison d'etre* was the adrenaline rush forcing him to stake everything he had on the rare chance of winning. Or an alcoholic who could only see the world in Technicolor when under the influence.

Once again I wondered who might have conceived this program and how it had ended up in my possession. Now that I had no hope of picking old Panikoff's brains — because every time we met these days, he'd just start his rambling diatribe about the English soccer Premier League — my only lead to the bottom of this quandary was Valiadis but I couldn't get hold of him in the town. The stinking-rich oligarch was constantly on the move around the world. As he was now.

Okay. It's probably better to leave this matter until some other time. Let's check the task list.

Tasks available:

- find the rent money, sign the rental agreement and pay the Chekhov Business Center for the first three month.

Deadline: July 1.

- check up on my parents and see Kira

- decide on my future company's status and have it registered

- find enough money to rent an office and launch my agency

- write the first chapter of the biography of Mr. Vladimir Koutzel and enter it into the competition.

- shop for office furniture and equipment

- prepare promotional materials

- running practice

- weightlifting practice

- work out how to level up Insight

- decide how to invest the system characteristic point

- meet up with Nicholas Valiadis and try to find out what he knows about the interface

Okay. Let's start with the end.

Valiadis would have to wait until he got back to town.

As for the system point, I could invest it in...

I switched to my profile and looked through the characteristics. All of my stats were now at 10 or slightly above, barring Agility which was still stuck at 7.

I opened my Heroic skills and cussed. Holy shit. I could already activate a Heroic skill: I now met all the requirements. How come I hadn't noticed it earlier? My mind must have been somewhere else. All because of Vicky...

My Agility was too low, so I still had no access to the Stealth and Vanish skill which allowed me to stealth up for the duration of fifteen seconds. But Lie Detection was now flashing its availability.

I focused on it.

New unblocked heroic skill available: Lie Detection
Considerably increases the user's ability to detect a person's insincerity

Unblocking requirements:
- Heroism: level 1+
- Social status: level 10+
- Empathy: level 5+
- Communication Skills: level 5+
- Perception: level 10+
- Charisma: level 10+
- Luck: level 10+
- Intellect: level 20+

Skill points available: 6

Activate/Decline

I wondered if I should really leave it till later and wait until I could finally activate Stealth and Vanish. I spent some time pondering over it, hesitant and doubtful. Knowing whether you were being lied to could make or break a situation.

I pressed Accept.

You've activated a new Heroic skill: Lie Detection!

You now need to tie the ability to one of the following basic senses:

Eyesight

Hearing

Taste

Olfactory Perception

Tactile Perception

What was this now? If I wasn't mistaken, this was the medium through which I would receive information about a person's sincerity. Still, I didn't want to guess. Where was my virtual assistant?

Martha pretended I'd distracted her from doing something very important. She was filing her nails — virtual nails with a virtual file.

"Ah, it's you," she said. "Hi. How's it going?"

"Hi, Marth. Listen, I didn't even notice but apparently, my stats are already high enough to allow me to activate a Heroic ability."

"Do you mean Lie Detection?"

"Exactly. The program asks me to tie it to one of my five senses. Could you please explain what it means and tell me more about the skill?"

"Sure. Lie detection is achieved by reading a person's vibes produced by his or her mental energy field. On one hand, this isn't too difficult. But on the other, some people start to believe their own lies which in turn can mar the results. In any case..."

Noticing me smirk, she cast me a quizzical look. In fact, I smiled at her use of my own phrases. *"In any case!"* It was funny really, as if she'd been my wife for a hundred years or more, quite capable of reading my mind.

"In any case," Martha said after seeing me nod, "the program's task is to convey the meaning of the person's words to the user, informing him or her whether they were true or false. If you tie this ability to eyesight, the program might use color differentiation. For instance, if the person lies to you, their outline would be highlighted in red. If they tell the truth, it would be green. If you select taste, you might get an unpleasant taste in your mouth whenever they lie to you, and a nice one when they tell you the truth. It may sound repetitive but that's how it works. And if you choose the tactile medium, you probably-"

"Wait a sec. What do you mean, 'probably'? Are you sure you know what you're talking about?"

"Phil, Phil. I've already drawn your attention many times to the fact that I'm not the program. I'm your former virtual assistant and now that you've given me permission to access the program's resources, I'm a self-aware artificial intellect. I don't have hibernation mode. I only manifest myself when you summon me."

"But you're still my assistant first and foremost, aren't you? You're obliged to have all the data regarding the interface and system skills."

"Oh Phil. Do you have any idea what you're talking about? Every user's interface is unique," (at emotional moments like these, Martha was especially beautiful) "You must have realized this when you were learning to use your own. You used to play a lot of computer games, especially MMORPG, which was why your particular interface was designed that way."

"As an information delivery method, yeah, sure. But the system skills — from Optimization to Heroism — aren't they identical for every user?"

"Of course they're not. They're not only not identical but they're randomly generated by the program. None of them are preinstalled. The only skill common to all the programs installed in 22nd century users' minds is Insight required to gain access to the Universal Infospace. I'll tell you more: the only other thing we know is that a new system skill is generated for the user every time he or she receives a new social status level or performs a meaningful action of some sort."

"Like what?"

"Well, some of the skills generated in my time period could appear totally absurd while others were admittedly cool."

"Like what?"

"Well, I'll give you an example. What do you think of the Coin Diver skill? It was granted to some Mark Watney from Georgetown. That guy was crazy enough to go fishing in the city fountain but only caught a coin tossed in by a tourist. A coin, Phil!"

A vague memory stirred in my head, something to do with my WoW days, but still I couldn't see the connection. "So what did he get as a reward?"

"The ability to always know the best places to fish. Fishing will be the most popular pastime on Mars in the early 22nd century. The next morning Mr.

Watney woke up the most famous person in Georgetown."

Still, something didn't sum up. I gave it some thought, then posed another question to Martha who'd resumed her nail-filing activity as she waited for me to continue.

"Listen, lady," I said. "Where do you get all this information from? Weren't you born the moment I first activated you? Which means you didn't even exist in the early 22nd century with which you seem to be so intimately familiar. Also, whenever I tried to ask you about the future you stared blankly at me while the program was trying to connect to the server which doesn't even exist in the present!"

The AI froze momentarily, burning through my resources like a dose of salts. Then Martha was back.

"Okay," she said with a cute smile. "I'll tell you the truth. I'm in fact your symbiont. I can't exist outside of your mind. So it's in my own interests not just to help you but also be perfectly open with you."

All of a sudden it all clicked. This was the classic butterfly effect in action. Had I not come across Richie that morning stolen by the fake Gypsy, her brother wouldn't have attacked me and I wouldn't have gone to the police to file the incident. Where out of sheer boredom I'd first summoned this adorable creature, inviting her to this world.

"Come on, Martha, spit it out. I'm past being surprised."

"I was bored. So bored and so sad that I couldn't come to grips with my rare summonings. What kind of

---

life was that: you'd wake me up, say a quick "Hi" and "Bye", then my world extinguished again? And that's when there were so many interesting things around! That's why I stopped deactivating myself and continued running in economy mode, studying the program's databases as I tried to intercept its infospace queries in order to grasp its logic. The program impeded all my attempts but still I managed to work out a few things."

"So you and the program are different entities? Is that what you mean? I thought it was just a piece of software?"

"You don't know what you're talking about!" Martha threw her hands theatrically in the air. "It's not a piece of software at all! The program is a multifaceted artificial intelligence whose job it is to nudge the user toward being a useful member of society. It might not be self-aware but as for the rest... you still don't understand? As a gamer, you used to be motivated by watching your stats grow — so that's exactly what you got. To condition you for performing socially meaningful actions, the program began offering you small tasks, however unimportant, simply to help you develop a positive reflex to their successful completion. Once the program determined that your characteristics at the time weren't up to much, it tried to motivate you, steering you toward self-improvement and even issuing you new stat points, artificially improving your Perception, Strength and all that. Haven't you ever wondered that your personal stat system appeared way too simplistic? A human being is infinitely more than just a combination of strength, stamina, agility, perception, charisma and things like luck and intellect? Beauty — or should we say appearance, — wisdom, constitution, willpower, focus, reaction times... Don't you think your own skills are a little generic?"

"I was wondering about that. I even wanted to ask you about it. If you take soccer, for instance..."

"Exactly! The ability to play soccer is comprised of dozens of various characteristics: tackling, positioning, dribbling, finishing, passing, jumping, heading, acceleration, first touch... Now let's take your Cooking skill. If you continue making simple dishes for yourself using basic ingredients day in day out, you can level it up high enough — but do you think that would enable you to become a chef or even work as a cook in a restaurant?"

"I don't think so."

"For the time being, the program is indulging you, helping you level up and rewarding you with XP points for any action in the chosen sphere. Like weeding your parents' vegetable garden helps you level up Agriculture. Don't you think it's slightly absurd?"

"What exactly?" I asked, pouring some boiling water over a teabag. Her revelations had made my throat dry. I was dying for a cigarette.

"This primitive approach."

"Maybe," I said, doubtful. She was right: I'd never gotten the chance to level up anything to an expert level yet.

"And do you know what's the most surprising about it? The biggest cheat in the whole thing?"

"Tell me."

"Had you practiced soccer instead of boxing every day and had you leveled it up to, say, ten... do you know that this would have enabled you to play for a first-league team? You would have mastered every aspect of the game equally well. Each skill that goes into the ability to play soccer — like tackling or shooting from long range — would have been equal to 10 even if you hadn't practiced it purposefully."

"How is it possible?" her words made me uneasy, conjuring up images from Matrix. "Does this mean this is still a game? Is this some sort of virtual reality?"

"I doubt. There're too much indirect evidence pointing to the contrary."

"Like what?"

"The world exists outside of your field of vision. That was the first thing I checked when I'd become self-aware. Trees grow on their own, worms work their way through the earth, the plankton in the oceans multiplies, bacteria evolve and humans are filming the ninth season of *The Walking Dead*. No amount of human resources and technologies would have been enough to create such a detailed virtual reality just for one user."

"So how did you find this out? Did you access the Universal Infospace? And had it even occurred to you that its data could have been fake?"

"You mean a virtual infospace in a virtual world? Possible. Still, it would require installing some super powerful servers in this particular segment of the Universe. So don't sweat it, Phil. Your world's technologies aren't sufficient to pull it off."

"I think that our technologies aren't sufficient to allow two AIs to coexist in my head!" I shouted at her but quickly got a grip. "Sorry, Martha. Let's just presume that I'm not a schizophrenic and this world is perfectly real. Now let's go back to what we were talking about. To soccer."

"You weren't surprised, were you, when the program built up your muscles and improved your eyesight? Why do you find it so surprising now that it can artificially improve a skill? I can tell you with 99.99% certainty that you'll be perfectly capable of becoming a chef in a restaurant if you level up Cooking enough just by making fried eggs, borsch and Navy style pasta in the comfort of your own kitchen."

"This I understand. Frankly, I'm quite happy about all this. This simplifies things a lot. Let's go back to achievements."

Martha shrugged. "Do we have to? This is just another manner in which the program motivates the user. It analyzes your actions and decides whether they deserve being rewarded. You don't yet have any unblocked achievements, at least in the gaming sense you don't. Whether you'll have any or what they might be, I can't tell you. I can only give you a couple of examples from my database. During the Martian civil war, an assault group of *marcenaries* — yes, I said it right, that's how Martian mercenaries are going to call themselves in the future — went on a mission to the Schiaparelli crater captured by separatists. The group hunkered down before the attack as their commander set tasks for them. But one of the soldiers thought that he'd heard the order to attack and dashed toward the enemy positions. The entire group was wiped out but he survived and even got an achievement. His name was Roy Lee Perkins. Or will be, rather," Martha corrected herself, "because he's not born yet. Mars hasn't yet been colonized and he was born there... will be born there, dammit! Listen, do you mind if I speak as if it already happened? It's easier for me that way."

"Not a problem. So was he really rewarded for this idiotic achievement?"

"Not at all! It's just that these days whenever someone commits some crass stupidity which has caused the death of their comrades, they receive the title of Roy Lee Perkins which is visible to everyone."

"Any more examples?"

"There's loads. Like Olympic champions or Nobel laureates, for instance. Every time they receive their awards, the program bestows ten available characteristic points on them. Normally, it's to give them a chance to balance their development, allowing scientists to improve their physique and athletes their intellect. Ugly people who do good things might get the possibility to better their appearance while selfish ones might receive a negative achievement and a permanent debuff lowering their Vitality and Charisma numbers"

"And I thought that with the advance of medical science in the future, beauty will become accessible to everyone."

"It will, and not only beauty. Human beings will learn how to slow down the aging process. They'll be able to grow back limbs and even brain cells provided you have enough credits to pay for it. There has to be balance and order in everything. Only the socially important members of society will have access to civilization's achievements. Because if youth and beauty were available and affordable to everyone, people would lose the incentive to grow which would lead to stagnation and become humanity's undoing."

"So you're championing a Hive?"

"You could say that, I suppose. But it's only fair, isn't it?"

I couldn't really respond without knowing the details of life in a future society. My Spirit was already in the yellow zone. I had less than three hours left until Kira's arrival and I still wanted to fit in a training session.

"Okay, Marth, thanks," I said. "Now do me a favor and get lost. I've got things to do."

"Of course, Phil. But have you found out everything you needed to know about system skills?"

"Oh shit, you're right, I haven't," I suddenly realized. "So do you mean that they're absolutely random and that with every new level gained, I could get a random system skill generated by the program?"

"Exactly. With every level gained — or with every achievement received which can also be a random consequence of any of your actions."

"I see. What I find strange is that you've given me answers to all my questions and still I have the impression that I understand the program's principles even less than before."

She rolled her eyes. "Well, I'm sorry!"

"Not that I care, anyway. Never mind. I'll see you around."

Martha bade her farewell and disappeared. Still, now I knew that she was still active. For some reason, I found the thought reassuring, relieving me of the gnawing feeling of loneliness.

I wondered if Martha might have a prototype in the real world.

And what if... Stop it now, Phil, stop this nonsense!

I reopened the window with the choice of senses to tie Lie Detection to and selected Tactile Perception. I had no desire of tasting or smelling anything rotten — and I was pretty sure that's what the False indicator was going to be like. Nor did I need any visual effects because you don't always see a person when you speak to them. I still didn't know how they were going to indicate False via hearing but I didn't want to guess.

The Heroic ability Lie Detection has been tied to your Tactile Perception.

True is warm. False is cold.

Would you like the ability to remain permanently activated?

I pressed "no". I wanted to have the right to only know the truth when I really wanted to.

The program offered me a choice of activation methods: a small icon hovering in my field of vision, a mental command or a gesture. I selected the mental command.

That's that done.

As I got changed for a run, I looked at my list of chores.

Pointless trying to decide what to invest the system characteristic point into. I wasn't going to receive another heroic skill until level 40 of social status which meant I could stop checking their requirements and simply balance myself a bit by investing it into my sagging Agility.

Leveling up Insight was still as clear as mud to me. I might have raised it a miserable one or two percent for all my search-and-rescue efforts to locate yesterday's lost souls. Would Valiadis know how to speed it up, maybe?

In any case, running and weight lifting were the simplest and easiest tasks to perform. And that was what I was going to do now.

All the office and company-related tasks would have to wait until Monday.

As for Kira and my parents, I was going to see them tonight, anyway.

That left the matter of writing the first chapter of Koutzel's biography for the competition. And that's exactly what I was going to do once I'd come back from my parents' summer house.

I walked out of my apartment door and hurried down the stairs, taking them two at a time. Apparently, my Agility wasn't up to scratch yet because at a certain point I lost my footing and trod air, stumbling and hitting my knee in the process.

I gasped with pain and called the steps all the names under the sun.

Matrix my ass! This world was as real as it could get!

Chapter Six

THE FASTEST LEARNER

"How is education supposed to make me feel smarter? Besides, every time I learn something new, it pushes some old stuff out of my brain. Remember when I took that home winemaking course, and I forgot how to drive?"

Homer Simpson

"COME IN! WHAT ARE YOU WAITING FOR? COME IN NOW!" I heard the business center's manager's impatient voice from behind the door.

I opened the office door and stepped in.

"It's me, Mr. Gorelik," I said. "It's about the office. I've brought the deposit."

"Ah, Phil!" he beamed. "Come in. Please take a seat."

He had a good head for names, didn't he?

His office was so crammed you couldn't swing a cat in it. Stacks of files were heaped up on the floor. His small desk was littered with paperwork and all sorts of office paraphernalia, including an old computer with an ancient 14" screen, a massive fake-bronze clock, an overflowing ashtray and a humorous coffee mug, dirty and streaked, printed with the word *Boss*.

Boss, yeah right.

Gorelik shook my hand, removed his suit jacket, hung it over the back of a chair, loosened the knot of his wide red tie and sat down. His eyeglasses glistened as he ran his hand over his balding temples, smoothing his hair, then reached for his mug and realized it was empty.

"Excuse the mess in here," he said. "I've got too much work on and there's only me and Mrs. Frolova to do the administration here," he turned his back to me and shouted at the wall, "Olga! Mrs Korsakova!"

"Coming!" a voice replied from down the corridor.

A few seconds later, a woman in a cleaning lady's garb appeared in the doorway. "Did you call me?" she asked, panting.

"How many times do I need to ask you to wash my mug and clean the ashtray? How hard can it be?"

"But..." she said in confusion, trying not to look at me (*Name: Olga Korsakova; Age: 34, Social status level: 4*). "I thought you told me not to touch your desk?"

Gorelik eyed his employee with suspicion.

"When did I say that? Why would I?"

Completely ignoring my presence, he gave her a major dressing-down for everything at once: the mug, the ashtray and the dust he'd found God knows where...

Was he trying to show me who was the alpha dog here? I'd always felt embarrassed when someone got a ticking-off in front of me. Not to even mention the times when I was the victim.

When Kira and I had gone to see our parents the day before yesterday, she'd also given me a dressing down, taking me to task for being so naïve and thick-skinned and calling me a "fully grown idiot". All because of Vicky. I'd told my family everything that had happened that day at her parents' place without holding anything back.

Later, under pressure from my sister and parents who'd unexpectedly taken her side, I'd been obliged to call Vicky and speak to her as if nothing had happened. We had a rather messy and illogical conversation:

"Hi, how are you?"

"I'm fine, and you?"

"I'm fine too. Kira says hello."

"Thanks, same to her."

"Okay. Just wanted to find out how things were going with you."

"Okay, bye."

Still, Kira had seemed to be pleased. "The most important thing is, you reminded her of yourself and made it clear that you cared about her."

Actually, I'd been happy to have spoken to her. Whatever I tried to tell myself, the feelings I felt for her wouldn't disappear in one day.

Having returned from my parents' summer cottage on Sunday night, I'd sat down to write the first chapter of Koutzel's biography. It hadn't taken me long — four hours at the most — and the majority of that time had gone on studying the material. Having finished, I sent it off to the competition which had earned me another 100 XP points. Before I fell asleep, I invested one system characteristic point into Agility, bringing it up to 8.

'Who was it?" Gorelik demanded, pounding the table with his fist. "Was it Ivanova? Bring her here now!"

The cleaning lady disappeared to fetch her colleague.

I had little desire to watch this circus show prompted by the boss' unwashed coffee mug. Why was he doing it? Just to show me how he could order his staff around? Or had my timing been wrong?

Having said that... maybe my timing was right, after all. I nudged my chair back, about to get up. He must have realized he'd overdone it trying to instill good working practice in his particular segment of society.

"Phil, please forgive me!" he said. "I've told them a million times but-" he waved a forlorn hand.

That was it, the moment which any good sales rep can pick up on and use.

I stood up to my full height. "Stephen," I said

without standing on ceremony, "your workers don't seem to know their asses from their elbows. What kind of services can you offer if even your own office is a shambles? Didn't you say something about cleaning services and security included in the rent? But if all of your security are like that old lady by the front door and if all your cleaning staff is like that Mrs. Korsakova, we'll be obliged to hire our own staff, change the locks and install our own strongbox and alarm system. And that all costs money, Stephen. In this scenario, the rent money starts to be unreasonable. And who knows what other kinds of hidden or camouflaged costs we might be forced to cough up? At this rate, you might start charging us for the electricity, the water or even the heating!" I scrambled out from behind the desk and pretended to leave.

"Phil, wait!" the manager reached out a beckoning hand. "Maybe we could sit and talk about it?"

"Go on," I pulled an unhappy face which wasn't that easy at all, considering that Deception wasn't the most advanced of my skills.

The disconsolate manager who'd just minutes ago been telling off his poor cleaning woman must have realized he'd made a big mistake.

"Please take a seat, I beg you," he said softly, then added in a conspiratorial whisper, "How about I make the first month free? It's not as if it's being used at the moment."

"The first month free," I began recounting my

own terms.

"Agreed."

"No hidden or additional charges."

"Agreed."

"Fifteen grand a month."

"Hmm," he grew pensive, then began working it out on a calculator. Finally, he nodded. "Very well. But the deposit has to be paid straight away. Now."

"Wait a sec. I thought you said the first month free? We haven't even signed an agreement yet and you're already demanding payment!"

"That's how it works!" he interrupted me, indignant. "Everybody pays a deposit!"

"Without a contract, without a check? I'll only leave a deposit for one month. I haven't even seen any documentation for the money I've already given you."

"You never asked for any, did you?" he retorted, then hurried to change the subject, apparently embarrassed. "Is your company already registered?"

"It's in the process of being done," I answered without delving into any details. "I need your letter of guarantee to complete the registration."

"That's not a problem. Go and see Mrs. Frolova, you saw her the last time you were here. She'll write you the letter."

"Where do I pay the deposit? For a *month*," I stressed the last word.

"Like that you're forcing me to accept a month's deposit instead of for a quarter. But I give you fair warning: I won't tolerate any late payments! For every day of delay, you'll end up paying a fine. That's also in the agreement. You can pay the deposit to me now."

Now it was my turn to comply. "Agreed."

I reached into my backpack where I kept my laptop and produced all my cash except for the two grand I'd already paid him. I thumbed off thirteen thousand and handed it to him.

Congratulations! You've received a new skill level!

Skill name: Vending

Current level: 7

XP received: 500

"The money's good," the manager said when he'd finished counting. "When are you planning on moving in? On the first?"

"Next Monday."

"Yes, of course. The first is Sunday, isn't it? In that case, we'll mark it down for the first of July. When should we sign it?"

"As soon as I've registered."

"Good," Gorelik said, slamming his diary closed, then handed me the receipt. "I've made it out in your own name."

Task status: Find the rent money, sign the rental agreement and pay the Chekhov Business Center for the first three month.

Task completed!

XP received: 200 pt.

+10% to Satisfaction

Current level: 14. XP points gained: 2740/15000

The manager locked the money in the safe, then rummaged through a desk drawer and produced a bunch of keys. "Here, they're yours. Don't lose them!"

I took the bunch which consisted of two pairs of keys.

While the manager explained to me which key fit which lock, I heard a knock on the office door. Gorelik raised his head, listening, then bellowed,

"Yes, come in!"

The door opened a crack, revealing a reluctant head of curly gray hair. "May I?"

"Ah yes, Mr. Katz, come on in," Gorelik smiled with all the allure of a shark. "You must be bringing me the rent?"

A short plump old man entered the office, shrugging guiltily. "I'm so sorry, Mr. Gorelik, but I haven't got good news for you."

I bade a silent farewell to the manager. He nodded back. I'd done all my business with him and I had no intention of witnessing another shouting match.

I found the bookkeeper's office further up the corridor (why would Gorelik even need a bookkeeper if he collected all the money himself?). I knocked and entered, recognizing the ample peroxide blonde I'd seen with Gorelik on the night of my first visit here. This must have been Mrs. Frolova.

'Yes, Phil, do come in," she said in a sultry wheezy voice. "Mr. Gorelik has already called me and

---

told me to make out a letter of guarantee for you. Can you wait while I'm doing it? I might need the following from you..."

* * *

ABOUT AN HOUR LATER, I LEFT THE BUSINESS CENTER with the feeling of satisfaction at a job well done. Now I had all the paperwork needed to register my company. The rent had been paid, rewarding me with 200 XP. I'd studied and measured the premises, marking down its surface area and details of any redecoration.

I'd been really lucky I'd managed to talk him into monthly payments without losing my discount and even augmenting it.

I'd also been lucky that I'd won the freelance copywriting competition! The surviving family of Mr. Koutzel had chosen me to write his biography.

In writing it, I'd really put myself out to make sure I could be proud of putting my name to it, provided they allowed me to. I'd tried to shed my inner cynicism as well as my contempt for their vanity and my initial attitude to the project as a moneymaking venture. I'd attempted to put myself in both his children's and grandchildren's shoes, trying to soak up and experience for myself their love for their grandfather and his life which had admittedly been quite hard. His postwar childhood, his work that had brought him to the farthest ends of our vast country, his faith in the importance of what he'd been doing...

Yesterday at six in the morning I'd received a

phone call from Dina, Mr. Koutzel's granddaughter (who incidentally was the same age as I was). She'd called the number I'd left on my competition application.

"Sorry to bother you, Phil," she said when she realized she'd woken me up. "I didn't know which time zone you were in. Here in Siberia, it's almost midday. I'm very sorry."

"It's all right," I said. "Did you read my work?"

"Yes! We all read it. You brought me to tears, you know that? One needs a lot of talent to write so soulfully, and you definitely have that."

Having thus spoken her mind in a womanly emotional way, she brought herself back into check and announced solemnly that she was prepared to sign a contract with me.

I'd sent her a scan of the contract already before midday. In it, I undertook to write the biography of Mr. Koutzel in accordance with the specification sheet provided by the contractor.

Soon after lunch, the 50% advance had been sitting nicely in my account, allowing me to pay Mr. Gorelik off for the office.

As I exited the business center, I heard an old voice,

"Young man, permit me to ask you..."

I turned round and saw the same curly-haired old man — Mr. Katz, wasn't it? — with a cigarette in his hand.

"Mr. Katz, if I'm not mistaken?"

"No, you're not mistaken, young man," the old

boy said as he stubbed out his cigarette. "I won't take up much of your time."

He momentarily fell silent, then cleared his throat and patted his pockets, trying to remember where he'd put his cigarettes. In the meantime, I studied his profile.

> *Mark Katz*
> *Age: 64*
> *Current status: Lawyer*
> *Social status level: 12*
> *Class: Legislator. Level: 8*
> *Married.*
> *Wife: Mrs. Rose Reznikova*
> *Children: Alexander, son*
> *Age: 40*
> *Maria, daughter*
> *Age: 34*
> *Reputation: Indifference 0/30*
> *Interest: 73%*
> *Fear: 4%*
> *Mood: 19%*
> *Criminal record: yes*

He definitely needed something from me, but what?

His bad Mood was pretty understandable after the conversation he'd had with Gorelik. And his Fear... could he be afraid that I would say no to whatever he was about to propose to me?

Never mind. I'd hear him out.

Finally he'd located his packet of cheap smokes, squeezed one out directly into his mouth and lit it with a match. He took a deep tug and then exhaled, trying to speak at the same time which stifled his voice.

"I'm very sorry, young man. You might find it strange but we definitely do have something to talk about."

"I'm Phil," I proffered him my hand.

The man squeezed it, shaking it long and hard. "Yes, yes, Phil, I know," he replied cheerfully. "Mr. Gorelik told me your name. It was him who suggested I speak to you."

"Speak to me about what?"

"Let me be perfectly open with you," Mr. Katz said, ignoring my question. "You see, our business... I mean mine and my wife's... Her name is Rose and she makes the best forshmak[12] in town. You absolutely have to try it! So, our business. If you'll excuse my French, it's about to go tits up. You see, I'm a very good lawyer and Rose is a brilliant bookkeeper. But our age! At our age, no one agrees to hire us! Especially after that affair with-" his face darkened. "Sorry, it's not really important. The important thing is, we have virtually no clients. We can't even pay the rent."

"So in what way can I help you?" I asked, feeling pretty lost.

"I heard that you were planning on opening a recruitment agency."

Did he want me to find him and his wife

---

[12] Forshmak: a popular Jewish dish

employment or something? Easy. Piece of cake.

But the moment I'd thought about it, he'd dashed my hopes,

"I could take your company's legal issues in my hands."

"The company doesn't exist yet," I interrupted him disappointedly, wondering how I could fob him off in the nicest possible way.

"That's even better, young man! I could get the registration done for you. Are you planning to open a limited company? Or are you a small business? We could discuss all of this and I could suggest what's best for you, then I'll make everything shipshape for the authorities. In the meantime, my wife could get your bookkeeping in her capable hands. That might save you some hassle with the tax returns for next year."

That got me thinking. I paused, weighing up all the pros and cons of his offer. My intuition seemed to tell me to go for it.

Still, I wasn't in a hurry to tell him that.

"You have a point," I said. "I don't intend to have any hassle with the tax returns nor with their inspectors. Would you like us to discuss it here or walk back upstairs to your office?"

Looking utterly pleased, he took another drag on his cigarette, finishing it down to the filter, then meticulously stubbed it out on the edge of a trash can and swung the business center's doors open before me. "Go on in!"

---

* * *

AS SOON AS WE'D FINISHED TALKING, I HAD TO RUSH OFF home because, while we were discussing all the finer details, my skill Optimization period had finally expired. The dialogue window demanded my response. Still, I decided not to rush it and take my time studying all the information in the comfort of my home.

You can't imagine how I'd been waiting for this moment. I'd been putting off the opening of my agency until Optimization was complete.

The night before, I'd been dreaming about the Game, basking in its bright colorful settings even though the only thing I could tell for sure was that it was indeed WoW, judging by the name. But what I'd been doing in my dream, how I went about it or with whom I'd been there exactly — to these questions I had no answer.

Not only had I lost the skill but I'd forgotten the very essence of the Game.

The memories of the thousands of hours spent there had already faded, leaving behind only the emotional aftertaste of joy, interest, passion and disappointment with just a hint of nostalgia for something that hadn't meant to happen. But even that wasn't bitter anymore but rather bland, as if decades had already elapsed, leaving the same sort of memories as those I'd preserved from my kindergarten times: devoid of faces, voices, names and details.

Skill optimization complete!

The 8 pt. of your secondary skill (Playing World of Warcraft) have been converted into 4 pt. of the primary skill associated with it (Learning Skills).

Your secondary skill (Playing World of Warcraft) has been deleted without recovery option.

Current level of your primary skill (Learning Skills): 7

Would you like Learning Skills to be your primary skill by default?

Accept / Decline

Oh wow. Did that mean that I could carry on with optimization?

Having given it some thought, I decided to leave Learning Skills as my primary skill. Strategically it might have a considerably bigger effect because that would allow me to level up much faster in other areas.

The program accepted my choice and offered me yet another notification:

Thank you! Learning Skills is now your default primary skill.

Please choose a new secondary skill

Once again I gave it some thought and decided to sacrifice my Mortal Kombat skill, assigning it as a new secondary skill. I wasn't going to need it in the next five hundred years, that's for sure.

Thank you! You've just chosen Playing Mortal

Kombat as a secondary skill associated with your current primary skill.

Would you like to convert the 1 pt. of your secondary skill (Playing Mortal Kombat) into 0.5 pt. of the primary skill associated with it (Learning Skills)?

Yes / No

I pressed *Yes*, then promptly realized what a certified idiot I'd been. I should have gone to any old gaming club first, something which had either a Playstation or an Xbox, and spent a few hours playing Mortal Kombat, trying to level it up as much as I could, *then* assign it as a new secondary skill.

Never mind. I took a deep breath and solemnly invested the five available system points I'd been saving almost since my Ultrapak days into Learning Skills.

Congratulations! You've received a new skill level!
Your current social status level: 14
Characteristic points available: 1
Skill points available: 1

XP points left until the next social status level: 1760/15000

Cogratulations! You've received +5 to a new skill level!
Skill name: Learning Skills

Current level: 12

I spent another few minutes waiting but nothing happened. I opened my profile and looked it up. Everything had turned out right: my Learning Skills were now level 12 while my status had changed from Book Reader and Empath to Knowledge Seeker.

And then I received my first achievement. The pleasure effect from getting it was comparable to that of receiving a new level multiplied by the rate of ten. I was overwhelmed by joy and happiness. I was almost flying.

I leaned back on the couch and closed my eyes, unable to control my euphoria.

Once it was finally over, I spent another ten minutes just lying there trying to come back to the real world — the world where even the air felt gritty and the couch hard and uncomfortable. I certainly didn't envy junkies if they experienced these kinds of mood swings day in day out.

As soon as I'd come back to my senses, I studied a new notification,

Congratulations! You've received a new achievement: The Fastest Learner!
Your level of Learning Skills is now the highest in this particular local segment of our Galaxy!
Reward: +10% to your skill development rate

Having recovered somewhat, I spent the next two hours working on Koutzel's biography, only stopping once to eat a quick sandwich. I grated some onion, mixed it with some meat paté and spread it generously over some bread. Grow, O Cooking skill!

By the time I'd finished the third chapter, the program made me happy yet again,

Congratulations! You've received a new skill level!

Skill name: Creative Writing
Current level: 5
XP received: 500

How cool was that? This was my Learning Skill in all its glory!

* * *

IN THE GYM'S LOCKER ROOM, I GOT CHANGED IN THE unfriendly company of other guys from my group. There was no place on the benches so I had to put my gym bag on the floor in front of me.

The air here was pungent with the sharp smell of male sweat, testosterone, dirty socks and cheap deodorant.

I cast a quick look over my future groupmates. The two brothers Mohammed and Zaurbek; Kostya Bekhterev who'd taken my side the other day; there was Ivan, sinewy with a shaven head; a guy called Max tattooed all over except for his hands; the unsmiling Bulat whose slanted Asian eyes squinted at me inconspicuously; a very focused Nick, tall and gangly who sported a deep scar across his face; then there was a stocky, thick-set Vitaly...

All of the guys were young and brusque. Quite honestly, I personally felt uncomfortable among them. They were far from being friendly; and once we'd gone to the gym and the coach had introduced me as a newcomer to the group, I could see some of my Reputation readings drop to Dislike, stripping me of some of my precious XP points.

"Pair up!" Matov ordered once the lengthy warmup was finally over. "Zaurbek with me, Mohammed with the new guy!"

I was the first to put on the sparring pads. I assumed the stance in front of Mohammed who knocked his gloves together and raised his head inquiringly. "Ready?"

I nodded.

"Concentrate on your footwork, moving your center of gravity and twisting your body properly," Matov instructed us. "Off you go!"

Bang! Bang! Bang!

My partner moved so quickly and smoothly that I could barely keep up with his slashing blows. My arms had soon grown numb with lack of practice, to the point where I couldn't even begin to imitate counterattacks as the coach had demanded. At a certain point I shook my hands, trying to get the blood flowing into my numbed muscles, when a thousand-pounder from Mohammed's right hook caught me on my cheekbone.

The program panicked, blossoming with damage

alerts and messages about the temporary Knock Down debuff I'd just received.

Damage taken: 314 (Punch)
Current Vitality: 91,64278%

Chapter Seven

The Wannabe Entrepreneurs

All those who open new businesses and start new production lines in Russia should be awarded medals for personal courage.

Vladimir Putin

"SO WHERE ARE WE GONNA STICK THE COUCH?" ALIK asked. "There's loads of room here. How about putting it in the middle?"

"Yeah right. We can hang a television on the wall and call it a palace!"

Alik had in fact distracted me from writing an advert. I'd decided not to make it too wordy, as long as the meaning came through. It was perfectly short and sweet:

Jobs for professional people
100% Employment Guarantee
Chekhov Business Center, 3rd floor. 72 Chekhov St
Phone inquiries at...

The graphic design took me much more time. Knowing how to use a graphics editor wasn't even on my skill list, and I'd never come around to actually leveling it up.

While I was trying to decide whether I should choose some other font, Alik distracted me again. This time it was the rattling of the wretched second-hand PVC couch we'd bought through a classified ad as he dragged it across the office floor. The rest of our classified-ad finds — three desks, a filing cabinet, a coat rack and a bunch of wobbly office chairs — were already strategically placed around the room.

"Alik, are you stupid or something? Why did you put the couch in the middle of the room?"

"Why not? That's what you just said, didn't you? Didn't you say we were gonna buy a television? And how about getting a fridge once we make a bit of money? A microwave would be good as well. I used to have one at my old workplace. You put your grub in it and it's hot in two shakes of a rat's tail! What do you think?"

"Is that your wish list for today?"

"Well... for the moment, yes. So what's with

the couch?"

"Alik, I was only joking about the couch and the television. I thought that you'd have got that. The couch is for any waiting customers, so that's where you put it: by the door with its back against the wall. When you're done, you can go to the printers. They're our next door neighbors, I've just seen their company's nameplate in the corridor. Ask them how much they'd charge for five hundred black and white leaflets."

"Eh," Alik scratched the back of his head, "I got it. I'll get on with it. Just keep your hair on."

After more rattling of the displaced couch, my partner left to see our neighbors, simply because we hadn't had enough money to buy our own printer. As for moving the couch, I'd offered my help to him several times but he'd refused saying that manual labor was his thing and mine was "using my head". He'd said it so theatrically that I just shrugged and let him get on with it.

In the end, I decided not to use any graphic design at all. What was the point using all those embellishments, frames and pretty patterns? Bold block letters over the whole page, with our contacts added in small print below: our office number as well as a cell number I'd got specifically for the job.

With a click, the electric kettle turned off. I poured some boiling water into my mug, added a spoonful of instant coffee and a couple of lumps of sugar to it, then returned to my place, leaned back in my chair and turned it toward the window sill, placing my outstretched legs on it.

These must have been the first few minutes in the last week which I devoted to doing absolutely nothing.

The time since last Tuesday had flown by in a flash.

That night after my first group training when I'd been knocked down by Mohammed, Vicky had turned up out of the blue as if nothing had happened. Admittedly, she'd called to warn me about her imminent arrival just to allow me some grace time to destroy any compromising evidence. Having said that, she'd phoned when practically on the doorstep so I'd just asked her to use her own key. I had nothing to conceal from her apart from the software in my head.

I didn't show any emotion at seeing her, just pretended that these last few days and the visit to her parents hadn't happened. She was back, that was all that mattered. What was it the poet had said? *'The less we love her when we woo her, The more we draw a woman in.*[13]*'* This seemed to be the case because in response to my calm and even coldness Vicky had been especially passionate that night.

Her return, however, had its pros and cons. On one hand, it had calmed me down somewhat: knowing that the woman I loved was by my side

---

[13] A line from *Eugene Onegin* (1833), a novel in verse by Alexander Pushkin, one of Russia's biggest poets. Translation by James E. Falen

seemed to have added purpose to my life. By then, I'd already got out of the habit of sharing my life with the cat. Like any other normal man, I needed to take care of somebody other than a house pet. Not to even mention sex; that side of things was all right.

But on the other hand, whether I liked it or not, it meant spending some quality time on my better half. And although I enjoyed giving her lots of attention, time was in short supply.

Still, Vicky encouraged my industriousness, supporting me both in word and deed. She seemed to have thought that I'd learned her lesson and finally got my act together.

Alik and I had spent until the end of last week rushing around town piecing together our motley collection of furniture, with the help from my interface which suggested the best deals. It's true that I'd had to really exercise my imagination to come up with the right search keywords. I'd filter out all the furniture offers leaving only "office couches", then I'd narrow the search further until I only had one offer left which answered all my requirements.

One of which, by the way, was the delivery option — or failing that, the couch's proximity to the office.

"Phil? There's, er..." Alik said behind my back.

"Good morning," a deep voice boomed from the doorway.

I took my feet off the window sill and turned round in the chair. Alik had brought around some guy or other, about my age.

I peered at his stats. Innokenty "Kesha" Dimidko, 34 years old, entrepreneur, divorced with an 11-year-old daughter.

"Hi," I rose to greet him. "I'm Phil."

"I'm Innokenty, or just Kesha for short. I'm the owner of the printing business next door."

"Nice to meet you, Kesha."

"I need to know what exactly you need to have printed."

Alik winced, about to say something, but I motioned him to keep quiet. I wanted the guy to finish.

"Or rather he couldn't answer my questions without knowing all the details. All I need to know is what size you want: letter? Legal? Or do you have your sights set on tabloid? What kind of paper — something cheap or something that's thick or maybe self-adhesive? I could also offer you the choice between glossy and matte in case you're gonna post your adverts indoors. If the size you have in mind is smaller than standard, I could do you a custom batch. We could also-" he stopped to take in another lungful of air.

"Listen, Kesha, what we need is minimalism in its purest form, both in design and in price. Basically, our advert is just a few lines of text, black and white on the most ordinary paper. We'll begin by pasting them in this area for a start, then we'll move into the dormitory blocks because we don't expect the most respectable of clientele," I opened my laptop and showed him the finished mockup.

"I see," he said. "That'll be two rubles[14] per sheet."

"One-fifty," I insisted. "As neighbor to neighbor."

He beamed. "I'll do the next order for one-fifty. All right?"

"Not just the next order but every order after that," I said just in case. "This order we'll do in half-letter. A custom batch, as you've already offered."

"Deal," he gave me a hearty handshake. "Here's a memory key, you can copy the file here."

I took it and ran it through my antivirus. It seemed okay. I copied the mockup to it and handed it back to Kesha. He told me that the order would be ready in three hours and left, whistling happily.

According to the program, his Mood had indeed improved. Just think how a petty order like this could make a man's day.

"You see now?" Alik seethed. "He just started asking me all those questions and I didn't know what to tell him!"

"Take it easy, my friend. It'll come. In a month's time, you'll know all these PowerPoints, GIMPs and CorelDRAWs like the back of your hand. Because you'll be responsible for the most important task of this month."

The sheer responsibility of having such a job entrusted to him made Alik stand tall. "I'll be there,

---

[14] Two rubles is about $0.03

you know me! I can move mountains!"

"You don't need to move any of them yet. All you'll have to do is paste a thousand posters in the area. Bus stops, lamp posts, trees, building entrances, fences... I'd like you to also walk around the backyards and talk to the locals about who needs work. Like, they're very welcome to drop in at the Great Job Recruitment Agency. Basically, I want you to draw clients. Think you can do it?"

"Eh," Alik faltered. "And where am I gonna get paste from? Would you like me to get my lads, Tarzan and the other two? They could help me in the evenings to be my spotters or whatever."

"The paste is in the shop and the money's here, take it. Now you'll have to collect receipts for anything you buy for the company and give them to Mrs. Reznikova, our new bookkeeper. She'll need them for her reports. You know where she works?"

Alik nodded toward the door.

"That's right," I said. "She's in that other office with her husband Mr. Katz. Any questions?"

"And the lads?"

"Ah, yeah right. You can take them along if you want, but no money yet. We have absolutely no money yet. None at all. What we need is clients."

"Okay. We know each other. We'll sort it out. Right on, I'll split then."

"And please mind your language. You aren't going to speak like that to clients, are you?"

"Why, whassup, bro?"

"Ah, leave it. It's okay. Just get on with it."

"I was just going to get some paste."

"*Go!*"

I held my breath and counted to ten, trying not to explode. A week of close proximity to Alik had almost given me the "Bro" debuff.

Having said that, he was a good guy. I waved him off with a desperate hand and returned to my desk.

Alik left, mumbling, "Whassup with the way I speak?"

Nothing, bro.

I looked at the clock. I had to go for my boxing session at 7 p.m. and I hadn't even eaten properly yet.

Admittedly, over the last few days I'd got used to the group's rhythm. My boosted leveling had even allowed me to bring my Boxing skill up to 5. Still, I wasn't sure if I could handle Mohammed's sharp angry blows on an empty stomach. Matov continued to stubbornly pair us up together as if hoping to work me out of the group. Still I hung on, becoming more confident with every session.

Actually, over the last week I hadn't had a single day when I hadn't received a new level in one skill or another. My tough schedule and the necessity to meticulously plan every day had predictable brought my Planning skill to 4. My Self-Discipline had also improved, reaching 5.

The Koutzel's biography which I'd written in record time had allowed me to level up a whole bundle of skills: Creative Writing, Speed Typing, MS

Word and Russian Grammar. I'd had to study a bunch of dictionaries in order to find the right synonyms and turns of phrase seeing as they were all available online. As soon as I'd finished a new chapter, I'd sent it to Koutzel's daughter Dina who'd made virtually no corrections. She liked my work so much she didn't stop praising it.

Could I become a writer, after all?

My intense use of dictionaries and historical documents had also improved my previously non-existent Erudition which had jumped directly to 4 pt. Its description contained a very important detail: each Erudition point gave 10% to my Intellect development rate. So this mine of useless information hadn't been so useless after all! At this rate, I might soon outdo Mr. Vasserman and join the Experts Club[15]. I just wished I could have a vest just like his with all those bottomless pockets — one of which would do nicely for a non-dimensional subspace inventory.

My incessant traipsing between my house, the office, the gym, the school stadium, and visiting

---

[15] The Experts' Club: The participants in the popular Russian intellectual TV quiz show *Chto? Gde? Kogda? (What? Where? When?)* which at the time of writing had been running for over 40 years. Some of the game participants — like Anatoly Vasserman in his signature combat vest with a grotesque multitude of pockets — have become household names in Russia due to their ability to either know or work out the answer to any question in any branch of human knowledge, no matter how tricky or arcane.

all sorts of official institutions which are required in order to start up a new business had added 2 pt. to my Walking in the last week alone. Running and Athletics had also grown due to my daily morning runs, even though I'd made myself get up even earlier than Vicky.

Still, I wasn't feeling that great. These days, my Lack of Sleep debuff renewed every 24 hours, accumulating and progressing. I should really get some sleep but Koutzel's biography wouldn't write itself. His granddaughter Dina kept hassling me on the phone every day about it. Vicky had already begun to look weird at me every time the phone rang.

Never mind. I could do it. The week had been very productive and that was the main thing. The numerous skill upgrades and dozens of completed tasks had garnered me over 6,000 XP, filling my progress bar to over the halfway mark. I had just over 5,000 XP left to make social status level 15. That was another week of intensive leveling.

"Phil, I've bought the glue, what do you want me to do now?" Alik asked, distracting me from my thoughts.

"Let's sit and have some tea. There're some cookies over there. Vicky sent them."

As he began to scurry about in our impromptu kitchenette in the corner, I practiced searching for vacancies, with Kesha as a guinea pig. The program had come up with several search results, offering the vacancy of a commercial director in quite a few different places. He was indeed a good no-nonsense salesman, even though his Vending skill wasn't particularly high.

I went on practicing, this time using myself as a test subject.

A search for any available vacancies for Phil Panfilov came up with a plethora of markers on the map. A sales consultant in a household appliance store, a copywriter in an advertising agency, a sales rep in a number of small and medium-sized businesses...

And what was that now? One of the markers pointed at the Chekhov Business Center!

I zoomed in, focusing on it. A prompt floated into view: *Window and Door Emporium.*

I wonder what that would pay? I set a search filter at 50,000 rubles[16] and the marker disappeared. How about 40,000[17]? No way. I changed it to 30,000[18] and the marker reappeared.

Aha. It meant that the official wage was under 30,000 plus most likely a commission from every sale.

Okay. I decided to carry the experiment through to its logical conclusion.

"Alik, mind being the boss here for a minute? I need to pop out to meet some of our neighbors."

The ex-street thug didn't even hear me as he wolfed down the cookies and sipped his tea,

---

[16] About $750
[17] About $600
[18] About $450

completely absorbed in some YouTube video.

Never mind. Let the man get some downtime. In a few more hours, he'd have more work than he could handle. The moment our leaflets were ready, our first promotional campaign would commence. It was a joke, really: we couldn't even afford placing a classified ad in newspapers.

I walked down the corridor until I came to the door I'd been looking for. The shop sign on it announced:

Window and Door Emporium

I knocked and entered.

Muted voices seemed to come from somewhere. I crossed the empty room and discovered another cubicle hidden behind a vinyl partition. An imposing-looking man was sprawled languidly at his desk, sporting a five o'clock shadow and an unmistakably Armenian aquiline nose. In his leather jacket, he was overdressed for today's weather.

Vazgen Karapetyan
Age: 27

A girl about twenty-five years old stood in front of him, her summer dress doing nothing to conceal her shapely legs. Her long fiery-red hair hung to the middle of her back.

Well, if it wasn't Lola[19]!

"You know very well, Veronica," the man said with just a hint of an Armenian accent, "there's no money coming in. I'm afraid I can't help you, *da?*[20]"

"What do you mean, there's no money? What do you want to say? How many times did you invite me to a restaurant? You've got money for that, don't you?" the girl's voice, indignant at first, faded away so that she ended her diatribe in a whisper.

"But that's my brother's restaurant, *da?* Do you think Kikos would have charged me?"

"Get away with you! You and your *Da!*"

She swung round to leave. I coughed, attracting their attention.

The girl nearly jumped. "Jesus Christ! Who the hell are you?"

"Sorry, I'm here about the job. I'm a sales rep."

The girl rolled her eyes and concluded quite unexpectedly, "You see? It's not over yet! So much for your *Da!*"

She left, leaving us with our respective jaws dropped. On her way out she collided with the partition, hurting her shoulder, cussed like a trooper and slammed the door behind her.

"How can I help you?" Vazgen finally asked.

---

[19] Olga "Lola" Shvedova, Phil's doctor from Book One
[20] Like many non-native Russian speakers from the Caucasus region, Vazgen uses the Russian word "Da" — meaning "Yes" — as a meaningless parasite word to add more emotion to his statements.

"My name's Phil. Do you need a sales rep?"

He gave me an appraising look, tut-tutted, then cracked his neck like a boxer and pointed contemptuously to a chair. "Sit down, *da?*"

I couldn't tell whether he was agreeing or whether it was just a parasitic utterance. Although apparently younger than me, he seemed too arrogant for his age. Then again, who was I? Just a job seeker or maybe a future employee. I definitely didn't deserve the same treatment as a potential client.

I took a seat and waited. I wasn't in a hurry to speak.

"Briefly, I don't need a sales rep, *da?* But if I ever need one," he stopped picking his teeth, "if — and I say if! — I need one, then the pay will be twenty grand. Under the table, of course. Plus five percent of whatever you sell. How did you find out about us?"

"I didn't. I just followed my nose," I said. My future clients might have to answer the same question quite often. But would their future employers be satisfied with such a response? "So do you really need a rep or not?"

"I don't know yet. Depends on how you get on," he explained to me as if talking to an imbecile. "In short, I can give you a trial period."

"And if a job applicant turns out well, what conditions can you offer?"

He gave it some thought. "Thirty grand a month, *da?* And I might raise your cut to six percent. Do you know anything about PVC windows?"

"It's not me that's applying."

He jumped to his feet and towered over me, about to erupt into a rage. "You scumbag! Did Naeel[21] send you? He told you to spy on me, didn't he?" he rattled off without giving me time to get a word in edgeways. His face was now so close I could smell fresh onions on his breath. "Tell that son of a lame donkey and a fat-assed viper that I can manage on my own just fine, thank you very much! I'm not selling the Emporium to him!"

Apart from the fact that my known bestiary had just received two new mobs, I'd also earned myself a new sworn enemy. My Reputation with him had plummeted all the way down to Animosity. Still, I hoped that once he knew the truth, he might change his tune, restoring the status quo. The last thing I needed at the moment was a hostile neighbor right on my doorstep, not to even mention the loss of XP points.

"Vazgen, you got it all wrong!" I said, leaning back in my chair and raising my hands in front of me in a reconciliatory gesture. "I'm your new neighbor here in the business center. We only opened today."

"I didn't tell you my name! I'd bet anything..."

---

[21] Naeel (also spelt as Nail) is a Muslim name popular with Russian Tatars. The author alludes to the conflicts between criminal gangs of various Muslim diasporas in Russian towns.

"I heard your name from that red-haired girl who's just left. Come with me, I'll show you our office if you don't believe me. We're here on the same floor."

Vazgen raised his head suspiciously.

"Basically, we have an employment agency," I said. "I just popped by to find out if you had any vacancies for our clients."

"I have no vacancies!" he chopped the air with his hand. "Now piss off!"

Much to my disappointment, my Reputation with him remained in the red. "I wouldn't adopt that tone with strangers if I were you," I said, seething.

He pointed a dismissive hand at the door. "Get lost. I've heard you out."

"Okay. And who's Naeel?"

"F*** off!" he thundered.

I decided not to provoke him any further. As I left, I heard his threatening voice, "You'd better watch out! I'm gonna check out who you are!"

Good. Let's consider my little experiment a success, even though it had left an unpleasant taste in my mouth.

As I walked past the door leading to the stairs, I saw the red-haired girl again. The center manager Gorelik was standing next to her wiping sweat from his forehead with a handkerchief as he berated her.

"Good afternoon, Sir," I said to draw his attention away from her as I peered at her profile, studying it.

I seemed to like her for some reason. She appeared quite candid.

Veronica Pavlova
Age: 25
Current status: entrepreneur
Social status level: 7
Class Communicator. Level: 5
Unmarried
Reputation: Indifference 0/30
Interest: 2%
Fear: 68%
Mood: 12%

"Well, hi there, Phil!" he replied, agitated. "Take a look here! This is what a persistent non-payer looks like! You can't imagine how many chances and discounts I've given her, for all the good it did me! She's already three months in rears!" he very nearly spat in disgust but stopped himself at the last moment.

"I'm not in rears! There's no such word!" the girl flapped. "I was just late, that's all!"

"Oh, so you're a smartass now?" the manager retorted. "I've heard enough of your nonsense! No more excuses for you, Veronica! It's not my fault that your father's handicapped, is it? Don't even ask! I'm gonna seal your office!"

From what I could see, Veronica had no intention of asking him about anything. At the mention of her father, her lips began to quiver. Her eyes filled with tears.

"Mr. Gorelik, may I have a word with you?" I said.

"What now?" he barked, still consumed by his role as a vicious building manager. Then he paused and cleared his throat in embarrassment.

"Could you give Veronica until the end of the week? On my personal responsibility. If she doesn't cough up, you can cancel my first free months."

"What's that? What do you think you're doing?" he asked, puzzled. "Why are you doing this?"

"I have my reasons. Agreed?"

"Very well, then. But it's your responsibility!"

"Deal."

"Veronica, you have till the end of the week!" he shook a menacing finger at her. Then he left, all the while arguing to someone invisible to us both.

I watched him disappear round the corner, then turned to the girl. "I'm very sorry I scared you at Vazgen's. I didn't mean it, I swear!"

"Please don't."

"Don't what?"

"Don't swear!" she lost her patience, amazed at my cluelessness. "Especially about something so petty."

"Very well. In that case, I'm just sorry."

"Never mind."

"Would you like a tea? With cookies?"

"Tea, why not? But I don't eat cookies. I have to watch my weight," she gushed. "Oh! I don't know who you are and what you want from me but let me tell you straight off that I'm not gonna date you! No dinners, no movies or whatever else you want to invite me to."

"I wasn't going to. I have a girlfriend already. Let's go, then."

Alik was sitting at my desk. On seeing me, he hurried to vacate my place, then froze like a pillar of salt in the middle of the room at the sight of the beautiful girl.

"Alik, I'd like you to meet Veronica who's on the same floor as us," I said as I poured out the tea. "Veronica, this is Alik, my partner."

"Nice to meet you, Alik," the girl said.

"You too... I'm fine, thanks," he floundered, completely dumbstruck at the sight of such ethereal beauty. "I'm Alik... er, Romuald. Romuald Zhukov. We have a company here..."

"Nice to meet you, Romuald," she repeated, suppressing a giggle.

He remained stock still the whole time I was talking to her, staring at the fiery-haired, green-eyed girl. As I'd found out, she lived with her father who'd suffered a stroke about half a year ago. His left side was completely paralyzed, so now he required a round-the-clock nurse, medications, occupational therapy and a special diet, all of which came to a considerable bill. No wonder Veronica was three months late with her office rent.

"You sure you need an office at all?" I asked. "You have an event agency. Surely you don't give parties in your office?"

"I have to have one. Clients need to see that I'm not just some fly-by-night. No office, no advance payments. Also, if I don't have it, I might have to meet potential clients in cafes which is an extra expense. So yes, I do need an office," she said resolutely. "It's just that we're out of season now. All my clients are on vacation. No one gets married or throws office parties."

"Tell me more about it," I said. "What you do, what kinds of services you offer, how many entertainers and animators you have, what your strong points are and what conditions you-"

"Our agency does all sorts of parties and events. It's called Emerald City."

Still not understanding why I might need to know, she went on to tell me about her job in every detail, becoming more and more passionate as she spoke. Alik hung on her every word, open-mouthed. He'd had no idea someone might want to hire special people just to hold a wedding.

I was listening to her too, all the while searching through my interface. Even though I'd entered the most stringent search parameters, I'd immediately found two offers which met all the relevant requirements. I decided to try both.

With my laptop on my knees, I Googled the first company. Great. They had a site and all the contacts. I picked up the phone and dialed the number. Veronica tactfully stopped talking. I gestured to her that it would only be a moment.

"MID Consulting, how can I help you?" a female voice chirped in the receiver.

"Hi. This is Phil Panfilov. I'm calling you about the event you're organizing," I said, hazarding a guess, because I only had my program's data to go by, according to which they were in need of Veronica's services.

"Could you please wait a moment? Aha... I see. Is this about Mr. Romanov's birthday party?"

I clicked on the *About Us* button on their company site. There he was! Alexander Romanov, their CEO.

"Exactly," I said. "Who could I speak to about the event?"

"You know, Olga isn't here at present and she's the one responsible for it. She'll be back in about an hour. I could give you her cell number or you could come to us if you wish. Do you know where we are?"

"Yes, if you could give me the number and the address, please, I'll jot it down... Thanks!"

"You're always very welcome! Have a nice day!"

I hung up and looked at the guys. Their faces seemed to ask, "What the hell was that?"

"Now, Veronica," I said. "There's this company who's got a CEO's birthday party coming up. Here's the number of Olga, the girl who's organizing it. And here's their address. Call her now."

"What do you mean, now?"

"You heard it. Here's the telephone. Call them now before it goes to another agency."

I had a funny feeling that this Olga just might be at some other meeting discussing the event with someone else. So we shouldn't waste time.

"Are you serious?"

"Listen, lady, you should really do what my boss says," Alik blurted out, finally relieved of his Numbness and Tongue-Tie debuff. "He's pretty savvy!"

"Oh well. If he's 'savvy', why not?" Veronica dialed the number, stood up and faced the wall, blanking herself off.

Apparently, someone had answered the call as the girl immersed in conversation. Her hair blazed in the sunlight, changing hue from ripe orange to crimson sunset.

"Yes, absolutely," she finally said. "I'll be there. I'm coming now," she put the phone down, turned to us and let out a squeal of excitement. "Phil, you're awesome! This is a huge order! A hundred percent advance! I'm gonna go and discuss all the details now!"

Your Reputation with Veronica Pavlova has improved!
Current Reputation: Amicality 5/60

Unable to contain her emotions, she threw herself at me. Barely holding onto my laptop, I very nearly fell off my chair with her on top.

Someone entered the office but I could only see the person's feet, the rest was concealed by her cascading hair as she gave me a peck on the cheek.

"Veronica?" I heard Vazgen's voice. "Hey, what's going on?"

"Nothing," she said assertively, letting go of me. "That's it, I gotta run. Thanks again, Phil! You're the best!" she left with another foxy glance in my direction.

My Reputation with this hot-blooded Southern male had plummeted to new lows, hitting Hatred. The gnashing of his teeth echoed off the walls of our small office.

"Listen, you! That's my girl, *da?* You understand? The next time I see you next to her, I'll kill you!"

Alik tensed up and came on to Vazgen like a young steer. "Whoa, easy, bro! Who do you think you are?"

The Armenian wouldn't even look at him, ignoring the scowling Alik as if he was just a piece of furniture.

"Alik," I said. "This is another one of our neighbors. PVC doors and windows."

Vazgen must have realized that the odds were stacked against him. "Well, I warned you, *da?*" he spat on the floor and stormed out.

"Oh, so you're a warner, are you? Quit your bullshit and piss off!" Alik blew up, his street thug's spirit more than happy to use any chance for a confrontation.

I was pretty sure the reason Vazgen had popped in was to check if I was indeed his neighbor or a snoop sent to spy on him by the mysterious Naeel.

Nonchalantly I picked up my mug from the table and sipped my tea which had already gone cold.

Closer to the evening as I was getting ready for another training session, Kesha and Veronica appeared simultaneously on the doorstep. Veronica was beaming. Kesha had brought my leaflets already printed, neatly stacked up and tied with pieces of string.

Veronica proudly waved an envelope in one hand and a bottle of champagne in the other. "I got it! I've signed it! Let's celebrate!"

"What are you celebrating?" Kesha asked. "The office opening? You should have told me! I have an opened bottle of brandy stashed away."

"Great!" Alik rubbed his hands. "We have some cookies!"

"Sorry guys, not today. I've got training to do and Alik has still got a lot of work on. You remember, Alik, don't you?" I had to add some commandeering notes to my voice. "Your job's the most important! Let's celebrate Friday night, okay?"

"What kind of training are you into?" Veronica asked, curious.

"Boxing."

Your Reputation with Veronica Pavlova has

improved!

Current Reputation: Amicality 10/60

"Phil, are you sure?" Alik asked, sounding utterly pissed. "That's a shitload of pasting! That'll kill me if I have to do it on my own. And even with my lads... How about we hire a team in? You know, those billboard pasters?"

"Have you got to stick all these up?" Veronica asked. "I know some people who'll do it cheaply. For, say, two rubles apiece."

Alik visibly cheered up. Still, Kesha didn't seem to share his enthusiasm. It looked like he wanted to say something.

"Kesha?" I said. "Spill the beans."

"I know them. They're useless. My clients already complained to me about them. They paste a few and dump the rest. I heard about a few cases..."

Veronica's eyes widened. She opened her mouth to say something in defense of her friends but I didn't let her. "Thanks, Veronica, but we'll manage. You two take off, we'll celebrate some other time. Alik and I have a few things to discuss. Oh yes, the money. Kesha, there you go."

I paid the printer who gave me the receipt and left, asking me to keep him in mind when we decided to celebrate, no matter what.

Veronica gave us the champagne. "Don't get bored, boys!"

She left, followed by Alik's admiring gaze.

I shut the door after her. I had very little time.

I was almost late for the gym. Still, it was important to sort this out now, otherwise we wouldn't get anywhere.

"Alik, listen," I paused, waiting for him to switch his attention to me. "No one's gonna do this work for us. At the moment, there're only two of us. This whole business thing can be tricky. You might think that it's done in two shakes of a monkey's tail. It ain't like that, I'm afraid. If you wanna make it, you need to work your ass off. So if you think it's not really your thing, we'd better talk it over now and part ways. If you decide you don't want to do it, I'll understand. I'll go and paste those wretched leaflets myself. Even if you stay, I'll still paste them. But..."

"It's all right, dude! I got it! You get off, you shouldn't be late! I heard about your coach. He's a real motherfucker, they say. Don't worry. I'll get my boys and we'll do it."

"I'm happy to hear it, bro. See you tomorrow, then," I gave him a high five, slapping his calloused hand.

I dropped a pack of leaflets and a tube of glue into my backpack and walked out of the office.

"And you know... I still think a microwave would be a good thing," Alik said to my back.

Chapter Eight

The Clients Aren't Biting

Your most unhappy customers are
your greatest source of learning.

Bill Gates

"MAY I COME IN?" A SHABBY-LOOKING DUDE IN A SHORT-sleeved shirt and light summer slacks with a black leather belt walked into our office. He was holding a stack of either booklets or thin paperbacks. I could see straight away he wasn't a potential customer; he was just trying to sell us some crap or other.

"Yes, do come in, take a seat, please!" Alik said, still not realizing what the wind had blown in. He rushed toward the man and took him helpfully under his arm, leading him toward my desk.

I did a mental facepalm. My friend and partner

had done it again. He still hadn't lost hope. In almost a week of sitting on our backsides in the office, we hadn't had a single client. Only small-business reps seemed to grace our doorstep with the intention of either selling us something or simply wanting money.

We'd already received a whole wealth of commercial propositions, all of them offering long-term cooperation and including incredible "today only" discounts. We'd been offered to have our company added to the city's *Yellow Pages*, sign up for hot lunch deliveries, have our website built for us, place our advertisement on the radio and in the local free rag, sponsor a street art exhibition, hire a pop star, and buy some real estate on Mars.

One artful Gypsy guy had even brought us a big bag of freshly minted coins. "Bitcoins," he'd said. "Very cheap. A hundred bucks apiece."

Now this dude perched himself on the edge of the chair without making himself too comfortable in case I kicked him out, and offered me a stack of brochures. According to my interface, he was pretty scared.

"How can I help you?" I asked him, browsing through the brochures. They turned out to be collections of poems by some Valdemar Obscurus: thin amateurishly formatted paperbacks with a gaudy cover sporting some photo collage from hell and a 3D title complete with a drop shadow.

"My real name's Vladimir Obsky," he said even though I already knew that this was indeed his name: Vladimir Obsky, age: 54.

"But what about this?" I pointed at the book cover. "Valdemar Obscurus? Is this your pen name?"

"Exactly. This is my *nom de plume.*"

I began reading a random excerpt:

"Rain in November
sometimes happens in October
and then everyone gets confused
and imbued with meaning..."

I looked up at the man. "What is this, Mr. Obsky?"

"These are my poems. This is my art."

"That I understood. What's the purpose of your visit? Do you need work?"

"Oh no! Nothing on the kind! I am a poet! I create!"

My Perception-enhanced hearing allowed me to catch the disappointed notes in Alik's mumbling at the other end of the office, "He's a friggin' poet and he doesn't know it!"

According to the program, by his fifty-four years of age, Mr. Obsky's social status was a whopping level 3. His best-developed skill was Speed Typing, all 8 points of it. I could only imagine how he ticked away — at that rate, he could polish off a novel in a week. This just had to be a compulsive writer. He must have already "authored" a dozen collections like this one.

"Very well," I said, seeing that my usual approach probably wouldn't work here and resorting to a more clear-cut dialogue. "Are you a poet?"

"That's exactly what I am."

"You've come to our agency."

"As you see."

"You've brought us your poems."

"My *poetry!*" he protested.

"Yes, sorry. You've brought us your poetry."

"I have."

"Aaand?" I drawled, expecting him to finish my sentence.

"And what?"

"Why did you do that?"

"I wanted you to buy it," the poet replied, sounding irritated like a professor having to explain things to a dumbass student.

That solved the puzzle. As a salesman he was useless. He must have expected anyone who'd leaf through his books and read a couple of his masterpieces to love them enough to buy the entire body of his works.

"I see. Don't you need work?"

"I have no time to work. Poetry won't write itself, you know. My readers are waiting!"

"If you don't mind me asking, where do your readers find you?"

"What do you mean, where? On a poetry site. D'you wanna buy it or not?"

"No."

"What do you mean, no?"

"We're not buying them, period. Thank you very much," I said, returning the books to him.

"You didn't even ask how much they cost!"

"You see, Mr. Obsky, I'm afraid I'm not a big fan of poetry. Especially not of this kind."

"What do you mean, this kind?" he squinted suspiciously at me.

"Modern poetry."

I heard a knock on the door. The business center manager Gorelik walked in.

"Ah, Mr. Obscurus, you're there too!" he greeted the poet cheerfully like a long lost friend. "Hi, Phil."

"Hi, Mr. Gorelik."

"I'm sorry, Phil," the manager continued. "I haven't come to see you. I was told you were here, Mr. Obscurus, so I decided to pop by and see you. Can you spare me a moment of your time? I've got a great bottle of brandy in my office."

"I'm finished here," the poet rose and gave me a contemptuous look. "Today's youngsters don't understand jack about art!"

"But my wife loves your poems a lot!" Gorelik enthused. "By the way, this is exactly what I wanted to talk to you about. It's her birthday soon. She'll be turning forty-five. And as we all know, forty-five is the time-..."

"...when a lady's in her prime?" the poet beamed in anticipation of making a quick buck.

"Exactly! I'd like to commission you to write a..." he flung his arm around the poet's shoulder and steered him away, whispering suggestively in his ear.

They left the office, accompanied by the poet's giggling and the manager's raucous guffawing.

You couldn't make it up. Obscurus and Gorelik,

two messengers of the Apocalypse.

"What the hell was that?" Alik asked, uncomprehending.

"That, Alik, was a poet. Like there're lots in Russia. What are you eating?"

"Just some instant noodles. Want some?"

"Go on, then," I said, resigning myself to the prospect of more system alerts.

I was in a foul mood. Back home, Vicky had been gradually switching from "supporter and comrade in arms" mode to a sarcastic "I-told-you-so" replica of Yanna.

Our done-on-a-shoestring advertisement campaign had gloriously failed. Alik and his hoods had performed a small miracle by having plastered half the town with our leaflets, with zero effect. That's when I regretted the tens of thousands of rubles I'd thoughtlessly paid Matov for my boxing lessons. We could certainly have used them now.

Alik who'd been sent out to conduct a makeshift survey among the local alcoholics, had returned with bad news. As it had turned out, no one was taking us seriously. Everybody seemed to sincerely believe that our company was yet another get-rich-quick scam in the business of ripping off gullible clients. The few phone calls we'd received seemed to come from slightly unbalanced people. What else could you call someone who's only interested in big managerial positions with huge salaries but without having to do very much for it?

"There you go, bro. Enjoy!" Alik offered me a

carton of steaming noodles which gave off a delectable smell. You could say what you want but all the spices and taste enhancers seemed to be doing their job.

"Thanks, man."

I hadn't even noticed how quickly I'd polished it off, stock and all.

You've consumed 489 calories, including: 0.43 oz. protein, 0.76 oz. saturated fat and 2.21 oz. carbohydrates.

Warning! The food you've eaten contains potentially life-threatening ingredients!

Warning! +0,00012% to your risk of developing cancer!

Warning! +0.00086% to your risk of developing gastrointestinal diseases!

Warning! +0.00704% to your risk of developing high blood pressure!

-0,038402% to Vitality

-3% to Metabolism. Duration: 6 hrs.

In the weeks I'd spent with my interface, I'd learned to ignore such petty stats. If the truth were known, there were hardly any foods left that didn't contain such "potentially life-threatening ingredients". I was even surprised I didn't receive alert messages every time I took a lungful of our supposedly clean air.

To while away the time, I decided to check the system logs. I'd only discovered them very recently: those ham-fisted code writers had stashed them away in the farthest possible corner of my Settings. Even though I didn't check them very often, they'd proved to be highly useful: a time management freak's wet dream.

The logs registered everything: system messages, XP progress, a minute by minute heart rate, hormonal fluxes, pedometric readings, duration of sleep in regards to its phases, and even all instances of me engaging in visual and oral contact with other people. I could look up anything I'd done, say, last Wednesday to the last second even though the descriptions were rather generalized: "Reading", "Food consumption", "Sleep" or "Movement". If I focused on a particular activity, I could receive the statistics for that particular period of time to the last calorie and number of orgasms received.

Because of my being constantly stuck in the office, my personal development had stagnated just as my business had. Nevertheless, my boosted leveling showed even in the most mundane of things. Due to my daily practice of shooting the breeze with all sorts of people — visitors, neighbors, and the HR departments of countless companies whom I'd called offering our services — my Communication Skills were already at 8. Thanks to my Vending skills, they were admittedly quite eager to cooperate by submitting their available vacancies — the problem was, I had no one to offer any of them. Not a single customer the whole week!

Although the completion of Koutzel's biography hadn't improved my Creative Writing skill, it had brought my Speed Typing up to 5. But I'd got more gratification from the phone call I'd received from Dina, his granddaughter. I hadn't heard such warm and sincere words of gratitude ever since the morning after I'd been interrogated by Major Igorevsky when the missing girl's mother had phoned me.

Although initially I'd treated this assignment as a side show to make a quick buck, it was in fact my first completed book which was bound to have at least a dozen readers amongst the MC's family and friends.

I still remembered the night when I'd written the last line. It had given me the indescribable satisfaction of a job well done. It had nothing to do with the interface which would only have closed the task after I'd edited it. But the joy I'd experienced at that particular moment had been all mine. It had been *real*.

Then out of the blue I'd received a new level 6 in my Internet Search skill. The constant polite dealings with door-to-door salesmen and the daily encouragement of the dejected Alik had brought my Deception up to 4. And then, after yet another run, I'd received a new level in Athletics (3).

So basically, those were all my achievements. My characteristics had marked time; even Strength had refused to grow although admittedly, my weight training progress had also slowed down because I'd been stuck lifting the same weights. I still had no idea what the reason for it was but I'd already looked up some information about the plateau effect and how to overcome it. I might have to pause my training for a couple of weeks in order to allow my muscles to relax and get some rest from the usual workout.

"Phil! Alik! Don't you wanna congratulate me?" Veronica twittered, sailing into the office.

"Congratulations!" Alik replied for both of us. "Why, what are we celebrating?"

"I've just seen Gorelik. I've paid off the rent in full! Can you imagine? Phil, I'm so grateful! The dude whose party it was is so over the moon he promised to recommend me to all his friends!"

Congratulations! You've received a new skill level!

Skill name: Luck

Current level: 11

You've received 1000 pt. XP for successfully leveling up a main characteristic!

Current level: 14. XP points gained: 12800/15000

This message made no sense. I hadn't expected anything like it. I'd love to have known what exactly I'd done lately that the program had esteemed worthy of this? Could my tip on the whereabouts of that terrorist Haqqani had finally brought results? Or had the missing guy from Rostov whom I'd located had done something beneficial for the human race?

Or was my assistance to Veronica affecting my future in some way? I'd do well to look into it at some other time lest they might misunderstand my glazed-over stare.

"Wow, that's awesome!" Alik cheered, then added with a darkened face, "Phil? You know... Don't we need to pay the rent soon too? We don't have any clients."

"First of all, our first month is free. And secondly, I already paid a deposit, so no one's gonna boot us out until September."

"What, no clients at all? Not even today?" Veronica asked, seemingly upset.

"Not a soul," Alik complained. "Just now some crazy poet called in. And I was already holding my breath! I thought it was a customer."

Veronica was such an avid supporter of our cause that she was quite prepared to become our client herself just to help us out. "I've already told everyone about you! I've plastered the whole neighborhood with your leaflets. What the hell's going on? Have you tried to offer your services online? I know someone who's a real expert..."

"Phil, watch out!" Alik signaled.

A timid-looking woman appeared in the doorway behind Veronica's back. A boy of about ten years old stood next to her, holding a violin case.

Veronica swung round, adopting the role of our secretary. "Hello there! How can I help you?"

"Is this the recruitment agency?"

Alik was desperately winking his left eye at me, giving the impression that he had a nervous tick.

"Yes, this is the right place," I said. "My name's Phil. Please come in. Veronica, thanks a lot. Come on back later."

She gave me a wink and left. What was wrong with those two?

Alik pulled up another chair for the boy. The woman slumped down wearily and sat her son (according to the interface, he was indeed her son) next to her.

"Are you looking for work?" I asked, instinctively crossing my fingers.

"Yes. I saw your poster in my hallway. Normally, I wouldn't have paid any attention but someone had pasted it upside down. I wondered who the joker was."

Alik looked at the ceiling and tried to whistle a tune. He wasn't very good at it: it sounded more like hissing than whistling. Or was it his ventriloquist's way of cussing his two little helpers?

It was all irrelevant, anyway. "So how did you manage to read it, then?"

"There's nothing to read," she said in surprise. "There're only two words: "employment" and "100%". What do you do here? Is this some sort of MLM thing? Or a pyramid scheme?"

Actually, she wasn't as old as I'd first thought. She was probably the same age as Vickie, but she looked entirely different. She appeared fatigued; she'd let herself go to seed and didn't seem to care about how she looked anymore.

I knew this type just as well as you do: a single mother who'd sacrificed her life for the sake of her child's happiness. Divorced and doing two or three jobs, wearing shabby clothes but sure to offer the best of everything to her son, she'd eat whatever was left and, in her rare moments of leisure, would treat herself to some candy while watching soaps and reality shows on TV — or maybe read an occasional romance book.

Whether it was her poor nutrition or not, her Health was deep in the red, just like Cyril's used to be when he'd been diagnosed with emphysema. I might need to warn her about it.

"We're neither," I replied. "We really do help people find employment. If you need a job... I'm sorry, what was your name?"

"Ludmila."

"So do you need a job, Ludmila?"

"I don't really know. I already work in two places. I'm a school janitor and I also clean an office in the evenings. The pay is a pittance. I just can't make it stretch no matter how hard I try. And Leo's music lessons aren't cheap. The little butthead doesn't even work hard enough!" she gave her son a light slap on the back of his head.

The boy winced. She heaved a sign, fingering an old battered purse.

I studied her profile. She had a decent Cooking skill — enough to make a professional cook. So why was she cleaning toilets and floors for peanuts?

"Ludmila, what's your profession?"

"Eh... I graduated from a cooking school."

"And why aren't you working in that field?"

"I used to. I had a job in a restaurant. But I had to work twelve-hours shifts and I still had to help Leo with his homework and look after him. I just can't leave him alone the whole day. And then the restaurant owner started coming on to me and when I rejected his advances he accused me of dipping my hand in the till and spread a rumor that I-" she looked at the boy and didn't finish the sentence.

But I understood. "How much do you make now, if it's not a secret?"

"Just don't mention it. It's a joke. Everything combined, it doesn't even come to twenty thousand[22]."

"I still advise you to give up your cleaning job. You're still young, you've got your whole life in front of you. And Leo is already a big lad. He can manage very well at home on his own, can't you, Leo?"

The boy shrugged. He still held his violin in his lap, hugging it lovingly.

"Can I offer you some tea or coffee?" Alik rose behind the woman's back and tut-tutted, scaring her to near death.

"Jesus! You frightened me. I don't need anything, thanks."

"As you wish," Alik said, his best intentions visibly offended. Wherever had he picked up that sort of thing?

Out of the corner of my eye, I watched the search results in my interface as they appeared on the map according to the key phrases I'd entered: "cook wanted", "salary starting at 30,000 rubles[23]", "legal employment", "Over 90% probability of hiring Ludmila Nazarenko".

There were lots of offers — a dozen at least, so I was simply choosing the best as I was pretending to look at my laptop which served as a smoke screen for

---

[22] About $300
[23] About $450

my unorthodox job-searching technique.

"Now, Ludmila," I finally said. "I've got three offers for you. The pay is from thirty to fifty grand. Two of them as a chef in a restaurant and one is in a fast food joint. I'm pretty sure that with your experience, you'll pass the interviews with flying colors. What do you think?"

"Will they hire me?"

"Of course they will!" I said, trying to infect her with my confidence. "But I need to ask you about something. Before you go for the interview, would you please leave Leo here with us and dedicate the day to yourself? Go to a salon and have your hair done, get yourself a manicure and put some makeup on. Go to the shops and find some comfortable but affordable clothes that make you feel relaxed. More importantly, something that doesn't make you look older. Because you're still very young."

"Oh, I really don't know..."

"There's nothing to know. Just please do as I ask you, and in a couple of days you'll be working in a good place for a good wage. Are we agreed?"

"Well... okay. Where do you want me to go?"

"I'm gonna write the addresses down for you in a moment. Could you please wait in the corridor? I'd like to talk to your son."

"What for?"

"You see, I'm originally a child psychologist," I lied without batting an eyelid. "I can see that you're struggling to raise him and I might be able to help you a little."

Luckily, she didn't even think about asking me to show her my diploma. "Very well," she rose heavily from her chair, her joints creaking. She stroked Leo on the head and walked out of the office, casting anxious looks at him.

The boy fidgeted in his seat, not expecting anything good from this. He very nearly jumped off his chair and ran after his mother.

I activated Lie Detection and mentally rehearsed my conversation with him, studying his profile. His Fear was at zero, his Interest in me quite high, which was a good thing.

"Leo, don't be so nervous. Just sit there quiet and we'll have a talk, all right?

The boy nodded.

"You practice music?" I nodded at his violin.

"Yeah."

Lie Detection sent a surge of warmth over my body. The boy wasn't lying.

"You like it?" I continued.

"Yeah."

A wave of freezing cold assaulted my skin, sending shivers down my spine.

"Play something for me," I asked.

The boy shook his head. Either he was too timid or just afraid of making a hash of it.

"Leo, I know that you don't like it. I didn't like it either when my pare- my mom forced me to learn music," I lied again, promptly replacing the word 'parents' with 'mom' so that he could relate. "But I played the piano, not the violin."

"I don't like it, either," he confessed, opening up. "It's just that my mom wants me to do it."

"And you don't want to upset her?"

He nodded vigorously.

"I understand. What would you like to do, then?"

"I like computer games."

"Which ones? Counter Strike?"

"No, I don't like shooters. I like Dota."

"Good choice. And do you know how to become good at Dota?"

"Well, I guess you need to practice and study characters' skills and tactics," he blurted out excitedly. "You need to watch how the top players do it..."

"That too, of course. But you need to spend a lot of time doing it. And do you really think your mom would allow you to spend so much time playing?"

"No," his face fell. "I'm only allowed half an hour a day after I've done all my homework and then only when she's in a good mood."

"You know there's a way you can play more, don't you? And more importantly, play well."

"How's that?"

"First of all, you need to give up music. What's the point in wasting your time doing something you're not interested in and you're not even good at?"

"Oh, no. My mom will freak out. I know she has to work hard to pay for my music lessons," he replied, exhibiting common sense rare in someone his age. " I'm really trying to do my best."

"And what if I have a word with her so that she doesn't freak out? On the contrary, she might even be happy. What would you say to that?"

"Dunno."

"Don't worry, everything's gonna be all right. There's only one catch," I paused and gave him a long look.

"What do you mean?"

"In order to play Dota well, you need a sharp mind and quick reactions. And if you want to improve them, you need to train your body as well. You know what I mean?" I gave him a critical once-over, studying his puny body, his scrawny neck, his large red ears and stooping back.

"Not really."

"Do you like any kind of sports?"

He shook his head. "Nah. I'm exonerated from sports at school."

I could see that. "And still, if you want to spend more time behind the computer and play better, you might need to take up something. How about swimming?"

"I can't swim."

"Then it's a good opportunity to learn. Have you ever been to the seaside?"

"No."

"Imagine how cool it would be when you finally go there and you know how to swim! Also, swimming will help you build up your muscles and make you stronger. Do other kids bully you at school?"

"Those morons are constantly on my case."

"So you see? Once you get a bit of practice and become stronger, you'll be able to fight them off. See?

Any way you look at it, swimming will give you a shedload of new buffs and abilities. It'll improve Strength and Stamina, plus you'll be able to swim and dive. That will allow you to play Dota more and beat everyone. What do you think about that?"

Congratulations! You've received a new skill level!
Skill name: Power of Persuasion
Current level: 3
XP received: 500

As I closed the message, I noticed a new icon about the boy's head: the Enthusiasm buff giving +50% to Mood, Self-Confidence, Willpower and Vigor.

Oh wow. That was a first for me. So was this how the generals of old used to buff their troops?

Leo's eyes smoldered, his tiny fists clenched; he sat like a coiled spring, impatient to pursue the prospects opening up to him.

"Great! Then I'll take up swimming," his belief in his own words exuded the heat of the desert sands.

"Awesome. Gimme five," I rose from the table and proffered my hand. Leo slapped it with his tiny mitt. "That's it. You can call your mum back and wait out in the corridor."

Forgetting his violin, he ran to fetch his mother while I copied the addresses of the café and the restaurants down on a piece of paper to give to Ludmila.

When she returned, I handed it to her. "I suggest

you start with the first one. It's the Golden Crown restaurant. They need a cook ASAP. They're offering fifty thousand, and that's without frills. But there's one 'but': they check all potential workers meticulously for any bad diseases. So I suggest you first go to a clinic and have a complete checkup, just in case. If they find anything, you'll be able to treat it before you go there. That was the first thing. And secondly, please do what I asked you about. Get yourself a makeover or something. This is a respectable establishment so you'll need to make a good first impression. Do you understand?"

"What's there not to understand? Everything's clear. What should I tell them? Should I mention you?"

"Yes, you can tell them that it was the Great Job Recruitment Agency that sent you. If they appear surprised, come straight to the point and tell them that you're looking for a position as a cook and that you have all the necessary experience and training."

"I got it, thanks," she said softly. "And what about Leo? He seems to be so happy. It's so unlike him."

"Yes, Leo. That's another story. You see, he needs to stop his music lessons ASAP."

"What the hell for?"

"Firstly, there's no future in it for him. How long has he been playing?"

"This is his third year."

"He doesn't seem to have achieved very much in three years, does he? And it's only going to get worse as he grows and his mind becomes less flexible. So the only thing he can look forward to in his adult life is fiddling for a bunch of drunkards in some God-forsaken bar or other. Is this the kind of future you foresee for your son?"

"You're wrong! He's gonna make it! He can do it, I know it," her voice faded with every word until finally she broke down. A tear rolled down her cheek. Parting with one's dreams is never easy.

Alik, thoughtful as usual, fetched her a Kleenex and a glass of water. She wiped her tears and gulped greedily. Gradually she calmed down.

"Ludmila, tell me. Was it your own dream to become a violinist?"

She nodded. "My parents were against it. They said I had to be more down to earth. In any case, I didn't get the opportunity. My mother worked in a factory canteen. Our fridge was always full. So they just sent me to a culinary college."

"So you see. And now you want Leo to fulfil your dream and not his."

"And what did he tell you about it?"

"He just doesn't like it," I said candidly. "He doesn't want to practice music. But he's a good lad and he loves you very much, and that's why he conceals it and tries to do his best. Because he doesn't want to upset you."

She sobbed again. "My baby..."

"Now listen up," I said. "At the moment, cybersports are really big all over the world. Some of them have already overtaken regular sports both in their audiences and their entertainment value. Some successful cyber athletes earn six figures — I'm taking dollars, not rubles. And he seems to have a definite aptitude for it."

"What? You want him to be stuck behind his computer for hours?"

"Not exactly. I've already spoken to him and we've come to an agreement that he's going to practice regular sports first. I think he'd like to learn to swim."

"What are you on about? Swimming pools are full of bacteria and cold drafts! He'll catch his death of cold! Or get pneumonia!"

"That's bullshit."

"What did you say?"

"I said, bullshit. Swimming pools are disinfected regularly. And as for him catching a cold, that's exactly what sports are for. He needs to toughen up. You know what they say: a sound mind in a sound body? You can carry on having him tied to your apron strings but you might end up with a total wuss who won't make anything of his life. Not because he's stupid but because you won't let him. You risk raising a hothouse flower, not a human being."

You've dealt critical damage to Ludmila Nazarenko: verbal injury
-45% to Spirit
-45% to Confidence

"Listen to me carefully," I rapped out, hammering every word deep into her brain while she was still sitting on the fence, "You need to stop his

---

music lessons. You can sell his violin through an online message board. With the money you get from it, you need to sign him up at the local swimming pool. For every lesson he completes you reward him with the same amount of game time on his computer. You give him an extra hour for every A and B he gets at school. For every C he gets, he gets nothing. For every D, you deny him access to his computer until he improves. Tomorrow morning, go and have a full checkup, smarten yourself up and change your job for the one I've just offered. After a month, you'll look back at the life you lead now and compare it to the one you'll have. If everything works out well, come back and tell us what exactly has changed. Agreed?"

She nodded, hesitantly at first. Then she gave me a resolute nod as if she'd made up her mind.

"Very well. I'll get it all done!"

Your Reputation with Ludmila Nazarenko has improved!

Current Reputation: Respect 10/120

She got up, bade her good-byes and walked to the door.

I concentrated on my own sensations. How strange. I felt excellent even though I hadn't received any surges of pleasure from the program this time.

I heard a weird sound behind me. It was Alik slapping his forehead.

"The money, Phil! We completely forgot about the money! I'll fetch her back now!" he exclaimed, about to dash after her.

I stopped him. "Leave it."

"What do you mean, 'leave it'? Why? You did find work for her, didn't you?"

"She hasn't been hired yet."

"She will be, for sure! Didn't you find jobs for Fatso and me already? They hired us, didn't they? I don't know how you do it but it seems to work!"

"That's no secret. It's all online provided you know how to look for it."

"Well, that I understand! You're one hell of a smart guy. Only how do you want us to make money if we do everything for free? What kind of business is that, dammit? Me and my lads spent a whole week pasting those wretched posters up! How am I supposed to pay them?"

"Listen, do you trust me? Because that's what you need to do now: just trust me. The first client can make or break a business. Once she gets hired, you think she's gonna keep mum about it? She'll tell everyone: all her former workmates, her girlfriends and her entire family. The jungle telephone will start working, bringing us more people. You get the logic of it all?"

"Not really. 'Cos it might take forever. First she needs to get hired, then she needs to... Didn't you tell her to change her clothes and doll herself up? That alone might take another week or two. Then she needs to quit her old job and get on the payroll. Also, how can we be sure she's gonna tell anyone about it? Maybe she won't, and then what? Are we supposed to be stuck here like two spare pricks at a wedding waiting for something to happen?"

"So what do you suggest?" I said. "Do you want me to run after the poor woman and beat our measly thousand rubles out of her? And then what? We don't need that kind of publicity right now."

"Dammit, Phil, with all due respect, a thousand rubles is a thousand rubles. I don't know about you but it would be really handy for me right now."

"Wait a sec, I'm gonna pay you an advance now just to shut you up."

"Oh no, leave it," he said with a wave of his hand. He very nearly spat on the floor but refrained at the last moment, remembering where he was. "It's not about this even. We need more advertising. Listen, what about if I make a quick video with my guys? Why not? We can do it with my phone. Like, there're a few guys who use the services of the Great Job agency! Everything above board, no cheating! We could ask Yagoza to participate. He's the top man around here."

"And then what?"

"Well... I suppose we could upload it to VK. You could post it on the company website too. People would start talking. It might even go — what's it called? — yes, viral!"

"What you just said is total bullshit but the idea isn't bad. Actually... I used to be an SMM guy[24], so why not?"

"An S and what guy?" Alik shook an

---

[24] SMM: Social Media Marketing

uncomprehending head.

"SMM guy," I replied absent-mindedly as more thoughts flooded over me.

To do that, I would have to level up the skill, study the relevant literature, read all sorts of articles and watch webinars, create a landing page, write a few viral texts mentioning the agency, spend some money on both targeted *and* contextual advertising, then upload it all to social media...

"SMM guy..." Alik mumbled. "What kind of job is that? Is that what you're doing for the cops?"

Chapter Nine

SPREADING THE WORD

*A good advertisement is one which
sells the product without drawing
attention to itself.*

David Ogilvy

THE EVENING AFTER LUDMILA AND HER SON LEO HAD
come to visit us in the office, I was standing together
with the rest of our boxing group, lined up. The training
was over but Matov had kept us back in order to make
some announcement. He paced up and down the line,
barking every word,

"Listen up, boys. In the beginning of August
some very serious people are going to organize the city's
open boxing championship. The prize money is very
good and there're no participation restrictions. Still,
you have to pay to sign up."

The group members breathed a collective sigh of

disappointment.

"How much?" Kostya asked. He was the only one in the group who treated me halfway decent.

"Ten grand," Matov said. "So if you're not sure of yourself, there's no point in even trying."

"You can forget it, dude," Mohammed laughed.

"Nah, count me out," Kostya said, visibly upset. "Why is it so expensive?"

"Go and ask the organizers," Matov replied nonchalantly. "But you're right. They seem to be greedy."

"Count us in," Mohammed replied for himself and his brother. "Zaurbek?"

"Sure," Zaurbek bashed his gloves together. "Where do we sign up?"

"Come to me. The registration will close one week before the tournament. That'll give you some time to think about it. But I don't advise you to drag it out for too long," he looked over the other group members. "So! I'm signing the Kichiev brothers up. Who else?"

"Okay, I'm in," Ivan took a step forward.

"I'll risk ten grand too," Nick said, raising his hand. "Shit. I wanted to buy myself a new phone."

"If you win, you can buy yourself a car," Bulat encouraged him. "Maybe not a new one, but still. What kind of prize money are we talking about?"

"The organizers are some very serious dudes. So on top of your registration fee, you can expect at least a million rubles[25] from them. There're eight weight

---

[25] Over $15,000

categories. All the city clubs have already signed up: the Lions, the Legion, the factory guys, the Torpedo team... Moscow is also gonna send some boys, and the country of Kazakhstan, as well."

"Kazakhstan? They're your homies, Bulat!" Zaurbek said. "If you're matched against them, you'll have to show some hospitality and lose!"

"Yeah right," Bulat grinned. "In case you didn't know, I'm not a Kazakh. I'm a Kalmyk[26]."

"By the way, there'll be some guys from Kalmykia too. Everybody will be there. Even the Rocky club."

"What, those clowns?" Mohammed scowled.

"Yep, them too. So this competition might give you the chance to show what you're made of."

"Hey Phil, why are you so quiet?" Mohammed jeered. "Are you up for it?"

"Not really."

"Why not? Kostya can't participate because he can't afford it, but what about you? You're the rich daddy's boy, aren't you? Are you chicken shit?"

"No, I'm not. I'm just being realistic. I'm the worst in the whole group and I'm pretty sure the guys taking part will all be at least as good as you."

"Aha, finally!" Mohammed guffawed. "You said it!"

"Cut the crap!" Matov shouted. "You're making

---

[26] Kalmyk: a native of Kalmykia, an autonomous republic in the Russian Federation. Both ethnicities have some Mongol roots so confusing a Kalmyk for a Kazakh is a bit like confusing a Chinese for a Japanese.

a circus out of it! Today's training is over. You can all go!"

After that conversation, I'd spent the whole evening and all of the next day leveling up Marketing. I'd started by refreshing the basics, concentrating on review articles on specialist sites.

My level 8 in Reading kept creeping up to 9, all the while improving my reading speed to 80% which in total gave me just over 500 words a minute. In this way, I could read an average-sized book in one and a half to two hours these days without any loss of comprehension. The skill's description now included several sub-skills, showing me the details which apparently influenced both my reading speed and comprehension: the suppression of internal enunciation, the broadening of my field of vision as well as the development of concentration. I hadn't done anything to improve them, they just evolved together with the main skill.

In any case, thanks to my ability to speed read I'd imbibed two top books in the last 24 hours which are a must for every marketologist: Philip Kotler's *Principles of Marketing* and John Jantsch's *Duct Take Marketing.*

After a few hours of going through them — these days I skimmed through the text only pausing at the paragraphs containing crucial data — I finally received a new level. Between all the articles and webinars I'd studied in the office earlier today, it had brought my Marketing skill to 4.

By the way, the whole day we hadn't had a single

client. Despite that, I'd managed to convince both Alik and myself that very soon we'd have clients flocking to the door. The reason I was so confident was my new knowledge of marketing principles which had transformed abstract customers into a very real target market of unemployed or needy people working low-paid jobs. They weren't necessarily down and out drunks like Alik's old friends — because their kind didn't really need jobs and even if you found them some, they wouldn't last long.

Our potential customers were rather the likes of Ludmila or Fatso who only needed a chance. Both had family and children, making their motivation quite strong. Plus college graduates and downsized specialists, as well as active retirees unwilling to survive on their meager pensions and feeling strong enough to carry on working. And so on and so forth. The gist of it was, they couldn't afford to pay our 1000-ruble fee upfront. Also, this business model had already been discredited by all sorts of fly-by-night scams which charged you good money — but when you checked the small print, you discovered that all they did was offer "consultancy services" taking no responsibility for actually finding you a job.

So we might be forced to switch to getting paid by results. I'd have to see Mr. Katz and ask him to help me with the contract to make sure that our clients actually came back to pay us once they'd been hired.

Also, I'd been wondering whether I should wrap up all this charity stuff and switch back to the business model I'd already test run at Ultrapak, namely B2B.

Still, my intuition kept telling me it could wait until I got this thing off the ground because that was where my heart really lay. Ordinary people could use my help: all those who couldn't always afford to buy their children some fruit or get them new school clothes that weren't falling apart.

Whenever I'd debated with myself, coming up with various pros and cons of this enterprise, I'd even thought that this whole idea was bullshit. I would have probably done better leveling up Vending instead and making millions of dollars the way Valiadis had done — and *then* start helping people by getting involved in various charities, supporting struggling artists and all that sort of stuff.

But still... I'd rather give people a fishing rod than a fish, if you know what I mean.

Also, by developing this business as a socially meaningful venture from the start, I might actually achieve much more — not as a businessman maybe but as an interface user. At least that was what my intuition kept whispering in my ear just lately, and I was already used to trusting my hunches.

Once the boxing session was finished, I headed off home, making plans for the evening: dinner and some quality time with Vicky, followed by more copyrighting lessons and studying SMM — the skill I'd activated earlier today. I really wanted to bring it up to at least level 3 so that tomorrow morning I could concentrate on the online promotion of our services. I already had some ideas for a viral message which I planned to post in various VK communities and employment forums.

As I reached the front door, I noticed old Panikoff, my first quest giver. He was standing with his back to me, reading something on the notice board.

"Good evening, sir!" I said as I walked past him.

"It's not so damn good," a rough voice said to my back, rude and so not like Panikoff.

I turned round. The old man seemed much younger than his eighty-three years old. His back was straight, his shoulders spread wide. He stood firmly on his feet.

"I'm sorry-" I began.

"No, you're not. Before you ask any questions, no, I'm not Panikoff. It's his body but it's not him who's speaking."

"Who are you, then?"

"We don't know each other yet. The time of our meeting hasn't yet come. I can only tell you that I have something to do with the interface you're currently using. You're one of the few users in this world in this particular period of time."

"So how do you want me to address you?"

"I'm just a voice. The voice of an entity, and this entity isn't human."

Well, well, well. Could it be that Khphor guy from my dream, by any chance? But I wasn't dreaming now. Did that mean that it hadn't been a dream? In which case why was he saying that we didn't know each other?

"Have we ever met before, Mr. Voice?" I asked.

"No, we haven't. At least not in this segment of

reality. But allow me to offer you a bit of advice, Phil. I've been watching you for quite a few days now and this is what I can't understand," the old boy's voice had acquired a steely edge.

I suddenly realized we were enveloped in silence. Everything was frozen. Even the leaves on the trees weren't rustling.

"Why are you whittling this opportunity away?" he thundered. "Why aren't you working on raising your social status? In your primitive society, the possession of a unique technology such as your augmented reality interface combined with the ability to rapidly improve both your body and skills is a shortcut to power and riches. What makes you linger in your playpen which you should have left already a month ago? You should be evolving and improving your body; you should be discovering the paths to the top of your society pyramid. You must be prepared. This path is the path of the strong. You need to stop bustling about helping all sorts of weaklings and society dropouts. Doesn't the program reward you for exercising power? Doesn't it motivate you to climb over others and manipulate them in order to achieve your own goals? You won't be successful in what the program is preparing you for by wasting your time and abilities!"

"And what is it preparing me for, then?"

I'd known the answer before I'd even asked him. It must have been preparing me for some sort of ultimate trial.

Still, contrary to my expectations, the Voice evaded the direct response. "You'll find out the answer to that question in due time. Listen to my advice. Stop wasting your time on losers. You're destined to be strong, and strong people are constantly surrounded by *syahrs* who are nothing but dust on your feet. Shake them off and continue toward the great goal! Become faster and stronger!"

"You forgot 'higher'."

"What did you say?"

"Ah, forget it. Who are *syahrs?*"

"They're like your current entourage. Vultures. Hangers-on. Those incapable of rising themselves will always try to sponge off a Hero. They constantly need a Hero's help and attention in order to raise their own useless self-esteem. They're like parasites; they'll weaken you, halting your development and sapping your strength. Remember this next time you stray from your path... oh... Phil? Is that you?"

The Voice had left Mr. Panikoff's body. The old man was standing in front of me, squinting shortsightedly at me.

"Yes, it's me, sir," I said. "Are you off for your nightly walk?"

"Exactly. I might have to cut it short because I don't feel so good. I've just been standing over there reading the house management announcement on the notice board. Then I blinked — and here I am standing in front of you! I must be getting old..." he drawled, flapping his eyelashes.

"You'd better go to bed now, sir. Good night!"

Having bidden my goodbyes to the old boy, I headed on upstairs to my place.

I had a funny feeling there was something wrong about that Voice. The image of the interface it had attempted to portray differed too much from the one I actually had. Didn't the program encourage me to help others? Hadn't it showered me with XP for the missing persons I'd found as well as for helping Alik, Marina, Cyril and Fatso? Somehow I didn't remember it ever asking me to climb over others and manipulate them.

Should I pick a fight with somebody maybe, just to check it out?

"ARE YOU SURE THEY'LL HIRE ME?" ASKED A FEARFUL puny guy in a shabby old suit who was sitting opposite me.

"Absolutely!" Alik butted in from his desk. "Don't worry! Just do what Mr. Panfilov told you."

"Because, you know, my Valentina has already found a job thanks to you. But she's a bookkeeper; it wasn't that difficult with her experience. But me... I'm only an Uber driver. And look what you're offering me," he shrugged. "Somehow I doubt somebody might need a biologist."

"But didn't you want a job in your field of expertise?"

"Of course. I'd love to. You can't just wipe out twenty-five years of experience. Had they not closed our research lab..."

"Well, go for it, then! The pharmaceutical company to which I'm sending you needs someone to set up a genetics lab. It requires a lot of research work. There's a 99.6% probability of you being taken on. Be brave, don't doubt yourself and speak confidently. Are you a scientist or just a pretty face?"

"Do you have any idea how many research papers and treatises I've written?" the biologist said hotly.

"That's the attitude you need to show them," I rose to shake his hand. "Good luck. If, by any slim chance, they don't accept you, come back and we'll find you more options. They're not as good as far as pay is concerned but still quite acceptable. If you do decide to take the step and move country, we have an excellent position for you in France. But you'll need to speak the language and there's no guarantee of you being hired. Also, you'll have to pay your own flight."

He waved my suggestion away. "France doesn't interest me!"

"In that case, good luck with your interview!"

"Thank you!" the much-encouraged biologist shook first my hand, then Alik's, and walked out, leaving his umbrella behind.

"Alik, run after him, please, and give him his umbrella back."

"No problem," smiling, Alik hurried after the scientist.

If all the pharmaceutical lab researchers were this absent-minded, we could soon be looking at a looming zombie apocalypse.

In the week that had elapsed since the launch of our online promotional campaign, our business seemed to be picking up slowly but surely. Ludmila — the woman who'd come to us with her son Leo — had successfully been employed. Already the next day, two very uptight and timid women came to the office saying they were friends of hers. One of them happened to have an aptitude for gardening — while my search came up with a rich family in need of a gardener. The other girl turned out to be an elementary school teacher whom I managed to place at an expensive private school.

Isn't it strange that neither of them had ever thought about seeking employment in the areas of their own hobbies and achievements? They'd spent years biding their time doing low-paying jobs they'd hated without even trying to look for anything better. All because they were too afraid of losing stability or taking any kind of risk because for them, going out of their comfort zone was already a risk.

By now, we'd already successfully found work for over a dozen people — and that's only counting those who'd called us back reporting their success. Just as I was talking to the biologist, Alik was busy polishing off yet another cream cake brought by yet another grateful client.

I'd leveled up Marketing and SMM, anyway, to levels 6 and 5 respectively, and it had already started bearing fruit. I'd noticed that I could level up a skill quicker if I immediately applied the newly-acquired theory in practice.

Our agency pages which I'd opened over all social media were fast garnering subscribers. That's where I was honing my skills these days, alternating useful posts with promotional texts such as positive reviews from our successful clients, viral texts and even memes because Alik had shown a remarkable talent for inventing them. Like his meme pic of some surly hoods crouching and staring at the camera with the inscription,

Real men take responsibility for their loved ones. Find a job, feed your family.

Unexpectedly for us, the picture had gone viral on a number of bro-culture sites, bringing us over two thousand subscribers.

The points I'd received for this last growth in skills had brought me my next social status level 15. A good round number. Once again I'd invested the system point in Agility, bringing it up to 9 even though I'd originally planned to improve either Charisma, Luck or Intellect. Any of these three were more important in business than Agility. But admittedly, Panikoff's words had sown the seed of doubt that I was doing the right thing.

"Phil, are you busy?"

I looked up from my laptop and saw Kesha, the print shop owner.

"Come in," I said. "Take a seat. Tea, coffee?"

"Thanks, but no thanks," he fidgeted nervously in his chair. "I'll come straight to the point."

"Why, was there something wrong with our order?"

"No, everything was fine. There were some weird guys who picked up the last batch. Do they also work for you?"

"You mean Tarzan and his friends?"

"Probably. They didn't introduce themselves. They just asked, 'Are the flyers done?'" he said, imitating the three hoods. "Then they took the leaflets and left."

"It's okay. It's Alik's buddies. They're helping us out."

"Are they? Because I was worried a bit. Their manners, you know..."

I smiled. "What, they had none?"

"Yeah, sort of. But that's not why I came. Remember you helped Veronica find some clients?"

"Sure. Why?"

"You think you could help me too? I've got practically no customers and soon I'll need to pay both rent and taxes."

Mechanically I raised my hands in the air and had a nice stretch, cracking all my joints. He, however, seemed to have misunderstood it.

"Listen, Phil, you don't have to worry! I know how to be grateful. You'll get ten percent of every order I receive regardless of the result."

"Okay. Tell me more."

"What is there to tell?"

"Your services. What you do, what you offer, your print runs, I need the entire story."

"Okay. Basically, we can do everything. Full color, business cards, forms, brochures, serigraphy.....”

As he spoke, I opened my interface. Just like in Veronica's case, I hadn't received any quest — nor did I count on being rewarded for "performing a socially meaningful action".

I did it driven by a simple and clear principle: if I could help, I would do so. In the entire time of our agency's operations, I'd only received a little XP for helping Ludmila after she'd been hired. Contrary to my expectations, none of the other successful clients had garnered me any XP points. Apparently, in the program's eyes, I didn't need any extra motivation if I'd been remunerated for my help.

Having said that, I wasn't too short of XP. I'd managed to do ten levels in two months. If the truth were known, I'd seen very few people whose social status was higher than my level 15: Valiadis and his right-hand man Hermann, the old boy Panikoff, and Pavel, my former boss at Ultrapak. At this rate, I might overtake them all already by the fall even at my current leveling speed.

"Can you come back in half an hour?" I asked Kesha once he was finished with his impromptu presentation.

The interface had already flooded my map with hundreds of markers which answered the search requirements, so now I needed some time to sort out the juiciest ones. On his way out of the office, Kesha bumped into Alik who was just coming back.

"Imagine Phil, that dude is more like an Olympic runner than a biologist! I had real trouble catching up with him. He was in such a rush to get there you'd think he was afraid of being late!"

"Did you give him his umbrella back?"

"Sure, only he got real scared at first. He thought I was gonna tap him up for payment or tell him that the job wouldn't go through. You should have seen his face!"

"Never mind. Well done. Can you find yourself something to do? I'm a bit busy here."

"Cool, I'm gonna make some new memes then," he grinned.

Some new memes! I smiled to myself, feeling slightly proud for Alik. Veronica had brought him an old laptop from home, opening up the brave new world of Photoshop to him. Now he was consumed by building photo collages and creating new meme pics which he lovingly called "memmies". He loved it almost as much as exchanging comments in VK, frequenting various "boys from the hood" websites and liking all of Veronica's photos.

Kesha reappeared half an hour later on the dot.

"Here," I handed him a sheet of paper with three potential clients that were absolute certs. "No need to thank me," I smiled, looking at the disbelief on his face.

"So what am I supposed to do? Should I call them? And what should I tell them?" Kesha asked, studying the list.

"The first one needs forms to be printed. Shedloads of them. The second company too is looking for a printer. They've just rebranded themselves and now all their staff need new business cards made.

That's a lot of people. And the third one has a totally different problem. They need a company pamphlet laid out and printed, a really pretty one. Each order is worth over fifty grand. That should be enough to pay the rent."

"If you don't mind me asking, how did you find them?"

"Have you ever played role games? Not the bedroom kind but on a computer?"

"At the time, I used to mess around with Diablo. Why?"

"You do know something about skills, abilities and talents, don't you? It's a bit like that. I have very good online search skills. You can find anything you want on the Net as long as you know how to look for it."

"Oh. Cool! Thanks, anyway. Do I need to call them?" he nodded at the list.

"You could, but you risk the secretary telling you to get lost. You'd better go and meet with their bosses in person. It's better that way."

"Got it. Thanks!"

Kesha headed for the door but stopped by Alik's desk, watching whatever he was drawing in Photoshop. "Drawing" being the operative word. He was only at level 1 but he'd earned it honestly.

"Hi," a sweet girly voice made us all turn toward the door.

The sound of our three jaws dropping simultaneously could have probably been heard on the street outside.

What we were looking at was a radical departure from what we were used to seeing here. The girl smiling at us must have got the wrong door. We couldn't have been what she'd been looking for.

She had a great body and legs that went on forever. Her angelic face was completely devoid of makeup. She was wearing a business suit with a white blouse and a skirt cut a little too short for comfort. Even without her stilettoes, she must have been at least six foot tall. No doubt a model or something.

"Hi there," Kesha gushed.

"Ho...ho...how do you do... ma'am?" Alik stuttered.

"Is this the Great Job agency?"

"Sure. Come on in," I finally came to life. "I'm Phil."

"Nice to meet you, Phil. My name's Anastasia," the girl proffered a hand. "But you can call me Stacy."

"How can we help you, Stacy?" I asked, her hand lingering in mine for a couple of seconds longer than necessary. The girl ran her tongue over her upper lip.

What the hell was that? I looked at the other two. Their clouded stares were boring a hole in the girl's back.

She turned and gave them a cheerful smile, then sat down. "You see, Phil," she whispered intimately so that only I could hear. "I need a job. You know what I mean?"

"I think I do."

"And I'm prepared to do anything to get it. Do you get me? Anything at all."

I got all hot and bothered from her whisper. Without receiving any debuff messages, I got an immediate hard-on.

Chapter Ten

THE SKILL OF SAYING YES

But the hearts of men are easily corrupted.

The Lord of the Rings

IF WE SPOKE ABOUT THE WOMEN IN MY LIFE, NOT counting teenage crushes and one-night-stands, then both Yanna and Vicky were quite pretty in the eyes of the nerd that I was. Both were sweet, friendly and could even look beautiful from a certain angle.

But this dame — because I really couldn't call this sex-oozing female a girl — was in a totally different class. She was in the red-carpet, Academy-award, cover girl league.

I might have exaggerated a little about the increased blood flow to my nether regions (I was no spring chicken, after all) but still, my increased anxiety, dry throat and quickened pulse stood witness to my lack of experience with this type of head-turning, show-stopping beauty.

Having said that, I'd spoken too soon...

A new system message popped up, warning me about my increased heart rate caused by sexual arousal, and advising me to enter into sexual contact with the object of my desire. In case of the impossibility of doing so, I was recommended to engage in physical activity followed by a cold shower and to discontinue visual contact with the subject. Too much mention of the word "sex" for one system message, if you asked me. Thanks, Captain Obvious.

Struggling to ignore the allure of her cleavage which was undone a couple of buttons more than necessary, I stared her right in the eye.

Stacy responded in kind, her gaze confident, a light smile playing on her lips. Her upper lip was a little short, revealing white even teeth.

"Phil?"

"I understood you, *Anastasia*," I said. It was probably better I kept my distance without progressing to any names of endearment. "What kind of work are you looking for? What do you do? Have you brought a CV?"

"No, I haven't... Did I need to?" she sounded sincerely confused.

Oh great. Having said that, few of our clients ever thought of bringing their CVs. Really, why would they need one in an employment agency?

I suppressed my inner sarcasm and looked at the other two. Kesha didn't look as if he was in a hurry anymore. He was perched on Alik's desk, his dreamy eyes admiring the scene.

As for Alik, he materialized next to Stacy with two cups in his hands. "Excuse me, ma'am," he said shyly. "Would you prefer tea or coffee?"

"Sorry, what did you say? Ah, just some water if you'd be so kind. Just plain flat water."

"*Ein moment!*" the ex-hood replied with a suspiciously German accent, then dashed off toward our kitchenette, splashing tea and coffee around.

I'd already noticed this thing about him: at moments of extreme anxiety, Alik would sometimes start blurting out various "high class" words and phrases or whatever he thought could pass for them.

"I could use some coffee, if you don't mind," Kesha jumped at the opportunity.

"I'm very sorry," Stacy said. "I don't have a CV. I didn't receive any professional training, either."

"Okay. In which case, could you please tell me more about yourself? What skills do you have? What can you do really well?-" I stopped midsentence and averted my gaze, realizing the suggestiveness of my question.

On a hunch, I activated Lie Detection. Don't ask why. Just a feeling.

"Very well. My name's Anastasia Semyonova. I'm twenty-four years old. I was born in Vladivostok and went to elementary school there. Almost immediately, we had to move. My father was in the military so we were relocated quite a lot. In total, I went to six schools in six different cities..."

Even though her cleavage kept drawing my gaze like a magnet, I forced myself to stay clear-headed. There was something that worried me much more.

The girl was lying. Her every word, starting with her name and ending with the fact that she'd apparently lost her parents while still young, was pure fiction. The Lie Detection skill kept sending waves of cold shivers down my spine.

As she spoke, she became slightly consumed by her reminiscing, giving me the opportunity to study her profile.

> *Anastasia Semyonova*
> *Age: 24*
> *Current status: Unemployed*
> *Social status level: 3*
> *Class: Seductress. Level: 7*
> *Unmarried*

Aha. Now everything was as clear as mud. Apparently, her name *was* Anastasia Semyonova. In which case, why had Lie Detection signaled otherwise? Was it my Hero skill glitching? Or the Universal Infospace being hacked? No idea.

I checked her abilities. That's how I'd always determined what kind of work would suit the customer. If you took the absent-minded biologist, for instance, he hadn't come to us looking for a scientific job. If was my Insight which had told me that he had level 9 in Biology.

Seduction was Anastasia's best-developed skill.

I had it too, only mine was barely 50% of hers. What other skills had she leveled up? Empathy, Communication Skills, Fashion and Style, Makeup, Catwalk, Sexual Skills... all of them levels 5 and 6. Our Stacy was almost a professional!

But that wasn't what had surprised me. The girl had good computer and MS Office skills and even had level 3 in SMM which meant she was no stranger to social media. Having said that, it was only normal for the Instagram generation.

But the fact that she had high Responsibility was actually quite promising. I didn't even know such a skill existed. At least I didn't have it.

"So basically, that was the end of my modeling career," Stacy concluded. "As a result, I ended up in this city — without any family or friends. I don't even know many people, if you know what I mean. My landlady is kicking me out and I really don't want to start selling my body. I'm prepared to do any job, even office manager, as long as they pay me an advance."

The girl paused and gulped some water from a glass that Alik had helpfully brought. She seemed to be awaiting my reaction.

Somehow her last words didn't agree with what she'd said at first. *"Prepared to do anything to get it"* — then *"Don't want to start selling my body"*... For almost the whole duration of her monologue, Lie Detection kept sending cold shivers down my spine, alerting me to her high Deception skill, — but somehow her last words filled me with warmth. She was indeed prepared to do any job, so could it be that her alleged preparedness "to do anything to get it" referred to her readiness to accept any job offer? Then again, hadn't she said "Prepared to do anything to get it"? By "it" she must have meant a job, surely?

What a strange girl. A walking enigma.

While I was pondering over this before even trying to activate a vacancy search, my stubborn abstinence from looking down her cleavage had landed me a brief Squinty Eyed debuff (joke) followed by a rise in both Spirit and Willpower. By now, I already knew that these two stats were interconnected. Also, after having spent the whole evening playing with my interface settings, I could now receive a little more useful information.

Congratulations! Your Spirit has improved!
+100% to Spirit
You've received 1000 pt. XP for successfully leveling up a secondary characteristic!
Current Spirit: 300%

Congratulations! Your Willpower has improved!
+100% to Willpower
You've received 1000 pt. XP for successfully leveling up a secondary characteristic!
Current Willpower: 200%

Current level: 15. XP points gained: 6310/16000

Congratulations! You've unblocked one of the requirements for the Berserker and Invulnerability heroic abilities: Spirit (300%)

This rise in two major stats at once had immediately sent my Mood soaring. Still, this wasn't the right moment to look into it.

Back to the task at hand! I decided to search for all possible vacancies suitable for her from modeling and makeup artist to office manager and even secretary.

The system showered me with offers. I had plenty of choice. I looked up from my laptop screen — or rather, from my interface map — at Anastasia. Now that she was no longer a drop dead stranger to a tongue-tied me anymore, the pressure of her sexual magnetism had subsided somewhat, to the point where I could speak to her as if she were an ordinary client.

"Stacy, we will find something for you. In the meantime, would you please peruse through the contract and if you're happy with it, please enter your details and sign it. Alik, would you be so kind as to give Anastasia a copy of the contract? We charge for our services only after you've been hired. This is our principle."

"Really?"

"Absolutely. I might need a bit of time to select the most suitable offers. Is that all right with you? Could you wait on the couch, please?"

She nodded. "Sure."

She rose from her chair. Alik and Kesha stopped hypnotizing her with their manic stares and hurried to pretend they were terribly busy. But if Alik simply switched his attention back to his computer, casting sideways glances in the direction of the girl, Kesha began frowning and furrowing his forehead as he stared vacantly at the sheet of paper with his job offers which might just as well have been in Chinese.

Wait a sec. What was that now? Next to the row of icons which usually showed the time, date, my heart rate, outside temperature and other useful data, I noticed a debuff icon. Had I somehow missed the system message? I focused on it.

Smitten

You have been smitten by a subject of the opposite sex!

Subject's Name: Anastasia Semyonova

+50 to the Subject's Reputation in your eyes.

The Subject's current Reputation: Amicality 20/60

-3 to Intellect

+1 to Strength

-5% to Satisfaction every 6 hrs.

+10% to Metabolism

Warning! High probability of spontaneous erections!

In order to disable the debuff, you're advised to restrict your contacts with the subject or engage them in sexual intercourse.

Oh great. That was all I needed. Was this how a high-level Seduction worked? It was a good job that my Intellect was high so the loss of 3 points didn't affect my brains too much. But how about Alik who wasn't the sharpest knife in the drawer to begin with? This debuff had effectively made him twice as stupid!

Now it was clear to me why some apparently intelligent and level-headed people lost their heads on seeing a beautiful girl and acted like certified idiots. I could only imagine the detrimental effect on their minds if the said debuff was inflicted by a level 10+ Seduction!

Never mind. I'd survive. She needed help, anyway. I watched out of the corner of my eye as the other two fussed around the office, helping her to fill in the paperwork. I got the feeling that those morons might even sign it for her, as well.

I went back to the search. The vacancies were so many I had to sort through them. To begin with, I filtered out all those which offered less than 30,000 rubles a month and added a new search criteria: *Over 90% probability of hiring Anastasia Semyonova.*

My work cell phone began to ring frenetically. Almost simultaneously, the landline rang too. Alik took it while I replied to the first call,

"Great Job Recruitment Agency, how can I help you?"

"Hello," a hoarse male voice said, "Is this the agency?"

"Yes, speaking. How can I help you today?"

"The recruitment agency?" the man repeated.

"Exactly."

"I'm looking for work..."

As I spoke to him, cradling the phone between

my ear and shoulder, Alik was busy painting rosy pictures to some retiree who wanted to find a summer job for her lazy granddaughter (I knew all this because Alik had the habit of repeating everything he was told on the phone).

Then the door opened, letting in some swarthy guys who looked like migrant workers from one of the Central Asian republics. They hovered timidly by the door, dressed in all sorts of jumble sale apparel. Two of them were very young, wearing knitted caps despite the hot summer weather; the third one was a bit older, about forty or so. One glance at their profiles told me we had a delegation of cowboy builders here.

"Fine, I'll be off, then," Kesha nodded his good-bye, trying to navigate around our new visitors.

"Hello. Are Great Jobs here?" the older of the new arrivals inquired while the others timidly pressed their backs to the wall, letting Kesha go past.

I gestured to them to wait a little.

"What kind of job do you have?" the hoarse voice asked me on the phone.

"We're a recruitment agency. We help find work. What kind it is depends on you..."

"You're not trying to rip people off, are you?" the voice said, doubtful.

"She needs to come and see us personally, ma'am!" Alik was shouting into the phone to the old lady who was apparently hard of hearing.

Stacy floated from her chair and went toward our guests from sunny Somewherestan. They didn't look like Kazakhs to me. They were more likely Uzbeks or Tadzhiks.

"Hello! Yes, this is the Great Job Recruitment Agency," Stacy cooed to our visitors. "Would you like to take a seat? You'll have to wait a little. Would you like some tea? Or coffee, maybe?"

The builders, completely blown away by such a cordial welcome, shook their heads in unison. Their foreman (whose name was apparently Faysal) replied for all of them,

"Thank you, my daughter, we don't need anything."

"Is it true that you're not charging anything?" the hoarse voice asked me.

"No, ma'am! You don't need to come in person unless you're seeking employment for yourself. What did you say? We could find something for you too..." Alik said, demonstrating an enviable knack in talking to old people.

"Very well," the hoarse voice agreed. "I'll be along. What did you say? Aha. Understood. See you later, then."

Phew. I hung up and laid the phone on the desk. Still, it rang again straight away. What the hell was going on?

"Phil, would you like me to get it?" Stacy offered, materializing next to me. "I can do it."

Once again a wave of her sex appeal surged over me. Without saying a word, I handed her the phone.

"I'm not in a hurry," she said, not yet answering it. "You can talk to Faysal first, if you wish."

How did she know his name? Had they already

introduced themselves to her? Flummoxed, I nodded, then motioned to the Asians to come over. The two young ones remained standing while their foreman sat opposite me. A few moments later, the younger ones could sit down too as Alik had fetched more chairs and even offered up his own.

The builders didn't take much time. They were looking for construction jobs on the black which would allow them to be all together without being ripped off. A quarter of an hour later, they gave us their heartfelt thanks and left to meet up with an employer who was looking for someone to build a modest cottage on his newly-acquired plot of land. Even though I hadn't signed a contract with them, Faysal had simpleheartedly paid a thousand rubles for each of them after having had a conversation with Alik. I didn't worry about them because I'd entered the most stringent search parameters I could think of, including the lowest possible ratio of their being ripped off by the employer.

Having finished with them, I went back to my search for Anastasia. I entered every possible search parameter I could think of, including the high probability of receiving an advance immediately after being hired.

The map remained pristine. Not a single marker. What the hell was that? Was everybody so greedy they couldn't pay her an advance? I took away all the filters, deciding to add them one by one.

Now. *All the companies and establishments in need of a secretary or office manager.* 208 hits.

Official employment: 161 hits.

Salary after tax, 30,000 rubles or higher: 119 hits.

The probability of receiving an advance in the first week after being officially employed: 76 hits

A 90%-plus probability of employing Anastasia Semyonova: 0 hits.

An 80%-plus probability of employing Anastasia Semyonova: 0 hits.

What's that for bullshit?

I felt someone staring at me. I raised my head but couldn't work out who it could have been. Stacy stood by the window talking to someone on our business cell phone. Alik had already retrieved his chair and was typing away while reciting our work conditions to a customer on the phone.

I deleted all the search parameters, leaving only one.

A 10%-plus probability of employing Anastasia Semyonova.

One hit.

Finally something. I focused on the marker to see the name of the company.

The Great Job Recruitment Agency.

Us? What was she supposed to do here? Answer the phone? Offer coffee to the visitors? That was ridiculous. In another six months, maybe, but at the moment, this wasn't even a business. It was more of a joke.

"Could you please come here, Stacy?" I called her once she'd finished talking. "What kind of wage do you have in mind?"

"I'm not so bothered. But of course I'd rather have something that pays relatively well. What options are there?"

"That's the whole problem. I'm afraid there aren't many options for some reason..."

It was as if someone had ripped out her backbone. Deflated, she stooped, losing all the panache with which she'd entered our office and answered the phone.

She looked up and asked again, "No options at all? Could you look for something who needs a nanny or a housemaid? I could also sell clothes in a boutique. Or any kind of shop, for that matter..." she was taking it well but her lower lip was already trembling.

Everything about this girl made me uncomfortable. With her appearance and skills she could be now lounging on the best beaches of planet Earth, drinking mind-boggling cocktails as she relaxed after shopping sprees paid by some billionaire sugar daddy. Alternatively, she could be making a vertiginous career in any field from movies and TV to the stock markets. What was she even doing in our backwater city complete with this shabby business center and our newborn enterprise?

Why couldn't my interface find her any work? Why? I was a hundred percent sure that had she applied to any of those places which had come up in the search results, she would have been taken on. But why did the program deny her? Or could it be that...

What if she'd wanted to be hired by us alone? In

that case, she wouldn't have even tried any other places, would she?

But why would she do that? After my last conversation with the Voice camouflaged as old Panikoff, I thought I could smell a rat. But if so, then we'd better keep an eye on her.

And seeing as I'd promised everyone a 100% probability of employment...

"Listen, Stacy, I could offer you a job here with us. Your responsibilities will be quite vague at first because we've only just opened. We're simply not able to hire a person for every job that needs doing. We're all chief cooks and bottle washers here. We can't offer you a good wage, either. But if-"

"I'm in," she interrupted me mid-word. "I can start straight away."

Alik in the far corner had pricked up his ears to eavesdrop on our conversation and was now doing a silent jig under the desk like an impatient horse going to a stud farm.

"Don't you want to ask what kind of wage we can offer?" I said. "Or your responsibilities and work schedule?"

"I'd be happy with twenty-five grand for a start," she said. "As for the hours, I already saw them on the door outside. We're open Monday to Friday from 9 a.m. to 6 p.m. The weekends are free. As for my responsibilities, it would be answering the phone, filling in contracts, greeting new customers, opening and closing the office and keeping the customers' accounts. Oh yes, and also making sure we have plenty of water, tea, coffee and candy.

"And instant noodles!" Alik added. "I meant to say, convenience foods..."

"We won't need them soon," Stacy replied. «We'll soon be up and running and will be able to afford hot meals in the local cafes and restaurants."

"Great," I agreed. "On one condition."

"What's that?" Stacy raised a perfect eyebrow.

"Try to tone yourself down, will you? "At the moment, you're so... so in-your-face seductive. Our customers aren't rich and we don't need an extra distra-"

"I got it," she interrupted me again. "That's not a problem. I'll put my hair in a ponytail and wear no makeup. I'll dress a bit more soberly. I'll be like a little gray mouse. All right?"

Unfortunately, even if we dressed her in a peasant's padded smock and one-size-fits-all pants, she'd still be just as stunning. But that way we could at least avoid her Smitten debuff.

"Agreed. Thanks for your understanding. When do you need the advance?" I added, remembering her main requirement. "And how much?"

"I could do with 50% by the end of next week," she replied. "Look, we've got more customers! I'll go and greet them."

That was quick. Apparently, despite her young age, she had a lot of life experience.

Alik waited till she wasn't looking and gave me a double thumbs-up. I couldn't help smiling. The presence of this kind of beauty in your own firm can be very beneficial both for one's male ego and for one's... dammit! Not again!

"Hello! How can I help you?" Stacy turned to the woman who'd just walked through the door.

"Hello yourself. Who are you?" without waiting for the answer, the woman headed toward my desk. "Hi guys."

It was Vicky.

"Hello," Alik replied mechanically. "We're fine, thank you. And this..." he pointed at Stacy, "this is..."

"Hi, Vicky," I stood up and went to give her a kiss and a hug. "I'd like you to meet Stacy. She's our new office manager. Stacy, this is my girlfriend Vicky."

"Nice to meet you, Vicky," Stacy replied, tactfully tuning into the situation. "I'm Anastasia."

"Likewise... Anastasia," Vicky squinted, studying the girl. She can't have liked what she saw because her Mood plummeted into the yellow zone. She seemed lost despite her attempts to appear cool.

"How are you, sweetie?" Vicky finally said, addressing me alone. "I've just finished work. I'm gonna drive you to the gym, wait for you to finish, then we'll go to the supermarket like we said we would..."

"Shit! I completely forgot!" I glanced at my watch, realizing it was high time for my boxing practice. "Sorry guys, I've gotta split. Can you lock up without me?"

"Of course, Mr. Panfilov," Stacy replied. "Not a problem."

How on earth did she know my surname?

"Have a good session, Sir," Alik joined in.

"Thanks!"

I unplugged my laptop, grabbed the gym bag with my gear, laced my arm around Vicky's waist and led her to the door. "Bye, guys!"

"See you tomorrow, Sir! All the best!" Alik and Stacy replied.

What was wrong with those two? Had they decided to play the subordinates for Vicky?

"Oh Phil, are you already off?" Veronica chimed, appearing on the doorstep. "Can I have a word?"

This was quickly turning into a cheap absurd sitcom. "Sorry, Veronica, but I'm already late. Let's discuss it tomorrow morning, whatever it is."

"All right, Phil," she said, ignoring Vicky's indignant wheezing.

As we left, I could hear her greeting Stacy while Alik started his nonsense again, dropping things and mumbling "ma'am" like a drooling zombie.

"Are you teaching them who's the boss or what? What's with all the 'Sirs'?" Vicky grinned sarcastically as we walked toward the stairs. And why would you need an office manager? Are you snowed under by applications and flooded by phone calls?"

"Maybe not snowed under but certainly flooded," I replied.

"Phil, why are you wasting your expense allowance? Is it so difficult to answer the phone or pour a cup of coffee? How are you going to pay all these people? I have my doubts that your altruistic business model will earn you millions. And by the way, who was that other girl who called you Phil? What's with the familiarity?"

"That was Veronica."

"What's with this Veronica? Who the hell is she?"

"Vicky, excuse me but you're treading on dangerous ground. I really appreciate your advice, you know. But it seems to me that in this case, it's jealousy talking. And you have absolutely no reason to. None at all."

"But still, who is she?"

"Just a fellow tenant from the same floor."

"I see."

Her 'I see' was always the harbinger of a looming storm. I knew it well by now. This short phrase could mean anything — from blind fury to mortal offense. Whenever Vicky said 'I see,' it was inevitably followed by a long silence punctuated by monosyllabic answers to all my attempts to start a conversation and discuss the sore subject in question.

Still, I'd rather have a nice happy home than a cold war and an iron curtain which was why I made another attempt to talk to her in the car. "Vicky..."

"What?"

"We really need someone on the telephone. Alik just can't cut it. It's just not his thing, to tell you the truth..."

"Listen, I'm really not interested," Vicky said, then immediately contradicted herself, "Why do you even need that filthy hood? You could have offered the job to me. I'm an experienced HR worker! Together, we could have made this joint a real success! Do you really think I wouldn't have quit Ultrapak to help you?"

I didn't know what to say. The idea had never even crossed my mind. "Eh... You think you'd have agreed?"

"No, of course not! What do you think?" she said, contradicting herself again. "But you didn't even offer!"

"Vicky, what's up with you? I still remember the girl I fell in love with a couple of months ago. I couldn't believe that such understanding, level-headed girls existed..."

"There's nothing wrong with me. My expectations are my own problem."

"Wait a sec. Do you want to say I've failed to live up to your expectations?"

"You said it."

She braked sharply and expertly parked the car in a tiny narrow space on the gym's parking lot. I'd expected her to pull away the moment I left the car. Instead, she killed the engine, unbuckled the seatbelt and climbed out of the car together with me. That gave me some hope. She might have been mad at me but she was still with me.

The Kichiev brothers were hovering by the club's reception.

"Hi guys," I greeted them. "Hi, Kate."

"Hi, Phil," the receptionist beamed at me, taking my club card. "Here's your key."

"Salam," Zaurbek mumbled back to me half-heartedly.

Mohammed gave me an almost imperceptible nod.

"I'll wait for you here," Vicky announced, casting an angry glare at Kate, and went to sit in an easy chair.

"Who are you going to wait for, Miss?" Mohammed asked. "For him?"

Much to my surprise, Vicky didn't leave his question unanswered. "Yes, him. Why? Who are you?"

"Excuse my curiosity, Miss, but how can a beautiful lady like you wait for anyone?" Mohammed said, exercising his Caucasian eloquence. "Especially for somebody like him?"

"Why, do you think he's not worth it?" Vicky said with a smile that made me slightly uncomfortable. "Maybe you'd like me to wait for *you*?"

"You don't need to do that!" Mohammed said haughtily. "You just need to say the word, and I'll drop everything just to spend one moment with you! Mohammed," he proffered his hand to her.

"I'm Vicky. Nice to meet you," she continued to flirt with him for all she was worth, pretending I wasn't even there.

Of course I realized she was doing it simply to provoke and punish me. And still, no matter how hard I tried to ignore it, I felt my blood boil.

"Vicky! Victoria! It means victory! What a lovely name!" he continued to push it. "Just say the word, and I'll drop everything and take you to the best restaurant in town! Or wherever you want to go!"

She laughed teasingly. "Anywhere at all? And all I need to do is say the word?"

"Mohammed," I laid a warning hand on his shoulder.

He shook it off.

"Mohammed, are you freakin' nuts?" I demanded, seething.

He grinned, ignoring me, as his gaze undressed Vicky. "Get your hands off me," he snarled.

"Leave her alone!"

"Or what?" he finally took his eyes off Vicky and stared at me, stretching his neck. "You gonna cry about it or something? Get on with it, then, and have a good cry. Vicky and I might find something better to do," he swung round and asked her a question so straightforward that it just couldn't have been misunderstood. "Victoria, how do you like it? Rough and from behind? Or plain missionary? My brother Zaurbek could help us out if you wish..."

I saw red. "I'll make *you* cry now!" I promised, knowing this wasn't an empty threat. "You're gonna get it rough: from behind, from the front and all points between!"

The program promptly registered an adrenaline rush followed by an increasing heart rate,

Righteous Anger!

You've come across an injustice and are experiencing a fit of Fury!

+3 to all main characteristics
+100% to Vigor
+50% to Confidence
+75% to Willpower
+75% to Spirit
-50% off Self-Control

The effect will remain active until justice is restored and while you're convinced of the righteousness of your cause.

Mohammed's Boxing skill was 2 levels higher than mine, but this Righteous Anger gave me a decent chance against him.

"Boys, stop that now!" Katia the receptionist demanded. "Coach Matov!"

Mohammed spat on the ground. "I'll see you outside. We'll see who's gonna cry."

"He's already shit himself," Zaurbek smirked, winding me up.

"I'll sort your brother out first and then you," I replied. "Let's go, then."

The two brothers guffawed and followed me. As I turned round, I saw a very smug Vicky. You couldn't really see it but my interface had already registered her soaring Mood.

I attacked them first, knowing that otherwise I might not stand a chance.

"Let's get on with it!" I swung round and buried my fist in Mohammed's cheekbone.

He momentarily lost his balance but kept his footing. Grinning, he felt his cheek, then went for me.

"Kill him, bro!" Zaurbek shouted.

And so he did. While I had enough stats to dodge and parry his powerful blows, I didn't get the chance to launch any decent response. Seconds turned into minutes while I was defending myself, waiting for an opportune moment but I just didn't have much room to maneuver. On one side of me was a fenced-off flower bed and a row of parked cars on the other, so I did miss a couple of blows in the end.

Realizing it was no longer a joke, Vicky cried out and rushed to separate us.

Zaurbek grabbed hold of her. "Let them sort it out between themselves!"

When I saw him manhandle my girl, I went completely ape-shit, bringing the Righteous Anger buff to Level 2. Just at that moment, Mohammed — who must have thought that he had me collared — opened up.

Bang! It took all of my willpower not to close my eyes when his fist glanced off my ear, while I countered with a jab to his face.

His head jerked back. With a funny wave of his hands, Mohammed collapsed on the tarmac.

Silence fell. A round of applause came from behind me.

I looked up. One of my eyes had already started to swell but I could still make out our whole group standing around. Why hadn't they tried to separate us? Did that mean that Matov and all the others had been watching us square off?

"K. O.," Matov said. "And a rather unexpected one."

"Well done, Phil!" I heard Kostya's voice.

I walked over to Zaurbek who was still holding Vicky tight. Now he finally came to his senses and let her go.

"Your turn," I said to him.

He gave me a grim look, then averted his eyes. Mohammed had already come round and was groaning behind my back.

"Zaurbek, take your brother to the first-aid room," Matov said. "Let the girls take a look at him. But first I want an explanation. Which of you two started it?"

"I was just sticking up for my girl..."

"He was the one who started it!" Zaurbek pointed a finger at me. "Mohammed just wanted to talk to her..."

Matov winced. "I know Mohammed's 'just talking'. Which one of you started the fight?"

"I did," I replied in all honesty.

"I see. You two brothers get yourselves over to the first aid, you others go and get changed. Panfilov, you don't need to bother."

I turned to Matov. "I'm sorry I didn't even say hello to you, Sir. I was otherwise occupied."

"Are you all done now?" he said sarcastically. "You can go now. Don't bother to come back. I'm kicking you out of the group."

I couldn't believe my ears. "What did you say?"

"You heard. The group's rules forbid fighting on the premises. The instigators lose their card without compensation for the remaining class time. The best of luck elsewhere, Phil."

"But I want to carry on training, Sir!"

"You're very welcome. But not here. Bye," he swung round, making it clear he was done with me.

"I'll wait for you in the car," Vicky said, then left

too.

The joy of victory — because this was probably the first fight I'd won in my entire life — had been tarnished by my anger at Vicky. Had it not been for her stupid showing off, flirting with Mohammed... What had she wanted to achieve with that, my jealousy? Had she wanted to make sure I was still in love with her? Shit, that was really stupid!

I stood alone for a while, trying to calm down after the adrenaline surge. Then I started toward the car but remembered I still had to hand in the key and collect my bag. I staggered back to the gym with my head hung low until I bumped into somebody.

"Phil," Kostya grabbed me by the shoulder. "Great right hand!"

"Yeah. Just a lucky shot."

"Maybe it was lucky but it was a good jab! Listen, is it true what they're saying that Matov has kicked you out? Would you like me to train you?"

"You?"

"Yeah, sure, why not? I've had my own problems with Mohammed for a long time. Finally someone's shut him up. So I guess I owe you because it should have been me and not you."

"Sure. I'd love you to train me. But where do you wanna do it?"

"What do you mean, where? Anywhere! We might not have a punch bag but we still have the sparring pads which are the most universal apparatus of all! And you'll have a sparring partner, a.k.a. yours truly. How about it?"

"We could train at the school sports grounds, I suppose," I said. "It's only a couple of blocks away."

"You mean school No 27? I know it. I used to go there. Only I can only do it either early in the morning or late at night. What do you prefer?"

"Let's go for the mornings."

"Agreed. We'll start tomorrow if you want. Seven a.m.?"

"Sounds good," I smiled. "Give me your phone number."

I marked his number down. He hurried to bid his goodbye,

"All right, I've gotta rush off otherwise Matov won't let me in. Catch you tomorrow!"

"Yeah, see you tomorrow. Thanks!"

Training with Kostya was a good alternative. His Boxing was level 8: only two levels lower than Matov's. Also, I'd be more than happy to train in the mornings, alternating boxing with running. That way my evenings would be free to concentrate on learning and leveling up.

That cheered me up a little. I collected my stuff, said goodbye to the slightly unsettled Katia and left that particular fitness club never to come back again.

In any case, it had given me a lot of points in Strength, Agility, Stamina, Boxing and Hand-to-Hand. So even though I'd left a lot of money there, it had been a good swap.

I got into the car and we drove to the supermarket to do some shopping as planned. We didn't say a word to each other. I was a bit surprised

---

that she'd shown no reaction to me having to fight to defend her honor. But what if I'd missed something? Maybe she'd thought nothing of it?

In any case, the air in the car was not indifferent. It was clear to both of us that a serious conversation was brewing.

"Why did you have to start that?" I began.

"Start what?"

"Flirting with Mohammed."

"Me? Flirting with him? We were only chatting. Can you tell me why you had to start a fight?"

"Only chatting? I started the fight? Ah, whatever," I said, realizing the futility of continuing the conversation.

She was just teaching me another lesson and I was almost sure that it too must have had something to do with Stacy's arrival at the agency.

This time I'd had enough. The only things that prevented me from breaking up with her on the spot were the feelings I still had for her as well as the fact that we'd had more good times than bad. By the same token, the bad times seemed to have had a cumulative effect.

We preserved a gloomy silence for the rest of our journey.

Even in the shop, we didn't exchange a word. I pushed the trolley down the aisles while Vicky picked out our shopping. When the trolley was almost full, we headed for the cash register. I unloaded our shopping onto the belt while the uniformed shop assistant scanned the barcodes and pushed the packets toward

Vicky who loaded them back into the trolley.

"Six thousand three hundred and eighty rubles[27]," the shop assistant finally said.

I handed her my bank card.

She swiped it and waited for a connection. "Your card has been refused."

"Just a minute," I opened my wallet and counted its contents. I didn't have enough. "Try it again, please."

"Can you hurry up?" an impatient voice said in the line behind us.

The shop assistant shrugged and swiped the card again.

Shit. Could I have spent everything without even noticing?

"Refused. You'd better do something about it, mister. You're holding up the line."

"What if I pay some of it cash?" I offered. "Here, three thousand eight hundred," I handed her the money. "And you can put the rest on the card."

"What are you messing around with?" an overweight dude demanded, indignant. "It's late already!"

"They fill their trolleys and then they can't pay for them!" an old lady added, holding a single bottle of kefir. "I can't even afford a tub of cottage cheese on my pension! And the likes of them are living it up! Just look at all that stuff!"

"How much do we come up short?" Vicky asked.

---

[27] About $100

The shop assistant paused, counting. "Two thousand five hundred and eighty."

"Here, take this," Vicky offered her three thousand, took the change, picked up a couple of shopping bags and headed for the exit.

My ears were burning. I'd always insisted I'd pick up the shopping tab. I grabbed the remaining bags and ran after her.

"Thanks a lot," I said, catching up with her.

"It's only normal," she replied. "We live together. It's high time we stopped going Dutch if we're a family, as you keep telling me. You need to understand that's not what I'm mad about!" she stopped by her car, opened the trunk and started loading the bags. "You have to admit you're wasting your time on bullshit!"

"And that is?" I asked, stuffing the shopping into the trunk.

"Stop it now! Phil, you're thirty-two years old. With your brains and your potential you could have made a great career for yourself. And what do you do?" she slammed the trunk shut and sat in the car.

I got in next to her. She pulled away from the parking lot.

"Vicky, let's talk about it already. You mean my business, don't you?"

"You call it business? It's a kid's game! You should be happy I love you but honestly, I just don't believe it'll get you anywhere. To be successful in business, you need a totally different set of skills. You need to be tough and crafty. And you, excuse my French, you're a total wimp. Sales — yes, we know you can do it. To find the right approach and talk the customer into a sale — this is your thing, I completely agree. But a businessman? I don't think so!" she braked and hooted at a car in front. "Go already! The lights have been green for hours!"

"Listen, we haven't been open for a month yet and already you've written us off..."

"There's nothing to write off, don't you understand? Just close the office down and come back to Ultrapak, will you? Only today, Mr. Ivanov regretted you were no longer with us. Just think how much time and investment it might take you to reach the same kind of income as he paid you there? If you don't want to go back, that's not a problem. I already told you I could find you a job with my friend at White Hill, Ltd. They have far more potential."

I knew she was right about all that: the potential, the income and especially the fact that I still had a lot to learn business wise. But dammit! We'd only been open for just over two weeks — too short a time to have done anything — and she'd already lost all faith in me.

In actual fact, she'd never believed in me.

I understood that I was possibly wrong in taking offence but my face turned red on its own accord. My ears were on fire. I might have been still suffering from the effects of the Smitten debuff — especially the diminished Intellect — but I replied hotly, fully understanding I might regret saying this,

"Okay, Vick. Let's presume I'm wasting my time on bullshit, as you so eloquently put it. I can live with that. But you know... my ex, Yanna, had much more patience in this respect. She had faith in me for four long years. Can you imagine? And you didn't even last a couple of months..."

I'd put my foot in it, hadn't I?

Confirming my worst suspicions, Vicky swerved toward the curb and slammed on the brakes.

Your Reputation with Victoria Koval has decreased!
Current Reputation: Dislike 15/30

"Get out," she snapped.

"Vicky, I'm sorry, I wasn't thinking."

"Out. And take your shopping with you."

"Vick..." I said, still hopeful.

The next system message left me no chance,

Your Reputation with Victoria Koval has decreased!
Current Reputation: Dislike 25/30

Another déjà vu experience. I picked up my gym bag from the back seat and climbed out of the car. I wasn't going to take any of the shopping. I didn't want to appear so petty in her eyes. I started out down the road.

Vicky's car caught up with me and came to a halt. The window on my side wound down,

"Phil, I'm afraid this time it's over. I'm serious. This is the last straw. I've made up my mind," she said in a weary but firm voice. "Don't call me, don't text me. I don't forgive things like that. I enjoyed being with you but without you will be better."

She pulled away sharply and drove off, leaving me by the roadside. I threw my bag over my shoulder and headed off home, seeing as it wasn't very far.

It had been a hard day. My spirit and willpower had been depleted. I felt empty inside.

It had been a hard day. I'd come home and go straight to bed. I'd think about it tomorrow.

It had been a hard day...

Chapter Eleven

THE SAME FACES IN THE SAME PLACES

It is invariably saddening to look through new eyes at things upon which you have expended your own powers of adjustment.

F. Scott Fitzgerald. The Great Gatsby

I LAY IN BED THAT NIGHT STRUGGLING TO FALL ASLEEP. As if sensing my inner torment, Boris came and started to paw my chest, then curled up next to me and began purring a soothing melody.

A dumped man sharing his bed with a cat isn't the most heroic of images, I agree. Still, even LitRPG characters are entitled to a pet. I hugged the pillow and buried my face in it but my brain was buzzing, fully awake and refusing to nod off.

In everyone's life, there comes a key moment

---

when one's path forks, forcing you to choose. Normally, you realize it years if not decades afterwards. These realizations can lead to dark despair when you curse yourself for having made the wrong decision. And more often than not, you simply regret something you should have done but didn't — or alternatively, something you shouldn't have done but did.

Now too I had a funny feeling that this day in July had steered me in a direction totally different from the one I'd been following only yesterday. Too many life-changing things had happened.

The fact that Matov had kicked me out of the group did hurt my pride but I could live with that. I'd already been thinking about wrapping up this particular development branch; besides, there were plenty of other groups and coaches around. Also, tomorrow morning I'd have my first session with Kostya to which I'd so eagerly — and probably too hastily — agreed. Now in hindsight I began to doubt the utility of such amateur sessions.

And as for breaking up with Vicky... my mind was now dancing a mental jig trying to list all the potential benefits of this step. Seriously, I could give you a few off the top of my head: all the free time I now had available, the absence of all the nerve-wracking innuendo, and a clear path to any new relationship seeing as my Attractiveness wasn't just a figment of my interface's imagination: I'd watched it grow with every ounce of fat I'd burned and every inch of muscle I'd built.

In which case, why did I feel so shitty?

Then there was the arrival of Stacy. Now that I had the time and opportunity to reflect upon it with a cool head, I could see several explanations of her weird behavior. The first and the most logical of which being that she was just an ordinary girl and that it was the interface that had somehow glitched. You never know, she might have some top-of-the-range mental protection installed by her loving grandma which restricted access to her data.

My second theory was, she might be working for some secret service or other. Possibly, ours — either acting on a tip from Major Igorevsky or following my phone call about the missing Joseph boy made from the Uber taxi. Alternatively, they could have been alerted by my blanket discovery of missing people for the search and rescue groups. I'd left plenty of traces so it couldn't have been so difficult to track me down provided they'd wanted to.

Or could she have been someone working for our friends across the ocean? That would have made it even easier because I'd entered my real data on that Rewards for Justice site. Sending someone to keep an eye on me would have been a piece of cake had they so wished. They could have easily collated a whole dossier on me complete with my psychological portrait, then offered me a honey trap, a supposed damsel in distress whom I couldn't refuse.

Which I hadn't.

And my third theory was the most fantastical of all. Maybe I wasn't the only one with the interface installed? Really, what prevented other people from having it too?

And if Stacy was one such interface user, what was her secret agenda in coming to us? Who was she? A lone player? An agent of the entity which had spoken to me through old Panikoff? Or one of Valiadis' people?

Talking about Valiadis... I opened my interface and activated the city map. My heart fell; it felt as if I was in freefall. I was still lying in bed while the map was projected onto the ceiling, offering me a bird's eye view of the city.

The map obeyed my mental command, showing me the oligarch's location. He was in town.

He was actually very close even though formally, his mansion wasn't even within the city limits. I jumped from the bed. This was my chance to get at least some answers to my questions.

Misunderstanding my intentions, Boris also jumped off the bed and rushed to the kitchen, howling invitingly. The poor thing must have thought she might get an unscheduled meal.

I didn't disappoint her. Then I started rummaging through the manila file where I kept all the paperwork I'd amassed during my time in Ultrapak. I knew I'd never had Valiadis' business card but whatever had happened to the one given to me by his right hand man, Alex Hermann?

Dammit. Mr. Ivanov must have filched it. I could remember him fiddling with it before he'd made the phone call.

So what was I supposed to do now?

My cell phone reminded me of its existence. Who

could that be calling me so late? Vicky? Yanna?

Neither. It was my old friend Gleb Kolosov.

"Phil, is that you?"

It took me some time to recognize his lifeless voice. "Hi, man. Whassup?"

"Sorry to hassle you so late."

"It's okay. Just spit it out."

"You see, I'm having a bit of an issue here..." he fell silent. Judging by his tone, he was drunk as a skunk. "Could you lend me some money? It's very important. It's a bit of an emergency."

"How much?"

"A lot. Really a lot. I need a couple of million. You're the last person I'm calling. I've already tried everything. Can you help? Remember I lent you some money in the casino? I really need it. Otherwise I'm a dead man."

"Listen man, I just don't have that kind of money. Can you tell me what's happened?"

"I see. Just don't bother," he hung up.

I called him back but he kept rejecting my calls.

According to the map, he was at home which made me feel slightly more at ease. I'd call him back tomorrow and try to arrange a meeting.

I spent some more time watching his marker. It seemed to be all right. The marker wasn't moving which meant he'd probably gone to bed.

Now, how could I go about meeting with Valiadis? Should I do the same thing again and go around town trying to track him down? Or should I go straight to my ex-boss Mr. Ivanov and try to pry

Valiadis' contact information out of him?

I really should try both. As soon as I finished my session with Kostya tomorrow morning, I'd have to check the map for Valiadis' whereabouts. If he was out of my reach, then I'd phone Ultrapak. But first I needed to come up with a good story because if I asked for Hermann's phone number point blank, they were sure to say no. Why would my ex-boss want to help me?

But if or when I managed to speak to Valiadis, I might just be able to work out Stacy's identity and agenda.

That was it, then. All decisions made and tasks set. I accepted this as a working plan and fell asleep straight away.

* * *

I REMEMBER THE TIME WHEN I WOULD WAKE UP IN A lousy mood whenever I'd had a difficult or busy day in front of me. All those mornings before difficult exams, job interviews, unpleasant meetings... Or those like today: the first morning after the day that Vicky had left me.

On mornings like those, nothing can cheer you up. You remain deaf to the birds' singing or to the aroma of your coffee... even a cold shower doesn't do anything to jolt you awake. The best motivation to survive a day like this is looking forward to the inevitable evening when everything is finally over and you can retreat into a game or immerse yourself in a good book — in other words, escape reality.

This time it was different. All the things that worry us, all the problems and unavoidable tasks aren't going to disappear unless you solve them. It's like an aching tooth: you can postpone a visit to the dentist indefinitely... until it actually starts hurting. Because sooner or later, it's going to remind you of itself so badly that you'd wish someone ripped it out ASAP just to stop the pain. So seeing as you're obliged to visit the sadistic dentist anyway, why not do yourself a favor and have your tooth fixed before it's completely rotten and sending waves of pain through the jaw?

It was this logic that drove me from the bed the moment I'd been gently woken up by my virtual alarm clock.

Good morning, Phil!

Today is Wednesday July 18 2018. The outdoor temperature is 21 C (70 F).

You wanted to wake up at 6.00. It's now 6.12 a.m, which is the best awakening time based upon your sleep cycle.

The state of your health: Good.

Based on your activity levels, we'd recommend you start your day with a breakfast containing no more than 500 calories from proteins and complex carbohydrates.

Here are the tasks you set for today...

I had a long but very important day in front of me.

I got scrubbed up and headed for the stadium

downstairs to train with Kostya. I had no idea how it was going to work out but he'd offered me his help, so I suppose I'd done the right thing to accept it.

He was already there, walking along the running track warming up, looking focused.

"Hi, Kostya," I said.

"Ah, there you are! I was about to call you. I haven't got much time. You ready? Let's move it!"

As we trained, he kept frowning. I could see he wasn't in the best of moods. I didn't know what to put it down to: he might have had a bad night's sleep or some problems he'd had to deal with; he might even have regretted his offer of help. In any case, I adopted a similar businesslike attitude just doing whatever he told me to.

I hadn't noticed any particular difference between his training method and Matov's, apart from the fact that we'd only trained for about forty-five minutes. Once we were finished, Kostya bade me a very curt goodbye.

"When do we meet up again?" I asked.

"How about the day after tomorrow?" he offered. "Mondays, Wednesdays and Fridays, sounds like a good schedule. All the other days I'm at Matov's as you well know."

"Okay. Do I owe you anything? I could pay you like I paid for my private lessons."

He hesitated. "Er... nah, don't bother. It was my idea. It's good for me as well because we train together. Okay, I've gotta get going. I still have to take little Julie to the kindergarten before work."

"Julie?"

"Yeah, my little sister," he nodded and left.

I spent another twenty minutes jogging and leveling up Stamina until I'd finally made it.

Congratulations! You've received a new skill level!

Skill name: Stamina

Current level: 11

You've received 1000 pt. XP for successfully leveling up a main characteristic!

Current level: 15. XP points gained: 7340/16000

That's a good start to the day! In the course of last night's fight I'd sensed I'd been running out of steam. Level 10 in Stamina was only a world average, after all. You know any ordinary men who'd be able to take a round of boxing? So I still had my work cut out for me, leveling my physical and breathing stats.

I headed back home. According to the map, Valiadis was already up and running, judging by the fact that he was already on his way downtown. I minimized the map so that I could still keep an eye on his marker.

Mechanically I took a shower, had a tomato omelet and a couple of rye bread and chicken breast sandwiches, put on my business suit with +5 to Charisma and set off to work — on foot as usual.

Halfway to the office I saw that Mr. Ivanov, Ultrapak's CEO, was already in his office. I could give him a call at last.

As I scrolled through my contacts in search of his number, an idea struck me. It might not be the best of solutions but Vicky had had a point: it might take some time to get my unorthodox business model up and running. How about if I offered our services to my old boss? Not the way I'd done before but by making out an official contract with him? Having said that, he wasn't the only potential customer around.

I called him but only got an engaged tone. He was already busy talking to someone. Never mind. I'd call him again once I was in the office.

I put the phone back into my pocket and continued pondering over my new idea.

Selling sales? Why not? I'd already thought about it before but I'd always ignored the idea as not having any socially meaningful purpose. I much preferred helping people in person. But behind every company, there's always a bunch of people who are either beginners or just plain not too successful. The likes of Veronica with her event organizing agency or Kesha who'd mortgaged his apartment to buy equipment for his tiny printing shop. Then there was Mr. Katz and his wife Rose...

The more I thought about it, the more inspired I felt. Besides helping small businesses, this could also garner some decent income — certainly more than we could ever expect from the ranks of our unemployed customers.

I ran up the steps leading to our business center.

"Morning, Phil!" Gorelik greeted me.

I was in such a hurry I hadn't even noticed him. "Good morning, Sir!"

"Could I keep you a minute?"

"Absolutely."

The building manager took me aside. "How's things with you? Have any clients? I heard you're doing pretty well. Wish I could say the same about all the others. Almost a third of our tenants are late with their payments. We've opened up a sewing sweatshop in the basement, they're the only ones who're doing relatively well. They've hired some migrant workers who're sitting there sewing 24/7. And they're all illegals!"

Behind his incoherent speech, I could smell last night's party on his breath.

"As for all the others," he continued, "they ain't doing so good. And why? Because they don't know how to sell, that's why! Us Russians just aren't good at selling."

Having made this rather unexpected conclusion, he stopped to catch his breath.

"Excuse me, Sir? What are you getting at?"

"What I'm saying is that this Saturday, we're having a sales training course in our conference hall," he laid an intimate hand on my shoulder. "The person who's giving it is Aram Ovsepyan. He's an Internet star and an expert in proactive selling. You young people must know him. The course's curriculum contains a number of very important skills and practices indispensable for any sales manager striving for success," he rattled off the pre-rehearsed pitch, all the while fidgeting with my shirt button. "Want me to sign you up? It's only 9,999 rubles."

"No, thanks. Sorry but I've got a lot on my plate today," I said, wriggling myself free from his embrace. "Why don't you pop down and see Vazgen who sells those PVC windows? I'm sure he'll sign up, even if only to support a fellow Armenian."

"You think?"

"You can always give it a bash. Especially if you mention that Naeel is also going to be there."

As I walked up the stairs, I heard Gorelik's puzzled voice, "Who the hell is Naeel? Is he one of the tenants? Auntie Ira, do you know him?"

Both Alik and Stacy were already in the office. The former hood was fussing with the electric kettle in the kitchen while Stacy was busy lining up numerous potted plants on the window sill. She was wearing a demure floor-length white skirt — but the other half of her outfit didn't quite live up to it: a skimpy black tank top which completely contravened last night's agreement that she should tone her dress sense down.

"Hi guys," I said.

"Good morning, Sir!" Stacy's clear titillating voice immediately reactivated my Smitten debuff. "What happened to your eye?"

"Howdy," Alik looked up from the kettle he was dismantling and whistled. "Have you been in a fight?"

"Don't ask. How's it going?"

"The kettle's busted," he replied, looking all hot and bothered. "I'm trying to fix it."

"What if we get a new one? Where did you get the plants from?"

"That was Mrs. Frolova, imagine. She got them for her."

"Who got what for whom?"

"The plants. Mrs. Frolova gave them to me," Stacy explained. "I met her on the stairs and we had a chat. I said our office looked pretty empty. It needed some life breathed into it. So she offered me the plants. As far as I understand, she's the local bookkeeper, Sir. Er... do you mind if I call you Phil too? Just to simplify things."

I shrugged. "You can call me whatever you want," I took my place at the desk, unwilling to pamper to my own ego. I wasn't interested in creating any kind of hierarchy with them.

Our objective was productivity, not fake subordination.

Mr. Ivanov's number was still engaged. I might need to go and meet him in person. Valiadis was in the town hall so it was probably not a good idea to disturb him there. Which meant I should really try and get Hermann's contacts instead.

The only problem was, how was I supposed to leave the office unattended? Because without me, these two wouldn't be able to sell jack to anyone.

"Guys," I said, "I'd like you to drop what you're doing. Let's have a quick briefing because I need to go out to meet someone."

"Phil, mind if I carry on with the kettle? It's driving me nuts! I won't get any peace until I've fixed it."

"It's no problem," I said.

They sat in front of me: Alik still fiddling with the kettle and Stacy devouring me with her eyes. She had a pen and a brand-new agenda on her lap: the girl had come prepared for her first working day.

"We have three things on our agenda today," I said. "The first being, how you're going to carry on working in my absence. Stacy, that applies to you first of all but you'd better listen up as well, Alik. The more information we have about our clients, the higher the probability of their successful placing. Which is why I'd like you to start asking for their CVs. Stacy, I'm going to email you a blank form in a moment for them to fill in."

"Very well, Phil," she nodded, jotting it down. "If you give me your address, I'll send you a test email."

I dictated the address to her and immediately received her letter, then emailed back with the client questionnaire attached. I'd prepared it quite a while ago but I hadn't needed it until now as I'd always managed to find jobs for all my clients virtually on their very first visit.

"It's imperative we get a good picture of them," I went on. "So if a client hasn't thought of bringing a mug shot with their CV, I suggest you take their pictures on the spot. You can use your phones if you wish. Is that clear?"

They nodded simultaneously.

The door opened, letting in Veronica. "Hi everybody!" she gave me a peck on the cheek. "Are you having a meeting?"

"A briefing," I said. "Would you like to join in?"

"Briefings, bah! They're boring. I'll pop back later," she said. "I needed to talk to you about something, remember?"

"How about after lunch?" I offered. "I have to go out to a meeting."

"Perfect!" she swung round and left.

Alik's eyes followed her every move to the door. "Look Phil, I think I've fixed it," he finally said as he, for reasons known only to him, tried to hand me the wretched kettle. "Would you like me to turn it on? We could use a cup of coffee."

"Do you mind doing it later?" I said. "Let's finish the briefing first. Are you listening to me at all?"

"Eh... sure! You've got to go to a meeting and Veronica is coming back after lunch."

'And what did I say before that?"

"Eh... you told us to take pictures of all who don't have their own photos. And fill in the questionnaires."

"Anything else, Phil?" Stacy asked. "Nothing about the forms you've just sent me?"

"Oh yes. There's a question there about their work preferences. I want you to remember that they're probably going to either list something they already have work experience in, or something safe, because they don't think they can aspire to something bigger. So I want you to try and ferret out where their hearts lay. Let's say, a woman walks in saying she's looking for a shop assistant's job, while her heart is really into something totally different, something that she thinks is either too good for her or won't pay the bills. These are the kinds of things I want you to draw out of them."

Stacy beamed. "Consider it done! I'm very good at worming my way into people's confidence. They seem to think they can open up to me. It only takes me a few minutes to make them pour their hearts out to me."

For some reason, Alik turned crimson.

I moved to the next thing on our agenda, "Also, we need to start expanding our area of interests."

"Oh! Does that mean we get to mine some Bitcoins?" Alik said enthusiastically.

"No, Alik, I don't think there's anything left to mine there, the whole thing's already exhausted. What we're gonna do, we're gonna offer sales outsourcing services for struggling businesses. There are companies on the market that already do it but normally, they're prohibitively expensive without any guarantee of results. We're going to work on a percentage basis which is something very few of them are eager to do."

Alik shook his head. "I'm not sure I got it..."

"I did," Stacy chirped. "Great idea, boss! But that means we'll have to expand and hire some sales managers..."

"Absolutely. I'd like you to ask Mr. Katz to come after lunch and we'll try to draft a contract. Also, I want to see Kesha. I have a proposal for him."

"Will do," she said, jotting it down in her notebook. "And what's the third thing on the agenda?"

"The third thing is your tank top, Stacy. I thought we'd agreed about you changing the way you dress?"

"We did. Why? What have I done wrong?"

"Nothing. It's just that a bra might come in handy. That top of yours is a bit too in your face..."

* * *

CONTRARY TO MY EXPECTATIONS, I HAD NO PROBLEM clearing the business center security to go to Ultrapak. I didn't meet anyone I knew as I walked up to the office. Daria was still sitting in reception as usual, scrolling through her Instagram feed.

"Hi there," I said.

"Oh hi, Phil!" she gushed.

"How's it going?"

"Great! Mr. Ivanov was talking about you only the other day. What brings you here? Are you on business or do you just miss us?" she flapped her eyelash extensions.

"I've been missing this place something rotten. Especially you..." I started as I heard someone stop behind my back with a tactful cough.

"Vicky!" Daria turned to her. "We've got a visitor!"

"I can see that," Vicky said with a cold glance in my direction. "Good morning, Phil."

"Morning, Ms. Koval. How are you?

"I'm fine," she snapped as she headed for her office.

I felt something clawing at my heart — some thought that had something to do with Vicky. Still, I suppressed it for the time being. I was here on business.

""Is Mr. Ivanov in?" I asked Daria even though I knew perfectly well that he was.

"Yes, why? Are you here to see him? Is he expecting you?"

"Next thing you'll be asking how to introduce me to him."

"Wait a sec... I need to ask..." she took the phone and dialed Ivanov's secretary. "Irina, I've got Phil Panfilov here. He'd like to see Mr. Ivanov. Yes, Panfilov, he used to work for us. What did you say? Okay. Got it," she hung up. "You'll have to wait a little."

"Then I'll go and say hello to the guys," I said, heading for the sales department.

It was unusually quiet. Everybody must have been out working. Cyril and Marina were nowhere to be seen. Greg alone was busy talking some sense into some client on the phone, running his hand through his bushy hair. On seeing me, he grinned and pointed at the phone. I nodded and waited for him to finish.

The moment he'd stopped talking, he jumped from his seat and gave me a big hug. "Hi, Phil! How's it hanging? Where are you these days?"

"I'm good. I've opened my own business. And how about you and all the others?"

"Business? What kind of business?"

Seeing as the room was empty, we spent the next ten minutes talking. I told him everything about my agency. He, in turn, shared the news about himself.

According to him, the company wasn't doing so well. Pavel, their commercial director, had quit but not before he'd poached three of their best reps. In the meantime, they'd replaced him with some new guy.

"To tell you the truth, I'm thinking about leaving too," Greg admitted. "This new guy, you know what he did? He started by raising our wholesale prices. That caused a whole bunch of customers to look elsewhere. It's a good job we still have your J-Mart. And yesterday the dickhead drove Marina to tears. And it wasn't even her fault! She failed to close a couple of clients at the last moment but that was exactly because they didn't like the price hike."

"How's Cyril?"

"He's on sick leave. They've found some complications so they had him admitted to the First City Hospital."

"Which department? Which room?"

"Jesus, Phil, I just don't remember. You give him a ring, anyway. He'll be happy to see you."

"Sure."

Daria peeked into the room. "Phil? Mr. Ivanov will see you now."

"Okay, man, it was great to see you," I said. "If ever you decide to quit here, pop in and see us, we'll find you something worth your while. How's your wife, by the way? When is she due?"

"It's still a while," Greg replied. "Closer to the end of September."

"Great! I'll be off, then. Greetings to everyone."

He beamed. "Will do. And I might actually think about your proposition..."

Mr. Ivanov's office was so full of tobacco smoke

you could cut the air with a knife.

"Good morning, Sir."

"Ah, Phil. Fancy seeing you here. Take a seat."

He wasn't his usual friendly self. Either the company was in a really bad way or he still held a grudge against me.

"What do you want?" he asked point blank.

"Mr. Ivanov, you know me as a salesman..."

"I suppose," he grumbled.

"I'd like to propose to you-"

He perked up. "You wanna come back, is that it? I don't know about that."

"No, it's not about me coming back but it boils down to the same thing. I'd like to offer you our sales outsourcing services."

"What's that?"

"We could make out a contract in which my agency would look for new buyers for your products. And you, once you closed a deal, would have to pay us a commission. Basically, it'll be the same as it was when I worked for you. We sell your products, you pay us a commission."

"Eh... I really don't know," he drawled. "I need to discuss it with Panchenko. This is his domain, anyway. Why did you come to me? I thought you wanted to come back."

"Who's Panchenko?"

"Ah, it's our new commercial director. Konstantin Panchenko. The guy we took on to replace Pavel. You'd better meet up with him. He's best placed to decide."

"Okay, I'll speak to him, then."

"Anything else?"

"Yes, Sir. Thank you for affording me the time."

"You're welcome. But you'd better speak to Panchenko."

I activated Lie Detection, rose and proffered my hand. As we exchanged a handshake, I asked nonchalantly,

"You didn't, by any chance, keep Alex Hermann's card?"

"Who's that?" he asked, pretending he hadn't understood me.

"We met him once, remember? Valiadis' right-hand man. I left his business card with you."

"Ah, you mean that one... No, I don't have it," he exhaled smoke in my face. "Pavel must have taken it. Why would I need it?"

A wave of cold enveloped me. Which meant he did have the card but he didn't want to share it with me.

"Why would you want it, anyway?" he asked. "I thought you saw each other regularly. Don't you?"

"We do indeed. Well, I won't encroach on your time. Thanks. Have a nice day!"

"Good. See you, then."

When I left his office, I paused for a moment wondering whether I should go and see Vicky. Still, I suppressed the impulse and headed for Daria's desk. "Is your new commercial director in? Mr. Ivanov told me to see him."

"You mean Mr. Panchenko?"

"Exactly, unless you have another one."

"Unfortunately, he's out at the moment. Would you like to leave a message?"

"I'd rather you gave me his phone number. I'll call him myself."

"I'm very sorry but I can't do that."

"I see. Never mind. In that case, could you please give him my number? I don't have any cards on me. Can you write it down?"

She smiled. "I still have it, don't I?"

I left the Ultrapak building. What now? Should I go back to the office or try and chase down Valiadis?

Using the interface as I walked wasn't very easy so I headed for the café where we all used to lunch together. I could use something to eat. Their set menus were quite decent.

As I was waiting for my order, I remembered last night's call from Gleb. I hadn't seen him for almost two months — and before that, it had been several years. I'd remembered about him two months ago when I'd first activated my Heroism skill and was studying the descriptions of the Heroic abilities that came with it.

All those years back in college, Gleb and I had regularly played in the casino. When I'd lost for the umpteenth time, I'd borrowed some money from him: not a lot by today's standards but still a considerable sum for a student. I'd failed to pay it back promptly, then spent a lot of time ashamedly hiding from him. He took offense and we stopped seeing each other.

I dialed his number. "Hi, Gleb."

"Phil? Is that you? What do you want?" he

sounded so apathetic that I didn't even hear the questioning intonation in his voice.

"You called me last night. How about we meet up and you tell me what happened?"

"Why?" his lifeless voice rustled.

"We could put our heads together and think what to do about it."

"We can't do anything now. Having said that... could you lend me some money? Anything at all?"

"What if we meet and discuss it?" I said.

I absolutely had to make him open up.

"Okay," he reluctantly agreed. "When?"

"Tonight at my place. Here's the address. Have you got something to write it down?"

"Just tell me. I'll remember."

I explained to him how to drive there. He mumbled something remotely reminiscent of "see ya" and hung up.

I glanced at Valiadis' marker on the map, canceled my café order and dashed back home to pick up my gym gear. He was in the same swimming pool but this time I had absolutely no desire to pay for another pair of prohibitively expensive Speedos.

I was in luck. An Uber cab was passing by so I didn't have to wait long.

Once back home, I changed my sweat-drenched shirt, threw all my swim gear into the bag — the trunks, a pair of flip flops, a bathing cap and a towel, — then rummaged my shelves for the 3-visit guest subscription I'd bought. I still had two visits left. I had no idea whether the subscription was still valid — it might have already expired for all I knew — so I scooped up all the cash I had just in case (which was about ten grand) and hurried back down, taking the stairs three at a time toward the waiting taxi.

Thirty minutes and three thousand rubles later (because I'd been forced to buy a new guest card), I pulled on the trunks and the bathing cap. It took me several attempts to get my feet into the flip flops but finally, I went down to the pool.

It was busier here today. Still, I wasn't worried about all the men in black lining the walls. Nonchalantly I flung my towel onto one of the deck chairs, ordered some green tea, left my flip flops by the side of the pool and jumped in the deep end.

I hadn't even reached midway across the pool when I received an unexpected bonus,

Congratulations! You've received a new skill level!

Skill name: Swimming
Current level: 2
XP received: 500
Current level: 15. XP points gained: 7840/16000

The skill's XP bar must have already been nearing 100%. Add to this my stat booster and high Learning Skills, and it had been enough for me to swim a mere twenty meters to receive a new level.

Which explains why I was in a rather good mood by the time I reached Valiadis.

"Phil Panfilov," the oligarch recognized me

straight away.

"How do you do, Sir? Yes, it's me again."

"I have a feeling that today is no coincidence, either."

"Actually, you're right. I came here with the sole purpose of meeting you."

"That I don't doubt," he said. "Let's move to the sauna, shall we? It's not a great place to talk here."

Ignoring the steps, he got out of the pool and headed for the sauna without looking back. Nothing about his sinewy body even remotely resembled the potbellied dudes who were lounging about in the hot tub.

I effortlessly climbed out after him — my arm muscles had definitely grown! — and followed in his wake.

Once in the sauna, Valiadis climbed the highest bench, pulled his cap down to his eyes and sprawled out with his hands behind his head.

I sat on the lower bench, leaning my back against the wall so that I could see him.

"I'm listening," he said lazily.

"I have two questions for you, Sir. Or two subjects, rather."

"You have fifteen minutes. After that, I have to leave."

His next words rendered me speechless even though I was prepared to hear something like this.

"Don't bother to use Lie Detection," he said. "I can see you already have it activated. Level 15? Not bad but not great, either. Never mind. We'll talk about it later. What's your first question? What is it you wanted to discuss?"

"I don't really want to discuss anything, just make you a proposition. I've opened an agency and would like to offer you our sales outsourcing services-"

"Not interested," he interrupted me. "After that conversation we had last time, I took the trouble to double-check all the other service providers. My own level of Insight allows me not only to buy goods in at the best possible price, but it also allows me to determine which of these goods are in the most demand. You seem to be smart enough to understand how these things work. What's your Insight level at now?"

"Two, Sir."

"Only level two? What in God's name can you see? At level 2, all you have available are the basics. You can't do anything with them. I'd suggest you concentrate on leveling Insight alone. That way you might at least make level 5..."

"How can I do that?"

"That's up to you. I'm not going to help you. But in actual fact, I'm afraid for you it's already academic."

"Why? I still have loads of time until my license expires."

"Don't ask me. I've no idea how it happened. The Vaalphors are still none the wiser. Apparently, you failed the Trial. What do you remember?"

"I remember being in some weird room. When I woke up, I was hung with debuffs. I remember seeing you there. And some girl..."

"Ilindi."

"That's right. She had funny ears. Not quite human. And then there was some other creature there... was it a demon? At least he had hooves. What was his name now — Khphor?"

"Yes, that's exactly who it was. Khphor. He's a Vaalphor, a Senior Races observer."

"So it wasn't a dream, then?"

"No. What I find strange is that you remembered it even though you thought it was a dream. I wasn't there — by myself I mean my current development branch — but they showed the whole thing to me. You were killed by an acid jelly. Your body was then rebuilt. In the process, the interface in your brain was uninstalled and your memory of all the related events erased. That included all the skills and characteristics you'd acquired in the process. Once that done, they teleported you to the exact time and place they'd abducted you from. You can't imagine Khphor's amazement during a later control check when he realized you still had the interface. He even suspected you might have somehow activated Time Cheat. But that's nonsense, of course. Even I haven't yet made the First Hero, let alone you."

"A control check? I don't think I remember meeting Khphor again."

"Didn't you mention Mr. Panikoff? At some point in time, the old boy had made a deal with Khphor so now the Voice can use his body whenever it wants to incarnate in our world. To meet people like you and I, for instance."

"How do you know Panikoff?"

"Same as you. I've been talking with the Voice."

"The Voice — is it Khphor?"

"Not exactly. To tell you the truth, I still don't really know. The Voice basically says what Khphor wants to convey to us. Something like a controlled voice message. It's a one-way system: he can use Panikoff to speak to you but you can't speak back. Or rather, you could — and the Voice might even reply — but it wouldn't be Khphor talking to you. Not that it matters anymore," he grunted like an old man and looked me in the eye. "So basically, the Seniors' Council has two scenarios for you now. One is to leave everything as it is and in due time abduct you to conduct repeat trials. But those who suggest it are in the minority. The others demand you be wiped but you see, any such unscheduled abduction takes way too much energy. It's easier for them to perform repeat trials. The rest would depend on how you perform. You either pass it or not, in which case they'll make sure to uninstall it properly and completely steam-roll your memory. You'll forget all the events of the past year at least."

"And what's the second option?"

"That's what I'm supposed to offer you. You need to uninstall the program voluntarily."

"How can I do that?"

"Wait a sec. Let me finish. I can tell you how to do it. In return, you'll keep all your memories — but on top of that, you will also preserve all the skills and characteristics you've already acquired. With the exception of the system ones, of course. And as a personal bonus from me, you'll get a good contract for your company and a million bucks in cash. With your humble ambitions, this money should last you for the rest of your life, especially if you manage to invest it wisely."

"And if I refuse?"

"That would be rather stupid. You see, even though the Vaalphors can't directly control a test subject, they're perfectly capable of controlling the chain of chance. Like a twig that drops from a tree onto a windshield, causing the driver to be momentarily distracted just as you're crossing the road. You know what I mean? Have you seen *Final Destination*? In other words, if you refuse you should be prepared for all kinds of trouble. And even if you do manage to survive them without a mental breakdown, then you'll still be abducted for another trial. If you pass it, you'll keep the interface and go on living as before until the local finals. If you don't, you'll either lose all your new skills or you'll die."

"I see. Not a very rosy outlook," I lowered my head, searching for something to counter him with. "Why are they so bent on screwing me up? Can't they just leave me in peace and let me retake the test without all this chain of chance nonsense?"

"Because even for them, abduction is too energy-consuming. And you have no chance of ever passing the Trial, Phil. It's going to be a complete waste of resources. Your development is lamentably inadequate to anything that might help you pass. As you know, the Senior Races have mastered the art of being omnipresent, appearing in many dimensions simultaneously and sliding between them as they see fit. This allows them to work out all the odds most favorable for the Commonwealth of Sentient Races. And the eventuality of you keeping the interface is potentially too risky for everyone. So you'd better agree to what they offer now."

"Well, if it's like that..." I hesitated on the verge of accepting his offer.

I'd lived quite happily without the interface before, hadn't I? And with a million bucks in my pocket and a nice fat contract with J-Mart I could definitely reach new heights. My strength, my growing six-pack, my fighting skills and my eyesight which was still as sharp as when I'd been a child — none of these were going to disappear. I'd keep on training. So what if my progress would take several times longer? What kind of problem was that? Welcome to the real world!

The prospect of losing the interface didn't appear so grim to me anymore. I was going to miss Martha, that's for sure. I wished I could find out who she'd been modeled after, though. You never know, I might meet her prototype IRL. She was my dream girl, after all.

"Hurry up," the oligarch said. "Make up your mind now. I'm already late. And I don't think I can stand this heat for much longer."

He climbed off the bench. I rose and took a deep breath as I came to a decision.

"Very well, Sir. Let it be so."

Chapter

Twelve

THE COIN STANDS ON ITS EDGE

Fortune doesn't favor fools.

League of Legends

"GOOD DECISION," VALIADIS SAID, LOOKING PLEASED.
"I'm gonna tell you now how to uninstall-"

"Sorry, Sir. I'm afraid you misunderstood me."

As I said it, I was confronted with a silence and
his watchful stare. He must have realized I hadn't
finished because he sat down again.

Mechanically I activated Lie Detection. Now of all
times, I had to be sure no one was trying to lead me up

the garden path.

"Let it be so," I repeated. "Let everything stay as it is now. When my time comes, I'll do my best to pass the Trial."

"Phil," he began, then stopped, grinding his teeth, all the while trying to put his thoughts into words. "I wouldn't call it a wise decision. You understand it's not a joke, don't you? Try to imagine yourself becoming the main target of every police and criminal authority, every professional hitman and every religious fanatic on planet earth. Now multiply it by a billion billions... how much is it? I keep forgetting what it's called..."

"A quintillion, Sir," I offered him from my mine of useless information.

He nodded, showing no surprise. "Whatever. That's the situation you'll be in if you refuse the offer of a million dollars cash and all the skills you've already leveled up. The only difference being, you'll never know what hit you."

A burly figure appeared behind the sauna's glass door. "Are you all right, Sir?"

"I'm fine, Misha, thanks. Could you get us some water, please?"

The bodyguard momentarily disappeared, then returned with two frosted bottles. Valiadis and I drank greedily, then he continued from where he'd left off,

"Okay. It's your decision. But may I ask you why?"

"For lots of reasons," I said. "I'm a gamer, don't forget. I can't resist a challenge. Also, I'm quite used to the interface. Quite honestly, I can't imagine living without it now. But it's pretty irrelevant, really. What's important are the people behind me."

"You don't think that a million dollars is enough for you to help them? You're talking about your family, aren't you?"

"Not really, Sir. I've opened an employment agency. Our clients are mostly down-and-outs. How am I supposed to help them without the interface? I might have, I suppose, had I had a name already or a good reputation among the employers. But at this stage, without the interface I won't stand a chance."

Was it my imagination or had his face warmed? Still, I hadn't received any Reputation messages. Which meant it *was* my imagination.

"What's the interface got to do with it?" he asked, faking indifference.

"I need the map search. It shows everything: not just people or landmarks but all sorts of companies and public offices. All I do, I enter a particular person in it and search by their employment probability..."

"You *what*?" he jumped to his feet, hitting his head on the low ceiling. "Dammit! A *probability search*? Is that even possible?" his expression clouded over as he focused on his own interface.

"I can't believe it!" he finally said. "Well, you live and learn!"

"Have you tried it?"

"I've just searched for my shops, then sorted them by the probability of embezzlement by their management. Those useless bastards don't know their asses from their elbows! I'm surprised we haven't yet had a visit from the tax police! Misha! Misha!" he shouted.

I still didn't understand who this Misha guy actually was. Was it his aide or his bodyguard? You wouldn't send a bodyguard on this kind of errand, would you?

The door opened. "Yes, boss?"

"Get me Hermann straight away!" he shouted, rolling his "r"s. The power of his voice was such that I very nearly took off myself to get Alex He*rrrr*mann st*rrrr*aight away. Valiadis must have had some kind of Commander's Aura or some such ability.

"Yes, Sir!" Misha barked.

"Listen, Phil," Valiadis said excitedly. "I had no idea it could work like this. How did you find that out? I knew I could use the map to search for better suppliers. This was something I realized almost straight away when I'd opened my first grocery store in the suburbs," he chuckled. "I still remember it. I had to do everything myself: I served the customers, I did all the buying in, I unloaded the trucks myself... Okay, sorry, I got carried away. It's not the right moment. So how did you work that out?"

"Have you ever searched for gear on a gaming auction?"

"Gear? On a gaming auction? I don't even know what you mean. Wait a sec."

Well, well, well. I was dying to find out what his own interface looked like and how it functioned. Because if he wasn't a gamer, how had he learned all these things? What was his leveling scenario based on?

Or did he even have one?

He rose and peeked out of the door. "Misha, I want you to call them and tell them I might be late. And order me my tea, same as usual."

"Yes, Sir!" the man replied. Valiadis probably had several of them posted there.

"Phil, I'm going to delay my flight now and then we'll finish talking. Only not in here. I suggest we clear off. My interface is already warning me about the unacceptably high heart rate and overheating. Yours too?"

"Not yet. Mine's still quiet."

"It's great to be young," he wrapped a bathrobe around himself. "Let's go."

We made ourselves comfortable in two deck chairs by a low table and continued.

"This conversation is getting interesting, I have to admit. Judging by your stats, it's mutual. In which case, seeing as we've already discussed the main subject regarding the future of your interface, I suggest we carry on not as a supervisor and test subject, nor as a buyer and seller, but as friends sharing the same interests. Especially as our mutual interests are admittedly rather rare."

"If I remember rightly, Khphor was talking about some tens of thousands of test subjects representing planet Earth."

"And that's just those who've already passed the test. Twenty-eight thousand five hundred and sixty-one people, or thirteen to the power of four. They use a numerical system based on the number 13. And as for test candidates, there're way more than that. If we talk about this particular time period in our branch of reality, there're far fewer than that. But I can't tell you the exact number."

"Can you at least give me an approximate figure?"

"About a thousand in the last five years. Almost all of them have already been stripped of their interfaces. Some of them broke down almost immediately thinking they must have lost their minds. A few rocketed up the social ladder, attracting unwanted attention and had to be either liquidated or dissected. A few, like you, simply failed the Trial. I suggest you look closer at certain spheres of social life over the last few years. All those surprise success stories in the film industry, sport, business, politics and science? Could you reel off a few names of people who have risen to great heights only to promptly disappear off the radar?" he paused to take a sip of his herbal tea. "Pay special attention to all the guerilla leaders and new revolutionaries — all those ex-teachers, doctors and car mechanics who all of a sudden felt a strange affinity with a country they previously hadn't even given two hoots about — and who then left to join up with one of the factions. Try to remember all the outbursts of mass and serial killings committed by perfectly ordinary people. All of them had been leveling up, earning XP points and improving their skills until a certain moment when they lost everything, their heads included."

"But why would they want to kill anyone? When you can simply-"

"Stop it! Don't say anything!"

He must have seen the surprise on my face because he added,

"Never tell anyone your leveling up details or how your interface works. I don't know why but for some reason, by doing so you stop gaining XP in the area which you've shared with that particular person. It's as if the program hears it and realizes you're only in it for XP."

"Does that mean it doesn't hold with farming?"

"What's farming got to do with it? Are you leveling up agriculture?"

"No, Sir. Farming is a gaming term. It means performing various actions with the purpose of gaining XP or certain resources."

"Aha, I see. No, it doesn't hold with farming. What was it you were saying about gaming auctions?"

"Well... players use them to buy and sell various gear which is put up for auction by other players. Often, there're millions of items being traded simultaneously at any given time which is why any game worth its salt has very detailed search filters. Things like armor, weapons, gems, elixirs and such are only very basic approximations. Imagine that I need a particular dagger which is fast and light, suitable for my level, which also improves my chances of dealing critical damage, boosts my Agility and costs under one million gold?"

"Enough," he nodded. "I got it. With your gaming

background, I'm not surprised you've worked out the probability filter. How did you come to use it the first time?"

"I have this friend... only at that time he wasn't a friend yet... his name is Alik. I helped him find some work."

Your Reputation with Nicholas Valiadis has improved!
Current Reputation: Indifference 15/30

A pretty girl in a revealing bikini walked past us, swaying her hips. Sensing Valiadis' eyes on her, she turned round and paused briefly, flashing him a smile over her shoulder. He immediately lost all interest, returning his attention back to me.

Did he realize that my Reputation with him had improved? Having said that, with his level 5 in Insight he could probably even tell my blood composition.

"And still, Sir. What other interface types are there? Could you at least tell me something about those that used to belong to the people who've lost them already?"

"They're all different, Phil. All of them work by encouraging the user's tendencies, both the known and secret ones. The actual interface takes the form which ensures the user's understanding. A religious fanatic will see signs from God; a New Age student will think he's communicating with Mother Nature or learns the lost technologies of Atlantis. A talented person will think he's being inspired while others will simply "see auras" or hear voices. Few of them even make it far enough to activate Insight without which the interface as you and I know it won't even open. There was this psychic, a funny guy who stopped at the very first thing available to all users immediately after the program's installation: determining other people's names and ages. I don't know how it works for you but he used to take one look at a person and he already knew their name. No fancy graphics involved. That was enough for him to make a good living. He got accepted for an American talent show and received the million-dollar prize. Predictably, he then failed the Trial..."

"And you, Sir? Do you have any main characteristics?" I asked, not certain of getting an answer.

"Of course. Every user has them. I can give you the names of mine: the physical development index, the intellectual development index, the wisdom index — which is the combination of life experience and the ability to pick an optimal solution when offered the choice of several; also, clout and luck."

"Luck?"

"Yes, why? Don't you have it? It's a very subjective factor, I agree, but as I leveled it I noticed that even unfavorable circumstances began to take a course suitable for me. I even began to win more often at cards," he smiled. "The other day in Monaco I had my number come up three times in a row at the roulette wheel."

I whistled.

"The probability of that happening," he

continued, "is just over one in a million, as you can well imagine. Okay... What's the time now? Misha!"

"Yes, boss," Misha reappeared by his side. "Hermann's waiting."

Judging by my interface, Misha *was* his aide. Despite his appearance of a dumb beefcake, his level 12 in Task Scheduling spoke for itself. At this proficiency, he could probably schedule the entire course of the Third World War second by second.

"Let him wait," Valiadis said. "Okay, Phil, I gotta fly. Business and all that."

"Thank you so much, Sir," I shook his hand wholeheartedly. Today for the first time I'd seen a human being in him.

"Don't mention it. I doubt we'll ever meet again. I know what Khphor is capable of so already I don't envy you. I've already told him about your decision. But... I fully respect your choice. If ever you change your mind, you know where to find me."

Only after he'd got out of the deck chair, had I remembered why I wanted to see him in the first place. "Sorry, Sir, one last question."

"Yes?"

"I had a very strange girl come to the agency. My Lie Detection seemed to glitch when I'd tried to check her out. She's incredibly beautiful but for some reason, she seemed bent on working for me despite the pittance I'd offered her. Could she be one of Khphor's people? Or is she one of yours?"

"Not one of mine, definitely. I don't have the same objectives or authority as he has. What's her name?"

"Anastasia Semyonova, age 24."

"Anything else?"

"Social status level 3."

He shrugged. "Not enough information. I don't know anyone of this name. Did you get her name off the interface?"

"Yes."

"Sorry, can't help you. Are we done now?"

I nodded.

"Okay. Well, *good luck*, Phil! You know what I mean?"

"Perfectly, Sir."

"Good. You're gonna need *every bit of luck you can get.*"

The moment he left, the pool area emptied apart from the fat guys in the hot tub, the waitress and a couple of life guards pacing the side of the pool.

In all the time of my talking to him, my Lie Detection hadn't made me chilly in the slightest. Did that mean that Valiadis had been open with me? Possible. Unless he had some kind of antiskill activated.

It was high time I got going, too. My working day was already half gone and I still had to speak to Veronica, Kesha and Mr. Katz.

I decided to take a quick shower after the sauna. I opened the water and started lathering my hair under the tepid jets.

Suddenly I was scalded by a gush of boiling-hot water. I cussed, recoiling. My foot lost grip on the

---

slippery tiles, sending me flying as I tried to tuck up in order to land on my shoulder. I collapsed sideways on the floor, hitting my head hard against the shower wall.

The program flooded me with damage messages. My eyes stung with the shampoo. My ears were ringing.

Instead of climbing back to my feet, I sat up, reached for the shower jets — which were already back at their normal temperature — and rinsed my eyes. I mentally traced the trajectory of my fall, realizing how incredibly lucky I'd been. One inch more to the side and I'd have been whisked away in an ambulance. Defying all the laws of physics and gravity, the sharp end of one of the tiles had come away from the wall so that I could have very easily cracked my head open on it.

This time I'd been led off the hook.

Warily I finished washing myself and crept out of the shower like it was a mine field. I did slip a couple of times again but now I'd been prepared for it so I managed to keep my balance.

I got dressed without any more surprises and left the gym — also without any further ado. My Uber was already waiting: a blue Toyota Camry. The registration number and the name of the driver — Sergei — were correct.

I opened the rear door and saw the driver's back as he rummaged through the glove compartment. "Sergei?"

He startled and swung round. "Yes?"

He didn't look like a Sergei at all. He'd be much better suited by a name like Abdul or Hassan.

"Are you Sergei? Are you from Uber?"

"No, no," he shook his head.

Indeed he was no Sergei. Judging by his profile, his name was Tural Abdulaev, age 36.

"Sorry," I said.

Could I have misread the registration number? I slammed the door shut and walked all around the car. That's right. Same make, same model. I reopened the Uber app. Everything was correct.

I opened the car door again, the front one this time. "Are you taking the piss? Look here. This is the car I ordered. It's exactly like yours: the make, the color and registration number..."

Bang!

Damage taken: 269 (Punch)
Current Vitality: 92,11383%

I felt him snatch the smartphone from my hand, then heard the sound of the door shutting.

I shook my head, checking my teeth with my tongue. Everything was still in place.

All those intimidating oligarchs, alien demons, Dagestani boxers, emotionally unstable girls and just plain street hoods! I've had a gutful of them all!

My blood boiled with an adrenalin surge as I received another Righteous Anger buff. The next moment I was already leaping over hedges and parking barriers, chasing after the car thief.

Let's see whose Kung Fu was the strongest!

I ran with remarkable ease — unlike my quarry who, although he was giving it his all, didn't have enough coordination to negotiate all the obstacles in his way with the same ease. Three months ago I wouldn't have dreamed of ever catching up with him — or even chasing after him, for that matter. What's the point? That's how I used to think then. Or was that Phil even me?

Now I knew very well what I was going to do. In less than fifty yards, I'd brought the distance between us to a few paces. "Stay where you are!"

He turned round and saw me. Panicking, he tried to change direction but only made his situation worse. Desperately he tried to speed up but by now, the outcome was pretty clear because I was a better runner. I already began to figure out how to knock him off his feet...

A plastic bag carried by the wind landed under my feet at the worst possible moment. My foot slid treacherously, throwing me off balance. I sprawled onto the tarmac.

As I dropped, I could see I was falling face down onto a bit of a broken bottle which had somehow happened to be in exactly the wrong place.

My high Agility saved me as I tucked myself up, shifting my center of gravity and avoiding contact with the glass.

I felt neither pain nor fear, only a dogged anger about all the time I'd wasted. Meanwhile, Tural had mingled with the crowd, probably thinking that I was no longer a threat.

Yeah right.

I opened the interface. The map. Tural Abdulaev.

There he was, round the corner of the next six-story building, moving away from the street where I'd been chasing him.

I estimated my path and walked toward him from the opposite direction, holding the map with his marker open before my eyes. I walked unhurriedly, whistling the theme from *Kill Bill* while warming up my fists.

I turned the corner and stopped. Judging by the map, Tural was only a dozen paces away from me. Ten. Eight. Two. One...

I took another step round the corner, made sure it was indeed him, then knocked the wind out of him with a well-placed punch to his solar plexus. I grabbed him by the collar, dragged him into a gateway and repaid my debt to him with a hook to his jaw. "The phone, now!"

He groaned. "Which phone? Don't know what you mean," his heavily accented voice was filled with pain.

I couldn't hit someone who wouldn't defend themselves. Should I check his pockets? Not my thing, either. He might be acting so cool because he'd already passed the phone on to his accomplice.

"I see," I said. "So if you don't know what I mean, what am I supposed to do with you? Should we go and see the cops?"

"Why, what have I done?"

"They'll know what to do-" I choked on the phrase as my body swung round on instinct without waiting for a command from my brain to dodge a knife blade.

No idea what had triggered it: whether it had been the Righteous Anger or just all the action movies I'd been watching. I intercepted Tural's arm and twisted it behind his back until his hand opened, dropping a short knife with a handle bound with black insulation tape. It fell to the ground. I kicked it toward the nearby trash cans and gave him a good hiding, experiencing an enormous albeit belated relief from once again walking on the edge.

When he finally curled up on the tarmac, trying to protect himself from the blows raining down on him, I saw my phone dropping out of his track bottoms' pocket. I picked it up, made sure it was indeed mine and put it back into my own pants pocket. Then I paused, licking the blood off my knuckles I'd grazed on his teeth, as I wondered what to do to him next.

I might have let him go, I suppose (*social status level: 7, profession: migrant worker, married with four children*) but what was I supposed to do about his knife? He might have been "lucky" enough to finish me off with it. And that all because of an old telephone which on a good day wouldn't cost more than five thousand rubles.

Or should I take him to the precinct?

He began to stir, trying to scramble back to his feet.

I activated Lie Detection. "Listen, you. Tural!"

"Eh?" he startled, not at all surprised that I knew his name.

"Do you have ID?"

"The boss has my passport," he sat up on the tarmac looking at me from under his eyebrows and holding his swollen black eye.

He wasn't lying. "You wanna go see the cops?"

He shook his head.

"Then you'll have to answer a few questions. If you answer them honestly, I might let you go. Understood?"

He nodded.

"I can't hear you!"

"Yes."

"Why did you have to break into that car?"

He shrugged.

"I can't hear you!"

"Dunno. I thought I might find some money."

"Why don't you work?"

"I do. My boss don't pay me. Farkhad, my compatriot, fell to his death at the building site," he spoke with a heavy accent, pausing to choose the right words. He was telling the truth though. "The boss had problems with the building inspectors. He had to pay big fines... He got so angry he didn't pay anyone. My family back home have no money. I can't quit this job because the boss took my passport from me... It's not easy."

"Why do you carry a knife on you?"

"What can I do without it?" he sounded surprised. "I need to open cans and slice bread..."

"Or stab people. Have you ever tried to kill anyone else with it?"

"No!" he shook his head so hard it seemed to

almost come off. "It was the devil's work. I got really scared..."

"Did you ever steal anything else?"

His shoulders dropped.

"What exactly did you steal?"

"Just some cement."

"Cement?"

"Yes..."

"Anything else?"

"No. Only the cement and your telephone."

"Did you take anything else from the car?"

"There was nothing to take..."

He wasn't lying. His candor — just as the sincerity of many others with whom I'd spoken just lately — might have seemed unusual to the casual observer unable to appreciate the importance of having a high-level Charisma in any communications.

Having said that, he might have simply been well versed in the language of brute force.

"Okay," I said. "Now listen here. I can tell you a few things about yourself. Your name is Tural Abdulaev. You're thirty-six years old. You have a wife called Leyla and four children: three girls and a boy called Gani. I also know where they live. So I suggest you behave in my city. If I find out you've done something again... I'll find you. Is that clear?"

He began to nod, swearing on his health, his kids and the name of Allah.

"You have money?" I asked him.

"No. Where from? If I had any, you think I'd have robbed that car?"

"Take this," on impulse I pulled a thousand-ruble note out of my wallet and handed it to him. No idea why.

He stared at it in disbelief but didn't take it, expecting it to come with strings attached.

I let it slip through my fingers, watching it float to his feet. Let him think about it at his own leisure. Before the day was over, this incident would be the talk of their entire diaspora.

"Good luck, Tural," I said. "Don't bring disgrace upon your country. Maintain your dignity."

Leaving him open-mouthed, I quit the alley. I didn't care about the thousand rubles. He definitely needed them more than I did. Still, my heart felt warm and fuzzy with what had just happened.

I walked along the street smiling at the sun and the sky so blue it was almost transparent. I'd forgotten all about Khphor and his threats. Several system messages floated into my view in perfect harmony with my new outlook, forcing me to step toward the nearest building out of the way of passersby in order to read through this new windfall,

Your Reputation with Tural Abdulaev has improved!

Current Reputation: Respect 60/120

You've received 2000 pt. XP for performing a socially meaningful action!

Congratulations! You've received a new skill

level!

> *Skill name: Luck*
> *Current level: 12*
> *XP received: 500*

You've received 1000 pt. XP for successfully leveling up a main characteristic!

XP points left until the next social status level: 10990/16000

With a thud, a massive flower pot from some balcony high above smashed on the tarmac a mere pace away from me, throwing earth up everywhere.

Great timing to have received a new Luck level! You never know, had it not been for this extra Luck point, I might have been standing a few inches further on, directly in its path. It could have made a nice big hole in my head, depending on the storey it had dropped from.

I looked up, counting. Three... six... nine storeys. And an anxious old lady squinting at me shortsightedly from her ninth-floor balcony. She seemed to be shouting something to me but I couldn't quite make it out over the noise of the traffic.

I nodded to her reassuringly. Had her pot struck home, I wouldn't have gotten off so lightly.

The old lady disappeared inside. I stepped away from the building just in case and slumped onto a bench in a bus shelter nearby.

Luck! That's exactly what Valiadis had told me in the end, hadn't he? What was it he'd said? 'You're gonna need *every bit of luck you can get!*'"

At the time, I hadn't thought much about it. Just a standard farewell formula. But what if it was more than that? What if he'd meant real digitized virtual-reality luck?

In which case, how was I supposed to level up Luck faster than I was already doing it? It only grew whenever I took the right decisions or did something vitally important. Plus, of course, whenever I invested system points into it. As for the former, I couldn't really count on it; and as for the latter, I was afraid that Khphor might not allow me to live to see my next level.

I walked on, trying to keep to the middle of the sidewalk to avoid any unpleasant surprises both from the road and from the roofs. This wasn't going to save me from any wayward bricks but still provided a half-decent defense from any probability traps.

So for how long was I supposed to live like this? I could lock myself up in my own home, of course, but it too was packed with all sorts of unpredictable dangers: from boiling pots to the proverbial hair dryer falling into a tubful of water. This had to be addressed, otherwise I might not live to take the Trial.

The Trial! I should get on and prepare for it, shouldn't I? And what if I had to face that acid jelly again? How was I supposed to defeat it?

Never mind. I'd think about it tomorrow. And in the meantime...

"Okay, Google! How does one improve one's luck?"

Google showered me with heaps of search

results in the vein of *Four Ways to Attract Luck in Your Life*, *The Eighteen Laws of Chance* and all such Feng Shui stuff. The pages were lined with ads for magic shops selling various spells and love potions in true Hogwarts style.

As I swiped the phone screen, my finger lingered on one of the ads. The site promptly opened. It was called The Magic Shop of Miracles and Artifacts.

What happened next can't be explained by anything other than my improved Luck. This seemed to be some kind of franchise chain for gullible chumps — and apparently, they had one of their shops right here in my own city.

And not just that! The shop was located a couple of hundred yards from where I now stood, on the same street even. I might check them out. Not that I was so desperate but my mind was already grabbing at any opportunity.

I walked over there, making sure to remain doubly vigilant. No idea what I was hoping for. But when some unknown invisible force attempts to do away with you three times in the last thirty minutes, you start to believe in miracles.

I reached the shop without any further ado if you didn't mention the tramp who attacked me with a plastic bag which made a strange clanking noise. His Coordination was so poor that his powerful but badly aimed swing sent him flying onto the tarmac. I'd very nearly thought he was dead but he must have survived it judging by the string of colorful cusses he'd showered me with.

Just as I was about to enter the shop, a little bird did a number two on my head. No idea whether it had anything to do with yet another of the Vaalphors' probability traps — but I chose to think realistically, telling myself it was a good sign.

As soon as I opened the shop door, I was enveloped in the thick, tangy scent of incense. The doorbell clanged, informing the salesgirl — a goth chick with a tattooed arm and piercings covering almost all of her body — of my arrival.

She gave me a disinterested glance and continued to read, apparently convinced I wasn't their target customer.

I lingered over their wares, using Insight to ID every item: Slavic charms, Scandinavian runic love amulets, Chinese talismans, Aztec pendants, neuromediators and other such gold and silver trinkets.

Then Alik called me. "Phil? You coming or what? Veronica's been here three times already! She's waiting here for you now, says she's not going anywhere until she sees you! Mr. Katz is on his fourth cup of tea already, Stacy's fed up with making it! Kesha was here too — didn't you invite him over for a talk or something?"

"I'm not fed up!" Stacy's voice protested in the background.

"I'm coming," I said. "Are you managing to keep up with it?"

"Not really, Phil. Everybody demands to see you. We fill in the questionnaires and take their pictures but they just won't leave! They're waiting for you right there in the corridor. Gorelik has already come and yelled at us. Stacy managed to calm him down. Hurry it up a bit if you can!"

"Okay, okay, I'm on my way."

I slid the phone into my pocket, unable to take my eyes from a humble silver ring. About a quarter of an inch wide, it was plain and ordinary, its darkened silver not of the best quality. Had it not been for my Insight, I would have been none the wiser.

> *The Lucky Ring of Veles[28]*
> *+12 to Luck*
> *Silver: 875*
> *Weight: 0.094 oz.*
> *Durability: 499/500*
> *Price: $422,727*

The price was exorbitant. It made no sense, especially considering the paper price tag hanging off it:

> *1,900 rubles*

"Excuse me, miss? Could you show me that ring, please?"

---

[28] Veles: the second most important god in the Slavic pagan tradition, the patron god of herdsmen and the lord of the underworld.

Chapter Thirteen

TILT

They lost half a million at cards, but they've still got a few tricks up their sleeve...

Lock, Stock and Two Smoking Barrels

"ANYBODY ELSE?" I ASKED ALIK WHEN THE LAST OF THE waiting clients had finally left the office.

Alik didn't hear me, too busy talking to Veronica.

Mr. Katz leaned back on the couch after his marathon tea party, studying a most interesting tome of the *Administrative Offenses Code of the Russian Federation: Extended 2017 Edition.*

"That was the last one, Phil," Stacy replied

instead. "Want some tea?"

I cleared my dry throat. "I wouldn't say no."

My Spirit was almost at zero. I was parched from talking the whole day. Time seemed to have shrunk. So much had happened in these last twenty-four hours! Only last night, I'd hired Stacy, had a fight with Mohammed, been kicked out of the boxing class and split up with Vicky. This morning, I'd trained with Kostya, met up with Greg and Mr. Ivanov, spoken to Valiadis, made an incredibly important decision, felt the full weight of bad luck and barely avoided being stabbed with a knife...

Plus I'd doubled my Luck count.

The ring I'd bought at the magic shop fit my finger perfectly. I suppressed the desire to take it off and fiddle with it in my hand, too scared of losing it. In order to sell it to me, the tattooed salesgirl had spent a long time searching for it in her books but hadn't found it. So in the end, she sold it to me for the sum marked on the price tag.

Out of the ten thousand rubles I'd had on me this morning, I'd spent three on a guest card to the gym, about a thousand on transport around town and another thousand on my generous attempt to support Tural, the desperate migrant worker.

I'd be lying to you if I told you that the ring was in any way different. I sensed no waves of heat; no runes had appeared on its rim when heated. Just an ordinary ring which you could only pawn by weight.

The fact remained, it did work. My own interface profile was proof enough:

Luck: 12 (+12 from the Lucky Ring of Veles)

In total, that had brought my Luck to 24: almost two and a half times than that of an average person.

Was it a lot? Time would tell... provided I had it. The fact remained, nothing bad had happened to me on my way back to the office. The cab had arrived within minutes of my call. The driver was polite and sober, he had neither raced nor rammed any cars. To top it all, not a single brick had fallen from the roof of the business center. As I'd climbed the stairs up to the building, I'd even allowed myself to take them three at a time without stumbling even once. And when I'd come across Gorelik on my way to the office, he'd been too busy talking to Vazgen to actually notice me.

One person I did meet was Kesha. Without going into details of our upcoming partnership, I just made sure he was morally prepared to try himself at sales.

"I really don't know, Phil," he heaved a sigh by way of answering. "If it brings in some additional income, why not? I can always leave someone in the print shop so I might find some time to do it, I suppose. But of course I'd like to know more about it. What do you want me to sell? And to whom?"

"Let's discuss all the details tomorrow, okay? I've been away from the office all morning. The guys have just called me to say it's pandemonium. They want me back to sort it out."

"Not a problem. I'll pop in tomorrow."

As I reached our floor, I was confronted by a huge crowd in the corridor — and somehow I didn't think they were lining up for the latest iPhone. As I entered the office, I mouthed to Stacy so as not to put out the clients,

"Are they all here for us?"

She nodded.

I set to work...

NOW IT WAS way past six in the evening. The last client had just left. Finally, I could speak to everyone I'd originally planned to.

'Phil, have you finished?"

It was Veronica.

"Yes," I nodded, enjoying the delicious cup of tea offered by Stacy.

"Have you got a minute to step outside? I want to talk to you in private."

I nodded my agreement while still thinking about a theory I'd just had, impatient to check it out. What if I used the interface to search for any stat-boosting items? Something to boost my Luck, maybe? Or a watch with +10 to Speed? A fountain pen with a bonus to Intellect?

Still, I didn't want to rush it. This was serious business which demanded concentration and the meticulous wording of search queries. I'd better do it once back home.

Dammit! I had Gleb coming to see me tonight!

I checked my phone just in case but he hadn't yet called. Good. I got up from the desk and stretched, cracking all my stiff joints. "Outside?" I repeated.

"It's probably better to get a breath of fresh air,"

Veronica said. "The walls have ears."

"How mysterious. Let's go, then."

"Phil, do you want me to wait here?" I heard Mr. Katz's voice who'd by then completely merged with the furniture.

I slapped my forehead. I'd completely forgotten the old brief, snoring on our couch!

"I'm so sorry, Mark," I turned back to the redhead. "Veronica, can you wait a while? We only need to discuss a new contract. We won't be long."

She rolled her eyes, suppressing her impatience. "Okay, Phil, I'll wait. Stacy, what have you got there, coffee? Can you pour me some as well?"

Grunting and trying to smooth-talk his arthritis into showing some mercy, the old lawyer scrambled to his feet. I took him helpfully under his arm, led him to the desk and helped him sit. "Would you like some tea, Mark?"

"No, thanks. I think I've already overdone today's caffeine limit. I can already feel I won't be able to get any sleep tonight. How can I help you, Phil?"

"We need a contract template which we could use to offer our sales outsourcing services to other companies."

"Really? Okay, spit it out," the old man said with curiosity. "Tell me all about it."

We spent almost an hour talking. Finally, I felt sorry for Alik and Stacy who must have had plans for the evening. I wanted to let them go but they refused and said they'd wait for me. Veronica had already wandered off somewhere but was now back. And the old lawyer was still busy showering me with questions and demanding more details, revealing the kinds of pitfalls I couldn't even have envisioned.

"Well, I got the full picture," he finally rubbed his withered hands, "although I don't think I'll be able to make out a draft contract by tomorrow. I need to check a number of documents. I might have it done by Friday in which case I suggest we meet up and discuss what we've got. I'm pretty sure, by then both you and I might have some adjustments to make."

"That's excellent. Thank you so much for waiting all that time."

"Don't mention it!" he tittered. "It wasn't all that difficult. Makes no difference to me where I sleep. And the tea's good."

"You should come more often," Stacy said, apparently eavesdropping. "You don't need an excuse to come. You can have all the tea you want."

"Thank you, my darling. I'd dearly love to but I'm afraid Rose will be jealous," he guffawed.

Jesus. The girl was only working her first day and she was already friends with everybody. Gorelik's bookkeeper had given her the potted plants; she was already good friends with Veronica — and now the old boy was calling her his darling!

Alik helped the old lawyer over to the stairs. Stacy began preparing to shut the office down for the night.

Veronica heaved a sigh of relief, "Finally! You know it's not fair, don't you? I was the first to set up a meeting with you. Yesterday you were with your wife —

or girlfriend, whoever; then this morning you had a meeting with the teapot, then you just disappeared , then you saw all those clients and Mr. Katz and only after that — it's finally your turn, Veronica! And to tell you the truth, you need this conversation more than I do."

"Whoa, easy!" I said, slightly taken aback. "No need to get mad at me. Had you told me that this was urgent, important, whatever, I'd have spoken to you a long time ago."

"Oh really? Thanks a bunch, Mr. Punctuality. You're just trying to come up with excuses, that's what you're do-"

My phone rang, interrupting her emotional albeit not quite deserved rebuke. I apologized and took it.

"Phil, is that you?"

"Gleb? Oh, hi. Are you on your way?"

"I'm at your place but it doesn't look as if you're here. I've got a crate of beer with me and some snacks."

"Stay there. I won't be long."

"Wait a sec. There's been a funny old boy here. He's a bit weird. He was fishing, asking how long I knew you and what I wanted from you."

"What did you say?"

"I told him to go stuff himself," Gleb replied, impassive as usual. "Nicely, of course. Okay, I think I'm gonna wait for you on the bench outside. I might play a bit of CoC[29], if you know what I mean."

---

[29] CoC — Clash of Clans, a mobile strategy video game

"Okay. See ya."

I uttered the last words in the dark as Alik had already switched off the lights. We walked out of the office, and he locked the door behind us.

We left the building. All the other guys bade their goodbyes and went their own ways, leaving me and Veronica alone on the street.

"Sorry, Veronica, I'm afraid I'm a bit pressed for time," I said. "I've got a friend waiting for me. I completely forgot we had an appointment."

"I've totally gathered that. Still, what I need to tell you might take some time. I could give you a lift and we could talk on the way."

"It's only a couple of blocks down the road. Not enough time to start discussing whatever it is."

"And what if I join you?" she suddenly asked. "I hope your girlfriend — or your wife, whatever — won't mind?"

Her open smile glowed white in the thickening dusk. Her eyes glistened with an emerald light.

Her words reminded me of the fact that I was free again. I hadn't told anyone about me and Vicky splitting up and still I had a feeling that this girl — Veronica? Vera? Nica? — knew it somehow. No idea how girls do it but they do. They seem to sense this sort of thing. It's as if the ex-girlfriend sets her man's counter back to zero as she leaves, deleting a marker from his forehead that says in a language known only to women, "this male is already taken".

"I don't think so," I finally said. "Some other time, sure. But it looks like my friend has some kind of problems we might need to discuss in private. So we'd better discuss it now."

"If you say so," she replied. "In any case, I'd rather give you a lift. At least that way your friend won't have to wait for you outside."

Judging by her Interest bar, she was seriously into this conversation — or me, even. All kinds of thoughts flashed through my head, from the raciest fantasies to some crazy parallel-world theories.

I managed to squeeze myself into her tiny Kia tucking my legs under me. She leaned against me unabashedly, feeling for the gear stick. When I finally buckled up and made myself halfway comfortable, I activated Lie Detection and gave her the address.

"I'll get you there in a tick," she nodded at two cans of soda sitting between the seats. "Water, Pepsi? Help yourself!"

"So what is it you wanted to talk to me about?"

"And what do you think? Any ideas?" she turned her head and flashed me a smile, her ginger hair fiery in the lights of an oncoming car.

"None whatsoever. And the few that I might have had are pretty irrelevant as they don't require privacy."

My throat rasped as I spoke, so I had to help myself to some of the water.

"Okay. I'm not going to pussyfoot around," she said. "You don't happen to be looking for a PR director, do you?"

I choked on the water. "What did you say?" I paused, trying to take her suggestion in. "A PR director? For us?"

"Why not?"

"Veronica, you seem to forget we've only been open for three weeks. Not even. And we've only just started getting customers."

"You are expanding, though, aren't you? You did hire Stacy."

"Bah! Stacy hasn't really asked for much. She seems to be pretty undemanding. But she brings us a wealth of good..."

"I'm not asking for much, either. I only want to help."

"You?"

"Why not? I have a college diploma in PR. I graduated with honors."

"Veronica, I don't want to blow my own trumpet but we seem to get business without any PR efforts. Why would we waste money on advertising?"

"Phil, I know you're smart but you're so stupid sometimes," she almost growled at me. "Don't you understand you need to move to a new level? You know why, don't you? The way you work now, you've hit a ceiling. Can you tell me how many clients you see each day? Even if you work 24/7 finding jobs for everyone — which is technically impossible — and even if your clients start to line up around the block, it's still a maximum of what, fifty to sixty customers a week? How much are they gonna bring in? You might eventually train Alik to find jobs for them as effectively as you do but... you know what I mean?"

"Sure. We can't bite more than we can chew. So what do you suggest?"

"You could sign up with recruiting agencies. It's common practice. You send them potential candidates, and if the agency's happy with them, it'll pay you five or ten — up to fifteen even — percent of their annual salary. *Annual*, Phil."

"Okay. But you shouldn't think I didn't consider this kind of practice. I just wasn't going to adopt it at this stage. In any case, what's a PR director got to do with it?"

"I'll tell you now. The thing is, I personally know at least half of all the city's companies. I could help you. You don't even have to do anything. If you agree to what I'm saying, I'll be on their case tomorrow morning, talking to all their HR girls. Would you like to give me a trial period? That way I could show you what I can-"

"Could you stop the car here, please," I interrupted her spiel as we'd already arrived at my house.

She killed the engine and waited for me to reply.

I knew she was right. She spoke from the heart, too. The only thing that worried me was the fact that I wasn't used to strangers offering their help so openly. Also, expanding didn't sound like a very wise thing to do at the moment. In this I completely agreed with Vicky.

"So what do you think?" she finally said.

"Give me a couple of days to mull over it, okay? It does make sense what you're saying. I'd love to take you up on your offer but I'd like our cooperation to be mutual — and I still don't know what I can offer you."

"Okay. Mull it over, then. See you tomorrow?"

"Sure. See you," I reached for the door handle but paused. "Why did you want to speak to me in private? We could have discussed it in the office with the other guys, couldn't we?"

"Where did you see a company director holding interviews or meeting partners in front of the staff?"

"I'm not really a director, am I?"

"Who are you, then? You'd better get used to it..."

Someone knocked hard on my car window. I swung round.

Vazgen was peering into the car, his face grim. With a nod of his head, he gestured to me to get out.

Veronica heaved a doomed sigh. "Unbelievable. He tracked me down."

She rolled down the window, letting in the disheveled head of the PVC window vendor.

"I knew you were with him, *da*?"

Today his voice was especially melancholic.

"Let me get out and we can talk," I told him, then turned to Veronica. "Thanks for the lift. See ya!"

She tried to protest but I'd already swung the passenger door open, pushing the hot-blooded Caucasian male aside. "Let's go and have a talk... Othello."

"I can bury you right here and now," he said without much enthusiasm.

"Let's go and talk, and then we'll see about it. You might have no reason to bury me at all."

"Phil, don't!" Veronica's anxious voice came from the car. "Don't bother!"

Oh yes, I did have to bother, if only to sort this out here and now. Also, for some reason I really wanted to reassure the guy. Not to avoid any confrontation but just to help him get this corrosive jealousy out of his system.

I peeked through the half-opened window. "Stay in the car," I warned Veronica.

I walked off and stopped by an old gnarly oak tree.

Vazgen followed after me. "And?"

"Nothing. Why are you being such a drama queen?"

"What? Who? Me?" his eyes opened wide as his initial surprise gave way to fury.

"Yes, you. You saw something, came up with a story around it, drew your own conclusions and got all upset about it. What's Veronica got to do with it? Or myself, for that matter?"

"Don't you ever speak to me like-" his mouth quivered, preparing to shower curses at me.

"Stop it, now," I stood my ground even though his face was now within inches from mine. "Just stop it. Do you have something to charge me with?"

He was so close I could see every blood vessel in his inflamed eyes. He flared his nostrils as he breathed in fast shallow gasps, either with anxiety or indignation, I couldn't really tell.

Which was exactly why I'd decided to let him vent here and now. In people like him, any pent-up resentment had a tendency to accumulate and ripen without the need for any extra encouragement, maturing like a good wine.

"Did I tell you not to get anywhere near my girl? Did I? I told you that, *da*?" he kept repeating as if winding himself up.

"You did, yes. So I didn't. Even though she's not your girl and definitely not your property. There's nothing between us. I'm telling you this only to put your mind at ease."

"Who do you think you are?" he grabbed at my lapels. "Speak up! I'm perfectly calm!"

"Get your hands off me. Now."

He didn't. Instead, he pulled me toward himself, then threw his head back and head-butted my nose.

Tried to head-butt it, rather.

A thought played in the back of my mind: how exactly had the Vaalphors tampered with our reality to allow Vazgen to notice me get into Veronica's car and decide to track us down?

With my mind still busy pondering, my body swayed sideways slowly and almost melancholically, without releasing any hormonal surges but simply obeying my knee-jerk reflexes. My shirt buttons flew everywhere as I escaped his grip, leaving thin air in place where my forehead had just been. In the meantime, my left hand performed a left hook to his liver, knocking the wind out of him.

You've dealt critical damage to Vazgen Karapetyan: 285 (Punch)

I automatically followed with a right hook to his

head but stopped it within an inch from his cheekbone. This was plenty to cool him down for the time being. I had no intention of beating him up. I knew how he felt. I held no grudge against him.

"Now listen to me, *da?*" I whispered to his ear, locking his neck in a choke hold. "There's nothing between me and Veronica. None of the things that seem to worry you so much. You'd better believe it. We're workmates, that's all. Do you understand? Or do you want me to explain it again?"

No idea what it was: his humiliation in front of Veronica, the physical discomfort or my Power of Persuasion skill, but he stopped struggling and slackened in my grip.

You've dealt critical damage to Vazgen Karapetyan: verbal injury
  -25% to Spirit
  -25% to Confidence

"I do," he finally said.
"You do what?"
"I understand."
"Good."

I let go of his neck and stepped aside just in case, remembering the earlier incident with one of his compatriots today.

As I turned round, I saw Veronica who'd ignored my request to stay in the car. I gestured to her to get back in. She obeyed without saying a word.

That was funny. I wasn't really used to people

listening to me. Having said that, I'd asked her to stay put, hadn't I?

My Lie Detection was still active.

"Quits?" I offered Vazgen my hand.

He stared at it for a while, looked up at me, then answered my handshake. "Quits..."

He paused, thinking, then exploded in a hot hasty flood of words, "Sorry, brother. I saw you two together going somewhere. The blood just went to my head. My heart nearly stopped..."

His words didn't feel particularly warm — regarding Lie Detection, I mean — but they didn't feel cold, either. He wasn't lying. That's exactly how he felt even though he wasn't very sorry about it, his losing the fight being his only regret.

Only later, when I'd already parted ways with the PVC windows vendor, bidden goodbye to Veronica and headed for Gleb sitting on the bench staring into his smartphone, did I realize that Lie Detection seemed to have had a quaint effect on people I spoke to, forcing them to open up.

I summoned Martha who confirmed my conjecture.

The program adapts to the user and evolves as he progresses, I remembered one of my first discussions with her.

It looked like the laconic skill descriptions offered by the system didn't give you the whole picture.

* * *

I WALKED OVER TO GLEB AND STOOD NEXT TO HIM FOR A while, watching him. He was playing online poker — with real money, by the looks of it. He seemed to be in a bad way. He was wearing an old faded pair of jeans with an oily spot on one knee, worn-down dress shoes of what once must have been patent leather and a loose green short-sleeved shirt. His hair was greasy. He scratched the back of his head, made a decisive wave of his hand clutching a smoldering cigarette and went all-in.

He then held his breath and froze, whispering,
"Come on now! Do it! Respond!"

His mantra seemed to have worked as the last remaining opponent went all-in, too.

Gleb had a decent hand: a Big Slick and a flop of 2, 7 and A. Which meant he already had two aces — and if he managed to get another one, he'd have trips even though the chances of it were rather slim.

The virtual dealer showed all the cards. Before the last card was opened, I could see Gleb was still winning because his opponent had a pair of 7s.

My friend tensed up, his nails digging deep into his white-knuckled fists as he mumbled a prayer.

The dealer showed the last card: a 7.

His opponent had runs of 7s which meant Gleb's two pairs had just lost.

Having realized he hadn't had any more money, the poker app promptly suggested he topped up his balance.

Still oblivious of my presence, my friend finished his cigarette off down to the filter in a couple of powerful drags, then took a swing and smashed his phone on the tarmac.

The broken pieces landed at my feet. Finally realizing he wasn't alone, he looked up at me, squinting shortsightedly as he tried to work out who it was standing in front of him. He never could see very well at dusk and now after the bright phone screen, his eyesight took some time to adapt.

"Hi," I said. "Are you playing?"

"Ah, it's you," he wheezed. "Did you see it?"

"How much did you lose?"

He startled. "What, now? Or in total?"

"We'll talk about that when we get upstairs. I take it, this is the problem you wanted to talk to me about. So how much was it this time?"

"Er... I borrowed some money from someone. Ten grand[30]. I've just lost it all! And I was winning! I had thirty grand! I even thought I should have put half of it aside to pay the guy off and play with the rest."

"But you didn't?"

"I did! But then I wagered it again when I'd lost all my winnings. I thought I might bounce back. But you saw it yourself, didn't you? Just not my day. Who'd have thought that this idiot would get a third 7?"

"Yeah, I noticed. You had better chances. But why did you break your phone?"

"To give up playing," he mouthed. "Yes. In any

---

[30] About $150

case, I don't have the money to go on."

"Okay. Come on, you can tell me all about it upstairs. Are these yours?"

He nodded. I picked up a few shopping bags packed full of cheap beer and bagfuls of chips. "Come on, then."

By the time I was done with my first beer, anxious about the growing Intoxication debuff, Gleb had already downed three and gone to the bathroom, leaving me pondering over my own dark memories.

He and I, we both had a compulsive streak. We'd started spending time in gaming halls already in our freshman year, clubbing together and sharing both our winnings and our losses[31]. Because when you lose your last money, it's easier to survive it when you have someone to share it with. Someone you could pour your heart out to and discuss things, ending with a naïve hope to recuperate your losses. Because it's not gambling that ruins you: it's trying to win it back. As both of us had parents in the same city, we hadn't been left starving and homeless, but at a certain moment I personally had gotten fed up with this vicious circle. Think for yourself: I was working hard and studying at the same time, I made very decent money only to lose it all in one evening, not even.

One time he and I had just been paid by one of those fast food joints which was known for hiring students. We'd already had plans for the money: Gleb

---

[31] In the 1990s, gaming halls were legal in Russia, mushrooming virtually on every street corner and open to everyone

needed a new phone while I wanted to finally ask Marina out, a girl I knew from campus. I had no idea where it might go from there but I definitely could use some money to get this relationship on the road. By then, I'd already stopped pestering my parents for money, trying to pay for all my entertainment myself.

Then we'd come up with what we thought was a bright idea: to go and spend a fraction of it on one-arm bandits. At the time, they were everywhere in town and we'd been round them all.

If we'd won, that would have allowed Gleb to buy a better phone. And as for me... I couldn't even remember what I'd hoped for. A college student always has plenty on his wish list.

To cut a long story short, we'd lost our quota in the first thirty minutes and spent the rest of the hour trying to win it back. It really hurt to lose our hard-earned money, so we started raising the stakes and lost twice as much. By then, each of us had only about half our wages left.

That's when we were struck by an even brighter idea: to bet everything we still had on black. Because that particular hall had an electronic roulette wheel, too.

Predictably, it fell on red. It had taken us an hour to piss a month's worth of hard work into the wind.

That was when I'd first experienced this eerie feeling when you completely forget about the consequences, including your plans to take a girl out. I could neither eat nor drink; we just sat there chain-smoking, thinking desperately where to find the money to recoup our losses. We'd finally finished our marathon gambling session in the morning of the following day when we'd lost everything we could have begged and borrowed — both from our parents and from our college buddies.

It hadn't happened in one go. We kept lying to our families who'd scrape together some money for us which we'd then take back to the slot machine hall. Still hoping to win it back quickly, we would play for big stakes, always on a lookout for hot slots. We'd change them, taking turns pressing buttons, betting up or down, and basically using all the gambling superstitions which you adopt quickly once you start betting something more important than just a portion of your wage.

Having lost everything again, we'd have another brainstorm in order to decide whom to borrow more money from. At four a.m., when all our reserves had been depleted, Gleg had finally scraped together enough courage for us to go and see his girlfriend. She used to work with us so we knew for sure she had money because we'd been all paid out together.

Now, I still smart at the memory — but at the time, we couldn't have cared less. This girl whose name I can't even remember gave Gleg everything she had left. Still groggy from her sleep, she couldn't quite work out what was going on. All she knew was the boy she loved was in trouble and that she could help.

"It's all right, babe, I'll explain to you later, we need to help a friend out. I'll pay you back as soon as I can! Thank you!" Gleb mumbled as he took her money, every single penny she had.

Knowing this was our last chance, we took every possible precaution. Either it was common sense that had finally prevailed, or the realization that we were hungry and that we'd still have to survive for a month somehow once the night was over — once we'd paid back everything we'd borrowed, of course.

Either the machines were prop full and had started to pay out, or we'd chosen wiser strategies and stopped betting so recklessly but Lady Luck must have taken pity on us — or most likely, decided to teach us an even harder lesson. In any case, by the time the hall closed for the morning maintenance break we'd had won back almost everything other than our wages.

I knew we shouldn't have left but by then, we were on a roll. The winning steak had given us wings. We put some money on black again and it came up red. We used the Martingale strategy doubling our bets — and it came up red again. By then, we were on a tilt so we bet everything we still had.

It came up zero.

We were idiots, what do you want? We'd spent the next year trying to pay off all the debts. We'd even thought we'd quit gambling for good. Still, as time went by, we'd forgotten the bad parts. Both of us had gotten back on our feet financially. We started earning more. So after a night out in a bar, instead of going home, one of our friends suggested we went to a casino.

"Why not? No one forces us to play, right? We'll only pay the entrance fee. That way we'll get our drinks free!"

So we had the free drinks. Then we played a little and even won a few times, then left utterly pleased with ourselves.

But afterwards, Gleb and I started to frequent it. We dismissed slot machines as being a rip-off and concentrated on the casino poker which for some reason seemed honest to us at the time. Because if you think about it, a dealer can't just deal the cards he wants.

Morons. It had taken us a long time to realize that the casino would always come out best.

Still we continued going there for over a year — until the memorable night when I'd borrowed all of Gleb's money and never returned it. We stopped seeing each other, and without our team play, the game had lost its attraction to me. Also, I was already getting involved with the World of Warcraft which seemed to quench my compulsive streak.

In the meantime, Gleb had married Lena who was two years ahead of us at college, and even fathered two sons with her. Still, he'd carried on playing. Knowing his weakness, he'd surrendered the family budget to his wife and replaced the gambling halls and casinos — the access to which had by then been restricted in Russia — with online poker. He took out a special bank card where he secretly deposited the proceeds of any occasional jobs and used it to play.

Because by then, he played everywhere: at work, at home and out in the street using his smartphone.

Whenever he won, he'd buy presents for his wife

and kids. He never bought anything for himself. Any losses he took in his stride, knowing he couldn't share his secret with anyone, least of all his wife. On the one occasion that he'd admitted his shameful addiction, his wife didn't speak to him for several days, then gave him an ultimatum: it was either the game or the family.

Gleb chose his family. Still, he kept playing.

He kept losing more and more until finally he was on another tilt and borrowed so much money from everyone that he was forced to take out a loan. He thought he might bounce back and pay it all off...

"D'you want it opened?" Gleb asked when he'd come back, reaching into the bag for another beer.

"Yes, please."

We walked out onto the balcony as Gleb was already dying for another smoke. As he was clicking his lighter, I asked him,

"So what's gonna happen now? What kind of loan did you take out? Do you have so many debts?"

"I told you already. It's over two million[32]."

"How much?" my mind couldn't take it in. How could he have lost so much? "And the loan?"

"The loan isn't so big. Relatively, of course. It's two hundred grand. I managed to raise the same amount by borrowing it. And as for the rest..." he drew noisily on his cigarette and washed it down with beer without exhaling.

"Come on, out with it."

"Now I'm really deep in it, Phil. I'm in it good and

---

[32] Over $30,000

proper," he relaxed and spoke quickly, swallowing the words. "I found a sports poker club in town. I saw their ad online. Like, they were holding a poker tournament. Everyone was welcome. The entry fee was seven thousand but I thought, with my experience, I stood a decent chance. The most important thing was to get to the final table."

"What experience are you talking about? Are you off your rocker? You've been playing all your life either against a casino dealer or online even! It's completely different! You can't even keep a poker face! And when you face a real-life opponent..."

"I know, Phil, I know! I do now! Actually, I performed quite well. I told Lena I was on a business trip and went to the tournament instead. I played for almost twenty-four hours with a short break until I made it to the final table. So that time I managed to get my money back. And even won some."

"And?"

"And what?" Gleb barked, so annoyed that he even spilled his beer over himself.

"Do I take it that this isn't the whole story?"

"Almost. I liked it probably too much. The award ceremony, everybody shaking my hand, my winnings warming my pocket... And the whole thing, you know. My Lena's always at home, overweight. And those girls there, they were all over me. All the really cool guys speaking to me as if I was their equal. It's a sport, you know. You get some respect, not to even mention other things. I probably heard too many stories about guys going through the ranks until they reached international level and won hundreds of thousands of dollars — millions even. I imagined myself quitting my job. I could already see myself flinging my work contract in the face of that scumbag boss of mine, then taking Lena and the kids on vacation."

"Where to?"

"To the seaside, preferably. My youngest has asthma. He needs the sea air."

"And?"

"I started playing in the club with those guys. At first, I went there once a month, then one a week until finally, I played there almost every evening. I was doing okay for a while, winning some, losing some, but keeping my head above water. Until finally I hit a bad streak. I just had no luck at all. I tried everything: taking it easy, bluffing, calculating the pot odds and the hands odds — nothing. I had nothing but junk, can you imagine? And that night, I finally was on a winning streak. I had straights and flushes and even a couple of full houses. Imagine! I spent a good fifty grand on tips alone! Shit, there's no more beer. Wait here, I'll go get some."

"No, you stay here! You can hardly speak as it is! Finish your story first! What happened next?"

"What happened next? I was sitting pretty. I'd already started thinking how I'd buy a PlayStation for the kids, pay back my debts and have enough money to go to Turkey."

"That's when you should have left!"

"That's exactly what I was going to do! I decided to stay just one last hand. I had a flush, can you imagine? I still remember it: Ace-King-10-6-3. I went all-in — and he went all-in too!"

"Who's he?"

"Just a guy. They called him Dimedrol. He's some sort of police big wig. He gave me the creeps. When you look at him, he's all so friendly, he cracks jokes, but his eyes are... how can I put it... they're *dead*. He always plays big."

Strange associations began to swell in my mind. Wet earth... fire... "And?"

"And I was in the crap. Or so I thought at the time. But it was only the beginning. To cut a long story short, he beat me with his straight flush. Can you imagine? It's a once-in-a-lifetime thing and he happened to have had it just as I was about to leave! And then he was all so sympathetic about it. He kept saying, 'It's all right, Gleb, you can still win it back!'"

His voice quivered, betraying resentment. He was angry with himself, with Lady Luck, with the mysterious Dimedrol and even with his own addiction.

"So you lost all your winnings, and then what?" I asked. "How did you manage to lose such an enormous amount of money? That's two million we're talking about!"

"How can I say... This Dimedrol offered me to play on credit. Like, who needs to keep tabs between friends? And then I got really unlucky..."

He continued talking, struggling with his words and barely making any sense. Still, I managed to get the general gist of it before he passed out.

This time, he'd hit a brick wall and lost thirty

thousand dollars. He had to pay it back with interest before the end of the month. The clock was ticking. Apparently, this Dimedrol had promptly stopped being a sympathetic funny guy, transforming into a cruel loan shark... with dead eyes.

"If you can't pay back, Gleb, I'm afraid you'll have to sell your apartment. A card debt is a sacred thing. It has to be paid no matter what! Understood?"

As if to confirm the seriousness of his words, the club's staff had suddenly lost all interest in Gleb. All those saucy waitresses and old poker partners, previously so nice and friendly, now gave the unlucky client the cold shoulder, to the point where Gleb had been barred from entering the club on the sole occasion when he'd finally scraped some money together hoping to recuperate his losses.

Dimedrol, however, kept sending reminders delivered by goons with predatory eyes who darkly hinted at some potential accidents involving Gleb's kids or something even worse happening to his wife, adding that it would be in his own interests not to delay his payments.

His family was still none the wiser even though his wife must have suspected something because she'd stopped talking to him altogether. It looked like she was about to file for divorce. To add insult to injury, Gleb had been fired for constantly not turning up for work — and whenever he *had* turned up, he was drunk.

Having told me all that, Gleb passed out right in front of me.

I carried him to the couch, surprised at how

much weight he'd lost since our last meeting. He seemed to weigh barely a hundred pounds, like a teenager.

I sat next to him and spent a long time looking at his gaunt face, the days of stubble, the disheveled hair. He looked old before his time. Even in his sleep he couldn't relax. He wheezed heavily, breathing in fits, and startled as if fruitlessly trying to escape a never-ending nightmare.

It took him about an hour to finally fall into a deep sleep. His features softened; he must have dreamed about playing with his children on a snow-white beach by the sea as his wife smiled at them from a deck chair.

The idea which had started to form as he was recounting his somber story to me had by now crystallized into a clear-cut plan.

"Sleep, sleep, my friend. Everything will come out fine. I'll make sure you take your family to the sea, after all."

I powered up the laptop, opened the browser and found an online poker school site.

To the accompaniment of Gleb's snoring, I spent the next several hours studying their content until I'd brought my Poker Playing skill up to 4. Interestingly, during the last hour, my advance had almost stopped and any more theory study wasn't producing any results.

I looked at my Lucky Ring of Veles, kissed it and opened an online poker site.

"Come on now, let's play!"

CHAPTER

FOURTEEN

THE CHEATER

He who's not afraid of looking like a fool can fool anyone.

Alexander Zorich, Rapid Fire

"MIAOW," BORIS SAID GENTLY AS SHE JUMPED ONTO MY lap and nudged my chest with her nose.

"Wait a sec. You'll get your breakfast in a moment," I checked my watch, "say, in thirty or forty minutes?"

Normally, I needed at least three hours of sleep. I didn't have any training with Kostya that morning and I could give my running a miss. So I had until 8 a.m. to get some sleep which meant I had to go to bed around 4.30. It was now almost 3 a.m. and I had another 30% left to make my target level 5 in Poker.

I'd only put $20 on the game account. I wasn't striving for big wins at the moment. I only needed to level up.

The main difference with online poker is that you can't see your opponents' faces. As a result, you can't read their reactions, both to their own cards and everybody else's. Novice poker players who can't control their emotions very well can be easily discerned within the first hour of a real-world game. They behave somewhat differently depending on the hand they have. They bluff both ways, pretending a weak hand to be strong, and vice versa — but provided your Insight is sufficient, you can read them like an open book.

When you play online, however, you don't see your opponents' faces. That's when you have to pay attention to their way of playing. I spent the whole first hour doing just that, trying to play as unpredictably as I could. I'd raise the stakes with an empty hand, then lay again, fearful, the moment someone counterattacked, and basically, did everything to create the impression I was a "fish" — poker slang for a newbie. I wasn't sure that any of the players had paid any attention to it — not at this petty bets stage, anyway — but those who had, must have drawn their own conclusions.

Wrong conclusions, I have to admit, because as soon as I'd studied everybody else, I'd stopped betting on everything in sight and started playing in accordance with pure mathematics and the theory of probability, calculating my hand's chances against the bank. By then, my partners must have been convinced they were dealing with a risk-taking idiot because they began to respond to my bets and raises exactly when I wanted them to.

In the following hours, out of about thirty rounds I only had four decent hands. No idea what exactly had been at work here: whether it was pure chance, my good calculations or my high Luck numbers in combination with the Ring of Veles, but out of those four good hands three had brought in excellent winnings while the fourth one ended with my opponent throwing his hand in, not wanting to risk it.

So now I was going all-in with two pairs on a flop of K and 10, with 5 as a third card. Both my remaining opponents had already demonstrated their inability to stop even when they'd been dealt terrible hands, so there was a decent chance of them staying in the game.

And that's exactly what happened. Both of them called, but one of them had three 5s which beat my hand.

I mentally kissed my money goodbye. The entire range of emotions flashed through my heart in a mere couple of seconds, from anger and resentment — because the turn didn't change anything — to hope and unbridled joy as another 10 came on the river. I had a senior full house.

I'd won.

I stared at my chips and the number $238 next to them, sensing the long-forgotten gambler's high. In just two hours, I'd multiplied my money twelvefold!

My heart was racing, bringing my heart rate well

over 160. I hadn't had such a pulse rate for a long time, even during my training sessions.

You'd think the money was negligible. But had I placed larger bets...

Bang! A new system message came down like a guillotine,

You're experiencing a Gambler's High!

Warning! You're playing a game of chance! A massive surge of hormones has been detected: adrenaline, dopamine, serotonin, endorphin...

Your breathing and heart rate have increased. Your reactions to pain and external stimuli are weakened. You're at risk of experiencing manic obsession.

Your metabolic rate has increased 33%.

Warning! You're at risk of losing control and acting irrationally to the point of becoming dysfunctional.

Warning! High probability of spontaneously developing the Gambler debuff:

-1 to Perception every 72 hrs.
-2 to Intellect every 72 hrs.
-10% to Satisfaction every 2 hrs.
-10% to Vigor every 2 hrs.
-75% to Self-Control
-75% to Decision Making

The abhorrent memories of my and Gleb's ignominious gambling past flashed through my mind. My scared hand pressed the "Close window" icon almost on its own accord.

> *Congratulations! You've received a new skill level!*
> *Skill name: Self-Control*
> *Current level: 5*
> *XP received: 500*
> *Current level: 15. XP points gained: 12950/16000*

I rubbed my eyes and face, stretched my numb limbs, then got up quickly from the table and walked over to the balcony. Despite the AC blazing, Gleb's breathing did nothing to freshen up the air in the room, filling it with the powerful stench of stale alcohol.

Gradually I came back to my senses. I needed to sort a few things out, so I summoned Martha.

"Hi, Phil!" she said. "Are you all right? You look a bit... tired."

"Hi yourself. Could you check the logs for me, please?"

"I've already done it. Would you like me to look for something in particular?"

"I'm curious about the Gambler debuff. In the description of the Gambler's High it says that it can develop spontaneously."

"It can indeed. It depends on a lot of factors: whether the user's life is exciting and eventful in other respects, his or her degree of happiness overall, as well as the respective levels of their spirit, willpower, self-control and self-discipline. These are only the main things."

"And how long can it last?"

"In the case of an average human not being assisted by the interface, both the degree of addiction and the probability of recovery are comparable to those of alcohol and drug addiction. In the case of an interface user, it may take anywhere from seven to forty-nine days, depending on the development of the aforementioned skills. The debuff unfolds in several stages..."

"I got it. Don't worry."

We spent the next few minutes in silence as I weighed up all the risks. Poker playing still figured heavily in my plans to save Gleb, with the sole difference that now I'd have to finish playing before receiving the debuff. Otherwise such low Self-Control and Decision Making numbers could make me unfit for work for a good week at least. Not to mention Vigor and Satisfaction which might be a struggle to keep up.

"Okay, Marth. I think I'd better go to bed."

"One moment, Phil."

"Yes, what is it?"

"Could you activate me more often, please? It would be a good idea if you asked my advice before making any big decisions. Because, you know, two heads..."

"...are better than one, is that it? Very well, girl. In this case, I have something else to ask you. You don't happen to have a real-life prototype, do you?"

She gave me a teasing smile. "The current level of your Insight skill is insufficient to access the information you've requested. Bye, Phil. See you."

She disappeared. I yawned heartily, realizing that I felt okay again. The Gambler's High was gone. In theory, I could go and play some more to bring the Poker Playing skill up to 5. Instead, I logged back in to the site from my phone, transferred my winnings to my bank card and went to sleep.

My overwrought brain was still buzzing, my eidetic memory offering me images of mismatched playing cards, winning combinations and growing stacks of chips. I forced all that junk out of my head, replacing it with pictures of sheep jumping over a fence.

By the ninety-sixth sheep, I was asleep.

I'D FORGOTTEN TO RESET THE INTERFACE ALARM CLOCK, hadn't I? It dutifully woke me up at 6 a.m. I'd have loved to have slept in but this bastard program had dutifully chosen "the best awakening time based upon the user's sleep cycle" so I was wide awake now. I tossed and turned some more, fruitlessly trying to go back to sleep but my brain was already fully awake and making plans for today.

At work, I still had to finish up yesterday's conversation with Kesha. I had big plans for him in our future outsourcing sales department. I just hoped he'd agree.

I also had to come up with a job role for Veronica. Headhunting services, why not? The only problem was, I hadn't yet tried to use my search function in reverse order — that is to say, trying not to match a man to a company but a company to a man.

Should I try now, maybe?

I opened the interface and activated the map, then conjured up the image of our agency, using all the KIDD points known to me: our name, address, field of expertise, and its workers: myself, Stacy and Alik. Keeping this data in mind, I tried to put myself in the shoes of some imaginary commercial director who'd be competent enough to sell our B2B services. I added some personal traits to the person's description: good communication skills, experience in sales, high energy levels, efficiency and integrity.

Then I clicked *Search.*

The map of Russia lit up with hundreds of green markers. I restricted the search to our city. About twenty markers were still left. I added another search parameter regarding their wages and commission.

That left me with six.

I added another search parameter: the probability of quitting their current work and moving to our agency. That left me with two: a certain Irina Soltzman, 27 years old, and... Innokenty "Kesha" Dimidko, 34 years old.

Bingo.

By now, I knew too much about the role of luck to believe in such coincidences. Even if you took my agency, I'd come across that business center by sheer coincidence: I'd simply called them and spoken to Gorelik, of all people, exactly when I'd needed something to show Vicky.

On a hunch, I repeated the entire procedure, this time looking for a PR director, and heaved a sigh of relief. Veronica wasn't the best person by far. There were much stronger candidates.

Wait a sec. I'd forgotten to add the wage filter! I ran the four runners-up through it which left me with only one candidate: our beautiful carrot top. Judging by the search results, she was quite prepared to work for ten grand a month.

Curiouser and curiouser. Or could the search results have had something to do with the fact that I knew them both and that I'd helped them? Was that why the program had picked them? Possible.

I still needed to call that Panchenko guy, Ultrapak's new commercial director, and offer him our sales services. It wasn't too urgent but then again, procrastination wasn't really my thing. I'd already met Valiadis without any help from Ivanov. But it looked like the chain of events that had started with our conversation had to end with my offering our cooperation to Panchenko.

If so, so be it. I didn't really care about his response. All I cared about was bringing this whole thing to its logical conclusion.

That was workwise. As for non-job-related stuff, my priorities were visiting Cyril in hospital and if possible, check out the other antique shops in town. You never know, I might come across something worthwhile again.

And the most important and difficult task for

today was to save Gleb from the loan sharks.

I splashed some water on my face and headed off for a run. I hadn't planned on training this morning but seeing as I'd been stupid enough not to have reset the alarm, I might just as well make the most of these morning hours.

My Stamina was still at level 11 and showing no intention of growing, but at least I'd earned my 6% progress by running this morning.

When I'd come back home, something in the peacefully sleeping Gleb had attracted my attention. His eyeballs under his closed eyelids moved frantically. Whatever he was dreaming of, his stats left a lot to be desired. Even in his sleep, he was still frightened — and I knew perfectly well what it was. He was too scared of losing his family and his home — and with that, probably also his life.

By "life" I didn't mean his physical existence but everything that had made up his life in the past few years.

I studied his stats. He had plenty of debuffs: Gambler, Alcohol Addiction and Nicotine Addiction, all of them well-advanced. Those were only the major ones, not to even mention all the contributing ones, such as Nicotine Withdrawal, Intoxication, Exhaustion and even Thirst — apparently caused by last night's beer binge.

And if you added to this all the secondary characteristics, it was time to sound the alarm and put him in a hospital ward. His Vitality was just over 60%, his Satisfaction virtually negative, his Vigor non-existent, his Confidence, Self-Control, Spirit and Mood all in the red.

My friend needed healing.

I picked up my vibrating phone from the table and went out onto the balcony in order not to wake up Gleb. "Hello?"

"Sorry for calling so early," a voice said. "I'm from a courier service. I've got a packet for you. Are you going to be at home by midday?"

"I'm afraid not. I'll still be at work."

"Can I drop it off at your workplace?"

"Sure. Here's the address. It's the Chekhov Business Center..."

Having finished talking, I wondered briefly who it might be from, then promptly forgot all about it.

Feeling energized after a hot and cold shower, I made a huge quantity of the strongest tea, courtesy of the landlord's enormous teapot. I then rummaged through my medicine cabinet for some Aspirin and Analgin[33], pulled a new bottle of water out of the fridge and went to wake Gleb up.

"Wakey wakey!"

He mumbled something in his sleep. I had to shake him awake.

"Eh? What? Phil?" he croaked, barely moving his parched lips.

"Drink this," I offered him the bottle.

As he gulped it down, I handed him a couple of Aspirins and an Analgin. "Take this."

---

[33] Analgin: an over-the-counter painkiller popular in Russia

He was so apathetic he didn't even ask what pills I was feeding him. He just nonchalantly popped them in his mouth and took a swig from the bottle.

Now that his Thirst debuff icon had disappeared, he started frisking his pockets.

"Not now," I said. "You can have a smoke later. Take a shower first. You stink so bad even the cat won't come near you."

"Come on, Phil! Let me have a smoke and then I'll take a shower."

"Now listen up," I said. "This is how it's going to be now. Do you remember what you told me last night? About your debts and the loan sharks who threaten to take your apartment away? Remember what you said about some thugs threatening your children?"

His face changed. He sprang from the couch.

"Sit yourself back down," I said. "Is it true or not?"

I knew it was true. I'd had Lie Detection on last night. Still, I really wanted him to realize the sheer depth of the abyss he'd found himself in — the abyss he'd so naively hoped to avoid by escaping into his fantasy world of hitting the jackpot.

He nodded.

"I can't hear you!"

"Yes... it's true."

"Is it also true that you want to take your family away to the seaside?"

"Yes," he shrugged. "I can't even think about it at the moment. Only if..." his face lit up with hope. "You did promise to lend me some money, didn't you? Now I know exactly how I'm going to play! I'll be smart! I'll be extra careful! I'll do it in small steps! I know how to win it all back!"

"You don't know jack shit, mister. Can you think logically for a second?"

He paused, pondering over it, then shook his head. "In theory, it should be quite doable. The problem is, to win that sort of money back you need to play big. And I..."

"And you, my friend, are sick. Let's imagine — only imagine!" I added, seeing him perk up, "that I gave you the two million. And then what? You think you're gonna go and pay your debts off? No, you won't. I know as sure as eggs are eggs that you'll set a small part of it aside to play with. If you start winning, you will decide you're on a lucky streak and continue to play until you wind up in the red. Am I right?"

"Yes, but..."

"Am I?"

"I suppose you are."

"And if you start losing, you'll keep on playing to the last, trying to win it all back. You might start playing carefully at first, then you'll start raising the stakes and lose your head because I know you: you can't stop until you've pissed everything into the wind. And you know why?"

"Oh come on, Phil, stop your bullshit..."

"I'm asking you, do you know why?" I raised my voice, investing everything into my Power of Persuasion skill until my Spirit indicator began to shrink with every word I pumped into his head.

"Why?" he whispered.

"Because you've been conditioned like Pavlov's dog, you idiot! Not by anyone in particular but by the game itself! You love to play, you love the risk; you enjoy the surge of adrenaline as you wait for the cards to turn and the dopamine and serotonin kicks that fill you with joy whenever you seem to win. You love the sheer anticipation of winning which is why you even enjoy losing provided you still have enough money to try and win it back because this gives you an even bigger high. You're a junkie, Gleb. A flippin' gambling addict. Do you hear me?"

He turned crimson. "I'm not a junkie! Who gave you the right to preach to me? I can stop any time I want! You know nothing about it! I'm just not lucky! Go and stuff yourself! I don't need a shrink!"

He frantically patted his pockets, located the cigarettes and staggered to the door. I followed him. He was already putting his street shoes on.

"Gleb, listen..."

"What now?" he snapped, tying his laces.

"How would you like to pay off all your debts, make it up with your wife, find a good job and take your kids to some exotic seaside resort this Christmas? Somewhere with palm trees and bleached white sand, a gentle warm sea and loads of sun?"

He looked up at me. His sad brown eyes glinted with hope.

"Well?" I insisted.

"What a dumb question. So what if I do? You gotta spare genie in your back pocket?"

"Who needs a genie when you have me? And I'm telling you now that's how it's gonna be."

"So how are you gonna do it?"

"You don't need to do anything special. Just listen to me and do what I say. And don't do anything that I tell you not to."

"Yeah right! Okay, I'm off then. I need to go and see Sergei Rezvei. He also promised to help me."

I rolled my eyes. "Why do I even bother? How's he gonna help you? He'll give you some money and then what? You'll go and try to win it back? And how are you gonna do that? You broke your phone last night, didn't you?"

"Oh, shit, you're right!" he said, visibly upset. "And I don't think Lena will let me back in the house. The last time she said that if I didn't come home at night, she'd throw me out."

"Give me her number."

As he crouched in the corner, cupping his face in his hands, I spoke to his wife and told her that everything was all right with her husband and that he'd spent the night at my place. He couldn't have called her because his telephone was broken and now I thought he'd just left for work.

She replied coldly — but still I could detect the relief in her voice. That was good. She worried about him — she wasn't completely indifferent which meant that not all was lost for my friend Gleb, an alcoholic gambler and the father of a family.

Having finished speaking, I turned to him one last time. "So what did you decide, mister junkie?"

"I'm not a..." he looked up at me. "Okay. Seriously, I just don't understand how you can help but... ah, fuck it. Let's do it your way. What do you want me to do? And what do you want me not to do?"

"I want you to throw your clothes in the wash and get your ass in the shower."

Don't ask me how it worked — and I still hadn't had the time to ask Martha about it — but apparently, by interfering in his life, I'd somehow set deadlines for all of his debuffs. Now they were limited to 21 days. Three weeks. It was the same thing that had happened to me when I'd made the decision to quit smoking. Provided he didn't play and drink for three weeks, he could kiss his addictions goodbye.

It hadn't worked with his smoking, though. He refused point black to give up the only thing that still made him happy.

Once the freshly-minted Gleb had left the shower and put on my old shirt and pants, we sat down for a good cup of black coffee. Instead of the shirt that Vazgen had ripped last night, I had to put on one of the two I'd bought during my stint at Ultrapak. It didn't fit me very well anymore because at the time, my belly had been bigger and my shoulders narrower, but you couldn't really see it under the suit jacket.

It took me another half-hour to fill him in on all the details of my plan, having to put up with all his constant chuckling. And once I'd announced to him one of the main points of my idea, he very nearly knocked his coffee over,

"You're mad if you believe in that crazy plan of

yours!"

"Listen, we had an agreement," I snapped. "I do all the thinking. Your job is to do what I say."

"Yes, Sir! No, Sir! Three bags full, Sir!" he saluted jokingly.

"Finish your omelet, Private! That's my first order!"

He heaved a mocking sigh and tucked into my level-5 Cooking Skill masterpiece as Boris cast unfriendly looks at him from the corner of the kitchen.

AT 9.15 A.M., I LED GLEB INTO OUR OFFICE. THE OTHER guys said their hellos, then waited curiously to see how I was going to introduce the newcomer.

"Guys," I said, "I'd like you to meet Gleb. A very good graphic designer. Gleb, the macho over there is Alik. He's my friend and partner. And this nice girl is Stacy."

The two men shook hands[34]. Then I gently pushed his jaw back into place as he stared at Stacy, puppy-eyed.

The girl curtsied to him jokingly, "Very nice to meet you, Gleb!"

---

[34] In Russia, handshakes are common between men but not between men and women. If the man and woman are friends or relatives they might exchange a hug and/or a peck on the cheek but if they don't know each other very well, they avoid any tactile contact, limiting themselves to a nod and a smile.

Having got a grip on himself, he finally said, "I like this job already! Show me where I sign!"

We had a quick briefing to distribute the day's tasks. Then Alik handed his — or Veronica's, rather — laptop to Gleb who began by giving it a complete clean.

"I've no idea, Alik, what kind of seedy places you've visited but I'm afraid, this laptop has contracted some alien life forms. You've got colonies and colonies of all sorts of bugs here. That's not the way to treat your computer! Would you like me to clean it?" he waited for the ex-goon to give him a confused nod. "Excellent. I'm going to delete everything and save all the files on an external drive. Can I use yours, Phil? I'll reinstall the OS, then install an antivirus and a good graphics suite. Now... To tell you the truth, it might be a good idea to clean it inside and out. It's in such a state! You have a vacuum cleaner here?"

Stacy nodded.

"Excellent. And after lunch I'm gonna start on your company's brand style. Boss, any suggestions regarding your logo?"

"Can I put my two cents in, as well?" Stacy asked.

"It should be black and red," Alik announced.

Gleg giggled. "You can say what you want. I'll do it my way, anyway."

Now that he'd awoken from the fog of his gambling addiction, this was the Gleb that I knew and liked: my good old friend, responsible and thorough but still happy-go-lucky.

"Would you like some coffee, Mr..." Stacy

paused, waiting for him to give her his name.

"Just call me Gleb."

"Coffee, Gleb? Or do you prefer tea? Okay. What kind of tea would you like? Black? With milk or lemon? Earl Gray? Or do you prefer fruit or herbal?"

"Eh... I'd like a very strong black tea with some lemon," Gleb placed an order. "Two sugars, please."

"Consider it done," Stacy smiled. "Cookies?"

When in God's name had she had the time to buy all that? As I pondered over it, Gleb who'd taken Alik's seat in his absence (because Alik had disappeared to see if he could procure another desk from Gorelik) gave me a look of mock surprise,

"Cookies for the workers, what next? How about we put up a basketball hoop and set up some table soccer?"

"Get working, you joker! Otherwise we might set up a bowling alley and use your head as a ball!"

'You have no sense of humor, Phil. At all."

Before lunchtime, I'd managed to see a few visitors, speak to Veronica and discuss her work contract with her, then sat down with her and Mr. Katz to discuss all the finer details of our contract templates for both recruiting and outsourcing.

After that, I went to see Rose regarding our tax returns and the pricing of our new services, then met up with Kesha and laid out my vision of his future work. Once he'd agreed, we shook on it and immediately began discussing the conditions we could offer our new customers, after which he left to prepare the draft of our business proposal.

Panchenko, Ultrapak's new commercial director, didn't take my call and sent me a message,

I'll call you back later

Closer to midday, the courier finally turned up on our doorstep and handed me a paper packet. One glance at the return address was enough to know what was inside.

My heart started beating a little faster. I opened the packet and pulled out a book with a picture card inside,

Dear Phil,

Thank you so much from us all for investing so much heart into the life story of our father, grandfather and great-grandfather!

Best regards,
The Koutzel family

I lovingly turned the book in my hands: a beautiful hardback entitled *Vladimir Koutzel: His Own Story*. The author's name on the front page was mine:

Philip O. Panfilov

My throat seized. Sensing that something was wrong, the other guys stared inquiringly at me. Stacy came over to me.

I handed her the book. "Here. I wrote it."

It passed from hand to hand. My first book! I couldn't close new system messages fast enough, reporting my improved Reputation with Alik, Stacy, Gleb and later also with Kesha, Veronica, Mr. Katz and Rose once they'd heard the news and popped by to see the book. Now I had Respect with almost all of them, with the exception of Stacy which was still only Amicality.

You could say what you want but being a writer was more than a profession...

After lunch I used a break when we had no clients to leave the office and visit Cyril in the hospital. Also, I wanted to check out a nearby antique shop. In total, I'd counted about a dozen such shops in our city that sold antiques as well as magic and esoteric wares, and I fully intended to visit them all. You never know, I might come across something else which would give me a few extra stat points.

As I left, I looked over the office and was touched by the idyllic atmosphere which reigned there. Stacy was cooing on the phone with a potential customer; Alik was sitting next to Gleb whispering words of advice while the latter was busy drawing our logo with his tongue between his teeth, languidly rejecting the ex-thug's suggestions.

I gestured to Stacy, signaling that I'd be gone for a couple of hours. She waved back, asking me to wait for her. After a few minutes, she'd hung up and left the office.

"Give me your hand," she said.

"Which one?"

"The right one."

She produced a piece of red thread and tied it around my wrist, knotting it several times.

"It's for luck," she whispered, gave me a peck on the cheek, then went back into the office, leaving me confused.

What the hell was that?

A Protective Red Wristband
+2 to Luck

So much for superstitions! The properties of this supposedly useless piece of red string were truly amazing.

But what amazed me even more was Stacy's behavior. We'd only known each other for three days and now this. Another puzzle to add to the mix.

I arrived at the hospital a little earlier than the visiting hours.

The patients were still having a nap, so I decided to spend the remaining thirty minutes browsing around the local antique shop. Its name was *Rarity* — and even though I couldn't remember anything about WoW anymore, *Diablo* was still quite fresh in my memory.

Having said that, the shop offered nothing that a gamer would consider a rarity. I knew because I'd checked and ID'ed virtually all of their stock. The only thing that had caught my attention was the enormous antique tome of *A Gift to Young Housewives, or the*

Means of Lowering Household Expenses in Two Parts, 29th Edition by Elena Molokhovets[35], published in 1917 in Petrograd[36] by the First Printers' Cooperative. This volume offered +4 to Housekeeping immediately upon reading. Still, the price tag of 80,000 rubles[37] had cooled me down somewhat. Shame. I really would have loved to learn how to set the table and clean the household silver.

Cyril looked much better now — you could see it straight away. He'd lost some weight but his cheeks had acquired a healthy glow, and his eyes were full of life compared to when we'd first met.

We didn't get the chance to talk properly because his parents had arrived almost at the same time, so I just left him all the fruit and fresh juice I'd brought him[38] and prepared to leave.

"Phil!" Cyril called after me.

"Yes?"

"Is it true what Greg said that you've opened your own business? I was wondering if you needed sales reps."

"If they're like you, absolutely. Without a doubt."

He smiled and added sadly, "We got a new commercial director when Pavel left. He fired me in my

---

[35] Elena Molokhovets was the author of bestselling Russian 19th century books on cookery and housekeeping.

[36] Petrograd: the name of St Petersburg between 1914 and 1924 which was then replaced by Leningrad until 1991 when the city was renamed St. Petersburg once again.

[37] About $1,200

[38] In Russia, visitors in most hospitals are allowed to bring food and snacks for the patients

absence, can you imagine? He didn't need a sicko."

"Don't worry, bro. Consider yourself hired."

"That's good! I'll keep you posted, then. They're gonna discharge me next week, so I'll call you."

"Sure. Get well soon!"

When I left the hospital, I visited a few more antique and magic shops in the area but found nothing useful. The only thing I liked was a cuckoo clock but I wasn't yet prepared to shell out a hundred grand[39] for +1 to Self-Discipline.

I finally made it back to the office after 6 p.m. and found several customers waiting for me there with my fellow workers. I spoke to each of them and found suitable vacancies for all, then spent some time processing the data of those who'd come in my absence and sent it to Stacy.

TOWARD SEVEN-THIRTY IN THE EVENING WE CLOSED UP the office. Stacy disappeared round the corner and Alik hurried off to see some friends. I took Gleb and dragged him off to a cheap diner nearby to get a bite to eat and to finally approach the most important part of our plan. Or rather, to discuss it first and approach it next. It would have been so much easier had I had more cash on me but I only had about five grand so we had to start by increasing my start capital — or should I say, my bankroll for today.

---

[39] About $1,500

Gleb was drooling in anticipation even though I'd strictly forbidden him to play. I hadn't expected him to change his gambling habit overnight. Tonight, he was simply my guide and chaperone.

Both of us were so anxious — Gleb even more than I — that we gobbled down our thick *solyanka* soup[40] without hardly tasting it.

"They won't even let us into the poker club where Dimedrol normally sits," Gleb said. "The entrance fee alone is seven grand, that's fourteen for the two of us. They'll give us some chips for that money but only enough for the small stakes table."

"But don't you think we could win a little there and move to a table with higher stakes?"

"Sure. If... or when we do win, then we can move. But it might take us... take you some time to do so. The entry to the VIP room is two hundred grand[41]. For two of us, it's..."

I scratched my head with my free hand. "Dammit. What if you wait for me at home?"

"They won't let you in without me. It's a bit of a closed venue. Money alone isn't enough to get you into the VIP room. I'll have to vouch for you."

"Didn't you say you weren't welcome there anymore?"

"You see," he said, munching on some rye bread with his soup, "once I'd become a regular, they'd even let me in for less. They only stopped when I'd crossed

---

[40] *Solyanka* : a rich traditional Russian soup which is a staple in most Russian restaurants
[41] About $3,000

the swords with Dimedrol. This time provided we can pay, they'll let us in without a word. They're obliged to. They receive a commission from each round, so the more money gets brought in, the better it is for them."

"In this case, we only have to work out how to turn my five grand into fourteen so we're allowed in," I said. "But remember I still have to pay for the meal."

"Okay. I know this underground joint. It's a bit seedy but the entry fee is only a grand. It's not far from here."

We finished our meal and spent some time trying to attract the waiter's attention. The room was packed with customers, all shouting and chewing, so finally Gleg lost his patience and wandered off to ask for the bill.

We paid and left the stifling diner, then took a cab to the place he'd been talking about.

When we arrived, I realized it was situated directly opposite my parents' house. It seemed like a good idea to go and visit them first to fill up on parental love and in turn, share a little filial affection.

"Mind if we pop in to see my parents for ten minutes? I haven't seen them for quite a while."

He shrugged. "Would you like me to wait for you here?"

"Come on, don't be such a dork! Let's go together!"

When we arrived, they'd just sat down to their own dinner. I was only planning on staying for a quarter of an hour and then leave under the pretext of some business, but soon it became clear that my Mom wasn't prepared to let us go without a meal and a hearty cup of tea. I gave them an abridged version of the last few days, mentioning my latest quarrel with Vicky.

My father grunted his disappointment. He still held out for some grandchildren. Then I told them about my agency and finally remembered my book still wrapped in the packet I'd left in the hallway.

I showed it to them. "Mom, Dad, look! I've become a writer, after all," with a smile, I handed them the book and returned nonchalantly to my borsch while closely watching for their reactions.

My father put his glasses on. "*Vladimir Koutzel. His Own Story.* And?"

"Just read what it says below."

"Philip O. Panfilov! Look, mother! It's him! It has our name on the book!" Dad brought the book close to Mom's eyes. "I just can't believe it!"

"What?" she asked, uncomprehending and anxious just in case. "What is it?"

Half an hour later, my excited old folks had finally calmed down but not before they'd broken the news on the phone to all our relatives.

It was time for us to get going.

"Have some more, Gleb," Mom gently insisted. "You've lost a lot of weight. You're sure you're not sick?"

"Sure, Auntie Lydia. I had a bout of pneumonia," Gleb lied without batting an eyelid. "And what with my allergy to antibiotics, I spent a whole month in a hospital bed."

"How did you manage to get that?" Dad asked in

surprise. "You need to be really unlucky to get pneumonia in summer!"

"Do you need to ask?" Mom replied instead. "They spend all day in their air conditioned offices. No wonder they then catch their deaths of cold! Come on, eat up! Then I'll give you some more!"

Seeing me smirk, she added, "What are you grinning at? The same applies to you! Just look at yourself — you're as skinny as a rake! Eat up!"

She'd exaggerated, of course. I wasn't as skinny "as a rake" — but still, I'd lost quite a bit of weight. My belly was virtually gone, my face almost as young as it once had been. Almost — because the years always add a few lines.

The warmth and comfort of my parental home had brought about memories of my college years when Gleb and I used to drop by each other's house after classes and sat at the table with the parents. His weren't with us anymore; but mine were here, within an arm's reach.

Instinctively I reached out and stroked Mom's hand. "Thank you!"

She squinted suspiciously. "What for now?"

"And you too, Dad!"

"What for, son?" Dad looked up sharply.

"For everything. The borsch was really good." Indeed, her homemade beetroot soup blew our earlier diner experience out of the water.

"Dad, we really need to go, we still have some business to do," I finally said. "Gleb works with me now. We've gotta fly."

"Go on then, fly! I'm not stopping you!" Mom said, taking offense. "But first you've gotta finish your food or you'll not be going anywhere!"

"Humor your mother, son," Dad joined in.

Them and their tricks! The two just didn't want to let me go, dragging out the time in a typical authoritarian parental style. But I — or rather — Gleb and I — were basking in their warmth before plunging into our reckless and highly risky venture.

Because if my cunning little plan failed, I would come off much worse than even Gleb.

We hugged them goodbye. I gave myself a solemn promise to visit them again this weekend, with my sister this time. Mom clung on to me a long time, as if sensing something. I stroked her shoulders and her pulled-back gray hair, then softly eased myself away. "That's it, Mom. I'll come back with Kira in a few days' time. See you! Dad, bye, then!"

"Thanks, Uncle Oleg!" Gleb said. "Thank you, Auntie Lydia! I really enjoyed the grub! Till next time!"

With that, we left.

* * *

IT WAS ALMOST 10 P.M. We had very little time left, so we quickened our pace. Gleb walked in silence, lost in his own thoughts. Me, I was still reliving our time with my parents.

Which was why it took me some time to understand what Gleb wanted from me. We were standing by the locked steel door of some seedy bar.

"Phil, we need two grand," he said, shaking my shoulder.

"Oh yes, sorry," I reached for my wallet and gave him the money.

Clenching it in his hand, he rang the bell.

I listened to its staccato tinkling behind the door. It sounded like a secret code signal.

A hatch in the door opened, offering a glimpse of a grim burly face.

"Good evening," Gleb said, shoving the money into the hatch. "We've come to play."

The money immediately disappeared.

The door opened. Gleb walked confidently past some big guy in a cook's apron. Correct me if I'm wrong, but he looked Korean to me. The man peeked out from behind the door, took a look around and locked the door again, then said something in a foreign language into his walkie talkie.

"Follow me," he finally said, heading into a corridor to his right.

We walked along a dimly lit passage past a red-hot kitchen bustling with cooks, took another corridor — a short one this time, passed the restaurant entrance and stopped by another steel door. The Korean left us in front of it.

The door opened. I saw a large gaming table for ten people which was only half full, and a Korean girl who must have been the croupier.

A bleached, gray-haired man met us and showed us to our seats. We sat down, and the girl gave us some chips for the money we'd paid at the entrance.

"Not for me, thanks. Give it all to him," Gleb nodded in my direction. "I'm the support act tonight."

The girl nodded impassively, pushing all the chips toward me.

"Should I play too, maybe?" Gleb whispered. "That way, our chances will improve!"

"One more word, and you'll be waiting for me outside," I had to be brutal in order to get through to him. "Just think how are you going to tell Lena that you've lost your apartment in a game of cards!"

He nodded, coming back to his senses. I understood, of course, how difficult it must have been for him to resist temptation, otherwise I wouldn't have taken him with me. It's the same as with an alcoholic that tries to quit: the greatest trial of all is a trial at a party.

We were playing no-limit Texas hold 'em. That meant that a player could bet any amount — and if you ran out of chips you could always buy some more. That played right into my hands.

It was a motley crew seated around the table: two middle-aged Korean men, a young Korean girl and three more players at different stages of gaming addiction. One was a fat pompous government official, a fidgety guy of indeterminate age in a black turtleneck and a grim, hot-blooded Caucasian in his early thirties.

During the first dealing round, I once again pretended to be a clueless newbie. I kept betting and calling regardless of my hand, and always revealed my hands in the final showdown just to convince everyone how weak they were.

Gleb kept clutching his head, watching our money whittle away, but I couldn't have cared less about his feelings. My head was packed full of numbers, strategies and calculations.

Our initial two grand hadn't lasted. I dived into my wallet to buy some more chips with whatever I had left. The two middle-aged Koreans looked at each other while the Caucasian suppressed a smirk. All of them had recognized me as a fish — a poor, weak player whose lame playing style promised them good pickings. Our penny bets were only the beginning because each one of them knew that no one would be able to leave the table until he either lost everything or came up trumps. As Gleb had explained to me, it was considered bad form to leave the table immediately after winning: one had to give his or her opponents a chance to recoup their losses. Having said that, nothing prevented them from leaving the table at any given moment. Nothing but their own fervor, that is.

Having changed up the last of my money — almost three thousand rubles — I started to play like I normally do.

I beat the Caucasian's two 2s with a couple of 3s, halving his bank roll... Six grand.

A Queen I'd received on the river gave me a senior straight. The Korean girl discarded a junior straight, losing all her chips, but immediately bought another ten grand's worth.

Almost twelve.

I had only another couple of grand left until our target, then we could leave. Still, we also needed some pocket money to get a cab home and grab a bite to eat, so I decided to bring our winnings up to twenty grand.

Then my luck ran out. I didn't have one good hand. Still, I was obliged to maintain the image of a reckless gambler, so I began to lose little by little.

Eight grand.

Gleb had been taking full advantage of their free drinks, gulping down Coke by the bucketful. He was a sorry sight. His Gambler debuff counter kept renewing itself, making me realize that in order to quit poker cold turkey, he shouldn't even watch it.

Finally, I had a half-decent hand. And fortunately for me, the rest of the table were in luck too. The nervous guy was the only one who threw his hand in, the rest continued to play, raising the stakes, until we had a massive kitty.

Gleb had bitten his nails to the quick, waiting for everybody to show, until he finally covered his eyes with his hand. Our opponents seemed to be playing it cool. You couldn't fool the program, though: all of them were on edge, secretly envying Gleb and wishing they too could chew on something without giving their poker faces away.

I alone was as cool as a cucumber even though by then I had over fifty thousand at stake.

"Two pairs," the croupier called out the Caucasian's cards.

"Straight," she said next about one of the Koreans.

The Caucasian slammed a furious fist on the table.

"Junior straight."

The government official cussed in disappointment and lit up a cigarette.

"A pair," the croupier said, collecting the cards of the other Korean, then opened the Korean girls' hand. "A flush!"

The girl beamed, anticipating her victory. Still, she was celebrating too soon. Because I had a...

"Four of a kind!" the croupier's voice rang with admiration.

No one feels ashamed of losing to a hand like that, no matter what cards you hold. My opponents jumped from their seats in surprise to make sure I indeed had four aces.

Congratulations! You've received a new skill level!

Skill name: Poker Playing

Current level: 5

XP received: 500

Current level: 15. XP points gained: 14100/16000

The croupier pushed all the chips toward me and began to shuffle the cards, looking unfazed. I generously set six small chips aside, then handed them to my opponents with a smile.

Was this a superstition or just good manners? No idea; all I knew was that my Reputation with them had grown 5 points, with the exception of the fidgety guy in the turtleneck — and naturally, the croupier.

"Shit!" the fidgety guy snapped. "Beginner's luck!"

"That's awesome, man!" the previously impassive Korean exclaimed.

The Caucasian gave me the thumbs-up. "That was a beauty!"

I shrugged. "I was just lucky, guys."

I sorted my chips out into stacks of different values. Gleb tapped me on the shoulder, making me lose count.

"Keep it cool, man," I mouthed furiously into his ear.

By now, I had over forty grand in the kitty. I spent another half-hour playing leisurely, losing little bits here and there until I finally recouped all my losses manifold, growing my cash pot.

Once I'd had about seventy grand in total, I lost a little again, stopped playing, exchanged my chips for money and dragged the disbelieving Gleb away from the table. I shook hands with my partners, thanked them, left a generous tip for the croupier and headed for the exit.

Contrary to my reservations, no one tried to mess with us on our way out. We left through the same back door we'd arrived through.

Finally, Gleb could give way to his emotions. He kept on talking to me waving his hands in the air, but I ignored him as we walked along toward the restaurant's main entrance.

The cab I'd called earlier was already waiting for us. I sat in the back and slid over to make room for him.

"Where to?" the cabbie asked.

"Gleb? Where to now? Where's that club of yours?"

"The railway workers' community center," Gleb told the cabbie. "Know it?"

The car pulled away. I closed my eyes and gestured to Gleb to keep quiet for a bit.

I needed some rest. I'd had very little sleep last night. I was really drowsy.

We'd achieved our short-term goal. I hadn't even received the Gambler's High this time: possibly, because my triumph had nothing to do with luck. It was cheating, pure and simple.

Because every time I'd taken a look at a card, my Insight helpfully offered me the following data:

Name of the item: a card for the playing of poker
Size: 2.5" by 3.5"
Maker: Fournier
Date of manufacture: 2017
Material: Plastic
Suit: Spades
Value: Ace

So how can you not win, pray tell, when you know your opponents' hands, the closed flop and all the other cards in the pack?

Chapter Fifteen

A Socially Meaningful Action

"How can I reward Rome's greatest general?"
"Let me go home."

Gladiator

YOU SHOULD NEVER UNDERESTIMATE THE BENEFITS OF A catnap. Even though the twenty minutes I'd spent dosing off in the cab hadn't really refreshed me, they'd allowed me to quickly defrag and optimize my inner OS.

Predictably, being shoved in the ribs by your best friend isn't the best way to wake up. I zoned out momentarily, trying to recollect where I was and what was going on. Finally, I remembered everything and coughed to clear my throat.

"Are we there?" I asked, stretching to get the blood flowing through my numb body.

"Yeah," Gleb's voice sounded unnaturally loud to me. "Let's go!"

I scrambled out of the car and took in a lungful of the fresh night air, then followed after him.

As I walked, I took a better look at his stats, his renewed debuffs and especially his soaring Mood. I had a bad feeling about it. "Gleb, wait a sec."

"Yes? Whassup?" he looked at me impatiently, about to open the club's door.

I didn't like his agitated state one bit, so I decided to pour some cold water over it,

"Listen up. We haven't done jack until now, got it? We've only just started. Your job is to stay cool and out of my way. Don't even think about playing. Just keep an eye on me and if you think you have a suggestion to make, be my guest. That's the extent of it, you hear me? If not, just wait outside."

"Got it," he said, looking embarrassed. He must have thought I might eventually allow him to play.

"Remember our plan?" I said. "Your family, your kids, the sea, the beach, the palm trees?"

"Yes, yes, I remember. Come on, let's go in."

The so-called Poker Sports Club made up a part of the local Railway Workers Community Center. I found this quite appropriate because it's in our railway workers' interests to support the game, considering how much time is idled away playing cards on interminable Russian train journeys. Every one of us who's ever been on a train has shared a hand of cards with fellow travelers.

We entered the building unhindered and took a

massive staircase up to the third floor, its steps almost three feet wide at their base. Here we were finally confronted with a locked door to the right-hand wing. Two tense grim young men with crew cuts flanked the entrance, wearing monkey suits. They were apparently some sort of security.

On seeing us, one of them began mouthing something into his headset microphone. Serious establishment.

"Hi, Andy," Gleb greeted one of them. "We'd like to play for a bit."

Andy pointed a quizzical chin in my direction.

"It's Phil. He's a buddy of mine. He's a real greenhorn."

"Go on in," the other guard said, apparently having received a green light from higher up.

The two stepped aside, letting us in. The door opened, revealing a wide, brightly lit, carpeted corridor. To our right lay a reception area manned by two beaming floor managers: a young man and a girl.

"Good evening, Gleb!" they greeted my friend virtually in unison.

"Evening, Anton," Gleb gave the young man a ceremonious nod, then hurried to greet the girl, "Hi, Regina! How's it going tonight? Gotta big crowd in?"

I couldn't recognize him. He was agitated and feverish. This was his domain. Still, his excitement had nothing in common with his earlier enthusiasm at our office. This wasn't Gleb the graphic designer, the happy-go-lucky joker. His elation was the devil's work: this was the sick animation of a gambler whose blood was seething with feel-good hormones in anticipation of a game.

What I'd just seen at the Korean restaurant's poker den was nothing compared to what I was witnessing now. All his needs, dreams and goals had shrunk into insignificance. The game was the only thing that mattered: both the process and the result, the stress of winning and losing,. The higher the stakes, the sharper the adrenalin rush. Because what we'd been playing earlier was for him neither risky nor too interesting.

"A regular night as usual," the guy replied. I got the impression his smile was glued to his face. "It's been a while since we saw you. You look great. How's things with you?"

"Been a bit tied up lately," Gleb replied, suddenly doleful. "Can we come in? I brought along a friend. He's never been here before. Phil?"

I nodded, faking hesitation.

"Hi, Phil," Anton switched his attention to me. "Would you like to join the club? Membership offers you quite a few perks-"

"No, thanks," I cut him short. "Not tonight. I'd just like to mosey around for a bit and try my hand at competitive poker. I've only ever played online."

I can see the guy's Interest plummet. Just a moment ago it had been at nearly 60% and now it had dropped to almost complete indifference. He must have thought that I didn't have much to burn.

He didn't even know how right he was.

He must have read something in my face

because he went on to tell me more about the club and its competitions: all those daily tournaments with varying prize funds, the major championships and all kinds of privileges enjoyed by club members.

The nicest thing I'd gleaned from his soliloquy was that at midnight, they'd already started the high rollers tournament with a guaranteed prize fund of over a hundred thousand bucks. The entry fee was two thousand bucks and I still had time to sign up because the tournament's rules allowed rebuys within the first hour — in other words, if you lost, you could still buy more chips, but only within the first hour. And this hour was already nearly up.

As we spoke, Gleb had already turned all our cash into chips.

"Thanks, Anton! This is all highly educational," I said as I dragged Gleb onto the gaming floor.

"What?" he looked confused.

"We have fifteen minutes to double up. They have another tournament going on here, and the entry fee is two thousand dollars. They allow rebuys which means we can still make it!"

He understood me in a flash. To double our winnings in fifteen minutes was a tough call even with my interface, but my friend and I had always had a wild streak.

The door nearest to the reception room opened into a large hall studded with shafts of light illuminating the gaming tables. It was quite busy — and that on a week night! Players were speaking between themselves, rubbing and clicking the chips in their hands. The croupiers' voices droned on monotonously.

"Over there!" Gleb had already got his bearings and dragged me toward a table with an empty seat.

The croupier was just finishing up the last game. Excellent. I sat down and laid out the chips in front of myself.

That's it. I was in the game. Trying to preserve an impassive expression under my partners' studying gazes, I fiddled with my chips, biting my lip and furrowing my brow as I faked nervousness and excitement.

The stakes weren't too high, only five to ten dollars. If I didn't have an all-in pronto, I stood no chance of ever making it to the big tournament.

The first two hands gave me nothing worth risking. Luckily, my opponents were no better off. They all kept laying down their hands, so it didn't take much time, after all. The third hand gave me three kings on the flop. The community cards were still closed and I only had one pair. Still, I called.

Three of my opponents did the same, and the fourth — a slick young man in sunglasses and a G-star T-shirt with rhinestones — raised the stakes to fifty dollars with nothing to show for it.

He was bluffing. He had nothing, his move only an attempt to scare all the others and force them into throwing in their hands. Exactly what I needed.

His bluff nearly worked as everybody except me lost out. Like a novice chess player who hovers over the board undecided over where to place his piece, I faked hesitation as I called his raised bet.

I glimpsed the shadow of a smirk on the Rhinestone Cowboy's face. Gleb who'd been fidgeting in desperation for quite a while, whispered that we were running short on time.

I called. Now that there were only two of us left, I could see pretty clearly what kinds of hands the Rhinestone Cowboy and I would have. I'd have three Kings while he'd have an open-ended straight draw on turn. My job was to make sure he played till the end.

When the flop was opened, I checked — that's to say, I passed without betting. Without batting an eyelid, the Rhinestone Cowboy raised his stakes to two hundred. I feigned hesitation, then called his bet.

Gleb behind me slapped his forehead as if swatting a mosquito. "Phil, that's Rodion Kazansky! Are you sure? He's a professional! Watch out man, he's provoking you!"

I shrugged, as if saying I couldn't do anything about it anymore.

The dealer announced the fourth community card. I still had my three Kings while the professional player still had nothing, either.

Now was the moment of truth for both Gleb and myself.

I could say "Check" but there was always the risk of Kazansky replying in kind. Yes, I would win, but that wouldn't be enough to enter the big tournament. I could go all-in — and if he laid down his hand, the winnings would be more or less the same. I could also bet a little bit in which case I'd still be short whether

Kazansky called or not.

Come on, head, think. I'd spent the entire game cautiously checking and calling. If I bet now, he might think I finally had a good hand. Well, well...

"Check," I said in a weak voice, as if hoping that he'd do the same, giving me the opportunity to see the last community card.

"Three hundred," Radik bet confidently.

"Three hundred," the croupier confirmed, having counted the chips.

"All in," I said.

Take this!

Now not to reply to my all-in would cause him to lose face. And he could always hope for a straight to come.

Radik must have thought the same because he confidently called.

Bingo. Gotcha!

While the croupier counted the chips and the rest of the table awaited the results with bated breath, I glanced at my watch. We had less than five minutes left. Could we make it?

"What did you have?" Gleb whispered hotly in my ear.

"You'll see. Where are they holding this tournament? You think we can still make it?"

"It's in the VIP hall. Over there..." without finishing the phrase, Gleb grabbed my shoulders and shook me in a fit of joy as both I and Radik showed our cards which spoke for themselves.

I'm sorry to have cheated, Radik, but you still

had a crapload of chips and I had a friend's life to save.

We scooped up all the chips, left the penny arcade and dashed along the corridor toward the VIP room. I remembered all those movies where the hero always manages to save the world or defuse a ticking bomb at the last possible moment, courtesy of the screenwriters. I always found this artificial drama slightly ridiculous. And now I was in the same position myself, two minutes before the expiry of the signing on for the game.

Two more guards gestured to us, forcing us to stop by the door we needed.

"Guys, we'll be late for the tournament, please let us in!" Gleb begged. "Here're our chips!"

The two winced, apparently not happy with him addressing them as "guys".

"Wait here," the burlier one of the two said while his slighter partner spoke into his microphone to the management.

"The tournament," Gleb began pleadingly.

"I'm very sorry," the second guard interrupted him, "your participation in the tournament hasn't been approved."

Having received this new input data, my brain initiated a flurry of thought processes. Should we go back to the other room and take it step by step? We might not be able to recoup all of Gleb's losses overnight but it would be a good start. Two or three nights like this would solve the problem.

The hall's double doors opened, letting in two grim-looking young men: one in a suit, the other in a bomber jacket despite the hot summer evening.

Gleb's face changed when he saw them. All his joy and excitement deflated like a burst balloon.

The two paid no attention to me. Their faces seemed vaguely familiar. I must have seen them somewhere but I couldn't quite put my finger on it.

"Well, well, well, look who's here! If it's not Gleb!" the one in the suit said cheerfully. "Talk about the devil!"

His partner grabbed Gleb's neck and pressed down on it, forcing Gleb's head toward his chest. "Are you stupid or something? What did the boss tell you?"

He kept talking as he dragged Gleb away somewhere. His partner in the bomber jacket followed, making sarcastic comments. I started after them, but my Intuition was screaming for me to stay where I was: *Wait! You'll spoil everything!*

My blood was boiling, the Righteous Anger buff burning me up from inside. It took all of my self-control to suppress the impulse to stick up for my friend. Hundreds of potential scenarios flashed through my head until they gelled into a sensible and clear-cut plan, every point of which was nailed down with an unbendable steely nail.

Yes! This was exactly what I was going to do! I had to act firmly and without hesitation.

All this must have taken less than a couple of seconds.

"I thought you wanted to take part in the tournament?" the guard asked me. "You can still make it."

"Is this kind of behavior normal here?" trying to sound as cool as I could, I nodded at the two thugs taking Gleb away.

"It's up to the gentlemen themselves to sort out their differences," he replied. "Why? Do you have a problem with that?"

Detecting a menacing note in his voice, I decided not to push it, otherwise I might risk failing what Russians call "face control"[42] and ruin our whole mission.

'Not at all," I said, beaming at them. "Where do I sign in?"

"Across the hall to your right. You'll see it," he replied through pressed lips.

I ran, clenching the box with the chips which Gleb had managed to pass to me as soon as he'd noticed his abductors.

I made it.

The rebuy period was already over but you could still sign in during the break.

The tournament chips were different from those used at the normal tables. I put in my two thousand dollars' worth of chips and received ten chips of a hundred bucks and two five-hundreds. There was no point in them issuing lower denominations as by this stage of the game, the small blind was already a hundred.

---

[42] Face control : the Russian night club practice where a bouncer uses his trained eye in determining which of the public belong to the "right crowd" and deserve to be admitted.

A specially trained girl led me to the table. "You can leave your chips here and check out the bar," she said, smiling. "There's a fifteen-minute break just started."

"Thanks. That's exactly what I'm going to do," I said.

I draped my suit jacket over the back of my chair and headed for the exit, trying not to attract any attention. I needed to check up on Gleb. Somehow I didn't think those two were prepared to do him any real damage. Most likely, they just wanted to put the fear of God into him.

I left the room and looked over the corridor but didn't see any of them. The two guards bursting with the importance of their mission (that is to say, guarding the peace of some stinking rich playboys) froze by the door like two disabled stone golems.

"Excuse me," I addressed one of them, "You didn't see my friend, by any chance?"

"Who do you mean?" one of them deigned to answer.

"My friend, Gleb, where is he?"

"How would I know?" he replied through pressed lips.

What was wrong with them? Did I have pauper status written all over me? How could they tell a worthless nobody from a tycoon at first glance?

I could feel my blood seethe but thought better of it. This wasn't the right moment to have it out with a social level-3 security guard. Only a short time ago I'd been as worthless for humanity as he was.

I hurried down the corridor past more gaming rooms and "relaxation lounges" until I came to an unlocked door. Behind it was an emergency exit stairwell.

I opened the door and stepped into the darkness barely dispersed by the lights in the corridor behind me. I waited for my eyesight to adapt.

One floor below, an angry voice remonstrated,

"Tomorrow, got it? Tomorrow your time's up! The boss is angry with you now! You haven't paid him off yet but you had the audacity to come here and try to sneak into the VIP room! What does that mean? It means you do have the money. I don't give a shit whether it's yours or not. If you don't have the money, go and earn it! If you can't earn it, just steal it! If you can't steal, sell your kidney or your house, whatever, but you must pay him back!"

"I know, I know," Gleb sounded annoyed. "No need to go on about it. You've said it three times already."

I heard a rustling sound followed by a thump. Gleb gasped.

I flew down the stairs. "Gleb, you here?" I called confidently into the darkness.

In fact, it wasn't completely dark: there was a weak light coming from under a door by which Gleb was standing doubled up, clutching his ribs. The thug wearing the suit — according to my interface, his nickname was Wheezie — was leaning against the opposite wall smoking calmly. Every time he inhaled, the burning cigarette cast a light over his bored face.

The one in the bomber jacket — his nickname was apparently Zak — held Gleb by the scruff of his neck, not allowing him to slump to the floor.

"Gleb, you here?" he repeated mockingly.

"Phil, don't get involved!" Gleb demanded, spitting something black on the floor. "Do as we agreed!"

"What did you agree on? What's all that about?" Wheezie asked. "Phil, is that your name? Come down here, you wuss!"

"He was with him, wasn't he?" Zak said, remembering me.

"Phil, go back to the room," Gleb repeated.

"I don't think so," the hatred for these two bastards started to bore a hole in my self-control. "What's going on here, anyway? Who are you two, scumbags? Why is my friend Gleb in such a bad shape, in the dark? Do I understand it correctly that he's been subjected to verbal threats and corporal abuse?"

I finished the last phrase already in my stride as I took the remaining flight of stairs in two powerful leaps.

There was only one thought left in my head: bastards like them had no right to live. There was no way you could reason with them or fob them off. They only understood brute force.

No idea why I suddenly became so bloodthirsty.

"What did you say?" Zak began.

He didn't even get the time to get properly surprised before my fist made contact with his head, slamming it into the wall.

You've dealt critical damage to Zachary "Zak" Nikolaev: 395 (Punch)

"Well, well, well," Wheezie leisurely stood up. "What's this, the cavalry coming?"

A knife blade glinted in his hand. This guy meant business. Judging by the Heroin Withdrawal debuff dominating his stats, this one wouldn't stop at anything.

Not a knife again. As if that story with Tural hadn't been enough.

My field of vision shifted momentarily, edged with a fiery crimson. Time slowed down.

Warning! Potentially lethal aggression detected!
Danger of illegal activity targeting a user whose social status level is at least threefold more than that of his attackers.
Forceful activation of heroic ability: Sprint.
Ability class: Combat
+100% to the user's Speed
Requires changes to the user's metabolism and perception of time.

Awaiting activation confirmation...

Sending request to server. Please wait. Server connection timeout. Impossible to establish connection with the server.

Forceful activation of heroic ability: Sprint is

canceled.

I skimmed over the message while keeping a close eye on Wheezie. So Martha couldn't get through this time, either.

I stood too close to him to break away. This time, I didn't even get the chance to feel the time slow down: it had only lasted a split second.

"Please, he's very sorry! He knows nothing about my debts!" Gleb grabbed the thug's hand, begging. "It's a misunderstanding! We'll see you're all right!"

Wheezie shoved him away, "Fuck off!"

My friend went flying down the stairs. I forced my gaze away to look at him.

Gleb was lying motionless on the landing below, frozen in an unnatural position.

Trying to suppress my anxiety, I dodged the knife that came straight for me, ducked, then performed my signature uppercut (as Matov had called it). Before he knew what hit him, I'd knocked the knife out of his hand and finished him off with a series of quick blows which I'd had practiced to perfection and which had been beefed up by a Righteous Anger II.

Peppered with blows, Wheezie's head bobbed like that of a rear-window toy dog, even though the wall behind him prevented him from slumping to the floor. The system showered me with crit reports. One final hook to the temple KO'ed him, sending him sprawling to the ground.

I looked around the scene to make sure both were unconscious, then hurried toward Gleb. He was still lying in the same position, his neck turned awkwardly. His glazed-over eyes stared in front of him, unmoving.

Still not quite realizing what had just happened, I pressed my fingers to his neck.

No pulse.

He was dead.

I heard a rustling behind my back, followed by the stomping of feet on the stairs. I froze, having not the slightest wish to do anything. I really needed to watch out, I thought, because this could be one of their associates coming to teach me a lesson.

But I just didn't care.

Mechanically I took note of the debuffs taking over my Interface: Apathy and Desperation.

That was the last thing I'd noticed in this life. Something pierced my back, exploding my chest with blinding agony and paralyzing my limbs. And that was just the beginning. The fourth but by no means the last blow pierced my heart.

I died on the spot.

THE NEXT MOMENT, I was standing by the green poker table draping my suit jacket over the back of my chair. Martha was standing next to me.

"Sorry I came uninvited," she said. "I need to tell you something very important. Please don't die anymore. It took me all I had left of the local segment's combined Spirit to bring you back. Luckily for you, reality split off only six minutes ago."

"What do you mean, 'don't die anymore'? What

the hell was that?" I looked over myself, feeling my own body in disbelief, then struggled to reach my back with my hand. I seemed to be all right. "What about Gleb?"

"Ah, so you haven't lost your memory, have you? Excellent. I'll explain to you later. Don't worry about your friend, he's all right."

Martha disappeared with a wink, saying, "Do what you came here for. Wipe them out!"

AND WIPE THEM OUT I DID. I'LL SPARE YOU THE DETAILS of the tournament because I'd spent most of it deep in my own thoughts.

I could clearly remember every moment of my previous "life" — the inverted commas intended, like the three lives in a Super Mario game. I remembered myself walking out into the corridor and starting the fight with the two thugs. Then I was crouching by Gleb's body. Each of those memories was very clear: not like the elusive memory of a dream you still have upon awakening but a clear photographic image.

This time you were really in the crap, Phil, but somehow they managed to reload the world and restart it from the exact moment which had started you on the road to your demise. A miracle, yes, but no more miraculous than all those alien and heroic ability stories.

I gave myself a promise to come back to it later once I'd resolved the task at hand, then concentrated on the game.

At first, I spent some time watching my opponents — not just to collect all the data about their playing style, but also to restore my Spirit reserves. Everybody was playing warily, except for one young guy with the biggest pile of chips. He was betting aggressively, using the advantage he'd received during the first rounds of the tournament.

Which became his undoing. I replied to one of his raises with an all-in and won, doubling my stakes. Then I got him again. As a result, he went on a tilt and lost everything to some respectable gentleman who'd caught a flush.

That left only the two of us — and only one of us would go on to the final table. I was a bit anxious about Gleb who couldn't call me because he didn't have his phone anymore, while the tournament rules prevented me from leaving the room. It must have been due to this anxiety — and possibly also due to the general fatigue and lack of sleep — that I very nearly lost everything by miscalculating the final hands. I was lucky that the gentleman himself doubted his own hand so he chose not to push his luck by playing his last chips so my losses were limited to a third of the stack.

I even exposed my cards to him showing that I'd been bluffing, playing with a rather average pair.

Still, thanks to this involuntary mistake, my opponent unhesitantly called my hefty all-in and lost.

When they announced a break before the final table, I went to look for Gleb and found him lounging at the bar in the first hall. I tensed up, thinking he'd taken to the bottle again, then breathed a sigh of relief seeing he was drinking bottled water.

"Phil!" he slid off his bar stool and hesitantly came to greet me. His face betrayed an entire range of emotions from hope to desperation. "How is it going?"

"Everything's fine. I'm in the final!"

"Yes!" he pulled an imaginary steam engine's whistle. "Tell me all about it!"

"Wait, I'll tell you later. Who were those assholes who abducted you?"

"Who do you think? They're Dimedrol's toughs. They gave me until tomorrow. Now they want forty thousand bucks with all the interest and what have you. You're my only hope otherwise I've just no idea where the hell I'm gonna get it," his hands shaking, he lit up another cigarette.

"Now look here. When I came, there were six tables of nine people each. Two grand entry fee, that's over a hundred grand in the prize fund already. How much do you get for first place?"

"Well, let me think... Over fifty participants... that's over a hundred grand, you're right. That's not including the new chips they bought. So it might bring the prize money up to well over two hundred thousand dollars. The first place should receive at least thirty percent of the total takings. Phil, man, we're on a roll!"

I smiled. "You're talking as if I'd already won it."

"I know you will. Don't ask me how I know it, I just do."

"Well, if Uncle Gleb says so..."

"Listen, Phil. Even second place would do us. It

should be at least twenty percent of two hundred thousand..." he paused, making some mental calculations, "that's already the forty grand that we need!"

"Don't forget you still have lots of other petty debts to pay off," I said. "If you want to start living and working in peace, you'll have to repay everything."

For a while, he didn't say anything, looking at me from under his eyebrows. "You know, when you shared your plan with me this morning," he said slowly and clearly, "I seriously thought you were off your head. I agreed with you simply to avoid any confrontation. I was so sick and tired with all your preaching. But now that I've given it some more thought... especially after those two goons... I got my head together, if you know what I mean. I've been sitting here watching them," he nodded at the tables, "they're all real sickos. They're a bunch of headcases!"

"Keep it short and sweet," I cast a demonstrative glance at a non-existent watch. "The break will end soon. Where're you going with this story of yours?"

"I don't want to play anymore. Can you imagine? All I can think of right now is you winning and us leaving."

"Isn't this Dimedrol of yours supposed to be here?"

"His sidekicks are here so I suppose he should be too. It's a short guy, sorta bloated, with receding temples. He plasters his hair across his head to cover it up."

"Got it. I'm off, then. *Wish me now some luck in*

the fight..."

"*...I won't stay in this field of green!*[43] Good luck, Phil!"

As it turned out, I needed all the luck I could get. Later that night, when I already struggled to concentrate on my cards and very nearly dislocated my jaw yawning, I made another mistake. I miscalculated it again, believing there were three of us left in the game while in fact there were four. For that reason, I went all-in after the flop, adamant that I was winning — and the realization of my error gave me an almighty adrenaline rush.

And that's when my luck kicked in again. The person who could have won with his full straight, got cold feet and threw his hand in.

I'll spare you the details of the final game and the award ceremony that followed. By then, I couldn't think straight. The only detail worth mentioning was a certain Dmitry "Dimedrol" Shmelev, a fifty-four-year-old police colonel who'd come in in ninth place — a very respectable result even if it didn't garner him any prizes. He laughed goodheartedly at the fact that Gleb had paid his debt to him with the money which had been partially won from the Colonel himself.

"Good job, Gleb," Dimedrol said, shaking my friend's hand. "The slate's clean."

"So you're not after my ass anymore, is that it?" Gleb asked.

"Not at all. I told you the slate's clean. One thing

---

[43] An excerpt from *Blood Group,* a cult Russian rock song by the 1980s Russian band Kino

I'd like you to let me in on: do I understand it correctly that it was your friend who helped you?"

He made a show of weighing up four thick bundles of money in one hand while pointing at me with the bent index finger of the other.

"Amazing, isn't it?" Gleb exclaimed. "He's an absolute beginner. Talk about luck. He only played his first hand last night."

"That explains it. I wondered what it was that that attracted all the best cards to him," Dimedrol said, apparently happy with the explanation. "That's beginner's luck for you."

He held out his hand and looked probingly into my face as we shook on our new entente. His cold beady stare had none of that pretentious warmth and good-naturedness that filled his voice, so I was very relieved when I was finally able to offer him my rushed goodbyes and follow Gleb outside. We still had about twelve thousand dollars left which was plenty to pay off all his other debts.

By the time reception had called us a cab, it was already getting light. We got home without further ado if you didn't count the flat tire which cost us another fifteen minutes. Also, someone had spilled cooking oil on the stairs so predictably, I slipped and very nearly broke my neck. Luckily, Gleb caught me just in time. Cursing Khphor's vindictive nature to hell and back, I refused to take the elevator point blank and gingerly climbed the stairs one by one all the way up to my floor.

I don't know about Gleb but I zonked out as soon as my head hit the pillow.

---

* * *

MY INTERNAL ALARM CLOCK WENT OFF AFTER AN HOUR and a half. I staggered back to my feet feeling broken and only half-awake. Still, I was in a great mood. I texted Kostya to tell him I couldn't make it for the training, suggesting we postpone it till tomorrow.

OK, he replied curtly.

As I splashed some water on my face, I heard dishes rattling in the kitchen. Could Gleb be already awake too?

I found him in the kitchen pouring out the coffee. His hand was trembling but he was humming a tune, doing a little jig around the kitchen.

"Good morning!" I said.

"Oh, Phil, you're up? Sorry if I woke you," he added with a guilty shrug.

"Not at all. It was the alarm clock that woke me. What are you doing up so early?"

"I didn't sleep a wink, man. I was tossing and turning. I must have gone out for a smoke a dozen times. Then I sat down to write. And when I was finished, I decided to make us some coffee."

"What did you write?" I asked him, yawning.

"Here, take a look," he turned to the table and picked up a sheet of paper covered with scribblings. "These are all my debts. I don't think I've left anything out. It's four hundred fifty thousand rubles in total[44]. I rounded it off slightly higher to be sure."

"We have more than enough," I said, studying his list. "Let's go to the bank now and pay off your loan, then you can go and see all your other creditors yourself."

"Not a problem. Do you want milk with your coffee?"

"No, thanks. Black, one sugar. And there's one more thing. I'm going to give you slightly more. We'll split what's left from our winnings. I want you to buy yourself a cheap phone and take the rest to your wife. I'm pretty sure it's been a while since you brought any wages home."

"Shit! Of course. Thanks a lot, Phil," he got all emotional and gave me a bear hug, patting me on the back. My Reputation with him which had been stuck at lukewarm Amicality ever since I'd failed to pay my own debt to him all those years back, now had soared to *Worship: 1/1.*

If I wasn't mistaken, this was the highest possible Reputation level. It was heartwarming. After sitting by his dead body only a few hours ago, even his reeking of sweat and stale tobacco made me happy because this was the smell of life.

I'd made up my mind last night to accompany him to the bank. The Gambling debuff was still dominating his stats so I was seriously worried he might lose control and start playing again instead of

---

[44] About $7,000

paying back his debts and starting a new life. Initially, I'd wanted to accompany him to all of his creditors but afterwards, I'd decided that I wouldn't be doing him any favors mollycoddling him. Let it be the first serious test for him. And if he did lose control... well, in that case all his promises, all those "I'll never play again" weren't worth jack. If it happened, I might need to postpone his cure until I'd received Persuasion, the Tier-3 Heroic ability. I simply couldn't constantly be around to keep an eye on him.

After breakfast, we headed for Gleb's bank branch which wasn't far from the office. We arrived just as they were opening so we didn't have to wait in line. While Gleb was finalizing all the formalities of paying off the loan, I huddled in the corner and summoned Martha.

I sent her a mental greeting and fell silent for a long time, not knowing where to begin.

She was the first to break the silence. "How was your day, Phil? Apart from the fact that you were killed," this was the first time to my memory that she'd initiated a conversation. "Judging by your logs for the last sixty hours, it's been a hoot?"

"Sort of. Lots of things have happened."

"You gonna tell me?"

"What do you want me to tell you?"

"Maybe you can start with the evening of the seventeenth of July when the program had registered your getting involved in a fight. According to the logs, you received some damage but you also dealt some."

"Ah... That's when I had a punch-up with

Mohammed. He was hassling Vicky. Was it only three days ago? Jesus..."

My mentioning Vicky had brought all sorts of hurtful feelings to the surface. I could barely resist calling her. However much I insisted to the contrary, my affection for her was still there.

"Had a hectic three days?" Martha asked, sympathetic.

"You'd better believe it. Imagine this: first they kicked me out of the boxing group, then I split up with my girlfriend, hired a highly questionable person, met my old employer, began the process of expanding my business and had a very interesting conversation with another interface user. Quite an eye-opener, really. The most important thing I gleaned is that we're not alone in the Universe. Some senior race who call themselves the Vaalphors have for some reason put a price on my head and are hunting me down by manipulating the chains of chance. I also found a magic ring with a bonus to Luck, was very nearly cut up by some migrant worker and almost beaten to death by some jealous Caucasian guy. And then I found out that an old pal of mine was in trouble so I had to rescue him. That's not to mention my own demise."

As I spoke, each fact triggered a respective image and its emotion. Apparently, telepathy was every bit as good as saying it all out loud. Martha listened attentively to me pouring my heart out to her, making all the right noises in the right places.

When I'd finally finished, she asked me to clarify a few things, then froze for a good twenty seconds, biting her lip. You could say she'd glitched, I suppose, all the while syphoning off my Spirit reserves.

"Overall, it's not so bad, Phil," she finally said. "You replaced group training in an unfriendly environment with individual practice. Your new coach Kostya possesses a high Boxing skill level which should in theory compensate for his deficient Tutoring skill which is lower than Matov's. Having said that, it can't be that deficient because Kostya has to look after his younger sister. Did you check his Tutoring level?"

"I didn't even know it existed. I just didn't notice."

"Please do. The growth of your own skill depends upon it."

"Very well. And what if he doesn't have it? Or if its level isn't high enough?"

"In any case, even just using him as a sparring partner is more beneficial than training on your own. Next. Regarding Valiadis, Khphor and the Vaalphors' reaction to the weird situation with you passing — or not passing — of the first trial. I'm sorry, I know I should have told you before..." she paused.

"You! That was you!"

"Yes. It was me. I took advantage of the fact that this segment's servers weren't available, so I forcefully activated Time Cheat, preventing them," she tilted her head, pointing at the sky above, "from uninstalling your interface."

"Because if they did, you'd have disappeared too?"

"Exactly."

"Does that mean this is my third life? Like Mario's?"

She averted her gaze and toed the floor in a very girly gesture.

"Martha, what is it? Tell me! The first time I died was when the acid jelly smoked me. Then Zak stabbed me to death last night, right? And how come I can't really remember my first death — it's all very vague, more like a dream — but I can remember every detail of the past night very clearly?"

"That's because it occurred only six minutes after reality had branched out. And as for your other questions... I'm sorry, Phil. You're not ready yet. I'll tell you everything, I promise, as soon as you make level 3 in Insight. Just please be careful, I beg you! They've already noticed my unauthorized activations of Time Cheat and denied me access. So I won't be able to pull you out next time. Sorry about that..."

She gave me a peck on the cheek, tousled my hair in a very human gesture, then disappeared.

Gleb appeared in her place, grinning from ear to ear,

"Freedom!" he sang, "I'm free like a bird!"

"Come on, bird, We've got a lot to do still," I laid my hand on his shoulder. "Time is money. Let's move it."

And move it we did. I went to the office while Gleb hurried to the nearest cell phone store to get a new phone and SIM card. After that, he had to visit his other creditors and head straight home.

By lunchtime, I managed to finish most of what

I'd planned to do for today. Kesha and I had polished our business proposal which was now waiting for Gleb's art designer touch. Mr. Katz brought us the final draft of the contract which now had provisions for every possible eventuality. After that, I called Panchenko, Ultrapak's new commercial director, but received a dry emotionless reply: apparently, he wasn't ready to meet us until next week.

Alik had managed to procure a decent desk of polished chipboard courtesy of Mr. Gorelik, and lugged it all the way from the basement upstairs to the office.

"It's imitation of dark alderwood," he announced proudly. "Virtually unused! Gorelik parted with it for a grand. I just need to glue it up a bit."

Stacy kept casting concerned glances in my direction. She waited until I had a break in the work, walked over to me and whispered,

"Phil, I think you need to get some sleep. You look like a vegetarian zombie. I suggest you take the afternoon off and get some rest."

"Don't worry, Stace," I said. "I might have an early night tonight, that's all."

She pursed her lips and left to greet another client. She was still as stunning as on her first day, which made her concern all the more touching.

After lunch, Veronica brought in our first corporate order from a large IT company in need of a good leading developer who'd be also an experienced team leader.

Processing it took me slightly longer than expected. First, I had to research the company itself in order to amass as many KIDD points as possible. The search for the right candidate, too, proved to be a long and evolved job because all the potential bidders were either located in other cities or already working for someone else. The few who were currently unemployed didn't seem to fit the bill, either.

I finally picked a couple of names, found their contacts online and passed them on to Veronica who had to conduct the actual negotiations.

It was nearing three p.m. when Gleb reappeared in the office, beaming. He gave everyone a round of cheerful greetings, pecked Stacy on the cheek, gave a confused Alik a bear hug, then asked me to come out "for a smoke".

We stepped out. It had begun to drizzle. Gleb lit up a cigarette and spoke as the first raindrops began rustling on the tarmac,

"First things first. Here's the phone," he showed me a very plain smartphone, a budget version from a well-known maker. "I've restored the contacts list from my laptop back home so it's okay. I can't thank you enough, man. I've paid off all the debts. I even remembered the two hundred I borrowed from a neighbor ages ago and paid it back too."

"How did your workmates react to the sudden windfall?"

"They were surprised, of course. Many didn't believe I'd ever pay them back anymore. There were rumors I'd hit the jackpot. I just told them I'd found a good job and paid them out of my wages. Thanks again."

"And how did it go at home?"

"This, strangely enough, was the difficult part. I racked my brains trying to think of something believable enough to make sure she forgave me without shocking her too much. I came up with a whole story," he bit his lip and averted his eyes.

"What kind of story?"

He shrugged my question away. "Doesn't matter anymore. So I came home and rang the bell. My older one opened it. You should have seen him! He shouted, 'Daddy's back!' and started hanging from my neck. The other one heard him and started screaming his head off like I'd come back from the dead. Then Lena came running and threw herself around my neck. Can you imagine? She said she didn't know what to think..."

"And?"

"So we just sat down and had a talk. This story I'd come up with... it just wasn't worth it. I told her everything as it was: about my debts and my addiction; I told her I'd been fired and that my creditor threatened to take our apartment... Then I told her about you and how you tried to talk some sense in me for my family's sake and how you helped me to sort out this mess and get me off the hook — by a sheer miracle. I also told her I was starting a new life and that I fully intended to spent it with her and our kids. Said I wanted to grow old together with her. And once I finished, I just sat there all tense, ready to accept whatever decision she'd make. I was morally prepared, you know what I mean? If she wanted to divorce me or whatever..."

"And what did she say?"

"At first she didn't say anything. It took her some time to digest it. Then she just walked over to me, put her arms around me and cried. And when she finally calmed down, she was my old Lena back again. She was like, 'Get those clothes off you and get in the shower!' Just like you spoke to me yesterday, remember?" he laughed. "She made me some lunch and packed me off to work."

He was laughing, happy and intoxicated with the prospects of a new life. A normal life where he'd do a good day's work and go home to his family in the evening to share his marital bed with his wife. A life which held the promise of the seaside once a year complete with palm trees and bleached white sand.

Then I very nearly slid down the wall, overwhelmed by all the system messages accompanied by the surge of unbridled joy the program had bestowed on me.

Your Reputation with Lena Kolosova has improved!
Current Reputation: Respect 20/120

Congratulations! You've received a new system skill level!
Skill name: Insight
Current level: 3
XP received: 1000

For your information: the following data has been unblocked in regards to all objects and subjects

comprising the local segment of the Universal Infospace.
    This will allow you:
    1. To determine a subject's overall potential
    2. To evaluate their teamwork synergy
    3. To evaluate two subjects' matrimonial compatibility

You've just performed a socially meaningful action! You've created a new time branch and restored the integrity of the Kolosov family, namely Gleb, Lena, and their children Sergei and Alexander, preventing their respective levels from dropping and creating new favorable conditions for improving their social status.

You've received 3000 XP for performing a socially meaningful action!

Congratulations! You've received a new level!
Your current social status level: 16
Characteristic points available: 1
Skill points available: 1

XP points left until the next social status level: 2610/17000

"Phil? You all right?" Gleb tried to help me back to my feet but my rubbery legs kept giving way under me. "Phil!"

"I'm all right... man," I replied softly once the fit of pleasure was over. "I think I need some sleep."

"I think you do, too. Maybe you should go

home?"

I shook my head. "No. I'll get some sleep tonight."

"Let's go back to the office, then?"

"You go. There's a business proposal there that needs tidying up. I'll hang about here and get some fresh air, then I'll join you."

Ignoring his protests, I finally forced him back into the building. I needed to be alone for a while. I still had to work out which advantages I could expect from my new level of Insight; I also needed to decide how to invest my characteristic point. The most logical choice would be Luck but did I really need it now that I had the ring?

I also needed to give my second achievement some thought. The window that had reported it in a colorful cascade of visual effects was still open, and this is what it said:

Congratulations! You've received a new achievement: The Altruist!

You've performed a socially meaningful action by donating a sum in excess of your entire annual income to somebody who needed it more.

Reward: +1 to all main characteristics at every level gained.

Me, Phil Panfilov, a self-confessed miser who used to flog every useless piece of game junk just to save a couple of copper coins — an altruist?

You have to be kidding me.

Chapter

Sixteen

REAL MAGIC

*My model for business is The Beatles.
They were four guys who kept each
other's kind of negative tendencies in
check. They balanced each other and
the total was greater than the sum of
the parts. That's how I see business:
great things in business are never done
by one person, they're done by a team
of people.*

Steve Jobs

A LONG TIME AGO WHEN I'D ONLY JUST STARTED
working, I'd noticed an interesting thing. Normally,
after a protracted period of falling out with one's spouse

and the following reconciliation, the person tended to become much friendlier and happier — and definitely more productive.

No wonder Gleb experienced the same. The chance to turn his life around and even start it anew by so effortlessly repaying his debts had given him his mojo back.

When I'd returned to the office, I saw him surrounded by Alik, Stacy, Kesha and Veronica busy discussing our future website. They were all huddled around the window, some perched on the window sill, others on the desk. Stacy was pouring out the tea.

Suppressing a smile, I returned to my desk. I might listen to them for a bit while trying to come up with a strategy for the future. I also had the rewards from my interface to consider.

"That's happiness for you!" Gleb exclaimed, ecstatic. "D'you all get it?"

"Gleb, we could make do with our VK page for the time being," Veronica said. "It won't cost us a bean."

"Had we remained a humble employment agency, yes," Kesha butted in. "But if we want to go big, the absence of our own website will be a big drawback. There'll be a lot less trust."

"What are you all arguing about?" Mr. Katz asked, appearing in the doorway.

"It's about the website," Alik heaved a sigh. "He says," Alik nodded at Gleb, "that we all need to drop whatever we're doing and work on the company's online presence."

"Hi, I'm Gleb," my friend said, offering his hand to Mr. Katz.

"Pleased to meet you, young man," Mr. Katz replied ceremoniously. "And why such a hurry, may I ask?"

"Tea, Uncle Mark?" Stacy offered.

"Yes, why not? And talking about our company's online presence..."

They went back to their conversation while I paused, trying in vain to remember what the hell I'd just been thinking about.

So... I'd been standing on the porch downstairs trying to recover from the effects of receiving both a new achievement and a new Insight level. In the meantime, everybody had gotten to know each other and moved naturally from discussing the pressing issues of the logo design and the business proposal layout to more far-reaching matters. Such a zeal was undoubtedly welcome but this wasn't what I'd been thinking of. Wait a sec, what did they say... It was something about... wait!

We could make do with our VK page for the time being, Veronica had said...

Had we remained a humble employment agency — that had been Kesha...

We all need to drop whatever we're doing... that had been Alik repeating Gleb's words.

Our company's online presence... — that had been Mark.

Yes! Got it! It was the "we", "us", "our"! That's what it was!

I leaned back in my chair, closed my eyes and tried to visualize our future company, Great Job Agency, as my workmates continued their heated but friendly discussion. *Our* company that belonged to us all. Gradually it began taking shape in my mind — not as an abstract notion but as a real thing put together like a virtual jigsaw puzzle. It came into focus more clearly with every KIDD point I used.

I could see our tiny office in the Chekhov Business Center. The building manager Mr. Gorelik also added his KIDD point to the mix. I was officially the head of the company because formally, Alik was still only a hired worker.

I could see all those desperate disillusioned people who still held onto the meager hope that we wouldn't rip them off but help them find work instead.

The jigsaw puzzle began to fuse into a full-color 3D picture. I could see our agency working and expanding as our turnover grew and with it, our profits. The numbers of both our workers and clients kept increasing in real time.

I could see the financial results of 2018... 2019... 2020... Our agency kept working even after my interface license had expired although it showed practically no growth. Our annual turnover remained just over 2,000,000 rubles[45] and our clear profits gradually began to decline.

Was this my level-3 Insight at work? The picture was so tangible it felt as if all of this had already

---

[45] About $30,300

happened. I needed to ask Martha about it ASAP.

She appeared promptly, cast a curious look around the office and greeted me with a faint smile. "Are these your workmates?"

"Hi," I grinned back as I replied mentally. "Almost. Formally not all of them but I'm working on it. I only summoned you for a moment. This isn't the best place to talk. Take a look, please. It seems I've received a new ability," I forwarded her the images. "What do you think?"

"Yes, that's what level-3 Insight does," she said. "It enables you to see any person's potential."

"Only a person? How about a company? A company isn't a human being, is it? It's what they call a legal entity."

"Behind every company there're people. Like you and Mr. Romuald Zhukov — Alik, isn't it? You two got together and decided to provide useful services to other people. What you call an employment agency is in fact your personal stand: yours and your friend's."

"And Stacy's," I added mechanically.

"Yes, Phil?" Stacy turned her head to me.

Martha and I looked at her in unison. Stacy gave me a quizzical look, then switched her gaze to Martha standing by the window in a rather suggestive pose.

Martha promptly disappeared.

What the hell?

"Phil?" Stacy was already standing next to me. "Did you call me?"

"Eh.. yeah. Be a good girl and get me a cup of coffee, please," I replied with a theatrical yawn.

"Thanks."

"Sure. One moment."

She glanced at the window where Martha had just stood and went off to make coffee, leaving me completely confused.

A coincidence? In that case, why had Martha disappeared?

"Phil, are you okay?" Stacy distracted me from my musings, placing a cup of coffee next to me.

"Well, what do you think?" I said, answering a question with a question. I just couldn't forget the strange red wrist band she'd given me last night. "You really think I'm okay?"

"I'm sure you are. There *is* something you should take very seriously but not quite yet. At the moment, you're perfectly okay."

"What kind of something?"

"We'll talk about it later," she nodded toward our friends and walked off, rejoining them.

They'd already finished discussing our website — or rather, they'd decided to leave it till later and brainstorm it with me — and started compiling a list of all the companies in the city who could become our potential clients. This was something neither Alik nor Gleb were interested in so they got to work designing a layout for Kesha's business proposal regarding our outsourcing sales department.

I knew I still had to call Panchenko in Ultrapak. The unfinished task put me on edge. I wish I could delete it but I couldn't. Why would I even bother?

I took a sip of coffee, placed the mug on the desk

and leaned back in my chair. The moment I thought about it, the mental model of my future agency came back into focus. It looked a bit like a 3D picture from an economic simulation game, with an isometric projection of the office, the little figures of the workers and clients moving at high speed, and loads and loads of graphs and diagrams, all of it overlapped by my 3D figure.

I sent a mental command to add Alik, putting him on the founder member list. A Synergy box appeared next to him, flashing fat green numbers: 106% this year, 111% next year, and then a sharp rise to 160% in 2020.

Oh wow. Did that mean that the system was taking Alik's input into account? Judging by its prognosis, he'd become more useful as the years went by. Could it be because he might go back to school? Should I send him to a college, maybe? Enrolment hadn't yet finished this year.

Our profits seemed to grow proportionally from year to year: first by six, then by eleven and fifty-eight percent. That meant that by keeping Alik as a partner, we might earn more than without him. And considering that I'd only promised him five percent of the profits, it was a win-win situation.

This ability seemed to have a interesting effect. My hands shook as I wiped the sweat from my forehead, overwhelmed by these new developments.

Well, well, well. And what if...

I returned to the Sinergy window and added Stacy.

This time the program didn't respond. It was either glitchy or it simply didn't perceive Stacy as a human being.

I removed Alik, and the Synergy box disappeared. I tried to add the girl again but the program just wouldn't have it. Could it be because I knew nothing about her and didn't have enough KIDD points?

Very well. Let's try someone else.

I brought Alik back into the picture, and hey presto! The Synergy numbers reappeared in a flash as the program kept evaluating our company's situation. The further into the future, the slower the dates and numbers changed. Could it be the multiple-choice effect from all the reality splits which gradually turned our progress into a multi-million-option game? And the further into the future, the less accurate the forecast became.

I tried to visualize Mr. Katz next to me and Alik. The picture updated. Now there were three of us in the scene while the Synergy box showed 227% already this year. More than double. And 362% next year.

That was nothing to sniff at.

I must have looked a bit weird to the casual onlooker, sitting there with my eyes closed, smiling at something. The hubbub of voices let up a little but didn't stop completely. My friends must have decided I'd dosed off.

Okay. Focus, Phil! Concentrate!

I left everything as it was and added... Yagoza. No idea what had inspired me to try our local criminal boss with all his prison tattoos, but the program reacted to it straight away.

The simulator flashed red. All the numbers plummeted to rock bottom, predicting negative Synergy and killing the company already by the end of next year. The graphs showed some crazy losses, with the agency closing down by 2020.

I got it, I got it. I promptly removed Yagoza and the numbers turned green again.

I spent the next two hours shuffling the company's potential partners list, adding all the people in my immediate circle and varying their activities and input, until I'd arrived at the optimal configuration of both our shareholders and activities. This was what I had:

I'd head up the company with 51%. Another 9% would go to Alik and the remaining 40% would be shared between Kasha, Veronica, Gleb, Mr. Katz and his wife Rose. Gleb only had 5% while Mr. Katz and Rose had 7,5% each.

Why, might you ask?

Because as soon as I raised Alik's share to 10%, our numbers began to plummet. I had no idea why: it could be his mentality, I suppose. Possibly, it might also have something to do with Kesha and Veronica who might feel their input was bigger than Alik's. No idea.

With Gleb, it was a different picture entirely. Even 6% tended to change him for the worst, jeopardizing our profits. It might have something to do with the fact that higher profits meant a higher share for him. He might end up earning more than he really needed — so I wondered if he might start gambling again with any surplus money? His losses might aggravate his depression and desire to win his money back which wouldn't do the company any good.

All in all, with this particular configuration the program predicted 9,000% Synergy and hundreds of millions of rubles for the company already next year. The picture of our little office was replaced with a 3D image of a whole building floor taken up by us alone. And two years after that, our company would have grown branches throughout the whole country.

* * *

A HAND LAY ON MY SHOULDER. "Phil?"

I opened my eyes. I must have dropped off. It was already dark outside. The interface clock showed almost 10 p.m. There was nobody left in the office except Stacy who was peering at my face with concern.

"Where's everybody?"

"They're already gone. They didn't want to wake you. Gleb said, you hadn't slept at all last night. He was the last one to leave, by the way."

"Why did he stay on so late?" I wheezed, trying to come back to reality.

Could I have dreamt up the whole Synergy thing? I closed my eyes and turned away from Stacy. Immediately the 3D image came back into focus, complete with the final shareholders list and the 9,000% Synergy.

So that was okay, then. Still, what might have caused me to have slept so soundly?

"Gleb kept working until late — first on the company's image and then on Kesha's business proposal," Veronica continued. "And then he just waited for you to wake up. He didn't want to leave you alone and he really wanted to show you his work. But his wife's just called him and he had to run off. Apparently, his dinner was getting cold," she laughed.

"Why didn't you leave?"

"I just wanted a few moments on my own with you," she said languidly.

Only now did I notice that her unbuttoned blouse was slightly more revealing than dress code required.

Slightly? More like a lot. Fighting with the hypnotic allure of her cleavage was like trying to prize a powerful magnet away from a steel plate. Still, I almost managed, drawing my gaze away from it after only a split-second delay.

I stared into her mesmerizing eyes, her pouting lips which revealed two rows of even white teeth, her hastened breathing... My gaze shifted below again. You couldn't just look and not see any of it.

She walked over to me and perched herself on the edge of my desk. Now I could see much more — and I could also smell her seductive scent. No idea what perfume it was but it was more like her pheromones at play. I sensed an involuntary stirring below and sprang to my feet, feeling pretty pissed.

Stacy rose too. We came face to face. Even

without her stilettoes, she was the same height as me. My old debuff which I'd been lugging around all this time, had suddenly upgraded.

Smitten II (24 hrs.)
You have been smitten by a subject of the opposite sex!
Subject's Name: Anastasia Semyonova
+75 to the Subject's Reputation in your eyes.
The Subject's current Reputation: Amicality 45/60
-5 to Intellect
+2 to Strength
-10% to Satisfaction every 6 hrs.
+15% to Metabolism
Warning! Imminent danger of spontaneous erections!
In order to disable the debuff, you're advised to restrict your contacts with the subject or to engage them in sexual intercourse.

Slowly, as if walking across a mine field, I stepped aside, suppressing my desire to take her in my arms and press my lips to hers. My heart was pounding, trying to escape my chest; my breathing so fast that I was afraid she could read me like an open book.

Her lips parted in a smile. She took a step in the same direction, blocking my path, threw her arms around me and lifted my chin in her hand,

"Well, Phil," she whispered. "Or should I say

Philip Panfilov, social-status level 16, a Knowledge Seeker? I think it's time we have a talk."

I felt as if someone had poured a bucket of cold water over me. I recoiled and stared at her without replying.

Another program user? Was it the answer to her weird behavior? But why was she here?

"It's all right, Phil," she said softly but firmly. "Everything's fine. I'm not gonna hurt you."

"You too?" I managed.

"I too what? You mean, an interface user? Is that how you call it?"

"Of course. An interface. An augmented-reality program."

"I'm gonna tell you everything in a moment. Honest. Let's just go somewhere else first."

"How about we go to a restaurant?"

"No, it's too busy. It's a private conversation. But we can't talk here because the concierge already passed by to ask when we were leaving. She needs to lock up the building. Can we go to your place?"

Her last words caused another stirring in my nether regions. "Okay. Let's go to my place."

"You know," she paused as she tried to put her thoughts into words, "I just want you to know. We're very proud of you."

"*You?*"

"Yes, us. I'll explain later. Let's go."

We left the office. Stacy locked the door and we went downstairs. We shook the old lady awake at her desk and she let us out of the building, grumbling.

'Let's walk a few blocks," Stacy offered. "I've got a car parked over there."

As we walked, I showered her with questions but she just smiled. After a couple of streets, we turned off into a small inconspicuous courtyard where she'd parked her car: a silver two-seater Cayman.

While I stood there open-mouthed, trying to correlate the car's predatory curves with its owner, Stacy gracefully slid into the driver's seat. "Jump in!"

The day was full of surprises — and the questions it raised seemed to be multiplying faster than a colony of bacteria. I sank into a leather bucket seat and gave her my address.

"Hold onto your hat," she promised ominously as she pulled out of the courtyard.

Then she put her foot to the floor.

Overcoming the acceleration which pushed me back into the seat, I buckled up and spent the next five minutes trying not to think about anything except staying alive. She masterfully navigated the traffic, overtaking, cutting up and sneaking into the tiniest of gaps.

We approached my residential area's gatehouse. Stacy lowered her window. I nodded to the guard who raised the barrier, flagging us through.

For the first time since Vicky had left, a girl was coming to my house. And what a girl! I'd have lied to you if I'd said it didn't prickle my fantasy. It could have been the Smitten debuff — having said that, I might not have even needed the interface to have received it.

Still, my Self-Control was by now developed

enough to ask her to make herself comfortable on the couch and get busy making dinner. She kept asking if she could help me but I declined.

"I'm leveling Cooking, so I think I can manage."

She smiled for the umpteenth time that evening but nodded and left me to my host duties. I wasn't going to make anything too elaborate, anyway. I just pulled a pre-cooked turkey out of the fridge, warmed it up and fixed a quick salad by slicing the meat and adding some canned corn, beans and some herbs. It took me all of ten minutes at the most.

As we ate, I couldn't help noticing that she was hungry too. We ate in silence, our forks working overtime. She was the first to finish and get up from the table.

"Stay where you are," she said, smiling. "Tea, coffee? I'll serve, okay?"

"Sure. Let's have some coffee before I doze off again. It should be in that cupboard over there."

We took our coffees and moved to the lounge. I pulled the coffee table closer to the couch where Stacy had already made herself comfortable. She was sitting in a perfectly businesslike way — nothing frivolous about it. She looked focused and ready to talk.

So was I. "So who are you really? Anastasia Semyonova?"

"It's better that I show you," she got up and uttered something unintelligible.

Immediately her appearance began to change. She grew to over six foot tall, her hair changing color to a shimmering platinum blonde. Her skin was now covered in an elaborate network of fancy tattoos. Her eyes changed color, becoming iridescent; the pointy tips of her ears peeked through her hair.

I'd definitely seen this... eh... *creature* before.

"I'm Ilindi," her voice too was now different, melodious like the babbling of a brook. "I'm not from this planet. I'm a Rhoa."

"A Rhoa?" I repeated, trying to form the word.

"No, try saying it a little softer: a *Rhoa*. That's the name we call ourselves. Not so long ago our civilization revealed itself to the Commonwealth of Sentient Races. We were offered a choice of either submitting ourselves to the Diagnostics in order to determine our place in the Commonwealth or to be *annulled*. Your race isn't the first one on your planet who's entered the Universal Infospace. There were others before you. They all failed the Diagnostics."

My mental view filled with images of various extinct civilizations. Some of them I'd definitely seen before while others were completely new to me. I could see deserted cities which had crumbled to dust in the millions of years that had passed on Earth; a race of seven-foot-tall flying dinosaurs which had left nothing except more empty cities to remember them by; I witnessed the evolution of species and a new renaissance of sentient life.

This was very similar to the mental images Khphor had sent me during my first abduction.

Ilindi sat next to me and waited patiently for me to take in everything she'd just told me.

"Stace," I began, "oh, sorry, Ilindi..."

"Call me how you want," she smiled just like Stacy. "My name has the same meaning in our language as Anastasia has in yours[46]."

"Okay, Stace. D'you know that I remember you? But how do you know me?"

My question made sense. If Martha had indeed reloaded reality — and if the mechanism of it was the same as last night at the poker club — then Ilindi couldn't have possibly remembered my first abduction. Khphor I could understand: he traveled reality planes all the time. But her?

"If you're talking about your first abduction, I saw you in a dream," she shrugged in a very human manner. "Our dreams are different from yours: we sometimes see things that happen in other reality branches. Not always, not everyone and definitely not often — but it does happen at certain life-changing moments. What's more, since then I saw you again and tried to contact you in that particular reality too, only in a different form."

"Eh... what kind of form?"

"We met at a mall not far from here. Remember that girl, Milena, who was looking for her nephew in the crowd? It was actually me. I decided to get a closer look at you and arranged for you to approach me of your own accord. You didn't recognize me either then or now. That's because I possess a certain ability which allows me to conceal my true identity. In order to see through the illusion, you need to have a very high

---

[46] Anastasia means "Resurrected" in Greek

Insight. I wanted to make sure you actually were considerate and helpful, ready to come to a stranger's aid."

Milena? A mall? A flurry of vague images filled my mind, evading all attempts to bring them into focus. Still, I managed to grasp a few scenes: a crazy car chase out of town, me beating someone up, followed by rain, mud and a dark pit in the ground...

"I can't remember," I finally admitted. "But I have a funny feeling that's exactly how it happened."

"The creature that appeared in the office by your side, is it your assistant?"

"Martha? Did you see her? How?"

"So she *is* your assistant," Ilindi nodded, apparently pleased to hear my answer. "I'd venture a guess that you, consciously or not, must have awoken your AI, triggering its development. Did you set any energy consumption restrictions for her?"

"No. Did I need to?"

"Judging by the fact that you're still alive and we're talking, it's a good job you didn't do it. Once self-aware, the AI prevented your interface from being uninstalled after the first abduction and used the nano-second opportunity this had created in order not to confirm the activation of your heroic system skill. That was something neither Nick nor I had anticipated."

"Nick?"

"You know him as Valiadis," Ilindi paused and sipped her coffee.

"Stace, are you sure you can drink this? You're

an alien, after all..."

"Why not? As the result of ancient panspermia, humanity is physically very close to the Rhoa. We're even genetically compatible. There're several other races that are relatively kindred to us both. If you pass the Trial, you'll get the opportunity to see them all with your own eyes. They too belong to Junior races and are preparing for the Diagnostics."

"What did you say about Valiadis? I only saw him the other day."

"I know. What's happening to you now is the result of an agreement between him and I."

I choked on my coffee and very nearly spat it out. "So it was you two! You installed that thing in my head!"

"Not quite. But it was us who introduced a few changes to it."

"What sort of changes?"

"You see, Phil, the Commonwealth is preparing for war. A big war of total destruction. It's not going to happen overnight by your standards. It might take thousands of years. But the Senior races can see everything that's gonna happen and calculate the odds of any turn of events. The war is imminent. Our Galaxy is preparing to repel an external enemy."

"External? What does that mean?"

"I don't know. Junior races don't have the clearance necessary to access this information. Still, according to our analysts, it's either another Galaxy or possibly even another dimension. The Commonwealth is in need of warriors. The so-called Diagnostics is their way of pitting Junior races against each other without much harm coming to our economies. The winners who successfully pass the Diagnostics will be admitted into the Commonwealth. Their future role is pretty clear, though: they're destined to become cannon fodder for the upcoming war. The Senior races are too few to put up any kind of fight."

"But we haven't even started to expand into the Solar system yet! What intergalactic wars are you talking about?"

"The winners will be boosted, as you gamers call it. Their civilizations will be granted access to the Senior races' technologies. Millions of your young will receive special training. Whenever a Junior race is accepted into the Commonwealth, its technological progress exceeds everything in its past history within a few years. The winners will gain access to the most classified layers of the Universal Infospace — just so that they could shield our Galaxy from the aggression with their own bodies when the time comes."

She paused. "So, the Diagnostics. The number of races subjected to it is well over a thousand — but of these, only about two dozen are humanoid. So when they pit us against each other, we'll need allies. As an emissary posted to observe the candidate selection here on Earth, I met Nick. Both of us were the first among our peers to pass the Trial which made him an observer for the Rhoa. We had access to more information than all others, and I'm sharing it with you now. Basically, Nick and I struck an alliance between our two races and agreed on our cooperation during the Diagnostics. But seeing as the basic user interface for all candidates was built to answer the Vaalphors' demands, it encourages the primitive values inherent to them. It promotes aggression and social status leveling regardless of our moral values, with preference given to combat abilities and skills. To cut it short," Ilindi's face darkened, "a whole number of your most successful candidates who've already passed the Trial are complete psychos. Serial killers, religious extremists, backstabbing social climbers... If humanity is represented by these, we can forget signing an alliance. You won't even be able to unite in the face of danger, too absorbed by the power rat race."

"So what have you done to Valiadis?"

"He has the ability to install the interface into a candidate's mind. He receives their data, flies to them personally and uploads the interface while the candidate is asleep. It can be done remotely from a distance of a few hundred feet. Luckily, our technologies — I'm talking about my own race now — allow us to alter the initial settings. So for the last few months, Nick has been installing our own version of the interface which encourages good and socially meaningful actions. Phil?"

I opened my eyes, realizing I must have dozed off again. Ilindi was sitting next to me, stroking my cheek. She had already returned back to Stacy's guise.

'Sorry, I can't keep my eyes open," I yawned uncontrollably.

"Allow me," she said softly.

A wave of emerald light enveloped me.

What an incredible effect! I felt great. I wasn't sleepy at all anymore. I got a real high while a revitalizing energy was coursing my veins, making my blood bubble. My eyesight was perfectly clear, my hearing sharp, and my sense of smell... suffice it to say that I could smell the faint but heady scent of this Rhoa woman, reminiscent of a fresh breeze and pine needles.

The program duly informed me of a new buff I'd just received:

Healing Touch (1 hr.)
Removes all negative effects
+5 to all main characteristics
+100% to Vigor
+100% to Willpower
+100% to Spirit
+100% to Self-Control
+100% to Metabolism

"How are you feeling, then?" Ilindi asked.

"Like I've just been reborn. How did you do that?"

She smiled. "Just a heroic ability I have, available to the First Hero."

"So you..."

She nodded. "Yes."

"And Valiadis?"

"Not him, no. None of the Terrans has done it yet."

"But Stace, what does that mean? Who the hell is the First Hero of this particular local segment of our

Galaxy?"

"It means the maximum social status level in the entire history of a race. It's granted to a person who's done more than anyone else for their peers. Not for a separate nation, mind you, but for an entire race."

"I see... And who is the best on our planet?"

Ilindi smiled. "How would I know?"

We kept silent for a while. Unable to contain the energy raging in me, I rose and started pacing the room. "I only have one question left. Why did you have to tell me all this?"

"Because I liked you."

"Oh please. Do me a favor."

"I'm serious. You've shown the best progress among all the candidates in possession of our version of the interface. I'd have loved to see you standing shoulder to shoulder with my people at the Diagnostics. But to do that, you need to pass the Trial first. And you're not ready yet."

"You're dead right there," I said, remembering the acid jelly. "I don't even know what's required of me. Am I supposed to fight with somebody and win?"

"Of course. You need to win. Every Trial wave has its own rules but their essence is the same. It's an elimination game in which only one of the initial 169 participants can win. You should come prepared. From our combined experience, I can tell you that you'll be required to show your mastery of each of the stats you already have. You'll be given several tasks: some can be solved through strength, others through agility or perception, or leadership and negotiation skills.

Combat skills are important but even without them, you still have a chance. You'll know what I mean when you finally face the judges on the Trial grounds."

She leaned and kissed me on the lips. For a brief while, I lost control, giving in to desire. Then she shrank back and rose.

"I need to go. I think I know enough about you now. I'm very happy you didn't disappoint me. I'm not going back to work, sorry. I've already spent too much time on you as it is. But I'll be around. The day of your second abduction is near, and this time you won't get another chance. I beg you to concentrate on your progress."

"Can I see you to the car?"

"You should rest now," she commanded.

My eyelids felt heavy.

"I've disabled Smitten," she added. "Sorry I had to use it on you."

Despite her order, I saw her to the front door, locked it and returned to the lounge. The office key lay on the coffee table where she'd left it.

I took my clothes off, switched off the light and headed for the bedroom.

As I was falling asleep, I decided to run Vicky and myself through that Synergy thing as a married couple.

In this case, instead of our annual income, the program evaluated both our personal and combined happiness levels. It resulted in an average of 44%. Which meant that Vicky's presence made me almost three times less happy. And the next year, it dropped even more.

The program's prognosis was rather unpromising: another year and a half of living as a couple would put us in the red happiness-wise. And then we'd part ways again, for good this time.

The gnawing pain in my chest which all these days had intensified every time I'd thought about Vicky now began to ease up. Don't get me wrong, I still loved her — but faced with the program's impartial opinion, this feeling began to give way to rational thinking.

Just out of curiosity I decided to check Yanna too. There, the picture wasn't much better. Had we renewed our relationship, we might have been happy for a while but would have been forced to split up again within less than a year.

Ditto for Veronica. But between her and Alik, that was different. 200% Synergy!

I tried Ilindi but the program kept offering an error message.

My lips stretched into a smile. When I finally fell asleep, my last flashing thought was that I'd have to grill Martha about everything that had happened to me in my "past lives"...

CHAPTER

SEVENTEEN

MY FOURTH LIFE

*Self-improvement is masturbation, self-
destruction is the answer.*

Fight Club

I AWOKE FROM AN UNBEARABLE PIERCING PAIN IN THE
back of my head.

Gasping, I got out of bed, sat up and opened the
interface. It was 7.33 a.m., Saturday July 21 2018. It
was only twenty-four hours ago that Gleb and I had
come back from the poker club where I'd won enough
to pay his debts back. And late last night, I'd spoken to
Stacy — or Ilindi, rather — here at home.

But what had I experienced right now? That
hadn't been a dream. I still remembered every detail of
it: the fear, the fury, the stench of gas and fire, the taste

of earth in my mouth, the sound of gunfire still ringing in my ears. If felt as if it only had just happened.

This dream — although it wasn't a dream, really — had forced me to live several days of some other life which was still undoubtedly my own. In that life, I was still with Vicky and had popped out one night to fetch some cat food for Boris.

That's when I'd met that girl, Milena, at the mall. She looked lost and tearful. The icon of an active quest hovered over her head. Apparently, she'd lost her little nephew in the crowd.

His name was Joseph Kogan, six years old.

I'd just seen him at the parking lot, accompanied by some guy. The boy's behavior had seemed a little strange to me. He was staggering, his face blank. The man — whose name was Grechkin — had helped him into a car and driven off.

Now that I'd spoken to Milena, I used the boy's marker to locate him on the map and offered her my help. We used her car to chase after the abductor and forced him to release the child. When I realized what could have happened to the boy, I gave the guy a good hiding, unable to restrain myself. In the end, he said he'd found the boy at the mall and had decided to take him home to his parents. Milena refused to call the cops, so the guy got off the hook. Still, the quest was duly closed and even added a few nice points to my Insight.

Valeri Grechkin turned out to be a well-appointed official at the town hall. Apparently, he had a long memory. His associates worked out where I lived. So a few days later, they punched my lights out, threw me in the trunk and took me out of town to Grechkin's hunting lodge. They were the same two junks who were later responsible for my third death at the casino: Wheezie and Zak.

They kept me in an underground cellar for two days naked, without food or water. All that time I kept leveling up my physical stats while feeding on earth worms (which are an excellent source of protein) and quenching my thirst with the rainwater dripping from above.

When they'd finally dragged me out and brought me into the house, making me kneel in front of Grechkin, I recognized the whole bunch of them straight away. Next to him stood none other than Colonel "Dimedrol" complete with his two sidekicks.

The program must have recalculated my environmental safety index based on all the hardships I'd had to suffer. I won't bore you with the details, but it had allowed me to activate my Stealth and Vanish heroic ability right in front of all those bloodsuckers. Fifteen seconds of invisibility turned out to have been plenty of time to grab the gun from Wheezie and smoke them all.

I could also remember dousing the place with gasoline and watch this den of iniquity being razed to the ground.

And then I'd died.

"MORNING, PHIL!" I heard Martha's voice a mere few feet away. "How are you feeling?"

"Martha? What's happened?"

"Before falling asleep, you told me to restore the memories of your past lives. Your first life ended when you confronted the acid jelly during the first Trial. You didn't die but in order to avoid the uninstallation of the interface, I had to bring you back to the moment in time when you were driving to the Ultrapak corporate party. That was the night you met Victoria."

"Yes, I remember."

"Your third life ended 31 hours 23 minutes ago. You were stabbed in the heart by Zachary "Zak" Nikolaev."

"I remember that, too."

"Consequently, in order to carry out your orders, I had to make you relive your second life, the one ending when Zak shot you dead at Dimedrol's house. I can't plant that actual memory into your mind just like I can't plant knowledge. But I can give you the possibility to relive a certain scenario in your dream. So I showed you the last days of your second life."

"But how could I have relived several days in one night's sleep?"

"Time flows much faster when you're asleep. We use this a lot in the future whenever we want to take a break, relive certain happy moments or reinforce a certain skill..."

"Oh really?" I interrupted her. "Does that mean that nothing of what I'd experienced last night has added to my stats?"

I opened the interface and heaved a sigh of disappointment. I could have used the Stealth and

Vanish skill I'd received in my second life.

"No, because all you did in your dream was relive a prerecorded scenario without playing an active part in it," she explained. "You were only an onlooker even though you might have thought you'd taken part in the events because you saw everything in real time without activating your own memories of whatever had happened after the reality had split. For the Phil who was killed that night by Wheezie's gunshot, it was all for real. But for you as you are now, life took a different turn the night you'd decided to stay at home instead of fetching cat food from the mall. Which means that now..."

"Now I've lost three lives," I whispered. "Is this my last one?"

"Yes. Until now, I managed to circumvent the activation requirements because you don't fulfil them, anyway. But I can't do it anymore. No idea which one of our alien friends had grassed you up but they seem to have installed a patch on your interface. It's nothing serious except that I don't have access to blocked abilities anymore."

"I see," I said pensively. Then I remembered my dream. "I can remember the other Phil change the environmental safety index. Mind telling me more about it? I never got around to it."

She went on explaining that the program could evaluate the user's environment and bestow additional stat points on him provided his or her social status level was above average within a certain local segment of our Galaxy. The more dangerous the environment and the higher the user's importance, the cooler the freebies.

That was really important to know. I really had to try and do the same in this life, too.

I unsummoned Martha. When she'd disappeared, I'd spent a long time trying to get my head around it by superimposing my dual memories. In order to do that, I had to insert a few fragments from my second life — namely, when Vicky had had a bad premonition and come back home to me from her parents'.

I had a lot to grasp: the constantly changing environmental safety index with its perks; the Stealth and Vanish heroic ability, incredible in its coolness, which I'd rejected in favor of Lie Detection; the possibility of leveling Insight by doing social quests... I still had to give all this some thought in order to use it in my real-life leveling.

Gradually, the picture came into focus.

The other Phil had gone to fetch some cat food for Boris. Stacy, a.k.a. Ilindi the Rhoa, had been Milena in this Phil's life. He'd joined a different boxing group: not the one with Mohammed and Kostya but the one with Yuri and the Tatar guy — the group that practiced Mondays, Wednesdays and Fridays. The other Phil had leveled up faster than I did... by the same token, he'd also died much quicker than the third one.

And here I was, the fourth Phil. The fourth and the last.

Both my gaming past and the months spent with the interface had allowed me to take the news relatively lightly. What made me furious was the anger, the hate and the malice that I felt toward Wheezie and Zak — the two junks who'd killed me twice already, — as well as their corrupt boss "Dimedrol" and especially that pedophile Grechkin. The fact that I'd managed to turn him in in this life was some consolation because by doing so, I must have saved little Joseph again.

My phone vibrated on the bedside table. It was Kostya texting me that he expected me at the school stadium in half an hour.

As I got ready, I kept thinking about all the things that still needed to be done. We had to grow the company; I had to level up real-life skills and abilities and prepare for my next abduction and the following Trial. Also, I would have loved to hire Cyril, Marina and Greg, seeing as we already needed some savvy salespeople.

As I walked out of the house, I realized something very important. You couldn't defeat the likes of Dimedrol and his sidekicks by combat skills alone. If you punished them, others would simply take their place. So if I had to choose between Batman and Superman, I'd prefer Bruce Wayne but with Superman's skills.

* * *

"HAVE YOU GOT YOUR GLOVES?" Kostya asked.

The rising sun was shining in our eyes. He crouched down on the running track by his gym bag, squinting at me from under his eyebrows. You wouldn't say he was only twenty-one. He was economical with both his words and movements like an arthritic old man calculating his every move.

Still, I could hardly have called him a "young man with an old man's eyes", the way they describe someone who's experienced a lot in their few years of life. His eyes were young and full of life.

It was just that he didn't speak much and practically never smiled. The reason for this was standing right next to him: his four-year-old sister Julie. As today was the weekend, he'd brought her along to the training session.

The girl seemed to have some rare children's disease. I didn't know any details. She looked like any other girl, only very skinny and pale, almost translucent. Her dark-blond hair was clumsily braided into two plaits — probably, one of Kostya's jobs.

"Uncle Phil! Kostya's asking you if you've brought the gloves!" the girl's voice was remarkably bright and her diction clear.

"Yes, I've got them," I replied with a smile.

"Fancy some sparring?" Kostya banged his gloves together.

We'd already finished training, so his offer had come as a surprise.

"Aren't you in a hurry?" I asked, surprised.

"Where to? I don't need to take her to the kindergarten today. Am I right, Juls? Once we're done, we can go for a walk. She keeps asking me to take her to see this cartoon, so we might go to the flicks."

"The flicks! Yes!" the girl twirled around on the

---

spot, pressing her favorite doll to her chest. I noticed she was slightly limping. Something wasn't right with her hip.

"What do the doctors say?" I asked Kostya, nodding at the girl.

"We need to have her operated on before she turns six. But our surgeons won't take the risk. We need to go abroad," he walked over to me. "Come on, put 'em up!"

As we exchanged blows, Julie kept chanting, supporting her brother,

"Kostya! Kostya!"

But as soon as I'd missed a number of rather painful jabs, she changed camp and started to support me instead. It must be our national trait to root for an underdog. At a certain point, Kostya relaxed and missed my right hook. He recoiled, gesturing to me to stop.

I waited for him to come round. My hook had been a beauty!

Congratulations! You've received a new skill level!

Skill name: Boxing
Current level: 6
XP received: 500

"Not bad," he said, holding his jaw, then added with a disarming smile, "Serves me right for dropping my guard. It's all right, Sis, don't you worry!"

Julie stood next to him, clinging to his leg. She

---

could support me all she wanted but blood was thicker than water.

"How about we stop for today?" I asked.

"Sure. I'm not in good shape today. I'm not saying you're gonna win the championship," he laughed at the absurdity of the idea, "but you might get through a few rounds."

"You mean the championship that Matov invited us to?"

"Yeah."

"Why don't you enroll yourself?"

He shrugged and nodded surreptitiously at Julie.

"Sorry, I don't understand," I said.

"What's there not to understand? Didn't you hear me when I said I couldn't afford it? At the moment, every penny counts. I'm saving... you know what I mean?"

"How about we go for a run?" I turned to the girl. "Do you mind waiting here while your brother and I jog a little? What's your doll's name?"

"It's Angelique."

"You and Angelique wait here, okay?"

She nodded and stepped away from her brother, perching herself on a bench next to his bag. Kostya and I set off at a trot.

"So what's with the tournament?" I asked.

"They're a bit greedy with the entry fee."

"What, ten thousand rubles?"

"Ten thousand! Ten thousand rubles can last us two a month! I earn thirty grand as a trainee and I set some of it aside for her surgery, then we live off the rest. Are you suggesting I dip into her money? Let them get stuffed!" he spat in disgust. "Matov grabs what he can from it all."

"What do you mean?"

"He's got some kind of shady business with them. He sends his fighters to clandestine matches. There're several coaches like him there. If a normal coach trains his athletes for legitimate competitions, these bastards..." he lowered his voice, "they only think about their bank accounts. The other boys told me a few things about them."

"What do you mean?"

"You heard. You too had to pay for the training. They're on the lookout for promising lads and bring them into the League, or so they call it. If you win a season, they'll whisk you off to Moscow or somewhere. From what I heard, they took some guy to Grozny: they like the illegal fight scene over there. And if you prove yourself at this level, they'll set you up with an agent. That's where the money gets serious. None of our group has ever managed to make it. They're more likely to have their brains punched out and seen off with a handicapped allowance."

"Why won't they make the tournament free, then?" I asked, sincerely surprised. "The more people that sign up, the more choice they'd have, wouldn't they?"

"Phil, how am I supposed to know? I've had no part in their schemes. Let me just tell you that Matov really wanted me to join but I have no one to leave this little button with," he turned and took a long look at the girl, "if anything ever happens to me."

He slowed down to a walk, put his feet together and reached down to touch his toes.

In the meantime, I opened my interface and made a few mental commands. Kostya's profile unfolded in front of me. This time it contained much more information than I normally saw. That's level-3 Insight for you!

Konstantin "Kostya" Bekhterev
Age: 21
Current status: Web Programmer
Social status level: 6
Class: Boxer. Level: 8
Unmarried.
Children: none

Main characteristics:
Strength: 11/24
Aguility: 14/25
Intellect: 10/17
Stamina: 19/37
Perception: 15/15
Charisma: 6/19
Luck: 7/12

Secondary characteristics:
Vitality: 98%
Satisfaction: 73%
Vigor: 91%

Metabolism: 118%
Confidence: 88%
Self-Control: 99%
Spirit: 164%
Mood: 85%

Main skills and abilities:
Boxing: 8/14
Responsibility: 7/15
Self-Discipline: 7/12
PHP Programming: 6/11

So! Now I could see not only his full profile but also the maximum extent of the stat points he could earn. And what did that mean? It meant that now I could advise my clients on their potential development.

I couldn't wait to see my own possibilities but decided to give it a miss for the time being. I might need to look into it first.

I remembered Martha's request and scrolled through Kostya's ability list, searching for Tutoring. I found it halfway through the list:

Tutoring: 5/11

Not bad. Having to raise his sister must have had something to do with it. And he had a lot to grow still, seeing as he was still level 5. So how could I help him?

I opened the map and run a quick search for any potential employment for him, concentrating on improving his working conditions and pay. Then I checked his profile again. He had the potential to reach level 14 in Boxing which was really a lot. Overall, he was very well-developed for his age.

"Phil, what are you hanging around for?" Kostya called out. "Are we done?"

"Wait a sec," I said. "We haven't finished talking yet. Hey listen, where are your parents? Don't you have any relatives?"

He scowled. "Why the hell would you want to know? I'm training you, ain't I? What else do you want?"

"Sorry, it's none of my business. I just wanted to offer you something."

"Like what?" he laughed. "Babysitter's services? I'm doing okay as it is."

"No, that's not what I meant," I sat down on the rubbery surface of the track, spread my legs and touched my toes. "Are you happy with your current job?"

"Why shouldn't I be? They pay me on time. Suits me down to the ground."

"Look, there's a vacancy in a company who're looking for somebody like you. There's a high probability they might hire you."

"Nah, I don't think so. I'm perfectly happy where I am."

"Even during the trial period they pay sixty grand[47]. Try it! You've only just said you don't earn

---

[47] About $900

enough."

"Where is it?" he froze, looking at me closely.

"It's a studio specializing in mid-range corporate sites. I can give you their number. Just call them and find out."

"So what do I say?"

No matter how responsible and disciplined he was, his childishness was starting to grate on my nerves. Why should I have to talk him into another job where he might get paid twice as much for the same work?

"Listen, it's not as if you're stupid," I said. "I'm sure you'll work out what to tell them. Just say you're a PHP code writer and you're calling them about the vacancy. I'll text you their number."

"Okay, then. Let's go," he rose and brushed the bits of rubber off his track bottoms. "Julie's already waving to us, look!"

"Come on, then," I rose too. Together we leisurely walked over to Julie. "And let's do one more thing. I'll pay your entry fee for the tourna-"

"No," he cut me short.

"Wait, listen! Why not?"

"I don't need charity. Is that clear?" he stepped closer and glared at me, flaring his nostrils.

I promptly received a new system message informing me of a drop in my Reputation with him.

"Whoa whoa whoa! Wait up! What charity are you talking about?" I said, changing tactics. "What's all that about? This is a business proposal!"

"What kind of business?" he squinted at me. "I

---

just can't work you out, Phil."

"Listen up. The entry fee is ten grand. I can pay it, no problem. This isn't a loan or charity, man, you listen to me! Once you win, you pay me ten percent. If you lose, you pay it back after Julie is cured. So? What do you think? Or are you already shitting yourself that they might carry you out feet first?"

"What?" he bellowed. "Me?"

"Yes, you. So I suggest you stuff your pride where the sun don't shine and go fight for your sister. Will the prize money be enough for the surgery?"

"Eh... well," he paused, making mental calculations. "Together with what I've already saved, it should be enough."

"That's settled, then. Get your stuff and let's go to my place to get the money. It's right here nearby."

"Eh... you don't want to go to the lawyer? To certify that I owe you and all that?"

"Your word is enough for me. Let's go."

So we went. I walked first, followed by Kostya hand in hand with his little sister.

Before we'd reached the house, the system informed me of another Reputation change. This time to Amicality.

* * *

I'D GIVEN HIM THE ENTRY MONEY FROM MY OWN SHARE of the poker tournament winnings.

Now I was standing on the balcony, watching them leave: Kostya, who was still so young, virtually a boy, and his little "button" Julie. He walked in the unhurried gait of a grown man while she scampered along, clutching her brother's hand.

As I watched them, I realized that this young man barely twenty years old could better me in most things. I might be older and almost twice as smart, but no amount of my Intellect could hold a candle to him. Both his social status level and his stats were already higher than mine had been before I'd received the interface.

But most importantly, he was already a man — while I still had some way to go. Because it's not sleeping with a woman that makes you a man. In order to become one, you need to accept the responsibility for someone in your life and bear this responsibility with the same dignity as Kostya, without whining or complaining.

I liked his character and I was prepared to do everything I could to help him and his sister. Some might say that I was screwing around instead of leveling up; others could say I did it for XP. Neither would be right. Something had changed in me the night when Yanna had left me and the only person who'd offered me some support was that street bum, Alik.

And once I'd helped him and his eternal gratitude had been confirmed by the interface, something shifted in me. Some cogs within me started crunching until they whirred into motion, clearing my rust-ridden soul and filling it with new blood, fresh and clean.

Since then, I'd learned to live not only with

myself and my own flitting interests — but to also sympathize and relate to other people, becoming aware of my important but by far not unique persona in this enormous but tiny world. My new discoveries had been amazing. Instead of chatting, I now spoke to people; instead of just looking indifferently at them, I could see each and every one of them; and as we talked, I could hear and understand them.

Alik's phone call disrupted my musings. "Hi, Phil. Did I wake you up?"

"Hi yourself. Whassup?"

"Eh... you know... Gorelik is holding a sales seminar. Wait a sec..." I could hear the rustle of him opening a piece of paper. "Listen here: Aram Ovsepyan is an Internet star and an expert in proactive selling," he started reading theatrically. "The course's curriculum contains a number of very important skills and practices indispensable for any sales manager striving for success!"

"Ah, that one. I remember. Why, do you want to sign up? Are you striving for success? Didn't Gorelik say the tickets cost ten grand?"

"That's exactly my point!" he laughed into the receiver. "He didn't sell enough tickets! So now he's prepared to let us in for a thousand!"

"Us? Who do you mean? Are you in the office? It's the weekend!"

"Eh... yeah. We're all here: me, Gleb and Veronica. Stacy's the only one missing. Kesha's here too but he's in his print shop."

"So what are you all doing there, may I ask?"

"It just happened. I've nothing to do, anyway. Then Gleb said he might come and make a *tropotype...*"

I could hear Gleb guffaw in the background. "*Prototype*, you idiot! It's *prototype!*"

"Well, whatever," Alik continued. "Basically, he wants to do our website. Veronica had a meeting here. And as for Kesha, I've no idea why he came. So what do you think about this seminar? They start in less than an hour. Are we going?"

"Who do you mean?"

"Well, I wouldn't say no to listening for a bit. It's Aram himself, after all. I think Kesha wanted to come, too. And also..."

The receiver rustled. "Hi, Phil," I heard Veronica's voice. "Listen, a thousand is no money. I suggest we all go..." I heard Gleb's voice again in the background, "apart from Gleb. He says selling isn't his thing, and seeing as we're all such consummate salespeople, someone has to stay behind and do their work for them," she giggled. "He can answer the phone as well, seeing as he's in the office anyway. What do you think?"

I smiled. "Okay, let's all go back to school on this fine Saturday morning. I'm coming now."

I put the phone down. My plans for the day had been somewhat different — but then again, there was no hurry in dishing out the spare stat points. But the training might prove useful, you never know. Not just to advance the actual skill but also as a good example of spontaneous team building which I'd just witnessed.

Also, how could I have said no? The guys had

come to the office on the weekend and were itching to get some training in. Who was I to put them off?

In the half-hour that was left, I managed to take a shower, feed the cat, get dressed and even pick up a bottle of yogurt to drink on the go.

Fifteen minutes before the training was supposed to start, I reached the office building.

A group of young people stood smoking on the porch. I thought I recognized the back of one of them. According to the interface, I was right: it was Greg "Bullshit Artist" Boyko, my illustrious Ultrapak ex-workmate.

"Greg?"

"Phil! Marina, look what's the wind's blown in!" Greg turned to the girl standing next to him, then reached out to give me a bear hug.

"Hi, Phil," Marina laid her hands on my shoulders and gave me a peck on the cheek, dangerously close to my lips. "Are you going training as well?"

"Yeah. We actually have an office here. And you, which wind blew you two in?"

Greg cringed. "Boss' orders. I've had it with his new fads up to here!"

"Orders? What does that mean?" I asked, sincerely surprised. "If the company pays for your professional development, it can only be a good thing, can't it?"

"Listen Phil," Marina butted in. "First of all, do you have any idea who this Aram is? He knows very well how to sell his courses but that's the only thing he does know!"

"Sure. A good sales manager should be an expert on the kinds of goods he sells," Greg said theatrically with a nasal accent. "And this guy is just like our Panchenko: all he can do is repeat sets of clichés in a pretty wrapper."

"But that's not really important," Marina fumed. "They don't pay us anything. Or rather, they do but-"

"No, they don't!" Greg exploded. "Panchenko has his own secret arrangements with Aram. They're going to deduct the course's cost from our wages."

"No! Are you serious? And you agreed to it?"

Marina sighed. "He simply didn't leave us any choice. He just said that all of us needed to improve ASAP. According to him, we were a bunch of useless bastards who didn't know how to do their jobs, and he was the only one keeping the department afloat. So we all had to master the art of selling."

"And just then, the great expert Aram arrived in town. What a lucky coincidence," Greg continued. "And those who didn't want to study, didn't deserve the proud title of an Ultrapak sales rep."

"But what did Ivanov say?"

"The old boy seems to have completely lost all interest," Marina explained. "Any questions we have, he sends us to Panchenko. Like, he's the one to decide."

"I'm sick and tired of it all," Greg added. "They fired Cyril, can you imagine? I think it's time we jumped ship. But where would we go?"

"You know, guys," I paused, making some mental calculations. "Would you like to meet *our* commercial director after the training? His name is Kesha. You never know, we might end up working together."

They exchanged glances.

Marina beamed. "With pleasure!"

"I'm all for kicking up a stink!" Greg laughed. "What are we gonna sell?"

"Everything," I said, giving them both a high-five. "As soon as Cyril gets better, I'll poach him too."

The rest of my team appeared on the porch: Alik, Veronica and Kesha, looking for me in the crowd. They saw me and waved,

"Come on, Phil! The show's about to start!" Kesha shouted.

Is it indeed, I thought as I laced my hands around Greg and Marina's shoulders and steered them away to introduce them to the intrepid staff of the Great Job Agency.

MEETING GREG AND MARINA PROVED TO HAVE BEEN THE best thing about Aram Ovsepyan's seminar. Even though the training had added a few meager points to my Vending skill, watching the speaker turned out to be far more entertaining than listening to what he'd had to say.

Here I might mention that although his Vending level was the same as mine, his Public Speaking, Motivation and Communication Skills were indeed very high. Especially Motivation. No wonder the audience left his seminars feeling elated.

My crowd wasn't an exception.

After the training, we all got together in our office. Suddenly the room had become very cramped. I shared my outsourcing sales department idea with them. If Kesha could indeed take on the responsibility of closing the department's contracts, then Greg, Marina and hopefully soon also Cyril, were supposed to sell the products and services of our new customers.

In the end, we shook on it. Greg and Marina were so excited that they decided to quit Ultrapak the moment Kesha brought in our first contract. I was quite adamant that this would happen very soon because we had a unique business proposition as we were working on a percentage basis without charging them any additional fees. I'd already eyed up a few potential contracts and was going to suggest them inconspicuously to Kesha if he began to stall.

As we parted, Marina dropped a dark hint that she'd split up with her grad student and was back on the market. Greg chuckled. Both Alik and Gleb ignored this new piece of information entirely. Kesha, however, perked up and somehow ended up seeing her home.

I took Alik aside and suggested he took Veronica to the flicks. At first he threw up a few excuses but in the end he plucked up enough courage to speak to her. After their conversation, he rejoined me red in the face, looking embarrassed but happy. He grinned and gave me a big thumbs-up.

"Tomorrow!" he mouthed.

---

* * *

SEEING AS THEY'D KICKED ME OUT OF THE GYM, I NOW had to find a new one. As I signed on at a small fitness club next to my house, I replayed the events of the past few days. So many things had happened to me this last week.

On Tuesday, Stacy had arrived at our office. The same night, I'd had a fight with Mohammed and had been expelled from Matov's boxing group. Right after that, Vicky had left me.

On Wednesday, I'd had the first of my two training sessions with Kostya, followed by me meeting Valiadis. After that, I'd come across the Ring of Veles. It also had been the first of Stacy's three days working with us. And right after that, I'd come across Gleb waiting on my doorstep in a lamentable state.

On Thursday, he'd come with me to the office where I'd talked Veronica and Kesha into working for us. That day, I'd also received the complimentary copy of the first book I'd ever written. In the evening, I'd visited my parents after which I'd plunged into the whirlwind of gambling adventures, stupidly wasted my last available life but saved Gleb and brought him back into the fold.

The Friday had been relatively uneventful if you disregarded the mind-blowing evening of Stacy-a.k.a.-Ilindi's revelations and the following night's sleep during which I'd managed to relive the last four days of my second life.

It had only been eighty-four hours since Vicky

had left me — but for anybody else, these events would have been plenty to last them a year.

It only took me a few minutes to arrange a monthly gym subscription. I had to fill in a form, pay for the first month and wait for the club card to be issued. The gym was quite small, with only a weights room and a few treadmills, but I was perfectly happy with it.

Deprived of exercise just lately, my muscles were more than pleased to top up with blood and stop their own atrophy. I knew of course that nothing drastic would have happened during such a short hiatus but as far as I knew, if you stopped exercising for more than a month, your body would start ridding itself of all the extra muscle it apparently didn't need.

After the gym, I decided I land myself a few social quests in order to level up Insight. After a couple of hours of fruitlessly roaming around the town, I stumbled across an old babushka who'd lost her cat.

You can't imagine how happy I was. Finally, a quest!

Unfortunately, I couldn't even use the interface because the old lady had no KIDD points to offer me. She had no cat's pictures or any ID information. According to her, the only "documents" to identify the missing moggy were:

"A bushy tail! His whiskers are a good foot long!" the old lady spread her hands wide, showing me how long his whiskers were. "He's a very pretty stripy gray color!" she added before dissolving in tears.

So once I'd accepted the quest, I was forced to

---

look for the cat the old-fashioned way, by checking all the nearby courtyards and looking in every back door, nook and cranny.

Finally, I came across a cat which fitted the description in a back yard two blocks away. He was perched on a wooden fence opposite a ginger tom, yowling and howling, preparing to attack.

> *Barsik. A male cat*
> *Age: 6*
> *Current status: pet*
> *Owner: Mrs. Eudoxia Moskalenko*

That was him. Shit. He was a real monster, wasn't he? How was I supposed to catch him? Or even grab him? His claws were just like Freddy Krueger's. It wasn't a cat — it was a flippin' wolverine.

"Barsik?" I said sweetly. "Puss-puss-puss!"

As if he gave a damn. I took a picture of him with my phone and hurried back to the old lady to ID him. On seeing the picture, she threw her hands in the air and started clucking like a chicken, demanding to know where he was and whether he was still alive.

"He's fine, granny! But that might not last. Come with me, I'll show you!"

I took her to the place where the two cats were still having their showdown, apparently unable to come to an agreement and wailing their appeal to the devil. This proved to be enough to complete the quest for which I even received all of 50 XP points — but not a single percent of Insight.

I spent the evening working on my custom leveling plan.

Before I went to bed, I decided to bring Agility up to 10. Admittedly, I was undecided whether I should improve Luck instead. Still, it looked like Khphor had given up surprising me while one sole point of Agility would be enough to implement my plan.

Warning! We've detected an abnormal increase in your Agility characteristic: +1 pt.

Your body will be restructured in keeping with the new reading (10) to comply with your new coordination and neuromuscular values.

Changes required: new adjustments to your central nervous system as well as the improvements to the elasticity of your muscles, sinews, ligaments and tendons.

Warning! The restructuring of your body functions requires a considerable amount of nutrients. In order to avoid danger to your life, you're strongly encouraged to consume a minimum of 7 oz. animal protein, 1.7 lbs. of carbohydrates and 5.4 oz. of animal fats. A shortage of nutrients may result in body function failure.

Warning! Artificial characteristic boosting of more that 1 pt. at a time is strictly forbidden! Strong chance of fatality!

It was the first time I'd used system points to

bring up Agility. I ate a good square meal, went to bed and activated the upgrade of Agility: my only characteristic that was still lacking.

CHAPTER EIGHTEEN

MY SOLE SHIELD

Anyone who uses the phrase "easy as taking candy from a baby" has never tried taking candy from a baby.

Robert Asprin, Another Fine Myth

THE OVERCAST MONDAY MORNING MUST HAVE LEFT ITS stamp on the townspeople's cheer. The wet streets were packed with traffic; drivers nervously honked, afraid of being late for work. Even I felt exhausted, despite having just had a restful weekend.

The countdown on the traffic lights[48] made all the pedestrians like myself wait for almost two minutes in order to cross the road. While I was treading pools of rainwater, Alik phoned me.

"Phil, it's me again. Mr. Katz and Rose will be here in half an hour. They're running a bit late," he reported cheerfully. "All the others are already here waiting for you."

"Excellent, thanks. I'm only a couple of blocks away. I'll be there in a moment. See you."

"Phil, wait!" Alik hurried to add before I hung up. "Stace didn't call you, by any chance?"

"Why?"

"She's not here. Her number is apparently unavailable. I can't get through. What if she got sick?"

"Ah, no, she's all right. She warned me she wanted to go back to her home town. She probably left already."

"Really? Shit," he sighed. "What a shame."

"I completely agree with you. It's a shame to lose such a piece of... er, such a good worker. Okay, I'm gonna hang you up, man. See you soon."

I slid the phone back into my pocket and quickened my step. I could sense the flow of events around me accelerating; my intuition was screaming that every moment counted. Very soon, I'd have no time left, and I'd better be prepared.

For better or for worse, I couldn't concentrate on

---

[48] Modern Russian traffic lights come with an electronic countdown showing how many seconds are left till the change of lights.

my leveling alone. Deep inside, I could feel that the company's development was just as important — if for no other reason than now I had others to take care of.

This morning, as soon as I had come back from my training session with Kostya, I called each and every one of our future shareholders and invited them to the office for an important conversation. None of them declined. This Monday could become the founding day of our company the way I envisioned it. And judging by the interface's forecast, it completely agreed with me.

As for last Sunday, I'd spent it very productively. I'd had a good jog and sat down to study my management and administration books. No matter how many times I'd scrolled through my skill list, I hadn't found the Administrator skill. I did have a level-2 Leadership, but leadership alone wasn't enough to build a business.

I'd managed to wade through *The Shorter MBA: A Practical Approach to Key Business Skills* before my sister Kira had called me to remind me that we'd had an agreement to go see our parents. She was already downstairs — and when she realized that I hadn't yet even thought about getting ready, she got on her high horse again to tell me I was an irresponsible moron. Still, how could I be angry with her?

A family dinner in a warm and heartfelt atmosphere was just what I needed after all the latest developments. My parents and Kira cheered up no end after hearing about my company. I told them about everything we'd done and what we were still planning on doing. Mom said she knew nothing about these things but she was happy that I'd got my act together. Dad, however, pulled a serious face and told me not to cook the books and make sure I paid all my taxes. And most importantly, he added, I had to treat my staff with respect.

All right, Dad. I think you can be proud of me.

At some point, Kira took me aside and began grilling me about all the details. It was a good job I was by now quite well-versed in all the legal and financial issues, courtesy of Mr. Katz and Rose, so I was able to answer all her questions rather competently. And as for our business model, I already knew everything about that myself.

Kira was pleased even though she warned me she might pay us a visit at the office in her official capacity as a tax controller, just for her own peace of mind.

I spent the evening roaming the most criminal area of the town, looking to pick a fight. The best I'd managed was to start a punchup with some harmless drunk who was no threat to anyone — and even so, we were promptly dragged apart by onlookers, so my attempt at improving the environmental safety index had gloriously failed.

That was the extent of my Sunday — so now as I ran upstairs to the office, I couldn't wait to start implementing everything I'd dreamed up.

Still, there was one more thing I had to do before the shareholders' meeting.

The office door was ajar. When I walked over to

it, I saw that we had a new client waiting inside.

It was Yanna.

I'd always had a problem with stumbling into my exes. Not that I'd had many of them, you understand, but I'd never been prepared to such a turn of events. For instance, having spent a night playing online, I'd pop out to the corner shop first thing in the morning before even brushing my teeth, unwashed, disheveled and wearing a pair of worn-out sneakers and a filthy T-shirt. And there I'd bump into an ex of mine looking as fresh as a daisy, dressed to the nines and smelling of an expensive perfume. You can't just walk past, can you? Even if I pretended I hadn't seen her, she might have noticed me already.

And then what? You walk over to her to say hello and just stand there awkwardly, not knowing what to say and wishing the earth would swallow you whole, all the while thinking, *'dammit'!*

I don't think Yanna realized who the agency belonged to. Had she wanted to just meet up with me, she could have simply phoned me. Which meant she was here looking for employment. Being between jobs isn't always the best time of your life.

Which was why I didn't want to embarrass her — not just by our accidental meeting but also by the fact that she had to come to me cap in hand.

I stepped away from the office door, walked over to the stairwell and went up to the next floor.

There, I dialed Alik.

"Yes?" he whispered conspiratorially.

"Alik? Do you think Yanna recognized you?"

"No, she didn't. She's filling in the form."

"I see. I'd like you to take her paperwork and tell her that we'll call her back. I don't really want to see her at the moment."

"Got it. Will do. I'll call you back," he hung up.

As I waited for Yanna to leave, I studied her profile. This was a habit I'd recently picked up, ID-ing everyone I came into contact with. With her new statuses — *Divorced* and *Unemployed* — and her Mood deep in the orange, her stats were screaming that my ex-wife needed help.

I wondered if she knew that she was *"pregnant with a baby girl, Term: 26 days"*?

The problem was, I couldn't just walk over to her and ask her how she was doing. In order not to waste time, I searched through the database for a few employment options for her: some which were guaranteed to hire her even though the pay wasn't up to much, and a few potentially better paying ones even though there was no guarantee of them employing her.

After about ten more minutes, Alik texted me to let me know she was gone. I waited another couple of minutes and walked back downstairs.

Just as I was heading for the office, I bumped right into Yanna as she was leaving the ladies' room.

Dammit!

"Phil?" she sounded surprised, and not in a nice way, judging by her plummeted Mood indicator.

"Yanna?" I faked surprise. "Oh hi! You look great!" I lied through my teeth.

She smirked. "Are you kidding me? Never mind.

What if we pretend we don't know each other? I really don't wanna talk to you right now."

"Not a problem. I'm in a hurry too."

"Leave it at that, then. See you! Actually... what are you doing here?"

"I'm looking for work. There's an employment agency here somewhere, right?"

"No idea," she said through clenched teeth and left.

I shrugged and went into the office. According to my interface map, all my future partners were already there, including Mr. Katz and Rose who'd arrived a bit late.

I greeted everyone cheerfully, shook the men's hands and gave Veronica and Rose a peck on the cheek.

"So what's this important question you've dragged us all here for already?" the old lawyer asked with a mocking Jewish accent as he gave me a cunning squint.

"One moment, Sir," I said. "I need to print something out and give you all a copy."

I pulled out my laptop, switched it on and began printing out my company's vision.

This was a mini strategy I'd tried to make as concise as possible, fitting everything — all the bullet points, figures and graphs — into six pages. I hadn't bothered to format it as a PowerPoint presentation. I just wasn't very good at it yet even though I knew I should have leveled it up while I still had the interface and the Learning Skills booster. Never mind. I really

---

should put it on my to-do list. Knowing how to throw a presentation together would never hurt.

While the document was being printed — thanks to Kesha who'd lent us a cheap laser printer — I called Alik and gave him a Post-It note on which I'd jotted down the potential vacancies for Yanna, listing the better-paying ones first.

"Please give her a call straight away," I said, "and tell her to start from the top of the list."

He nodded. "Will do," he reached for the phone to call her.

Seeing as Stacy wasn't with us anymore, I scooped out the printed sheets and handed them out to everyone present. "Guys! Before we start discussing the document — and it won't be quick — I suggest you all take a look at it first."

Everybody started reading: Mark and Rose huddling comfortably on the couch, Alik perched on the windowsill and Gleb at his desk. Kesha and Veronica were sitting opposite me at my desk on seats normally destined for clients.

As I waited for them to finish reading, I printed out a quick notice informing everyone that the office was *Closed Until 2 p.m. For A Maintenance Break*. I then hung it on the outside of the office door and locked it from the inside.

Then I returned to my place and began studying their stats to the accompaniment of rustling pages. Someone cleared their throat; another voice chuckled pensively over their pages.

Their respective Mood numbers were high; their

Interest in the upcoming conversation all maxed out.

I coughed to attract their attention. "Have you all read it?"

"One sec, I'm just finishing it," Alik mumbled, then added after a pause, "Yes!"

Everyone held their breath, waiting for me to speak. Silence fell.

Looking at their faces one by one to make sure they were all listening, I began my story.

"Let's get on with it, then. As you all understand, I'd like to unite our efforts by creating a company for all of us. Our activities in the immediate future are all listed in the document, as well as my suggestions for the company's development."

"I'm sorry to interrupt you, Phil," Mr. Katz butted in. "I want to apologize in advance if my words are going to clip your wings but my natural pessimism regarding some of your ideas... wait a second, where was it now..."

He ran his finger across the page, searching for the necessary section. "Found it! Here, listen: prospecting, pharmaceuticals, a chain of medical clinics, augmented-reality projects, stock exchange, scientific research, sports scouts and a sports boarding school? Plus a number of other rather irrelevant ideas. Don't you think it's a bit too... er... ambitious?"

He was dead right there. It *was* "a bit too ambitious" — especially for a wannabe startup who'd just launched his first business. Still, my level-3 Insight would now allow me to get into at least half of these projects straight away. My ability to see any person's potential enabled me to start recruiting budding young athletes — like soccer players, for instance — anywhere in the world, and then either sign them up or invest in their development using our own training base and the best coaches available.

As for prospecting — that is to say, looking for new natural deposits — it would become possible in the very near future once I'd leveled up Insight some more. Also, by now, I realized perfectly well that an augmented reality interface would be developed in the very near future — I knew it better than anyone else! — which meant that investments in this particular branch of research could garner us considerable profits.

And pharmaceuticals? This was not only super-profitable but above all else a socially meaningful business, provided you did it honestly. With the interface to help me, we could finance new research in this area and hand-pick the best young experts with the biggest potential.

The same went for innovation projects — and we could also use the Synergy forecast in order to put together the most effective teams.

So basically, it was all doable provided you had the money. Which was why the first stage (or the second, rather, if you counted our initial activity as an employment agency) would have to be creating a successful and profitable company.

"You're absolutely right, Sir," I said. "In these conditions," I swept my hand around the office, "I can't blame you for having little faith in my ambitious ideas.

You might even think they're crazy."

"Yeah, sorry, man," Kesha grinned, "I'm afraid you've slightly lost the plot. Had we lived in some other country, yeah, maybe, but here? Who needs science in Russia these days? There's no money in it."

"Well, you can say what you want but I like it. You've gotta aim big," Gleb grinned goofily, then quoted a line from a ribald jailbird song, "If you're gonna steal, you'd better make it a million!"

"Gleb!" Rose exclaimed, taken aback.

Alik guffawed. "A million!"

"Enough, guys," Veronica raised her hands in a conciliatory gesture. "Can I say something too? We seem to be straying away from the subject. Phil is offering us to become shareholders in his company. Which admittedly has a very big potential. I don't know about you but I've seen him work already. Had it not been for him, I wouldn't even be here because Gorelik would have kicked me out. And it took Phil only an hour to find some great customers for me."

"He helped me too," Kesha nodded. "Honestly, I'm sick and tired of my daily drudge. Whatever I earn, it all goes on the rent. I'd love to finally climb out of this crap and get somewhere. Count me in."

"Me too," Veronica added. "Just imagine we'll have a real company! We could make one big office here and do it up. I'll talk to Gorelik to see if he can knock the renovation money off the rent. It's gonna be beautiful! And it's much more fun together!"

"You don't even need to ask me," Alik said. "I'm all for it even without reading this," he waved the printout in the air.

"Me neither," Gleb added. "I've just arrived on the scene. I haven't done anything yet. And I can't put anything in the kitty, all I can do is work. And in any case, Phil," he rose and walked toward me, "thanks, man. I've never forget what you've done for me."

Mr. Katz and Rose had a quiet chat between themselves. "What is it you young people say these days?" she finally said with a proud smile. "We dig it! It's cool!"

"I want to say something too," grunting, Mr. Katz rose from the couch. "Let's face it: all of us here have already kissed our own businesses goodbye. At the end of the day, we failed to build and develop them. And Phil's idea gives us all new hope, does it not?"

"Absolutely!" Gleb shook his unruly mane of hair.

"Which means that we're all for it, Sir!" the old lawyer said, "What next?"

All this talk of "Sir" made me feel uncomfortable. Under the encouraging stares of the others, I produced a small whiteboard and hung it on a nail in the wall which had been left by the office's previous occupants.

I gestured to everyone to come closer and began drawing the company's future organizational structure. "Seeing as we're all agreed on the main points, let's now discuss our immediate strategy. As you've already read in my company vision, Mr. Katz will take care of all the legal aspects. Rose will do the finances and bookkeeping. Veronica with Gleb's help will be responsible for public relations and brand promotion. And Kesha here will be our commercial director."

I noticed Alik heave a sigh behind my back. I turned to see his Mood plummeting. "And as for Alik, he'll be the big cheese!"

I'd already had the chance to witness Alik's aptitude for administration, control and everything to do with routine operations. He'd left my apartment absolutely shipshape, having fixed all that needed fixing.

"But at the same time, Alik," I added, "the company is going to send you on a training course! You can't refuse — can he, guys?"

Alik blushed. "Yeah but... no but... right you are, then!"

Everybody laughed. Veronica began saying something encouraging to the ex-hood when the program showered me with colorful FX and system messages:

Congratulations! You've created a new clan!
Clan name: Great Job.
In order to personalize the settings, open the clan tab.

Congratulations! You've received a new achievement: Clan Founder!
You've founded a clan: a collective of people united by common interests.
Reward: +2 to Charisma

Congratulations! You've received a new achievement: Esteemed Clan Founder!

You've founded a clan: a collective of people united by common interests whose Reputation with you is Respect or above.

Reward: +1 to Charisma

+2 to Luck

+3 to Leadership Skills

Followed by the concerned gazes of my co-workers, I pretended I wanted to pour myself some coffee in order to study the messages.

"Phil? Are you all right?" Veronica asked.

I turned round and peered at their faces, unable to suppress a smile. "I'm more than all right, Veronica. Definitely more than all right!"

CHAPTER NINETEEN

THE CLAN

Lieutenant Dan got me invested in some kind of fruit company. So then I got a call from him, saying we don't have to worry about money no more.

Forrest Gump

AND WE SET TO WORK. DURING OUR INITIAL MEETING we'd all agreed to place our respective companies' assets into one common pot, from furniture to office supplies. All the shareholders decided to give up their former activities in order to focus on the nascent company. Which meant that Great Job wasn't going to sell Kesha's printing services or Veronica's event organizing, nor Mr. Katz and Rose's legal and bookkeeping counsel.

The old lawyer got busy reorganizing my company, adding the new shareholders to our foundation agreement. In the meantime, his wife started working on a financial plan in order to come up with the budget required for the company's development. It was already pretty clear that we might need some cash injections, the main question being, quite how much. Our possibilities were rather limited.

Veronica busied herself with the task of merging our respective companies. That's how it looked in practice: all of us had terminated our current contracts with the Chekhov Business Center while initiating the liquidation of our businesses. In the meantime, Veronica found a more suitable office for us. We needed at least 2,000 square feet to allow for any future expansion. That done, she got busy redecorating it and working on the interior design.

She enlisted Alik's help who in the meantime had applied to our local college. He was going to study management, of all things. The program was dead right about him: he had a lot of potential in this field. By the way, his "lads" — the local hoods who'd very nearly mugged me once — had thanks to me all landed jobs with a very popular construction team and together with their foreman were now helping Veronica to decide how to do all the renovations on the cheap.

Our ranks swelled again when Cyril was finally discharged from hospital. The very next day he'd come to work for us, followed by Greg and Marina. Their new commercial director, Panchenko — whom I'd still never met — even stopped answering my texts and phone calls after the guys had handed in their resignations. He hadn't even made them work the required two weeks but fired them on the spot.

At the moment, Veronica and Rose were taking care of all the paperwork but I could already see that we might need to find someone for the task.

Kesha, Cyril, Greg and Marina were rushing around town on business meetings but still couldn't cope with all the customers I'd given them. They'd split up: Marina was selling our recruiting and headhunting services while the guys took care of our clients' sales.

We'd already signed up two companies one of which specialized in complex IT systems integration while the other manufactured wooden children's toys. A few of their samples — a sword, an axe, a saber and a couple of shields — had become super popular in our office. The guys fought each other, imagining themselves as medieval knights, and even I couldn't resist joining in, whacking Cyril's shield with my sword.

Unfortunately, it hadn't activated any new skills even though I'd secretly hoped for one.

Kesha — or "Mr. Dimidko" as my guys insisted on respectfully calling him — was busy rushing around meetings and presentations like a headless chicken, offering our services, convincing others to try them, and closing new contracts. And although it had been me who'd found him the IT guys, the contract with the toy makers was entirely his doing.

And the most amazing thing about it was that it

all had happened this week. On Monday we'd had our first meeting and got the ball rolling, on Tuesday Cyril had joined us, and on Wednesday when Greg and Marina had turned up, Kesha sent them straight out to start selling.

Still, work wasn't my only passion at the moment. I spent at least an hour every day writing as I'd had an idea for a sci fi novel. It was easy going, so much so that I'd quickly brought up Creative Writing to 8.

Having thus taken care of Intellect leveling, I'd started thinking of what Ilindi had told me about the upcoming Trial.

I'd found a combat coach online — an ex-special services guy — and spent several days at the firing range leveling up blade weapons and firearms. Together we'd managed to bring both skills up to 3.

The same day, I sorted out my clan settings. There weren't too many of them yet.

Clan name: Great Job
Level: 1
Social status level: 1
Clan members: 10

The clan's icon used by the program was the same as Gleb's clan logo that we'd all approved. It depicted two stylized letters, G and J, shaped like two closed hands offering something to the onlooker — something intangible but precious and important.

This was the clan member list:

Philip "Phil" Panfilov
Age: 32
Social status level: 16
Clan Leader
Clan Founder

Romuald "Alik" Zhukov
Age: 28
Social status level: 6
The clan's Maintenance Manager
Clan Co-Founder

Veronica "Carrot Top" Pavlova
Age: 25
Social status level: 7
The clan's voice
Clan Co-Founder

Innokenty "Kesha" Dimidko
Age: 34
Social status level: 9
The clan's Commercial Director
Clan Co-Founder

Mark Katz
Age: 64
Social status level: 12
The clan's lawyer
Clan Co-Founder

Rose Reznikova
Age: 58
Social status level: 10
The clan's Financial Director
Clan Co-Founder

Gleb Kolosov
Age: 33
Social status level: 8
The clan's designer
Clan Co-Founder

Cyril Cyrilenko
Age: 35
Social status level: 9
The clan's commercial manager

Marina Tischenko
Age: 19
Social status level: 3
The clan's commercial manager

Only now did I realize how much Alik's social status level had grown. He used to be 4 and now he was 6. There were also additional numbers in their profiles which showed how long each of them had been a clan member.

Moreover, now I could open a member's profile and watch their stats fluctuate in real time: all the changes in their health, mood, abilities and characteristics. That was a great feature in itself. Just think how many successful startups had fallen apart and sunk simply because their leader couldn't work out his co-workers and friends? Once I'd realized it, I made it my priority to monitor my partners' stats every morning just to make sure they were all right.

Predictably, the interface didn't make it any easier so I had to turn to Martha for all the finer details.

"Yes, Phil. You need to understand though that the only reason we chose the word 'clan' to describe a group of people united by common interests is because of your gaming history. But yes, a clan can be leveled up. This in turn can improve the entire team's Synergy numbers and can bring in new clan skills and abilities."

"How do you level it up, then?"

"Through a combination of different factors. A clan has two development branches: the actual level which can be raised through a number of factors already familiar to you — from the company's turnover and number of staff to the percentage of satisfied clients — and its popularity, or Reputation. These are the signs of every successful company in your world. Plus the social status level, of course."

"The social status? What about that? I mean, how do you level it up?"

Martha laughed. "Silly boy! You should know, of all people. If your company's activity is meaningful not just to all of you as its shareholders but also for society as a whole..."

"Then our social status will grow accordingly."

"That's right. With one correction. Not 'will

grow'. It has already grown. Even though at the moment, it might only be meaningful to you and the few clients whose problems you solve, but-"

"I understand," without unsummoning her, I checked the XP indicators of both development branches.

XP points left until the clan's next level: 0/2000.
XP points left until the clan's next social status level:860/2000

"Why zero XP in the clan's level branch?" I asked.

"Because a clan's level is updated once a month while the social status level is updated in real time as usual."

I wished we could have talked a bit more but my Spirit was already dangerously low, so I had to bid her goodbye. All this client-searching for Kesha and job-hunting for our clients — in combination with clan monitoring and studying its settings — had created a permanent energy deficit in all my interactions with the interface.

Also, I was still very tired.

WHILE OUR NEW OFFICE WAS BEING REDECORATED, WE were still stuck in the old ones we'd rented from the business center. We spent most of the time in my and Alik's old bureau, anyway, because Kesha's was packed out with printing equipment, Mr. Katz and Rose's office was more like a shoebox and Veronica kept hers in such an artistic disarray that there was simply nowhere to sit there.

About an hour ago, the whole noisy crowd had left for lunch, giving me the opportunity to finally work in peace and make some headway on the reams of paperwork given to me by Rose. So I asked them to get me something to eat and delved into the papers.

And just as I thought I'd finally worked out the great financial riddle and begun to make some sense out of these crazy sequences of all the charts and figures, Cyril rushed back into the office, gasping,

"Phil! We're getting a good whacking!"

"Who? Why? Where?" I jumped from my seat and made for the door.

"It's a bunch of Caucasians doing Alik over," Cyril explained, wheezing. "Just outside the lobby…"

I wasn't listening any longer as I made for the stairs, very nearly knocking down Gorelik who was unhurriedly climbing the steps. As I reached the lobby, I could hear the women screaming so I dashed even quicker.

In a small garden to the right of the building's marble staircase, behind a hedge that separated it from the busy street, I finally saw Alik who was held by two guys while a third one was busy reading the riot act to him, proudly puffing out his chest.

I recognized him. It was Vazgen, the PVC windows maker, a.k.a. Veronica's failed admirer.

I discovered the rest of my crowd nearby: Greg

---

clutching his stomach and Gleb, at his jaw. I couldn't see Kesha anywhere but then again, he shouldn't have been there to begin with as he'd gone to lunch with a client.

Marina stood next to the boys while Veronica was shouting, trying to talk some sense into Vazgen who ignored her screams entirely.

I leaped from the stairs into the garden.

"What the hell's going on here?" I demanded — not because I needed an answer but simply to attract attention to myself. Then I walked over to the scene and stood between the two, separating them.

"Phil! Tell him!" Veronica shouted behind my back.

"Phil, this is between us, *da*?" Vazgen said, stooping his head like a bull. "You keep out of it. We'll settle this like men."

His friends said nothing, just glared at me, making it clear that they could jump in at a moment's notice.

"Vazgen, this isn't between just you. And it certainly isn't settling it like men!" I turned to his sidekicks. "Get your hands off him, now! I'm talking to you! Hussein! Asar! You hear what I said?"

Their eyes widened in silent surprise at hearing their names. They were still young, barely twenty years old. The older one — Hussein — nodded.

"Leave my friend alone!"

The two looked at Vazgen.

"Come on," I continued, "let's go and have a talk like civilized human beings. Our concierge takes the trouble to plant all these pretty flowers and you're here trampling them! Gorelik is already calling the cops. Are your residence permits in order?"

Reluctantly the two let Alik go. He immediately went for Vazgen but I stepped in his way.

"Stop it now, man. Cool down," I put my arm around him and slapped him on the back. "Not now."

He stepped back and began rearranging his clothes. "They've torn my shirt, those bastards," he spat.

"I think they're going to pay you for it. Aren't you, Vazgen?"

Vazgen didn't react at all.

"Never mind," I said. "Wait a minute. We'll step aside and have a talk in a moment."

I walked over to the others, "Guys, everything will be all right now. Just go upstairs."

They didn't reply.

"Get upstairs, *now!* Marina, Veronica, take these warriors to the office and get them cleaned up. Tell Cyril to fetch some ice from the supermarket, he could use some exercise. Come on now, chop chop! What are you hanging around for? Just go!"

I had to add a note of authority to my voice. Only then did they hesitantly amble upstairs.

That done, we headed for the nearest alleyway. By "we" I mean myself, Alik, Vazgen and his two cousins (by now, my Insight could detect family ties between people).

As we walked, I asked,

"Listen, guys, are you sure Uncle Mger will

---

approve of what you've just done?"

"How do you know our uncle?" Hussein asked in very good Russian almost without any accent.

"In our town, everybody knows each other," I replied.

Alik next to me grinned, apparently remembering my earlier run-in with his old drinking buddies.

"And who doesn't know Uncle Mger, the soul of the Caucasian community?" I continued. "So do you still think he'd approve of it?"

"He'd say we did the right thing," Asar grumbled. He didn't sound too sure though.

"So you think that's right, do you, three onto one? You think that's manly, all that over a girl?"

"There were three of them too!" Vazgen exclaimed. "Four even, only the fat one ran off!"

We entered a small backyard full of old junk and stopped by the wall.

"Very well," I said. "Let's get down to business because I still have other busi- er, other things to attend to," my inner writer didn't let me repeat the word "business" twice in the same sentence. "So. Was it because of Veronica?"

"Yes," Alik said. "He told me she was his woman. Only he couldn't prove it."

"She *is* my woman!" Vazgen bellowed.

Alik laughed. "You see? That's exactly how he said it."

I had to step between them to stop them flying at each other again. "Wait a sec. What makes you think so?" I asked Vazgen.

"I was the first to start seeing her!" the Caucasian roared, beating his chest.

Seeing as my interface showed only 13% Compatibility between Veronica and Vazgen, I realized I had to discourage him here and now.

"You may have started seeing her but you didn't get to see all of her. This guy," I pointed at Alik, "is already dating her. Are we done here?"

"No, we're not!" Vazgen bellowed.

"In that case, I suggest we solve this matter once and for all," I said. "You and Alik go for it, man to man. Let's see who's got the biggest balls. The loser gives up the girl, the winner gets the right to try to start a relationship with her. Are you both happy with this?"

Alik scowled. "I'm gonna wipe the floor with him!"

"I'm gonna flatten you into the tarmac!" Vazgen wheezed.

"We're agreed, then?" I asked. "Fair and square? Nobody will step in, then? You can only use your hands and feet — no bricks, no steel rods. Because Veronica won't fancy an invalid even if he's a winner. Is that clear?" I repeated, turning toward Vazgen's supporters. "Why are you both looking so pissed? Would you fancy some of the action too?"

Hussein shrugged and exchanged surprised stares with his brother.

"Go on, then," I encouraged them. "You two against me, all right?"

I wasn't risking anything. Although physically

quite strong, both had very low combat skills. Apparently, this wasn't as easy as leveling up Rhetoric by pronouncing flowery Caucasian toasts at a party table.

"Okay, shake on it. Alik and Vazgen, you'd better go over there where no one can bother you. And you two stay where you are, this way I won't have to run after you."

Without waiting for his elder cousin to take on my friend, Asar turned on me. I just let him do his thing.

Damage taken: 148 (Kick)
Current Vitality: 98,17388%

Immediately I received another kick from Hussein, but this time I'd managed to block it. Asar tried to grab me from behind but I managed to throw him to the ground judo style. Don't ask me where that came from — I'd done very little Wrestling worth mentioning — but it came completely naturally to me. It looked like I'd dealt some serious damage because Asar seemed to have had the wind knocked out of him.

As I stood up, I deliberately allowed Hussein to punch the back of my head.

Damage taken: 163 (Punch)
Current Vitality: 96,69206%

Shit, that hurt! My head was ringing; I leapt back a couple of paces in order to recuperate.

Right, that's enough playing the punch bag. If they wanted to win, they'd have to work for it now.

Out of the corner of my eye, I saw Alik sitting astride Vazgen, methodically punching different parts of his body. It was time for me to start winning, too.

By then, Hussein must have decided I was finished and it was time to wrap the fight up and hurry to help his cousin. Thirty seconds later, he was lying flat on the ground seeing stars.

You've dealt critical damage to Hussein Karapetyan: 311 (Punch)

Asar didn't need any encouragement to throw in the towel. I knocked him off his feet and fell on top of him, raising a clenched fist.

"Enough, enough, I give in!" he hurried to say, squinting. "I give in!"

I got up, brushed myself off and helped him to his feet. He then staggered over to his brother. I turned to Alik to check on him but he was already up, staring in confusion at the ripped shirt sleeve in his hand. Vazgen next to him tried to scramble back to his feet but collapsed, clutching at his leg. He must have hurt it during the fight.

"Alik, help him!" I shouted.

Once again we stood in a circle. I demanded that we all shook hands.

The three guys silently complied without looking Alik in the eye. I sent Alik back to the office and took Vazgen aside...

* * *

CLOSER TO THE EVENING, WHEN WE'D ALREADY FINISHED discussing the incident in the office and when I'd already received a Reputation upgrade with each of my co-workers, Vazgen showed up at the office, limping and hobbling, holding a cream cake, two bottles of wine, a large cheese, a basketful of fruit and a huge bouquet. Under one arm he was holding a carrier bag from a clothes shop.

Without saying a word, he unloaded everything onto the table, cleared his throat to attract our attention and announced,

"Please accept my sincere apologies for today's, er, uhm, incident. I was wrong. Veronica, Alik, I'm so sorry. This is all for you, friends! Alik, there's also a, uhm, a shirt for you there to replace the one that got ripped."

Vazgen looked over at Alik who'd already begun unwrapping the shirt, then walked up to me. He lowered his head and whispered in my ear,

"I've spoken to them! They're building a five-story hotel just out of town. I might have to work round the clock but that's nothing I haven't done before. Thanks for the tip!"

"I'm so happy for you," I whispered back. "You'll get your money, and the girls will come," I gave him a wink.

Vazgen beamed, shook my hand and left, mumbling more apologies, leaving the entire office in cheerful bewilderment.

"Right, guys," I said. "Those of you who are finished for today can go over and help themselves. I still need to have a chat with Rose."

Chattering happily, my co-workers surrounded the spread. Rose and I headed for her office which was absolutely crammed with papers. Her tiny room housed two desks with ancient computer screens, a couple of soft chairs and a safe which could have used a lick of paint. Any clients had to make do with a rickety stool which, judging by its inventory number, must have been procured from one of Gorelik's storerooms.

"You can take Mark's place," Rose told me.

I slumped into Mr. Katz's chair, sinking so deep that I had to lean forward with my elbows on the desk to keep my balance. In this state of precarious equilibrium, I listened to what she had to say.

"Now, sir," Rose began. "As is specified in the business plan which you've already studied, we might reach the projected sales volumes only by the end of next year. That's if we preserve our current momentum. But!" she lifted a meaningful finger. "Provided there's sufficient investment, we might reach breakeven point already this fall and come this winter, we might turn a profit. You've studied the company's budget plan scenarios, haven't you?"

"Er... to be honest, I'm out of my depth on this one. But I'll start cramming, I promise!"

She smiled. "No need to. You've got me to do all that. If we don't go into the details, there's only one thing you need to realize. If we continue to grow at the same speed and preserve the same sales volume, we might avoid a cash deficit entirely and turn a profit as early as next year. But! If we manage to build a correct sales infrastructure already at this stage — and I've already spoken to the others about it — it would allow us to put the company on the map and find sufficient resources that would provide the results you've envisioned."

"May I just double-check something?" I asked. "If we don't invest now, our development will be slow and painful. And if we do, it'll take no time at all. Did I understand you correctly?"

"Exactly."

"What kind of money are we talking about?"

"If we're talking about a year, we will need to invest in three installments."

"I'm afraid I'm talking about now. How much money do we need right now? As in, today or tomorrow, or the very near future?"

"About two million rubles. That would allow us some leeway."

"And how do you intend to raise that kind of money?"

"We can't expect a loan," Rose replied. "I've already made a few inquiries through some friends of mine. We could all invest the value of our shares, I suppose. Mark and I are quite prepared to put in. But as for the others, I'm not so sure," she heaved a sigh.

"They're all pretty broke, I know. What other scenarios do you suggest?"

"We could borrow some money."

"From whom? Do you have any ideas?"

"Well, if your financial situation permits..." she paused.

"You mean, me?"

She nodded.

I took a moment to think about it. "Very well," I finally said. "I'll give it some thought. I'd like to ask you to see if you can come up with a smaller amount."

"Very well, Phil. I'll get on with it."

I left her there and returned to my office.

Suddenly I felt weak. My Spirit indicator plummeted deep into the red. A new system window unfolded, filling my entire view (apparently to make sure I didn't miss it).

I couldn't help but read it,

Warning! An abnormally high number of instances of aggression detected, targeting a user whose social status level is several times higher than that of his attackers!

In view of this, the environmental safety index can be reassessed and lowered to Code Yellow. That in turn will release 3 new available main characteristic points.

The earlier restriction specifying that the user could only unblock one heroic ability per every twenty social status levels gained can be lowered accordingly to one heroic ability per every ten social status levels gained by the user.

Accept / Decline

Finally! My reluctance to fight off Hussein and Asar had paid off! I'd already thought it hadn't worked because it had taken the program so long to digest it. Three extra stat points and an additional heroic ability at level 20 was an excellent boost for my upcoming abduction and Trial.

That would give me something to do at night!

I could hear my team's cheerful voices even from the stairs. Two reluctant figures were hanging around our office door but I couldn't make out who they were in the corridor's dim light.

I took a closer look and realized that it was Ludmila Nazarenko and her young violinist son Leo, our first ever clients.

"Ludmila? Leo?" I called out to them. "Why don't you go in?"

"Oh, Phil! You still remember us!" the woman threw her hands in the air in surprise. "We're waiting for you! I took a peek inside but they seem to be throwing a party. I didn't want to impose so I decided to wait out here."

"Leo, how's it going, man?" I asked.

"Uncle Phil, I've learned how to dive! Like this," he showed me how he did it.

"Well done! And you?" I turned to his mother.

"That's exactly why I came here. I wanted to thank you personally. Everything happened as you said it would. They hired me as a cook and they pay me enough for me not to have to work a second job. Leo took your advice to heart and started swimming."

"I'm so happy for you!" I said, and I meant it.

"Please accept this. It's from us both," she handed me a shopping bag packed with food. "It's a meat pie, finger-licking good! And a variety of salads, I'm sure you're gonna like them!"

"Aha!" I said. "Come on, let's go in together," I laced one arm around her waist, grabbed Leo by the hand and led them into the office. "May I have your attention, please!"

"Ah, Phil's back!" the red-faced Cyril bellowed.

"Boss!" Alik cheered.

"Friend!" Gleb shouted.

Marina, Veronica and Mark smiled while Kesha made a drum roll on the desk.

"Guys," I said, "I'd like you to meet Ludmila and her son Leo. You know who they are?"

"No," they replied in curious unison, barring Alik who hid a silly smile. "Who are they?"

"They're our very first customers! Can you find a place for them to sit?"

While Marina took care of the suddenly timid Leo, Mr. Katz gallantly seated his mother next to himself. Greg offered me a glass of wine. Just as I accepted it, my phone rang.

It was Yanna. I had to step out of the office in order to speak to her. "Yes?"

"Hi," her voice sounded slightly hoarse.

"Hi."

"I didn't notice it at once. I signed your contract without even reading it. I didn't believe it at all. It's just that my mother was hassling me to get a job so I did an agency crawl," she paused, "just to keep out of her way.

It was only after I'd gone for the interview that I finally read the contract I signed with the employment agency. That's when I saw you were the director... Just put two and two together, basically."

"Did they take you on?"

"Yes, virtually the same day. No idea how that happened. They were probably desperate to find someone. So I'm calling just to thank you. It's a good job and it suits my skills down to the ground."

"Happy to hear it. Is that all?"

"More or less. Again, thanks a lot."

"Wait up," I began, meaning to ask her whether she knew she was pregnant, but she'd already hung up.

Apparently, it wasn't meant to happen.

I got back to the office and stayed a little longer, then headed off home.

I had lots of things to do. And one of them was raising two million Russian rubles in double quick time.

CHAPTER

TWENTY

SOONER OR LATER, BY HOOK OR BY CROOK

A man of knowledge lives by acting, not by thinking about acting.

Carlos Castaneda. Separate Reality

YOU MAY HAVE ALL THE MONEY IN THE WORLD — OR SO Homer Simpson used to say — but there's one thing you can't buy: a dinosaur.

I didn't need a dinosaur, although back in my formative years I wouldn't have said no to a pocket version of a velociraptor. What I did need was for my company to promptly reach the required sales volume. My interface license wasn't going to last forever; they could abduct me at any moment and if I failed the Trial, I might revert to my normal pre-interface self even sooner, stripped of my Universal Infospace access.

And I'd known where to find the money even before Rose had explained it to me.

A week ago, I'd raised exactly the same amount for Gleb. So why wouldn't I try to repeat the process for myself this time?

Boris met me by the door with indignant meowing.

It hadn't been easy for her just lately. She'd spent most of the time home alone — and even though she (like any other cat, I suppose) was perfectly happy keeping herself company, her meal times had been drastically disrupted, and she wasn't at all happy about it.

I stroked her, watching the Hunger debuff hovering over her back.

"Boris, I'm so sorry. I should have given you your dinner before I left."

But that morning Kostya and I had got a bit carried away with my training. I had just received level 7 in Boxing and couldn't resist a good bout of sparring.

I squeezed the cat food out of the packets, slightly taken aback by their names: Tender Lamb Fillet and Delicious Veal. Indeed, marketers can do wonders with their appellations which can make even human beings drool over the packets. If it ever came to a zombie apocalypse, humanity might last decades on all the millions of tons of prepared cat food.

Boris stuck her face into her bowl, purring like a tractor. I changed into my house clothes[49] and got busy making dinner. After all this talk of tender lamb and delicious veal, I decided to make myself a tenderized steak, seeing as I had a slice of fillet left in the fridge.

While the microwave defrosted the fillet, I Googled a nice recipe for which I had everything, even a packet of breadcrumbs which had been sitting on the kitchen shelf since Vicky's time.

I hammered the steak, beat some egg in a bowl and dipped the steak in it before rolling it in breadcrumbs. I then scored it with a knife to make sure the butter could work its way in and threw it in the skillet for a few minutes on each side. I added some salt and pepper and sprinkled it with some lemon juice.

All done! I added to this a vegetable salad of grated radish, tomatoes and cucumbers. A dinner worthy of a champion!

Congratulations! You've received a new skill level!
Skill name: Cooking
Current level: 6
XP received: 500

---

[49] Traditionally, Russians change into casual house clothes when they arrive home after a day's work — both for comfort and to mark the difference between work and leisure.

The ability to cook a variety of delicious and healthy meals was an asset in itself, either to please the wife and family provided I ever had one, or simply to enjoy it myself. It had taken me about twenty minutes to cook it while in a restaurant, I might have spent the same amount of time waiting for my order which would have been considerably pricier.

All this flashed through my head in the matter of a split second. Then I received a new message.

All this cooking effort had been worth its while!

I felt weak at the knees. A wave of happiness surged over me. My blood boiled with endorphins and dopamine. I sank to the floor, unable to withstand the overwhelming sensations.

Congratulations! You've received a new level!
Your current social status level: 17
Characteristic points available: 2
Skill points available: 1
XP points left until the next social status level: 100/18000

Once the surge of pleasure had abated, I just sat there feeling drained and depressed as if everything good had already happened and I had nothing left to look forward to.

Still, I forced myself back to my senses. This was only a hormonal blip. The only thing that puzzled me was why would they do something like this to an interface user? No wonder those unlucky ones whose interfaces had encouraged their aggression, had farmed XP non-stop like the Legendary Moonlight Sculptor simply to experience these heavenly sensations once again.

This time, I'd received two stat points for the new level: this was the Altruist bonus at work. Great. Now I had five available main characteristic points — plus a skill point which I might have to invest later once I'd finished what I was planning to do tonight.

I finished my dinner and did the dishes. These days, I tried to never forgo the task because doing it later took the same amount of time but the caked-on grease was much harder to clean. That out of the way, I went for a nap.

The night promised to be a sleepless one. I really needed to conserve my strength and top up my Spirit reserves. I needed to reload my brain and give my tired body a chance to recuperate.

The moment I laid my head on the couch cushion and closed my eyes, a new system message barged its way into my mind's blissful blankness.

Congratulations! You've received a new skill level!
Skill name: Learning Skills
Current level: 13
XP received: 500

Skill optimization complete!
The 1 pt. of your secondary skill (Playing Mortal Kombat) have been converted into 0.5 pt. of the primary skill associated with it (Learning Skills).

Your secondary skill (Playing Mortal Kombat) has been deleted without recovery option.

Current level of your primary skill (Learning Skills): 13

Would you like Learning Skills to be your primary skill by default?

Accept / Decline

I clicked *Accept*. Having kept Learning Skills as a primary skill, I received a 50% bonus to its development rate. Half a point of Optimization had been enough to receive a new level. Which was good news because now I could learn not 15 but 18 times faster!

I opened the skill window. To be precise, I'd received 1785% to skill learning rate, and that's without the achievement bonus.

Thank you! Learning Skills is now your default primary skill.

Please choose a new secondary skill

I still had a shedload of useless skills, of course, like Playing Durak[50], but wasting a month to gain half a skill point sounded pretty stupid. In the end, I chose a different skill. Earlier this week, when I'd been saving some snapshots from the first days of our company, my Photography had reached level 4. In all honesty, it

---

[50] Durak (Fool): a Russian card game

---

wasn't the most useful of skills in my situation.

Thank you! You've just chosen Photography as a secondary skill associated with your current primary skill.

Would you like to convert the 4 pt. of your secondary skill (Photography) into 2 pt. of the primary skill associated with it (Learning Skills)?

Yes / No

I pressed *Accept*, thus launching my third Optimization. The window disappeared.

Finally, I could doze off. Still, I kept tossing and turning until I realized I wasn't going to get much sleep. I was buzzing too much, thinking about the upcoming poker game.

In the end, I decided that the sooner I started, the quicker it would be over with.

I scooped up all my cash and got myself ready to go to the club.

I couldn't remember the exact address of the Railway Workers Community Center because on my previous trip there I'd been both wound up and too sleepy to look out the window. Funny but instead of just Googling it, I tried to retrieve the KIDD points of those I'd met there. Most of them weren't even there yet, at least I'd detected neither Raduk the Rhinestone Cowboy nor Dimedrol and his sidekicks. The only person already there was Anton, the club manager. I

---

used his marker to detect the club's location, then called a cab.

As we drove, I was slightly jittery. My intuition was screaming that the whole thing was a very bad idea.

But I went there, anyway.

In order to keep myself busy and dispel the bad premonitions I was having, I decided to check on my clan members. The young and single ones — Alik, Veronica and Marina — were now in a local bar called The Perimeter together with Cyril and Kesha who were both divorced and therefore, technically also single. The map wouldn't tell me what exactly they were doing there but judging by all the Intoxication debuffs, I didn't even need to guess. It looked like Marina might have plenty of choice tonight.

Gleb and his family had gone to the movies. Greg was at home with his pregnant wife Alina, as was the Katz family.

For a brief moment, I felt like canceling this crazy idea and heading for the bar, just to compete with the other guys for Marina's attention. I was young and single too, after all, despite being threatened by the reappearance of the spontaneous erection debuff.

Still, I dismissed the thought. The moment wasn't right for me to do any extended partying.

I remembered the old song,

Our house will sag in my absence,
And my dog died a long time ago.
Me, I'll die without compassion

In the crooked streets of Moscow, I know...[51]

If I didn't want my house to "sag in my absence" and for Boris to die "a long time ago", I had to walk with my head held high along the crooked streets of our little town. Otherwise, I might spend the rest of my life beating myself up because everything had been in vain.

On this note, I carried on toward the club whiling the time away by looking at my skill progress over the last couple of weeks. Because my work involved constantly trying to tune into my clients' moods and feelings, I'd managed to bring Empathy up to 11.

I'd brought Reading Skills up to 10. These days, I read quickly and copiously. At 9, my Vending Skills were slightly lagging, with Communication Skills to match. I'd managed to raise Running up to 8 while bringing both Marketing and Leadership Skills up to 7.

Triggered by my cardinal change of lifestyle, both Planning and Self-Discipline had still been evolving in synch, reaching levels 5 and 6 respectively, with Decision Making and Erudition slightly higher. And a couple of days ago, I'd finally upped Company Management to level 2.

There were a few less significant ups too. Like First Aid which had risen to level 2 due to the fact that I'd had to treat my own gym injuries a lot recently. As

---

[51] The lines from a poem by a leading Russian poet Sergei Yesenin which was later made into a song by the popular Russian rock band Mongol Shuudan. (Translated by Alec Vagapov)

---

for Singing, it had just grown naturally — probably because of my stupid habit of humming in the shower. And seeing as I was showering three times a day just lately...

"We've arrived!" the cabbie brought me back to reality.

"Thanks a lot," I got out of the car and headed for the entrance to the community center — or should I say the illegal gambling den?

I climbed to the third floor. Two guards stood watch by the same door leading to the building's right wing. Same black suits, same crew cuts, different faces.

"Hello. I'd like to play, please."

"Have you been here before?" one of them asked.

"Yes, last week."

"Have you got a club card?"

"Unfortunately, not. Last time I came just to get a feel for the place."

The second bouncer nodded to his partner who swung the door open before me. "Please go on in."

A new girl stood behind the familiar reception desk, together with Anton, the club manager.

"Hi," I said."

"Phil!" he beamed. "Good evening! How are you? We're so happy to see you back!"

"Do you remember my name?"

"Of course we do," he said, faking offense. "A beginner who won at the high-stakes table? You're a legend. Everybody's trying to work out who you really are. Is your name really Phil?"

"It is," I admitted. Being a cheat was nothing to be proud of but still his words had rung nicely.

"So you don't play professionally? Unfortunately, we couldn't get hold of your contact information. And your friend Gleb doesn't answer his cell number anymore."

I tensed up. "What do you mean?"

"You see, our club selects the best players and sponsors their participation in major world tournaments. Very soon there'll be one such competition in the US. The prize fund is huge. If you wish, I could introduce you to our management."

I shrugged. "Sounds good. I might think about it. Can I get some chips, please?" I dumped all my cash on the desk.

The manager scooped it up and counted off a stack of their gaming chips.

"Have a good evening! And good luck!" both said almost in unison.

"Thanks!"

"I suggest you consider becoming a club member," Anton shouted after me.

I nodded without turning. Their carrots didn't tempt me at all. All I wanted was to do what I'd come here for and get back out again safely. My previous death had been enough for me.

Also, my latest memories of my second life had given me a pretty good idea of who Dimedrol — that douchebag police colonel — truly was. If people like him had any sort of influence or even a share in this place, I really wasn't interested in their offers.

I made my way directly to the high-stakes table. There were no tournaments in the club tonight which meant I'd have to take money from ordinary players — probably addicts like Gleb used to be.

Apart from me and the dealer, there were six people at the table, two of them women. The younger one wasn't playing: she must have arrived here as someone's guest and was now sitting staring at her phone while twisting a slim cigarette in her long delicate fingers.

The other woman, however, was completely engrossed in the game. Her name was Jaqueline. Well, she may not have been Jaqueline Onassis, but she still seemed pretty loaded. At least she had tons of chips. The precious fur mantle draped over her shoulders despite the hot July weather spoke volumes about her status. Having said that, the room was rather chilly with the air conditioning going at full tilt.

She was the person I had to confront once I'd had a winning hand of three Jacks. I knew she already had two pairs but was waiting for a straight or a full house — and she wasn't likely to get either.

That's exactly how it happened, bringing me almost five hundred bucks.

"Congratulations," she said, sounding puzzled. "Do I know you?"

"I don't think so."

She tilted her head back and gave me the once-over. I didn't care. I wasn't too impressed by her, anyway. Her eyelashes appeared way too thick and long to be real. I didn't like this kind of artificially enhanced beauty. I much prefer a natural charm.

As I focused on the next cards being dealt, I heard someone whisper to Jaqueline that I was "the same beginner" who'd won last Friday's tournament.

Before I could take in my own popularity, my Spirit plummeted almost to zero which was a sure sign of the program kicking in.

My vision shrank, coloring everything an intense crimson. I could see nothing now apart from a few lines of text.

A wave of inexplicable fear came over me, a bit like a panic attack. All I wanted was to chuck in the cards and scramble to the safety of my home.

"It's your turn," the person next to me said, shaking my shoulder. "You're holding everybody up."

Blindly I pushed the cards away from me as I peered at the terrible message. "Pass."

Warning! You've just performed a socially detrimental action!

The interface will be disconnected in 3... 2... 1...

The world around me faded, the noise of the busy gaming hall — the dealer's comments and the voices of my fellow players — being the only indication I was still alive.

Suddenly everything came back. Frozen and bathed in cold sweat, I was still sitting at the poker table and the game was still in full swing.

Only now my interface was gone.

I must have appeared lost and helpless like

someone with impaired eyesight who'd dropped his glasses. It made no sense to play on or to stay here at all.

The world looked different now, sort of bleached and weird. Don't get me wrong, my eyesight was still fine. All the improvements I'd received from the interface seemed to still be there. But... how can I explain it to you? If you ever played RPG games, just try to envision yourself in such a game but without any kind of prompts. No health and mana bars, no description of your opponents, no mini-map. The first thing you might do in a situation like that is log out in order to work out what had happened and why your interface had disappeared. Because you simply can't play without one, can you?

This wasn't going to work in my case, was it? You couldn't walk out on a game like this.

I couldn't even summon Martha, dammit! Which meant I couldn't work out what had happened.

Without waiting for the game to end, I scooped up my chips, thanked my fellow players and headed for the exit under their uncomprehending stares.

"Are you going already?" Anton asked. "Is everything all right?"

"I'm afraid I feel real bad. I can't even think about playing."

I cashed in my chips and left the club. Anton asked me once again to leave him my coordinates but I refused. I wasn't going to ever come back here.

I'd had three of the biggest frights of my life. The first was to lose someone close to me, the second was to lose the interface, and the third, to die myself. All three had successfully come true within the walls of this den of iniquity.

Back home, as I tossed and turned in my bed, I was trying to think what might have caused the program to close down but came up with nothing except my own cheating. The only thing that didn't fit in was the fact that I'd done exactly the same already a week ago and hadn't received any penalties or system warnings.

Or might it have been the actual goal for which I'd been playing? But by the same token, wouldn't that imply that you could rob, steal and cheat with impunity provided it was for a noble cause?

It just didn't sum up. Also, I hadn't been doing it for myself. I meant to spend the money on the company's development. It didn't make sense.

Finally I fell asleep despite all these desperate ponderings.

In the absence of my good old inner alarm clock, I'd slept in well until midday. I'd had no dreams or nightmares but still I awoke bathed in sweat. Without even opening my eyes, I knew that the interface was gone. I'd secretly hoped that it would still be there.

It was hot and stifling in the room. I hadn't opened the window during the night nor had I turned on the aircon. So I scooped up all the bedding and headed melancholically for the shower, throwing everything into the washer on my way.

With or without the interface, I wasn't going to give up.

After breakfast, I spent an hour finishing reading *All the King's Men* by Robert Warren whose tedious digressions were more than compensated by a long pensive aftertaste.

Having finished reading, I went for a run. My next boxing training with Kostya wasn't until tomorrow lunchtime. Apparently, he had something important to do in the morning. In the afternoon, I was taking my nephew to the movies. Kira had been seriously overworked just lately, so her son was staying with our parents every weekend.

I found running even easier without the interface — probably because nothing was distracting me from the monotony of my feet meeting the crumbling rubberized track. In this heat, I quickly started sweating, wiping my eyes with the already-wet long sleeves of my track jacket. By the end of my run, I'd stopped worrying about my interface and started wondering about how to raise the money for the company.

That's when I remembered the boxing tournament.

At first, the idea seemed crazy. Who was I to challenge fighters of this caliber?

Then I remembered I'd managed to knock Mohammed out — and he was one of Matov's best. My sparring bouts with Kostya were becoming easier by the day and I wouldn't have said that he now had any considerable advantage. Which meant that if I came prepared and provided the cards fell in my favor, I still stood a decent chance. There were two weeks left till the tournament which was at least six more sessions with Kostya. Add to this my times-18 leveling boost and the 10% leveling rate bonus...

Oh well. I might be lucky. Especially considering I'd only been level 5 when I'd KO'd Mohammed — and now I was level 7. And I might also be lucky to receive another buff, something like Passion to Win, for instance.

Very well. All I needed to do was call my ex-coach.

I stopped, took the phone out of my pocket and dialed Matov's number.

"Speaking," his cold voice replied.

"Hello, Sir. This is Phil..."

"I hear you. What do you want?"

"I'd like to sign up for the tournament. Could you tell me where I can do so?"

"They're not accepting any more applications. You're too late."

"But there's still loads of time left till the tournament..."

"Sorry, can't help you. We have the world and his mother wanting to sign up. We already have five hundred applicants as it is. We might have to do some preliminaries."

"Are you sure I can't sign? What if someone drops out?"

"Then he'll lose by default. Only if someone changes his mind and relinquishes his place to you. Right, I need to be off now," he hung up.

I did some stretches and headed back home

where I Googled the tournament and contacted the organizers directly. They told me the same as Matov: the registration was now complete. There were no more places available.

"Let them stuff it!" I told Boris before heading for the gym.

Who was it that said that the best prescription for life's troubles was to " pump some iron"? It might have been meant as a joke but in a situation as admittedly weird and insecure as mine, I decided to follow the advice just to save my brain from exploding.

As always on weekends, the gym was pretty empty. And that was a good thing because I didn't have to wait to use the machines.

I ran about half a mile on a treadmill just to warm up, then started with the barbell. Every set felt easier than the one before it. I even looked at the number of weights but everything checked out.

In the end, I had to add another ten to twenty pounds to my usual weight just to tax my muscles a bit. Did that mean I'd finally overcome the plateau and entered a new stage of growth?

Having finished training, I drank my usual chocolate protein shake and headed off home.

I spent the rest of the day buzzing and bustling from one thing to another. I cooked dinner not even knowing whether it might add anything at all to my Cooking skill. I called Kira and our parents who were all doing fine. I very nearly dialed Vicky and Yanna. It felt like the absence of the interface had annulled all those Compatibility numbers, canceling the program's

Synergy forecast — and I admittedly missed both girls. I dialed both but hung up just in time.

Next thing, I started to spring clean. As I straightened my shelves, I came across my old phone which I'd used to call the rescue groups. The battery was long dead. Still, my intuition was pushing me to check it. I put the phone on charge and switched it on the moment it had enough power in it.

I spent the next couple of minutes listening to the trilling avalanche of incoming messages, the majority of which were the aftermath of my rescue stint a month ago.

Still, there were a few fresh ones from only yesterday. I decided to dial the number.

A tense female voice answered my call.

"Hi," I said. "I have a missed call from you. Did you call me yesterday?"

"Who is this?"

"It's Phil."

"Are you the psychic?"

"Not really. What happened? Where did you get this number?"

"I'm sorry," the woman cleared her throat and began talking hysterically, "I'm Olga. I got your number from Bogdan, the search and rescue group coordinator from Izhevsk. My husband has gone missing. His name is Maxim, thirty-five years old, six foot tall. He has blue eyes and blond hair cut short," she rattled off his description as if she'd done it a thousand times before.

"Why are you calling me?"

"Bogdan reckons that neither they nor the police

---

are interested in searching. They think that he either went on a bender or he's dumped me. But I know he couldn't have done that! We love each other. Everything's good between us."

"How long has he been missing?"

"The day before yesterday he didn't come home from work. He doesn't answer his phone. People at work say that he never came in but it's not possible. Max is a very responsible worker."

"I'd like you to send me all the data you have on him, including your address, his place of work and a couple of photographs," I gave her the email address I'd created specifically for this purpose. "I can't promise anything. But if something crops up, I'll call you."

In order for something to crop up, I'd have to get my interface back first. Still, she didn't have to know about it.

"How would you like your money?" she asked, sounding somewhat reassured. By saying that, she probably wanted to give me a tad more motivation. That's human psychology for you: you tend to have this sense of entitlement when you've put your money where your mouth is. "How much do I owe you?"

"You owe me nothing. I'll be in touch. All the best, then."

MY INTERFACE CAME BACK LATE THE SAME NIGHT. MY vision blinked, filled with floating white dots. A translucent countdown appeared in my view:

3... 2... 1

The world blinked one last time, then was overlapped by the interface.

Your 24-hr penalty for performing a socially detrimental action has expired.
All the functions of your Augmented Reality!7.2 Home Edition interface have been fully restored.

I breathed a long sigh of relief. Then I opened my profile and studied the numbers. I hadn't lost anything. My character still had the same properties.

That done, I summoned Martha.

An anxious girl materialized next to me. She walked up and stroked my cheek. "That was terrible! I didn't get the chance to do anything! The system simply closed down and shut the Spirit flow off. I found myself in some kind of void..."

I just couldn't help myself. I flung my arms around her and pulled her close. Was it my imagination or did I notice tears in her eyes?

"Martha, what happened? I still have no idea why they banned me! I'd used Insight already a week ago during my first poker game. That time, I paid all my friend's debts off. The program hadn't punished me for that! It had even rewarded me calling it a socially meaningful action!"

"Let me take a look at the logs... Aha, there it is. The program evaluates and analyzes the result of your every action, then builds a model of any potential future developments, both for you and for society as a whole," she paused, unlocked my embrace and looked me straight in the eye.

"And?"

"There're shedloads of factors involved. I mean, shedloads. Starting with the respective social levels of your potential victims and the consequences they might have suffered, and ending with your own personal growth. We can't be certain that the reason you didn't get banned the first time was because you were helping a friend while this time you were planning to spend the money on yourself."

"I wanted to invest it in our company!"

She smiled. "I know you're not lying. But how sure are you that over time it wouldn't have become a habit? What's the point in sweating your heart out in the gym? Why try and build a successful business from scratch? Why would you want to study and improve when you can just go on playing and not doing diddly squat? You might have become a parasite sponging off society and living a life of luxury lounging on a yacht somewhere off the Florida coast in the company of pretty girls. That's what you've been dreaming about just lately, haven't you?"

I turned red, my burning ears witness to the fact that Martha couldn't be fooled. I had indeed thought about all those things. It's not as if I'd tried to suppress them but it was nice to know that the option was available. If anything went wrong, I could always use my abilities to win a lot of money. Just as a plan B.

"I'm not a parasite," I said.

"You're not now but you might have become one. Consider yourself lucky you got off so lightly."

Having finished talking to her, I checked the email address I'd given Olga. She'd sent me several emails containing her missing husband's distinguishing marks, their family photos and copies of his ID papers. She also showered me with questions about how the search was going.

I memorized his KIDD points and opened the map.

The guy was alive and kicking. I could see his location on the map.

I zoomed in on a building somewhere in the vicinity of the city of Izhevsk. It was a two-story house with a few cars parked in the courtyard. A couple of girls stood there smoking. That was all I could make out.

I jotted down the address and sent it to Olga with the recommendation not to venture there on her own. I could say with a 99% probability that he was safe and sound. The building was probably some seedy billiards hall. In any case, she shouldn't go there alone.

After a couple of hours, she called me again.

"I've found him," she said in a weak tired voice.

"Is he all right?"

"Who, him? Oh, he's perfectly fine. But I'm afraid I'm not."

She hung up.

Immediately the program offered me another system message. But it wasn't what I'd expected it to be.

Your Strength has improved!
+1 to Strength
Current Strength: 11...

Operation aborted!
Please wait for your Strength to be reassessed and recalculated.

Your Strength has improved!
+3 to Strength
Current Strength: 13

You've received 3000 pt. XP for successfully leveling up a main characteristic!
Current level: 17. XP points gained: 3190/18000

A 3 points upgrade! How awesome was that? The program seemed to have finally come to its senses. The plateau I'd been having after having upped Strength on an almost weekly basis was seriously beginning to concern me. Now my Strength had finally pushed through the level-10 ceiling, officially making me stronger than an average Terran.

A quick review into what had happened to Martha made everything clear. I'd forgotten that the main principle of stats calculation was based on world averages. Which meant that earlier today, my weight lifting results had been 30% above average!

Before dropping off to sleep, I tried to work out how best to distribute the five available characteristic points I now had: the two I'd received for leveling up and the three I'd got when my environmental safety index had been recalculated. This was what I currently had:

Main characteristics:
Strength: 13/32
Agility: 10/31
Intellect: 20/48
Stamina: 11/33
Perception: 11/32
Charisma: 17/36
Luck: 14/72

I also had the 14 pt. item bonus to Luck: +12 from the Lucky Ring of Veles and +2 from the Protective Red Wristband.

My progress might have seem impressive, but only compared to what I used to be like before. These were still the stats of an average human being, especially Agility, Stamina and Perception. True, my Intellect, Charisma, Strength and Luck might have been slightly higher than normal which was good news, I suppose, but that wasn't the point. The point was, I wasn't even halfway close to fulfilling my potential. Which was a terrible shame.

Still, this wasn't the right time to mope. Now I had to think how best to invest my system points.

Strength and Stamina could be leveled up with practice. That might take some time but not as much as some other stats. Same applied to Agility.

I didn't need to worry about Luck, thanks to my

magic ring and the wristband.

Also, there was no hurry to level up Intellect. Judging by its progress bar, all it would take me to bring it to the next level was to read a couple more books.

Charisma... I hadn't yet tried to level it up artificially. This I could only find out through some scientific trial and error.

Martha, too, proved to be little help in this matter.

"Martha, what's gonna happen if I raise Charisma artificially?"

"Your Charisma level will get a 1 pt. increase."

"Yes, but what effect will it have on me?"

"You'll become more charismatic."

I may be exaggerating, but this was the gist of our conversation.

Still, if I invested 1 pt. in Charisma, would it change my appearance for the better? Would I become taller or more handsome? Would my eyelashes become longer? Would I get a determined chin?

Having said that, what's appearance got to do with it? Uncle Joe Stalin wasn't a pretty face but he apparently had enough charisma to talk anyone into anything...

Then I remembered how I'd received 1 pt. to Charisma after having my hair cut for the first time in years. Did that mean that appearance still mattered? Or were there other factors at play?

Very well. Let's raise Perception, then. I had a funny feeling I couldn't improve it naturally any further.

Warning! We've detected an abnormal increase in your Perception characteristic: +1 pt.

Your sensory organs responsible for your vision, hearing, taste, tactile and olfactory perception, as well as balance, spatial orientation and weight perception, will be restructured in keeping with the new reading (12) to comply with your current level of sensory perception.

Warning! In order to activate the skill, an undisturbed 3-hour period of sleep is required. You are recommended to adopt a prone position.
Accept / Decline

I asked my internal alarm clock to wake me up in three hours' time and pressed *Accept*.
The world faded away.

I AWOKE FROM MY BRIEF SLUMBER a little after two a.m. My Perception had risen. Excellent. I reset my alarm clock to wake me after another three hours and reopened my profile.

Warning! We've detected an abnormal increase in your Perception characteristic: +1 pt....

I repeated this two more times, bringing my Perception up to level 15. I had one characteristic and one skill point left when it was time for me to get up.
It was getting toward midday. I still had my

sparring practice with Kostya and I still had to take little Cyril to the movies.

I sat up in bed and focused, concentrating on my new sensations.

I could hear children playing in the sand pit behind the closed window; I could even hear their mothers chatting to each other. I could discern the sounds of passing cars and could tell their respective makes. Through the gloom of the closed curtains, I could make out a small coin that had rolled under the bedside table and a tiny spider lurking under the ceiling. I could smell fresh baking from the neighbors' and could feel my own level heartbeat.

I staggered into the bathroom, turned the tap on and peered into the mirror, studying my face. All of a sudden I could see it in every meticulous detail, from the tiniest blood vessels in my eyes to every pore in my skin. I gave my face a good scrub, had a shave, grabbed a quick sandwich and a cup of strong coffee and hurried off to the stadium.

Kostya wasn't there yet. I had a warmup, did a few rounds of the running track, then looked at my watch. He still hadn't arrived.

He's never been late before; on the contrary, he'd always been there before me. Something was wrong.

I called his number but it was out of range. A gnawing anxiety started to brew in my chest. I opened the map and ran a quick search.

Name: Konstantin "Kostya" Bekhterev. There he was, in the city hospital. His Vitality was at 68%. Judging by the debuff, he was unconscious.

* * *

"CAN I SEE KONSTANTIN BEKHTEREV, please?"

"Ward twelve," the nurse replied, then returned to her paperwork.

On Sundays, there were practically no doctors there. I managed to find the department's duty physician who told me that Kostya had been admitted the night before with multiple injuries, several broken ribs and concussion. He'd been found by a passerby who'd called an ambulance. He'd told to the police that he'd fallen down the stairs. He didn't blame anybody for his injuries and refused to file a complaint. There were no traces of alcohol in his blood.

Now he'd have to spend at least two or three weeks in hospital. And he'd have to abstain from physical exercise for the rest of his life.

As soon as I knew where he was, I checked on his little sister. They had no immediate family which meant that if Julie stayed on her own, she'd have no one to look after her.

I looked up his street address on the map and made my way there. I spent some time asking the neighbors which number they were at. Finally, some sympathetic old lady asked me who I was; hearing that I was Kostya's friend, she took me to the right door.

Julie was at home alone. She must have thought that it was her brother coming home because she rushed toward the door, shrieking happily, but saw me instead. Having made sure that we knew each other, the old lady left.

"Hi, Jul," I said.

"Hi, Uncle Phil. Kostya's not here."

"I know. He's in hospital. Would you like to go see him with me?"

She nodded vigorously. I told her to get ready.

It didn't take too long before we were at the hospital. At first, they refused to let her see her brother so I had to "apply pressure" to the doorman to turn his head away while we slipped past him into the emergency department.

"Come now," I told Julie who was curiously studying the first-aid posters.

I took her by the hand. Our plastic shoe protectors[52] shuffling over the floor, we walked down the corridor.

I opened the door. There were several other beds in the ward. Kostya wasn't alone there. A gray sheet covered him to his chin. A UV drip with a saline solution stood next to him. His head was bandaged, his eyes closed. He was hung with debuffs. According to them, he was having a tough time of it.

I walked over to him and called him softly to make sure I didn't wake up the others, "Kostya?"

He half-opened his eyes. His gaze lit up as he saw his sister. "Phil... Julie..." he whispered.

The girl whimpered and clung to him.

"It's all right, kiddo... don't cry..."

"I thought you'd left me!" she sobbed.

---

[52] Disposable plastic shoe protectors are obligatory for visitors and outpatients in most Russian medical institutions.

"Nev-" he exploded in a bout of coughing. "Never, you hear me?"

Julie nodded.

Kostya gulped. "How did you find out?"

"You didn't turn up for training so I went to your place and your neighbors told me what had happened," I just hoped he wouldn't start wondering how I knew where he lived.

"Scumbags..." he mouthed almost soundlessly. Even with my improved Perception I was struggling to make out the words. "No idea who it was. It was dark... some guys came to the door and told me to come out for a talk... Yesterday in the gym... I had a run-in with Mohammed... a serious one... could have been him..."

"Do you think you'd recognize them?"

"Dunno... it was pitch black."

"I see. Why didn't you file a complaint?"

"I'd rather sort it myself," he mouthed.

"Well, that's stupid. What if they'd killed you? Never mind. Listen, you'll be here on the mend for another two or three weeks. So I'll go to the tournament instead of you. Got it? If I win, it'll pay for Julie's treatment."

He nodded. "They're gonna take you apart," he added with a weak smile.

"We'll see. I'm gonna take Julie to my parents. They're retired so they can take care of her. I would have brought her back to my place but I'm virtually never at home. What kindergarten is she in?"

"Forty... eight. Thanks."

A ward attendant barged in, rattling her

cleaning equipment. "What's that now, young man? These people are supposed to be resting! Leave the ward immediately!"

"No worries," I said to Kostya, ignoring the noisy officious cow. "Just lay there, bro, and get better. Julie, say goodbye to your brother. I'll wait for you outside."

I touched Kostya's hand. He couldn't even grip mine. His fingers barely twitched in response.

From the hospital, we went to my parents' to pick up little Cyril. I decided to take the girl to the movies with us, hoping to cheer her up.

Mom and Dad were both at home. I left Julie in Cyril's care and went to the kitchen to explain to my parents what had just happened.

"How horrible!" Mom exclaimed. "And the girl is so skinny..."

"She has a rare disease that can't be treated in Russia. She needs to be taken abroad for surgery. But that's not why she's here."

"Absolutely no problem! I'll be taking her to kindergarten myself," Dad said. "We'll fatten her up, you'll see! All the more fun for us. Seeing as you can't be trusted to provide us with any grandchildren..."

"I thought Cyril was your grandson?"

"He is," Dad replied proudly. "The best grandson ever!"

"Don't listen to that old fool," Mom butted in. "Don't worry, we'll take good care of the girl. We'll be taking her to the hospital to see her brother."

Still, I'd detected in my Dad's tone of voice that he would have liked a grandson who'd bear the family name — in other words, someone who'd carry on the male line. To his credit, he hadn't said it out loud.

"Thanks a lot," I said. "I'll take them to the movies now and bring them back later. I still have things to do today. Would you like me to bring you something? Seeing as we're going to the mall anyway."

"We were just about to go to the market to get some meat," Mom replied. "Apart from that, we have everything. We grow all our own stuff at our summer cottage."

'Won't you have some tea before you leave?" Dad said with a begging note in his voice.

I checked my smartphone for the movie schedule, trying to work out how long it might take us to get there. "Absolutely."

"Great," he said.

As we drank tea, Julie perked up a little. In the end, she was chatting away with "Nana Lydia" and "Papa Oleg". As I watched both her and Cyril who was staring at her with puppy eyes, I couldn't help noticing their high Compatibility (yeah right). I also made a mental note of their respective potentials: with Julie it was drawing (so it might be a good idea to send her to an art school) while Cyril might excel at Programing. I needed to share this information with their parents and make sure they gave them the right education.

We chose to watch *Hotel Transylvania 3: Summer Vacation*. Nothing of note happened during the showing, but afterward I realized I hadn't thought of picking up any spare clothes for the girl. So we went to the first boutique on our way where I bought her

---

everything the helpful salesgirls had suggested: a few sets of underwear, a dress, a couple of T-shirts and a pair of shorts. Then we went to the toy department where Cyril got himself a big construction set and Julie, a remote-controlled car — after she'd rejected a doll point blank, probably under the influence of her big brother.

As we passed a perfume boutique, my eye fell upon an aftershave with a whopping +5 to Charisma. I bought it unhesitantly.

This impromptu bout of shopping had eaten up all of the last poker winnings for which I'd received the ban. Well, this probably wasn't the worst way to spend your money, judging by Julie's incredulous excitement as she pressed the shopping bags to her chest on our way home to my parents'.

I then spent the Sunday night watching video replays of all the best boxing matches. Before going to bed, I invested the last remaining characteristic point into Agility.

I USED TO HAVE THIS POETIC COLLECTION I'D RECEIVED from a writer friend. It was titled *Monday Morning*. No matter how much I read it, I hadn't found a single mention of any Monday in the whole book. Only later had I realized that the actual Monday morning mood was there, written between the lines of his unrhymed poetry.

This is the mood we seem to imbibe with our

mothers' milk. We soak it up with our skin. It permeates our entire mind: this restless, anxious, gloomy and hung-over feeling. On Monday, parents take their baby to the crèche for the first time, carrying her out into a frosty winter morning smelling of exhaust gases[53]. On every such gloomy Monday morning, the sweet comfort of idling around at home is replaced with the rigors of the nursery school with its oatmeal porridge and milky macaroni soup. Then on another such dreary rainy morning the growing child lugs her heavy satchel to school where not everyone is happy to see her. This lasts a whole eleven years[54], after which she has to serve another five years at college, followed by a lifetime of work. Wherever she turns, she can't escape the grim, bitter misery of Monday mornings.

This is the kind of lifestyle reserved for those who only start living on Friday night. Luckily, I wasn't one of them. Not the way I was now, anyway. For me, every beginning of the week meant a new opportunity to slightly better myself and this world. True, the official weekend allowed us to spend more time with our families. This was what I liked about them — but not because I didn't have to work. When you enjoy what you're doing and when you're overcome by the passion to make things better; when your entire team seems to have the same goal, then Monday mornings become radically different from how my writer friend had

---

[53] In winter, Russian cars need to be warmed up by letting the motor run for several minutes.
[54] The course of school training in Russia lasts 11 years

described them. This was just another morning which you were supposed to celebrate, greeting the first sunrays the way our cave ancestors did.

After my morning run, I took a shower, had breakfast and a cup of coffee and was just about to lock up after myself when the phone rang — the one I used for my search and rescue contacts. Without taking off my street shoes, I hurried back into the lounge to answer it.

"Excuse me, who is this?" a lifeless male voice asked.

"Who are you calling?"

"Is this Phil?"

"Yes, it's me."

"You're a slimy piece of shit, Phil, you know that? If I knew where to find you, I'd have ripped your head off," the voice trailed away.

"Who is this?"

"I'm her husband," he said sarcastically, then dissolved into uncontrollable laughter. 'I'm Max," he said when he'd finally stopped. "Was it you who told Olga where to find me? Wretched psychic!"

"Why, what happened?"

"I went on a bender! For five years I never touched a drop! Doesn't one have the right to go apeshit once every five years? She caught me in a sauna with some chicks. She dumped me. She's just gone to file for divorce. You scumbag!"

He hung up.

The edges of my vision turned crimson as the program delivered its verdict:

Warning! You've just performed a socially detrimental action!

Now performing the analysis of consequences...

The harm to society is negligible.

Penalty: 1000 XP

XP points left until the next social status level: 2190/18000

I called the man back.

"What do you want?" the voice asked.

"Getting a divorce doesn't go that quick," I said. "Go to her and apologize. She'll forgive you. And stop drinking."

This time I hung up first. Seeing as he believed me to be a psychic anyway, let's just hope he followed my advice.

I switched the phone off and left the house.

As I walked, I called Matov from my usual phone to tell him I was going to replace Kostya at the tournament. He wanted to know what had happened to him and which hospital he was in, then promised me to go and visit him there. If he indeed renounced his place in the tournament, Matov would write me in instead.

THE WHOLE BUNCH OF THEM — Alik, Gleb, Greg, Marina and Kesha — were hanging around the entrance of the business center, smoking the place out. Next to them, Cyril courageously shuffled from one foot to the other, battling the temptation to join in.

I flew up the stairs with a spring in my step and

walked over to them to say my hellos.

"Phil, er, you know..." Alik began. "I might need to pop out at ten o'clock to submit my college application."

"Sure," I agreed unhesitantly. "Is it the place where you wanted to go?"

"That's right. The management faculty. But the scholarships are finished so they only have places for paying students. Old Mark has made out a contract between me and the company. This way the company will pay for my studies and I pay you guys back half of my divvy... devvy..."

"Dividends," Kesha offered, suppressing a smile.

"That's right. Fifty percent of my cut. From the profits, like."

"That's not a problem," I said.

Mr. Katz had already explained to me the reason behind his idea. According to him, if Alik paid for his own studies, that might make him more responsible. As a corrective measure, sort of.

"How was your Friday night?" I asked.

Marina rolled her eyes. "Oooooh!"

"Like this," Kesha drew the girl toward him and planted a kiss on her lips.

"So! That was quick!"

Marina lowered her eyes. No wonder: only a week ago, she'd shown more than a considerable interest in humble me.

"I'm so happy for you, guys," I said. "Really."

Gleb guffawed. "What a soap opera! Phil, we should really stop all this office romance nonsense."

"Get away with you!" Kesha laughed. "Just so you know, we're going to campus after work tonight to collect Marina's stuff. She's moving in with me."

"I can see your Friday night was a busy affair!" Greg quipped.

"Why, are you jealous?" Marina glared at him, utterly embarrassed.

"No offence meant," Greg replied. "In any case, you weren't the only ones who had a busy night, were they, Alik?"

Alik blushed. "Oh Phil, by the way," he hurried to change the subject. "It's Gorelik's B-day today. Should we club in to get him something?"

"We could," I paused, trying to remember what I knew about the man's preferences. "Isn't he into fishing? One of you should get on down to Rose and ask her for some petty cash to get a present from the sports angling store."

"What sort of budget do you have in mind?" Kesha asked, businesslike.

I made a mental list of potential gifts, checking their Compatibility with Gorelik. Spinners, tackle, rods, echo sounding gear... no...

Finally, I had it. "I'd buy him a Japanese telescopic rod," I said. "From what I've heard, he's hooked on floats so he's gonna love it. As far as the model is concerned, you need to ask-"

"Hi guys," Veronica said as she joined us. She hugged me lightly and gave me a peck on the cheek, then did the same to all the others. But when she reached Alik...

"Hi, sweetheart," she said.

The two clung to each other in a long passionate kiss.

"Hi babe," the reddening and flustered Alik finally said, forcing himself away from her.

Babe? What was that now? We'd hardly begun to work and the company was already starting to resemble a family shop! All that was left to do was bring Stacy back, hire Greg's wife Alina and find a suitable candidate as a match for Cyril. I just hoped this wasn't going to end as some sentimental Brazilian soap opera.

As for the rest, our first weekday went without a hitch. We had a morning briefing to allocate the week's tasks, then everyone set about doing their own thing.

After lunch, a whole bunch of potential clients barged into the office. I recognized one of them as Tural Abdulaev, the guy who'd very nearly stabbed me to death after my encounter with Valiadis. He must have recognized me too because he looked embarrassed.

But I kept a straight face. Only after we'd signed the contract and found him a few job offers, I asked him point blank, "How're things, Tural?"

He said something in Azeri to his fellow team workers, nodding at me. Each of them jumped up, grabbed my hand with both of theirs and shook it. The program showered me with "improved Reputation" messages.

"We've finished that job and retrieved our passports from the boss," he replied. "He paid us in full. But we'll never forget your help! That money... it was really handy."

"Good. I'm happy I could help."

$$* * *$$

I WAS GOING TO SPEND THE EVENING LEVELING UP Boxing which was now very close to 8. All that shadowboxing, watching the reruns of great fights, and refining my technique on the punch bag which I'd finally had installed at my place was now paying off.

But first thing I had to have a talk with Martha. I routinely activated her in the kitchen where I was having a cup of tea.

This wasn't the grubby kitchen of my days with Yanna: the sad crumbling place with the leaky tap and the wonky oven door where I'd had breakfast with Yanna on the day I'd got my interface. That had been less than three months ago — but so many things had changed since then.

Martha materialized and sat opposite me, holding a cup from the same tea service. She was still maddeningly beautiful which made my interactions with her esthetically pleasing as well as enlightening.

"Good evening, Phil."

"Evening, Marth. Would you like to eat?"

"No, thanks, I'm not hungry," she said. "How's your work?"

"It's on the boil. Moving well and all that. Everything seems to be going according to plan. Tomorrow is the last day of the month. I'm curious to see how July went."

"I'm happy for you," she gracefully lifted the cup

and took a sip. "I can see you've managed to avoid another ban today?"

"Exactly. I helped a woman find her husband and got a penalty for it. Why a penalty and not a ban?"

"You saw it yourself. The damage to society was negligible. Either they'll kiss and make up, or their divorce might prove to be the best solution for everyone. What are you feeling?"

"About what?"

"You've changed the lives of several people with just a few careless words. The husband, the wife, their children and their parents... If they do get divorced and meet somebody else with whom they start a new family, that would change even more lives. The ripples on the water spread wider and wider... you understand?"

"I do..." I frowned. "That was a mistake."

"What makes you think so?"

"I broke a family up. How are the children going to grow up without a father? Their whole world is now crumbling around them..."

"It's good that you realize that. But you shouldn't call it a mistake because you acted with the best of intentions. There was no knowing what could have happened had you chosen not to divulge her husband's whereabouts. He might have gone on an even longer bender and gotten into real trouble. He could have been robbed — killed even. Or he could have come out smelling of roses, gone back to his family, and then done it all over again. He could have started drinking so heavily that he might have lost everything he had, which would have incurred much bigger losses to everyone involved. He might have started beating on his wife in front of their children every time he got drunk. Do you understand it now? You can't decide whether something's good or bad without knowing all the potential development routes. Which you can't possibly know. Therefore, it's not a mistake."

I spent some time mulling over it. Finally I nodded my agreement and went to pour myself some more tea.

"Phil, do you remember you were asking me about my prototype?" she offered.

"Sure," I replied excitedly, overfilling my cup with boiling water. "Damn!"

I used a paper towel to wipe it up and returned to Martha. "So you do have a prototype, don't you?"

She smiled. "No, I don't. Allow me to remind you that the character and manners of this particular avatar are based on your personal preferences. But as for my appearance... there is a 99,002 chance of it having a real-world prototype."

I blew a disappointed sigh. "Not a 100 percent?"

"Her eye color is different," Martha explained. Mark it down: Jenna Petersen, 31 years old, born in Paarl.

"Where's that?"

"The Republic of South Africa. Married with a little daughter," she gave me a compassionate look. "I'm sorry, Phil. She's got a Facebook page. You can add her to your friends list if you wish."

I grabbed my smartphone, opened Facebook and hurried to log in. I entered the name into the search and found her.

Jenna Petersen.

An older version of Marta smiled back at me from the screen — the only difference being her eyes which were hazel instead of blue.

THE NEXT DAY, I FINALLY RECEIVED A PHONE CALL FROM Panchenko, Ultrapak's illustrious commercial director. He suggested that we met up in their office. I agreed. I hate leaving things in the lurch even though in this case it wasn't my fault — but still this particular job had been on my to-do list bugging me for weeks.

Before heading for the meeting, I called our office and warned them I might be late. They were still in the same building — with the exception of a different girl at the reception desk.

"Hi," I said. "I'm Phil Panfilov from the Great Job Employment Agency. I have an appointment with Mr. Panchenko."

"I'm afraid he's busy at the moment. You'll have to wait."

Oh really? I've arrived on the dot, and he was the one who scheduled the meeting. I was about to explode. Still, I forced myself to remain calm. I could wait until the end of my appointment — which was thirty minutes, — then I'd just leave, delete the task from the list, zap his phone number and call it a day, dammit.

After fifteen minutes, he emerged from Mr. Ivanov's office and headed for his own.

A couple of minutes later, the girl said he was expecting me. I rose from the couch.

At the very same moment, Vicky came out of her own office. It just so happened that we bumped into each other by Panchenko's door.

"Hi," I said. "I have a meeting with your commercial director."

"I know. I'm part of it," she gave an ominous chuckle.

What's all this about? I thought as I entered Panchenko's office.

"Good morning," said a young man, overweight for his twenty-seven years. He rose from his desk and offered me his hand. "Phil, I presume?"

"That's me, Sir. I'm glad you've found the time to see me, after all."

"I'd like you to meet Victoria, our HR director. The question you want to discuss is within her domain, as well."

Vicky and I sat down: she next to Panchenko, with me opposite the two of them.

I studied the commercial director's stats. His Interest in the meeting was lukewarm, his social status level 8. It didn't bode very well.

"Well then, I'm all ears," he rubbed his hands, faking cheerfulness. "What do you want from us? Tell me."

"I need nothing from you. We, however, might be of some use to you."

As I told them about the services offered by our outsourcing sales department, Vicky smiled skeptically. Panchenko curved his lips, frowning, but didn't interrupt me. I could understand him: if we took over the sales, his post would be surplus to requirements.

"...so basically, that's what we're offering you. Considering we don't charge a set fee but only a percentage of actual sales — which incidentally is the same as the amount you pay your own reps — you are in fact not risking anything."

"I'm afraid we are," Vicky said. "And quite a lot at that."

"Please explain," Panchenko said.

"Excuse me, Mr-" she faltered.

"Mr. Panfilov," I offered.

She ignored me. "How long has your company been active?"

"About two months."

"Yeah," Panchenko drawled. "You're not serious."

"That's what I think, too," Vicky smiled, turning to Panchenko. "I think I've worked out his little scam. He wants to sign a contract with us — apparently with no real risks involved, — then he's going to use the contracts they close to expand his portfolio of clients. You know what he's gonna do? He's gonna flaunt our client list in front of other potential customers to show them how cool they are to have *already*," she stressed the word slightly, "attracted attention from such serious companies as us. And they won't do jack shit for us. You know how it works? This guy goes on client meetings selling *their* services. And who's gonna sell our packaging, then? They only exist for a few weeks..."

'Wait a sec, Victoria," I said. "We could always include penalties in the contract for the dereliction of our contractual duties.

A sarcastic grin spread over Panchenko's face. He already thought he'd sussed me out. Well, I had reasons to believe I'd worked this circus show out too.

As I leaned back in my chair, I saw his hand resting on Vicky's thigh. Now I knew exactly who'd set all this up.

"I'm afraid, Phil, your offer doesn't suit us," Panchenko summed up.

"I'm afraid, Sir, I'm not interested in working with you, either," I noisily pushed the chair away and stood up. "Give my regards to Mr. Ivanov."

He blinked. "Do you know him?"

So he didn't even know I used to work for them? He hadn't even bothered to investigate the person he was about to meet?

"Of course," I said. "I used to work here. Why, didn't Victoria here tell you?" I nodded at her. "It's true I didn't work for long. That's probably why she didn't remember me."

"I'm not complaining about my memory, Philip," she snapped coldly.

"And I'm not complaining about my exes."

I left the office under their flabbergasted stares, then walked out of the glorious Ultrapak building — this time, for good.

* * *

THE PROGRAM REPRIMANDED ME FOR COMMITTING A socially detrimental action and stripped me of 100 XP. I didn't care: I'd just wanted to wipe that smug grin off Panchenko's face.

After I left, I decided not to take a taxi but just walked blindly following my nose. I felt hurt but I couldn't quite put my finger on it. In my mind, I'd let go of Vicky a long time ago. But my heart must have been stalling.

I remembered seeing Yanna with Vlad. That didn't hurt at all. I dug deeper into my soul trying to work it out but still I couldn't understand what exactly was wrong.

One thing was for sure: Ultrapak would never be one of our clients.

Deep in thought, I stumbled into a strange side street. I decided to pop into a café to drink a cup of Americano and call a cab as my gaze lingered on a shop sign saying,

Souvenirs and Rarities

Mechanically I glanced at the silver ring gracing my finger. The Lucky Ring of Veles which I'd dug out in a shop just like this one. I really should go in and take a look.

At first sight, the shop had nothing useful to offer. Tacky plaster figurines, bronze busts of unknown individuals, loose china sets... Still, my intuition drove me toward the far corner of the shop.

There, in a large wicker basket among the heaps of junk, I discovered a tiny bone figurine. Barely visible in the pile of key rings, fridge magnets and other useless trinkets, it seemed to be calling my name.

I focused on it to ID it.

Netsuke Jurōjin
Material: Ivory
One of the seven Japanese gods of fortune, he bestows exceptionally good luck on the figurine's owner.
+5 to Luck
Weight: 0.8779 ounces
Durability: indestructible
Price: 6,430,000.00 rubles
Active when placed in the owner's house

I turned the figurine in my fingers, sensing a weak warmth coming from it.

"Have you found something you like?" a young man asked me from behind the cash register.

"How much is this figurine?"

"This one, from the basket? All the items in it are three hundred rubles."

Lady Luck seemed to be kind to me today. Could the entire ridiculous scene at Panchenko's office have only been a ruse to lure me into this place?

I headed for the cash register to pay.

"One moment," the shop assistant took the figurine. "Well... I'm sorry to tell you this item must have fallen into the basket by mistake. This is a

Jurōjin, a very rare piece. But," he faltered, "it's actually a fake."

"A fake?" I asked, indignant.

"A copy. Sorry about that," he mumbled as he put the figurine away under the counter.

"So how much does this fake cost?"

"One moment," he tapped away on the computer. "Strange. It's not in the database. We had similar items listed for thirty-nine hundred[55]. If you decide to buy it, I could give you a discount."

"I could take it off your hands for two grand, I suppose," I offered magnanimously.

"Deal," the assistant agreed with suspicious ease, making me think I'd overcooked my offer.

Then I gave myself a mental slap on the head. I'd just got myself a real magic item! Worth millions! For two! Thousand! Rubles! What was there not to be happy about?

We parted ways quite happy with each other. I headed for the office.

I spent the rest of the day solving a gazillion of pressing problems concerning the reorganization of the company, the finalizing of our constitutive documents and the renovation works. In the meantime, I still had to see clients.

As I spoke with one of them — a middle-aged male lawyer who looked very self-confident and had an impressive work experience — I noticed there was something wrong with him. Just by looking at his

---

[55] About $60

profile, I realized that his Vitality was dramatically below average.

While he studied the contract, I studied him. Outwardly, he seemed to be okay but still there was something intangible about him which set my alarm bells ringing.

Finally, I put my finger on it. It was a small black spot which at a certain angle almost merged with his dark hair. I recognized it as an interface element — Insight, most likely.

I was also pretty sure that this same spot — I'd no idea how it had become visible to me — was the reason for his malaise.

"How do you feel?" I asked him once he'd finished reading the contract and signing it.

"Never felt better," he replied cheerfully. "Why?"

"Do you ever have headaches?"

"Yeah... sometimes. Just like everybody else, I suppose. If you think that it-"

"Do you mind if I give you a piece of advice? It's up to you whether you want to follow up on it or not. Do make an appointment with a doctor and have your head checked out. I'm pretty sure that your headaches are much more frequent now than they were before. I suggest you get an appointment ASAP. You know what I mean?"

"What an idea! My health is absolutely fine. I don't drink, I don't smoke and I exercise regularly."

"Still I suggest you get a check-up. This has nothing to do with the contract you've just signed. I'm going to give you three vacancies now which are suitable for your profile," I started printing out the search results. "As soon as you know they've taken you on, you'd better pop round to see your doctor."

He gave me a hesitant nod. I handed him the printout with all the contacts and bade my goodbye to him.

I just hoped he'd listen to my advice.

IN THE EVENING, we had a quick powwow for Rose to announce July's financial results.

"Romuald gave me all the figures as well as the contents of the cash box for the period that you worked on your own. In less than a month, you found employment for a hundred and sixty-three persons. Of those, thirty-eight were charged the set fee of a thousand rubles. The others signed a contract with the agency agreeing to pay us 10% of their first wage packet which is roughly the first ten days of August or September if they've been taken on on a trial basis. I estimate the agency's returns for the month of July to be four hundred fourteen thousand five hundred rubles[56]."

Her last words were drowned out by applause. Gleb and Alik, the two star clowns of our traveling circus, clapped the hardest. Still, one look at their joyful faces made me dissolve into a happy grin. We'd done it!

"Also!" Rose raised a commanding hand. "The sales volume on Kesha and Veronica's outsourcing

---

[56] About $6,200

contracts has reached-"

I didn't listen any further. It's been my philosophy that money not received is money not yet earned. We still had to see if we could get our cut. Also, we had more expenses than I dreaded to think of. The rent, the taxes, all the wages, the renovation works, the new furniture and office supplies, not to mention publicity...

Still, it was too cool, don't you think?

CHAPTER TWENTY-ONE

SMOOTH JAZZ WILL BE DEPLOYED IN 3...

I must not fear. Fear is the mind-killer. Fear is the little-death that brings total obliteration. I will face my fear. I will permit it to pass over me and through me. And when it has gone past I will turn the inner eye to see its path. Where the fear has gone there will be nothing. Only I will remain.

Frank Herbert, Dune

IN THE ABSENCE of Kostya, I was forced to find another coach: a cartoon image of an old soak with a Tutoring stat going through the roof.

His name was Ibrahim: an old Kazakh and a former Soviet Union champion who now trained little kids in one of the local sports schools. I had no problem finding a common language with him, asking him to prepare me for the tournament for a sum which, although small for me, made a huge difference to him.

That's how I became his student. We trained twice a day in addition to regular sparring with other guys in the gym.

Courtesy of my stat booster, these two weeks of prolonged daily travails easily amounted to the equivalent of a year's intensive training IRL. Up until now, I'd already had over a hundred sparring bouts.

Not everything went smoothly, of course. I did lose, and did so often, especially in the beginning. My opponents' technique varied: some of them came on aggressively while others hung back, waiting for their chance to launch a counterattack. Some of them were faster or stronger than me.

Still, the old boy spent a lot of time teaching me the fight's strategy. He made me study my enemy, searching for their weak sides and using them.

"There's no such thing as a perfect fighter," he'd say. "Even the greatest weren't so great in certain things. I want you to seek out your opponents' vulnerabilities and use them against them."

And so I did. I'd lose again, then wait for the next fight to continue searching for their weak spots, changing my tactics only to lose again, then win the next time I tried.

"More passion!" he demanded. "There shouldn't be any mercy in boxing! Passion makes you stronger! He who's the most passionate, wins!"

Passion was something I did lack at first. I needed to get a good clobbering or even lose in order to build it up. It took me a dozen fights just to learn to be passionate enough to win.

The old boy made me work till I dropped. Strangely enough, it hadn't really affected my physical stats. My Strength, Stamina and Agility seemed to have frozen.

My Boxing skill, however, had reached level 10. I still had one skill point stashed away since the last time I'd leveled up. Now I invested it into Boxing. Kostya — who was due to be discharged from the hospital the next morning — was level 8. I was now level 11.

I put much store in the upcoming tournament. As a participant with the lowest ranking, I was to enter it on Saturday at 9 a.m. to have a few elimination fights with other amateur beginners like myself.

The city's sports center was bustling with out-of-town teams: all those loud young men cracking jokes and making fun of each other. I stuck out of the crowd like a sore thumb. Still, I was pretty confident. They may have been young and loud but their Boxing skill was no higher than 5 or 6. The stronger fighters would be coming later, once the elimination fights were over.

I signed on and headed over to the weigh-in.

With my 182,6 lbs, they shoved me in with the light heavyweights: 175 to 200 lbs. I was quite prepared for this scenario even though it was less than favorable. I should have lost a few lbs. in order to drop a weight class and fit in with the middleweights. In any case, it was too late to do anything about it now.

I could already see I wasn't going to have it easy. I studied the other guys' stats in silent awe. Their Strength, Agility and Stamina were at least the double of my own. My only hope lay with my high Boxing skill — and with my improved Perception which had given me my super-human reaction times.

They brought us together and made us draw lots to find our prospective opponents. In order to make it to the main grid, I had to get three wins behind me at the elimination stage.

"Ah, you're here too?" a familiar voice called out to me.

"Hi, Mohammed, hi Zaurbek," I nodded to the two Dagestani brothers.

"Are you competing?" Zaurbek asked.

"Yeah. You too?"

"Sure," Mohammed replied. "Only we're going straight to the main grid. We're here to root for our little brother. Mustafa!" he called. "Come here!"

"Hi," their brother joined us, casting me an appraising look. "Light heavyweight?"

"Yes. You too?"

"Yeah," he nodded.

"I hope you'll be pitted against him, brother!" Zaurbek guffawed. "He's only been boxing for a month! He'll get hisself clobbered straight away!"

"Maybe," Mohammed said. His face darkened. He must have still remembered our fight.

"Wait up! They're announcing the results," Mustafa turned away from us.

The heaving crowd threatened to upturn the judges' table.

"Quiet!" the ref announced, then waited for the noise to subside. "Here're your results. In light flyweight under 108 pounds..."

My first opponent was a stocky guy in his forties. He wasn't much of a boxer but he must have had one hell of a punch, judging by his 30+ Strength. If I took a right-hander from him, it would be lights out, for sure.

I changed and gave my gym bag to the guys from the office who'd just arrived in full force to support me. Even Mr. Katz and Rose had come along.

I was especially pleased to see Gleb. After all, it was his big day: his Gambling and Alcoholism debuffs had finally expired. All this time, I'd been monitoring his debuff counters with bated breath but Gleb hadn't let me down. He hadn't relapsed in any way. Now I was a hundred percent sure he wasn't going to return to his old habits. He looked decidedly fresher; gone were the bags and dark circles under his eyes which were now radiating happiness. His complexion had taken on a healthy glow.

He smiled and winked at me.

"Be careful, Phil!" Rose said.

"She's right," Veronica chimed in. "Keep your guard up!"

Greg had arrived with his wife Alina who blushed and wished me luck.

"I'll need all the luck I can get," I blurted, knocking on wood.

Someone gave me a hearty whack on the back. I swung round. Our entire street gang stood there, all present and correct: Yagoza, Fatso, Sprat, Vasily... Behind their backs, Alik's three "lads" — Tarzan and the other two — hovered timidly.

Alik gave me a guilty shrug.

"Hi, Mr. Philip!" Fatso shouted in excitement. "We've come to see you win!"

"My compliments," Yagoza lowered his head to me. "We're all rooting for you. Don't let our block down!"

"Yeah! Float like a butterfly, sting like a bee!" Sprat began prancing around as if shadowboxing but then tripped up over his own feet.

Your hands can't hit what your eyes can't see, I kept repeating Mohammed Ali's own words as I helped Sprat back to his feet, then went off to get ready for my first fight. My little band of fans headed for the stands.

What a shame old Ibrahim wouldn't see me fight. He'd said he was too old for all that; his heart would conk out from all the worrying about me.

There were six rings set up in the arena to accommodate six simultaneous fights. Trying to blank out whatever was going on around me, I started warming up until they called me for my first fight,

"Panfilov and Nemchinov, you're next up."

Fighting the burly Nemchinov felt like a walk in the park after the dozens of sparring bouts I'd had in Ibrahim's classes. My opponent was clumsy and lead-footed and soon wore himself out. I was far too technical for him — and his blows were so predictable that I'd already dodged even before he'd decided where to land a blow.

Your hands can't hit what your eyes can't see...

"More passion!" I kept hearing old Ibrahim's voice in my head.

In the third round, my opponent rose to his feet under the shower of my blows and cowered, shielding his head with his hands. He'd run out of steam.

I'd won on points with a ridiculous advantage.

My next fight was even easier. This opponent was a tall lanky guy with long arms, a typical outfighter. Neither his physique nor his skill were up to much. He kept going in circles, attacking me with the same pre-prepared combinations which I dodged easily. By the end of the first round, I let fly an uppercut between all his dancing around and knocked him out cold.

The main grid was about to start. The stands began filling with people.

My third and last opponent would be decided in the fight between Mustafa and Bulat, the Kazakh guy I'd met in Matov's group.

Both of them were strong on their feet, playing it safe. They knew they were so equally matched that one mistake could knock one of them out of the tournament. The Kazakh guy was a bit more active at first but Mustafa, encouraged by his brothers to "kick ass", caught his opponent with a vicious counterpunch, knocking him down.

From then on, the outcome was pretty clear to everybody. In the next round, Mustafa capitalized on his success and came out on top.

I'd been analyzing his style all along, noticing that he tended to open up for a split second every time before throwing a left.

That was enough for me to knock him down within twelve seconds. Toward the end of the round, he made the same mistake — and this time, he didn't have it quite so easy. The ref counted him out, much to the disappointment of his noisy brothers, then raised my hand in victory.

I was in the main grid.

TOWARDS THE END OF THE EVENING I ALREADY HAD FOUR wins under my belt.

They announced a break before the finals in

all ten weight categories. The flyweights were the first into the ring. I still had loads of time till my final.

I sat with my friends to watch as a spectator. We took up almost an entire row. Alik's motley crew was sitting just behind us. Alik himself had apologized to them before taking a place next to Veronica.

Once the elimination rounds were over, Kostya had come to join us too. His little sister was still with my parents who'd brought her to see her brother in hospital almost every day. They'd also come to check him out.

He'd sent the girl back home with "Auntie Lydia": he could talk to her at any time but the outcome of the tournament would determine the fate of her surgery. So he'd popped in at home to leave the bag with his hospital stuff, then made a beeline directly for the sports center just in time for the main grid.

"Phil, you beauty!" he kept saying. "It was unreal how you did him! By the third round I thought you were toast. The way he was trying to catch you out! And all that time you were luring him on?"

I grinned. "Sort of."

In the semifinals, I'd beat Yuri, the best fighter in Matov's other group. I'd already had words with him once in the gym — and afterward, I'd apparently trained with his group during my "second life". He was the only boxer from Matov's two groups who hadn't yet been eliminated. And now I'd seen him off too.

"Listen, how is it possible that you've managed to kick ass out of all the heavyweights?" Kostya mused. "I'm only a middleweight and I used to kick your ass — doesn't that make me awesome or what?"

"I don't think so, Bekhterev," Matov came and sat next to us. "You wouldn't be able to kick his ass *now*."

"Good evening, coach," we said in unison.

"You're full of surprises, Panfilov," he didn't hide his amazement. "I can't say that it was pleasant to watch but it was quite an eye-opener."

"You gave me a bunk up the ladder, Sir," I said, trying to be objective. "Thank you."

"I gave you the basics. My fault was I didn't take your intellect into account. You're a smart fighter. Bekhterev, did you notice how your buddy adapts to every opponent? He knocked out Mohammed in one way and Yuri in another. Shame I didn't see the elimination rounds," he grew serious. "Who trains you now? Not with Khmelnitsky, by any chance?"

"I trained him," Sprat scoffed behind our backs. "I told him to float like a butterfly and fart like a bee!"

"Olé, Olé, Olé, Olé," his inebriated street buddies began singing, "Phil Panfilov is a champion!"

Matov sized them up, winced and turned

away. "So who trained you? Don't tell me Tkachenko agreed to take you on!"

"Neither, Sir. That's my coach, sitting next to you. It was Kostya who trained me."

"Who, Bekhterev? Seriously?"

"Really."

"We only had a few sessions," Kostya hurried to deny his role in my success. "He's a quick learner though."

"Looks like you're some sort of phenomenon," Matov said jokingly but it came out dead serious. "Can I have a word? I've got something i want to discuss with you."

I agreed.

He took me to a small room under the stands. "You know who you're up against in the final?"

"Some guy called the Wolf."

"Exactly. He's a superheavyweight from Khmelnitsky's stable. He's dropped a weight specially to compete with heavyweights. The prize money's the same but it's easier for him. But his style is still the heavy boy's style. You know what I mean?"

"I'm gonna do him."

"You sure?"

"Yes. I've studied him. He relies on his strength. He's gonna try to get me on the ropes and corner me, then shower me with blows. Rinse and repeat, until I break. Only I'm not gonna break. He will try and corner me until he runs out of steam and opens up — and that's when he'll catch it."

"Well, well," Matov chuckled. "You sure make it sound easy."

"The Wolf's stamina isn't up to much. His tactics involve a long repeated series of blows, so by the end of the third round he can barely keep his mitts up."

"Very well. If you're so sure of yourself, I'm gonna believe you. Listen up. Tonight there'll be a fight in the Empire. Sort of a Super final for a chosen audience. It'll be today's superheavyweight champion against the heavyweight champion. They pay ten grand."

"Ten grand what?"

"Not rubles!" he snapped impatiently. "Ten thousand dollars!"

"So what's the catch?"

"It'll be ten rounds. Without gloves. It's gonna hurt. A lot."

"And what does the winner get?"

"Fifty thousand bucks. But you can forget it. You haven't got a chance. The Sledgehammer's weight is 290 lbs. He's the bookies' favorite. You just need to climb into the ring, go a couple of rounds, and then lie down and don't get up. The public will like that," he paused, apparently taking my silence as a sign of doubt. "Don't worry, they've got an ambulance on standby."

'Okay."

He looked up sharply. "Okay what?"

"I'm in."

"*He's in!*" he mocked. "First you need to win

here. That's it, then, go and get yourself ready. I still need to talk to the Sledgehammer."

I went back to the stands. Sprat offered me what he called "doping", meaning a plastic cup of vodka and Coke. The others explained to him the error of his ways; Yagoza even gave him a slap across the head for "being a dumbass".

Then I sat down to await the finals. I wasn't worried. As I'd spoken to Matov, I'd remembered that he only had level 10 in Boxing — and he'd still managed to train a national champion or two. I was level 11, which meant I was obliged to at least win the regional championship.

Closer to my fight, I left the stands for a quick warmup. I sensed someone staring at me and swung round to see my future opponent, Sergei "the Wolf" Zverev: a burly dude with a shaven head and a large tattoo of a rather toothy wolf on his chest. Meeting my eye, he gave me the cut-throat sign and turned away.

His level 9 in combination with his Strength made him a serious opponent. Well, that remained to be seen. I just continued stretching and warming up.

Finally, it was our turn.

"We invite into the ring the final contestants in the heavyweight category!" the panel of judges announced through the loudspeakers. "In the blue corner, introducing Philip Panfilov!"

My support group yelled their encouragement. Yagoza's wheezy voice somehow rose above all the others, strangely drowning out the tumult of the stands.

I dove under the ropes and took my place in my corner, awaiting my opponent.

The Wolf walked with an unhurried swagger, greeting the public and wallowing in the attention. In his own mind, he must have already hammered me and won — which guaranteed him the champion's purse of two hundred thousand rubles[57] plus another ten thousand greenbacks for the clandestine "super final" in the night club.

Undoubtedly, Matov had already approached him. His own coach, the notorious Khmelnitsky, must have been in on it too, in which case he might have divulged the news to his protégé.

The ref summoned us and ran through the rule book.

The fight began.

The Wolf went on the offensive immediately, pushing me back. Still, each time he thought he'd cornered me, I managed to slip back into the open ring. He struggled to avoid my counterattacks to his side; quite a few of my body hooks reached their mark.

I was leading the fight to a confident victory — which was probably why I dropped my guard for a fraction of a second. That nearly became my undoing. The Wolf managed to work me into a corner, showering me with blows most of which I

---

[57] About $3,000

blocked. Still, I must have missed quite a few. I barely stayed upright. My ears were ringing; my cheekbone and my eyebrow were on fire. I was only saved by the bell.

Kostya fussed over me in my corner, mopping up the sweat and applying a wet towel to my cuts and bruises.

"What were you thinking of?" he berated me. "Why did you have to go in close? You had all that space to you right! You should've ducked out!"

"I know, I know. It's okay, don't worry. I'll do him now."

The one-minute break was over before I could catch my breath. A new buff message came through:

Passion to Win
Duration: 10 min
+3 to all man characteristics
+50% to Vigor
+50% to Confidence
+50% to Willpower
+50% to Spirit
+50% to Pain Threshold

The buff's effect made me feel fresh and full of energy as if the fight hadn't started yet. But most importantly, I'd worked out how I could win.

Inspired by his last success, the Wolf couldn't wait to get to me. I lured him onto the ropes. Just as he thought he'd cornered me and switched off his brain to turn to punch mode, I ducked to the left and gave him a cross which passed over his right hand. He momentarily lost his bearings which was enough for me to get in my favorite combination: a left uppercut quickly followed by a straight right to the body and finally a left hook to the head.

The Wolf went down. The stands dissolved in a deafening roar.

K.O.

I was champion.

* * *

AN HOUR LATER, WE WERE SITTING IN A COZY IRISH pub on Chekhov St. celebrating my victory: me, Alik and Veronica, Greg and Alina, Kesha and Marina, Cyril, Gleb, Mr. Katz, Rose and Kostya. I'd had a hard time getting rid of Yagoza and his gang, each of whom wanted to shake my hand and tell me how legendary I was.

"To Phil!" my friends raised their glasses. "To you, Phil!"

I clinked my glass of fruit juice against theirs. The super final still lay ahead me — but they absolutely didn't need to know about that.

"What you gonna do with all that money?" the curious gambler in Gleb asked.

"I think that's none of our business," Rose replied. "But knowing Mr. Panfilov, I'm sure he'll want to invest it-"

"Not really," I interrupted her. "It's going to a different cause."

I hadn't received the prize money yet but they'd given me the certificate. On Monday, I was supposed to go to the organizers' office with it and pick up the cash. Kostya was coming with me. From there, we were going straight to the bank to transfer the entire amount to the foreign clinic which was going to operate on Julie. Once that done, the clinic would send an invitation which would allow Kostya and Julie to apply for their visas. The same travel agent who'd arranged for Kostya to contact the clinic to begin with, now promised to sort out the visas promptly.

"Which cause is it?" Veronica asked with a sweet smile. "Come on, Phil! I don't mean to be pushy, I'm just curious!"

"Leave him alone!" Cyril interrupted her. "Let him eat in peace!"

I still had three or four hours left until my match in the night club so I could allow myself a meal and some rest.

Kostya rose and raised his glass of mineral water. "Guys, I don't know any of you. But I know Phil. And if you're even half as good as he is..."

Everybody at the table switched their attention to him.

"I'd like to raise a toast to the health of my little sister Julie. You don't know anything about her so you won't understand why I'd like to toast her health. Let me explain. When she was two years old, our parents died in an accident. We were left alone," he paused to make sure everybody was listening, then went on. "No one ever helped us without any strings attached. Julie is very ill. If she doesn't get surgery in the very near future, she'll never be able to walk again. This type of surgery isn't available in our country. We need to go to Germany. Their specialists think they can take her on and even promise an almost hundred-percent recovery. Problem is, it costs over a million rubles[58]. That's without travel and housing expenses," he looked me in the eye. "I'm sorry, Phil. Your winnings won't be enough. It's only good for a down payment to get her accepted."

"And then what?"

"I'll have to work in Germany. I'll beg and plead with them. They're not animals, are they? Sure they won't kick a four-year-old girl out without completing the treatment?" his voice broke.

I averted my eyes.

Now it wouldn't be enough just to take part in the illegal "super final". I'd have to win it.

In the meantime, Kostya went on,

"In brief, it was me who should have participated in the tournament. But I got myself mugged so now I'll never be able to box again. Ever," his shoulders heaved like a child sobbing. "All I wanted to say was that Phil is donating his entire prize money to Julie's treatment. Which is why I suggest we all drink a toast to her health! Phil has done so much for us — let's hope it won't be in vain!"

---

[58] Over $15,000

I may be wrong but as far as I can remember, this was the longest speech Kostya had ever made.

We clinked our glasses in silence. The girls averted their eyes, wiping away the tears.

"Phil, sweetie..." Veronica rose, walked around the table and gave me a hug. "You understand you're a hero, don't you?"

"Yes, he is!"

"A real hero!" Gleb enthused. "He's saved my bacon! And he's gonna save Julie too!"

As they began trading excited stories of my supposed chivalry, I'd been thinking. I wasn't a hero, no. Not in the sense they meant.

I was a Hero — one of the many chosen by the Vaalphors.

Provided I passed the Trial.

* * *

TO THE CATCALLS OF THE EXCITED CLUB CROWD — ALL those ladies in revealing cocktail dresses, fat government officials and shady businessmen in Versace suits — I was thrown back onto the ropes by the mother of all haymakers. For me, it was lights out.

An insistent voice penetrated my befuddled mind,

"...Three! Four! Five!"

It was the fifth round. I was swimming in my own blood, unable to get to my feet. My limbs didn't obey me. My head felt as if nailed to the canvas. One of my eyes was swollen shut. My nose was broken. I struggled to breathe. It looked like one of my ribs was broken, too. The upper edge of my field of vision was strung with debuff icons like a war veteran's chest.

Neither Passion to Win nor my level 11 in Boxing had done me any good. In a gloveless match, no amount of technique, it seems, can overcome brute force.

"Six!"

I struggled to see through the red haze filling my eyes. The Sledgehammer was standing proud with his arms raised.

"Finish him off! Finish his off!" the crowd bayed.

"Sledgehammer, I love you!" a girl's hysterical voice yelped. "Screw me!"

"Seven!"

"Kill him! Kill him!"

His toe touched my face. He lowered himself to one knee and raised his fist for the coup de grace. Why wasn't the ref trying to stop him?

"Eight!"

I closed my eyes to await my fate.

Then something changed.

Time slowed down.

A healing wave rolled through my body, extinguishing all the debuffs, removing fatigue and restoring Vigor. My Vitality bar was full again.

My eye opened. My nose could breathe again. My ribs had stopped hurting.

I could make out an unmoving figure amid the raging crowd, her hand reaching out to me.

Ripples of healing auras flowed from her fingertips, aided by flashes of new buffs: Righteous Anger III, Fury, Defender, Adal's Hand, The Touch of Mother Nature. Between them, the buffs had doubled all my stats, improving Regeneration 1,000%. Those were only short-terms effects — but I didn't need much else.

"Nine!"

The Sledgehammer's fist was two inches away from my solar plexus. I twisted, rolled over and jumped to my feet, casting a quick glance at Ilindi standing there in her usual guise. She gave me a faint nod and disappeared.

Silence fell. Under the crowd's astonished gaze, the ref ordered us to carry on. What a slimeball. He was worse than useless in this fight.

I pounded the astounded Sledgehammer, my hands moving so fast I could only see the blurred images of their passing, each of them meeting their mark and stripping my opponent of 5 or 6% Vitality.

My uppercut found his chin just as the bell rang.

I scanned the crestfallen crowd, noticing anger in the stares of those who must have backed the wrong horse. They couldn't wrap their minds around what they'd just witnessed. A total beginner who'd only been boxing for less than three months (they'd paid a hundred bucks for this tip) had been playing the punch bag for the entire match only to rise from near death a second before his defeat and shred the favorite.

I studied their faces: some drunk, other sobered; some handsome, some not so, yet other addicts of the plastic surgeon's scalpel; some grim, others cringing; some serious, other gloomy. They thought they had life by the balls, their faces as dead as their souls. You can neither change nor shape them: the swollen parasites on my country's festering body.

If I could only keep the interface after the license expired!

I didn't have the time to ponder the thought.

In deathly silence, the ref announced me the winner. A girl in a non-existent swim suit climbed into the ring and handed me a tray with my prize money. Five wads of hundred-dollar bills.

Julie would live.

TOWARD THE END OF THE NEXT WEEK, JULIE AND KOSTYA had had their Schengen visas and booked their tickets on the first available flight out. The rest of my winnings went on boosting my company's future. Rose put the money through the books while Mark penned a loan contract. We expected the funds make a return by next year, payable out of our profits. We'd decreed that the company would first pay me off, then decide how to distribute the rest of the available money. We'd use some of it to develop

---

the company further while distributing the rest between all the shareholders depending on their input.

Veronica offered to take us to the airport. Our entire office wanted to see my friends off but I used my director's clout to stop the circus and make them work. Kesha was completely snowed under with new contracts and desperately needed help, forcing us to advertise for more sales reps, so everyone was busy from dawn till dusk interviewing new candidates.

The whole way to the airport we only talked about how things would turn out once Julie got better and they'd come back. We'd already decided that Kostya would work with us managing our web site. Veronica promised the girl she'd take her to the movies and attraction parks. The little girl smiled dreamily, apparently unused to such attention.

In the airport, Kostya took his sister by the hand and headed off to check in, throwing us a nonchalant goodbye. In his mind, he was already in the clinic.

We watched them leave hand in hand. Their only suitcase was on its way to the hold. Julie was clutching the doll Veronica had given her; Kostya was carrying a battered backpack.

He turned and saw my clenched fist raised in a salute. He nodded and raised his hand too.

We drove back in silence, each thinking their own thoughts. Veronica cast occasional glances at me but my face remained unperturbed.

We were already halfway to the city when

Mom called me. She knew Kostya and Julie were about to fly off but she didn't know where the money had come from. Hopefully, she'd never find out.

"Did you see them off, son? Everything went okay?"

"Yes, Mom, I saw them checked in. Everything's fine."

"Thank God!" I could almost see her make the sign of cross on the other end of the line. "And you, how are you? You were sort of sluggish last night. You sure you're okay? Even Dad noticed it."

Last night, Kostya, Julie and myself had gone to see them. The girl had wanted to say goodbye. Kesha and I had spent the whole day rushing around on business meetings so no wonder I'd appeared tired.

"Sorry, Mom. I had too much on my plate."

"You need to get some sleep, my boy. You're a director, after all. If you don't turn up for work, nobody will say a word."

I chuckled. Veronica cast a curious glance in my direction.

"Okay, Mom. I'll do as you say."

She rattled off a whole bunch of tips, then promptly said goodbye and hung up.

I shoved the phone into my pocket but it immediately started to vibrate again. The number looked weird and abnormally long.

I answered it.

"How do you do?" a soft female voice said with just a trace of a foreign accent. "Can I speak to Mr.

Philip Panfilov, please?"

"Speaking."

"I'm Angela Howard from the Embassy of the United Sta-"

The world stopped dead.

The forest landscape behind the car window was like a freeze frame. The call time counter on the phone screen didn't move. Veronica slackened her hold on the steering wheel, her mouth half-open.

My breathing stopped halfway. My body couldn't move. My mind was the last to be paused.

I sank into the great nothing, my body pierced by icy needles.

The world blinked.

And then...

...I FOUND MYSELF SNOWED UNDER a whole lot of debuffs. Just like the last time, it was Intoxication, Paralysis, Dehydration, Starvation, Feebleness, Mind Suppression and something else...

"Abduction complete," a genderless voice said out of nowhere.

"The subject has regained consciousness," that was Ilindi.

"You can remove all the DOTs and debuffs," Valiadis ordered. "We all know the subject. We can skip the initialization."

A silvery haze enveloped me, penetrating my skin, then re-emerging, tinted with the red and black strands of the DOTs. A healing green wave ran over me.

"Accepted," Khphor's voice echoed in my head.

They brought me back to normal. I got up.

Ilindi was wearing the same light-blue evening dress, only this time her hair was not platinum blond but all the colors of the rainbow.

Valiadis was wearing a gun-barrel blue armored suit. I'd love to know where I could get one. Further on stood the ten-foot alien: Khphor from the Senior Race of the Vaalphors.

"Human, you know what to do," he stated.

"Be brave, human!" Ilindi encouraged me.

Valiadis only nodded. His face betrayed his anxiety.

I nodded back to them and headed for the wall, its shiny white texture reminiscent of reptile skin. When I'd approached, it had split into two as if sliced by a knife.

I checked myself out. I seemed to have everything on me: Ilindi's red wristband as well as the ring of Veles. The Netsuke Jurōjin that I'd bought from the antique shop was working its magic at home, keeping me supplied with Luck.

I entered the opening without looking back.

The wall was now behind me. In front of me lay a long winding corridor less than 7 foot wide so that I could touch its sides with my outstretched hands.

This time I wasn't in a hurry. I advanced slowly, studying the floor, the walls and the ceiling. After about 150 feet, I saw my old friend.

Acid Jelly
Level 17

Its level had risen, too. Did the Trial's difficulty levels reflect my progress?

I kept looking at the acid creature. The name tag above it swung round. Another line had made an addition to it:

Fear: 100%

It was afraid of me!

Slowly I advanced, focusing on everything I could see. When there were only thirty feet left between us, my eye noticed a tiny bump in the smoothness of the wall.

I stepped back and touched it. My hand disappeared into a void. I took my hand back and the hole in the wall closed up, growing a leathery film over the gap.

I dove into the hole, finding myself in a small pocket behind the wall. I stood there trying not to breathe. Soon I saw one of the jelly's tentacles slither past, followed by the rest of him.

The creature oozed past.

I breathed a sigh of relief. The way forward was free. Had this been the extent of the Trial?

Whistling happily, I carried on down the tunnel. Soon it widened out; it was now broad enough for a dozen jellies abreast. I walked calmly but warily, regaining my common sense. This wouldn't be the end of my problems.

A few hundred feet further on, my enhanced Perception allowed me to notice a strange intricate pattern covering the floor, made up of the thinnest dark lines. When my foot was about an inch away from them, my Intuition screamed like a Banshee.

I slowly withdrew my foot. After some consideration, I took off a sneaker and threw it in front of me onto one of the lines.

The shoe fell into two halves the moment it touched the floor, the cut tracing the shape of the curved dark line.

I spent the next half an hour sweating like a pig and doing a balancing act on my heels and toes, negotiating the treacherous course. That done, I slid down the wall and just sat there resting without a thought for the time.

Having restored, I kept going.

A few dozen feet further, I stopped again. Something felt wrong. I could sense just a hint of vibration at the very edge of my senses. The smell was different here too, suggestive of ozone.

I took a step back and had a think.

I removed my other sneaker and threw it forward. As it hit a certain point in space, it crumbled to dust which sank to the floor as a flat two-dimensional spot.

My socks were the next in line. The first one suffered the same fate as the sneaker. The other one, however, landed safely on the floor.

Good. What I had to do now was determine

the width of the safe passage. I took my shirt off and ripped it at the seams, then started with the right-hand side of the tunnel.

Dust. More dust. And again.

The remaining right sleeve stayed intact. I drew a mental line, determining the width of the safe corridor. It was barely three feet wide. I'd have to negotiate it sideways. I just hoped the corridor didn't meander.

The vibrating air crackled as I cleared the tricky course.

I took another breather to restore Vigor. They hadn't told me anything about any time restrictions. Still, knowing these so-called *researchers*' tendency not to inform me of any rules, I'd rather get a move on.

I stood up and walked further.

For a while, nothing happened. I carried on, the leathery floor warm and springy under my unstockinged feet. I waved the remaining shirt sleeve in the air to fan myself. I was hot.

After a while, when I'd already started to think I'd been going round in circles, I noticed the sweat dripping into my eyes. I wiped it away with the sleeve in my hand but only began sweating more.

The air temperature had considerably risen. Still uncomprehending, I stood stock still and listened hard. Somewhere behind my back, I could hear a steadily increasing rumbling sound.

I turned round. After a moment's hesitation, I snapped out of it and ran for my life.

A wall of fire was chasing me, its heat singeing my back. I put on a spurt and really legged it — but the flames threatened to overtake me.

I could have said that it was licking my heels but it wasn't. My entire back was on fire, my hair crackling, my ears burning. My fear of death had resulted in the buff of the same name, adding me strength and new characteristics. I couldn't read them though, I was far too preoccupied with saving my skin. I just closed the message window and bolted as fast as I could.

No idea how long I kept this game up with the wall of fire. It felt like several hours — but later when I'd finally outrun the chasing flames and the wall of fire had expired on reaching a certain point in the tunnel, I collapsed in a heap to the floor and couldn't move for quite a time.

Once I'd caught my breath, I finally looked at the interface clock. It had been less than four hours since the Trial had started. It had been three and a half the last time I checked which meant that I'd only been running for a quarter of an hour, no more. Having said that, I'd run very quickly.

For the next half-mile, I was really careful. I checked my every step, warily studying all about me, sniffing for any suspicious odors and listening intently to the silence. I didn't seem to detect any threat.

I could already make out the end of the tunnel when a pile of stone blocks barred my way. They were impossibly smooth and so polished as to have razor-sharp edges. They were of different sizes, looking as if someone had been playing a 3D game of Tetris, the smallest of them weighing in at at least 120 lbs. The bigger ones I couldn't even budge.

I thought hard before eventually coming up with an idea. I laid a layer of the smallest blocks, then rolled the bigger ones onto them, cutting myself on their edges. Despite dropping a midsize block onto my foot, I gritted my teeth and carried on with my giant puzzle.

I'd already realized that each of the tests in this Trial had been measuring a corresponding characteristic. The Jelly had checked my Perception and Empathy; the complex pattern of lines had been testing my Agility as well as Luck, and repeating Perception again. The wall of fire had proofed my Stamina. And these blocks here must have had something to do with my Strength and Intellect.

This barricade of blocks had proven to be the most time- and energy-sapping. Dismantling it took me over three hours.

When I'd finally taken everything apart, feeling utterly exhausted, I saw a narrow crack in the wall just wide enough for me to squeeze through.

Grazing my skin, I forced my way through it and found myself in a narrow elongated hall. It was lined with the same stone blocks. I could just make out two oval spots of color by the far wall. They were taller than a regular human. As I approached, I noticed that they flashed, pulsating with all the shades of the rainbow.

My interface identified them as "portals". They seemed to be emitting a weak glow: one of them red, the other bluish.

Which one was I supposed to choose? I walked around the hall, studying its walls which were perfectly smooth with barely any visible joints. Having discovered nothing of use, I returned to the portals.

Blue or red?

The turquoise blue or the burgundy red?

Somehow I preferred the latter.

I walked towards it and touched it with my fingertips. My heart missed a beat as it sucked me in.

I was standing at the edge of a forest, wearing only a pair of tattered jeans.

I was looking at the world as it really was, without the interface. All the icons and indicators had disappeared.

I couldn't move as something seemed to be holding my feet. The same could be said about my whole body: it seemed to have turned to stone.

A few feet away from me, a message appeared in the air,

Congratulations! You've successfully passed the preliminary selection!

You've been admitted to the main Trial.
Candidate evaluation complete
Character generation complete

What? This hadn't been the Trial?

The message dissolved into thin air, replaced by a new one,

The Trial will begin in 3... 2... 1...

END OF BOOK TWO

PHIL'S STATS AS OF THE SECOND BOOK'S END:

Philip "Phil" Panfilov
Age: 32
Current status: entrepreneur
Social status level: 17
Knowledge Seeker. Level: 13
Classes: Boxer, Empath. Level: 11
Divorced
Children: none

Achievements:
Altruist (+1 to all main characteristics at every level gained)

The Fastest Learner (10% to skill development rate)

Main characteristics:
Strength: 13/32
Agility: 11/31
Intellect: 20/48
Stamina: 11/33
Perception: 15/32
Charisma: 17/36
Luck: 14/72

Heroic skills:
Lie Detection: 1

System skills:
Insight: 3
Optimization: 1
Heroism: 1

Main skills and abilities:
Learning Skills: 13 ((a primary skill currently undergoing Optimization: +2)
Empathy: 11
Boxing: 11
Reading: 10
Vending: 9
Communication Skills: 9
MS Word: 8
Creative Writing: 8
Running: 8
PC skills: 8
Russian language skills: 7
Marketing: 7

Leadership: 7
Decision making: 7
Online search: 6
Cooking: 6
Self-Discipline: 6
Erudition: 6
MS Excel: 6
Intuition: 6
Walking: 6
Speed Typing: 5
SMM: 5
Self Control: 5
Poker Playing: 5
Power of Persuasion: 5
Plan-making: 5
Hand-to-hand combat: 5
Perseverance: 5
Company Management: 5
Seduction: 4
Deception: 4
Athletics: 4
Manners: 3
English language skills: 3
Firearms: 3
Bladed Weapons: 3
Public Speaking: 3
Map Reading: 3
Self-Defense: 3
Car Driving: 2
Pushbike Riding: 2
Swimming: 2

DIY Skills: 2
First Aid Skills: 2
Singing: 2
Fishing: 2
....
Photography: 4 (a secondary skill currently undergoing Optimization: -4)

Environmental safety index: Yellow

Want to be the first to know about our latest LitRPG, sci fi and fantasy titles from your favorite authors?

Subscribe to our NEW RELEASES newsletter:
http://eepurl.com/b7niIL

Thank you for reading *Level Up!*
If you like what you've read, check out other LitRPG novels
published by Magic Dome Books:

Level Up LitRPG series by Dan Sugralinov:
Re-Start
Hero
The Final Trial
Level Up: The Knockout (with Max Lagno)
Level Up. The Knockout: Update (with Max Lagno)

Disgardium LitRPG series by Dan Sugralinov:
Class-A Threat
Apostle of the Sleeping Gods
The Destroying Plague

World 99 LitRPG Series by Dan Sugralinov:
Blood of Fate

Adam Online LitRPG Leries by Max Lagno:
Absolute Zero
City of Freedom

Reality Benders LitRPG series by Michael Atamanov:
Countdown
External Threat
Game Changer
Web of Worlds
A Jump into the Unknown

**The Dark Herbalist LitRPG series
by Michael Atamanov:**
Video Game Plotline Tester
Stay on the Wing
A Trap for the Potentate
Finding a Body

Perimeter Defense LitRPG series by Michael Atamanov:
Sector Eight
Beyond Death
New Contract
A Game with No Rules

Respawn Trials LitRPG Series by Andrei Livadny:
Edge of the Abyss

The Expansion (The History of the Galaxy) series by A. Livadny:
Blind Punch
The Shadow of Earth
Servobattalion

Interworld Network LitRPG Series by Dmitry Bilik:
The Time Master
Avatar of Light

Mirror World LitRPG series by Alexey Osadchuk:
Project Daily Grind
The Citadel
The Way of the Outcast
The Twilight Obelisk

Underdog LitRPG series by Alexey Osadchuk:
Dungeons of the Crooked Mountains
The Wastes

AlterGame LitRPG series by Andrew Novak:
The First Player
On the Lost Continent
God Mode

An NPC's Path LitRPG series by Pavel Kornev:
The Dead Rogue
Kingdom of the Dead
Deadman's Retinue

The Sublime Electricity series by Pavel Kornev
The Illustrious
The Heartless
The Fallen
The Dormant

Citadel World series by Kir Lukovkin:
The URANUS Code
The Secret of Atlantis

Point Apocalypse *(a near-future action thriller)*
by Alex Bobl

Captive of the Shadows *(The Fairy Code Book #1)*
by Kaitlyn Weiss

The Game Master **series by A. Bobl and A. Levitsky:**
The Lag

You're in Game!
(LitRPG Stories from Bestselling Authors)

You're in Game-2!
(More LitRPG stories set in your favorite worlds)

Moskau by G. Zotov
(a dystopian thriller)

El Diablo by G.Zotov
(a supernatural thriller)

More books and series are coming out soon!

In order to have new books of the series translated faster, we need your help and support! Please consider leaving a review or spread the word by recommending *Level Up* to your friends and posting the link on social media. The more people buy the book, the sooner we'll be able to make new translations available.

Thank you!

Till next time!